THE ROGUE HEARTS SERIES

A Perfect Love

A Perfect Match • A Perfect Secret

Donna Hatch

This is a work of fiction. Names, characters, and incidents are the product of the author's imagination. Any resemblance to actual persons living or dead, business establishments, events, or locales is entirely coincidental.

Cover art and interior format by Lisa Messegee, The Write Designer

Published in the United States of America

The Rogue Hearts Series

A Perfect Match

Donna Hatch

DEDICATION

To my fans who wanted to know how the story of Genevieve and Christian began, this prequel is for you.

CHAPTER 1

ENGLAND, SUMMER 1818

Genevieve Marshall gazed out of the coach's window, her joyful anticipation of reuniting with her friend fading at the sight of the dark, grotesque abbey. Why, all it needed was the clichéd dead tree, complete with a cawing crow, to make an ideal setting for a Gothic novel. Genevieve couldn't imagine a drearier place in which to have a house party.

"I can hardly believe Matilda grew up here," Genevieve murmured.

Indeed, the structure seemed determined to inspire melancholy rather than Matilda Widtsoe's irrepressible liveliness.

Mama pushed back the curtain and peered out. Auburn ringlets, the same color as Genevieve's, framed her face and contrasted with her lace cap. "Good heavens, what a cheerless dwelling."

Chuckling, Papa set aside his newspaper to admire the view. "That 'cheerless dwelling' is Bainbridge Abbey, built in the eleventh century to withstand sieges."

Genevieve sent him a wry smile. "I don't suppose you can promise a few ghosts to add to the ambience?"

"I'll speak to Admiral Widtsoe." Papa's chocolate brown eyes crinkled.

"Tell your ghosts to stay out of our bedchamber," Mama said primly. "I'll not have our privacy invaded by their shenanigans."

"I'm sure they can be reasonable," Genevieve quipped.

She studied her Mama for signs of undue fatigue or distress. One can never be too careful with a weak heart. However, despite a two-day journey, Mama's color remained good at the moment. Still, as soon as they reached the abbey, she'd see to it that her mother rested.

Genevieve resettled into the seat cushions and imagined her reunion with her friend Matilda Widtsoe. It seemed a decade since they'd last conversed, but it had only been a year. Letters were no substitute for lively conversation, although the capitalized and underlined words and the prolific use of exclamation points certainly reflected Matilda's passionate manner of speech.

And who was this young gentleman who'd captured her friend's heart this Season and occupied a large portion of Matilda's letters? Genevieve fairly tingled with anticipation. She must determine if this young man was worthy of her friend.

The coach bumped over the curving road and stopped in front of the to the ominous structure's main entrance.

As Genevieve took Papa's hand and stepped out, she looked up at the dark building. "Oh, my."

"Look at the gargoyles on the parapets." Papa pointed. "This is truly a well-preserved structure. I'm happy to see they didn't make any additions to try to modernize it."

"Mrs. Widtsoe said they've updated inside," Mama said. "They even have modern bathing rooms with shower baths." She raised her brows.

A bath sounded delightful after the dirt and grit of the road. But not as delightful as reuniting with Matilda.

While footmen shouldered the family's trunks, Genevieve followed her parents up the front steps. They'd no sooner been admitted into a cavernous great hall than a squeal of delight and a bundle of ruffles launched itself at Genevieve and hugged her until she let out a squeak herself.

"Oh, Jenny, you're here at last! I have so much to tell you!" Matilda drew back enough to let Genevieve breathe.

She'd forgotten their height difference. Though Matilda stood at average height, Genevieve barely reached the tip of Matilda's perfectly English nose. They grinned at one another.

Matilda curtsied to Genevieve's parents before resuming her bobbing as if her excitement refused to be contained, her honey-colored curls echoing every bounce. "Welcome, Captain Marshall, Mrs. Marshall. We're so happy you're all here. I trust your journey was not too tiring?"

Before Mama and Papa got off more than a few words, Matilda said, "Good, good. Mrs. Pearce will see you settled." She took both of Genevieve's hands into hers, and Matilda's words started tripping all over themselves in her excitement. "Oh, Jenny, I can't wait for you to meet him. He and his father are attending the house party. Isn't that wonderful? His father is an earl, you might recall, so it's quite an honor that they're coming, but of course, that's not why I adore him. Oh, Jenny, he's handsome and stylish and polite and even a bit mysterious, but I'm sure he'll be more forthcoming here with so many opportunities to converse." With her hands still entwined with Genevieve's, Matilda started hopping up and down with more vigor, her curls keeping pace.

Genevieve laughed weakly in the face of such a force of nature. "I look forward to meeting him. I only hope he's good enough for you, Mattie."

"Wait until you meet him! Oh, just wait!"

"Good heavens, child, show some decorum," came a voice from behind them. Mrs. Widtsoe approached, shaking her head, a resigned smile touching her lips. "Welcome, Captain and Mrs. Marshall, and of course, welcome to you, Miss Marshall."

Admiral Widtsoe arrived, greeting Papa heartily and bowing to Mama and Genevieve.

Mrs. Widtsoe asked, "Would you like refreshment first, or to rest in your rooms?"

"Tea would be lovely," Mama said. "But I do believe I ought to rest soon thereafter."

Genevieve cast an anxious look at Mrs. Widtsoe. Catching her meaning, the perceptive lady suggested, "Shall I send a tea tray to your chamber so you might rest without delay?"

"Thank you, that might be just the thing," Mama agreed.

Genevieve disentangled herself from her exuberant friend with a promise to return momentarily. After ensuring Mama got her tea and was resting comfortably, her heart medicine within reach if needed, and good-naturedly enduring Mama's calling her 'little mother,' Genevieve changed out of her carriage dress, freshened up, and followed a maid to the parlor. The longed-for bath would have to wait until after Genevieve enjoyed a coze with Matilda.

In the parlor, decorated in shades of rose and pink, Matilda arose from a settee where she'd been perched and cast a glance at her mother who sat speaking with a group of matrons. "We're going for a walk, Mother."

The lady nodded and gave them a loose wave. Matilda glided, with hardly any bouncing, to Genevieve. Taking her arm, she tugged her outside. The moment they stepped through the French doors onto the terrace, Matilda's flow of words began, as did her bouncing. With her blue eyes shining and her cheeks pink, she painted a lovely picture.

"Oh, Jenny, I have been waiting for this moment for ages! I just know you're going to love him. I declare that I will do anything to secure a place in his heart. Wouldn't it be lovely if he chose the house party to propose?"

Genevieve nodded. "Indeed it would."

Matilda pressed a hand dramatically over her heart. "There has never been a more perfect man in all the earth. I am most violently in love with him!"

Smiling, Genevieve couldn't help tweaking her friend just a bit. "Weren't you violently in love with the Duke of Suttenberg last year?"

Matilda waved away the past. "Oh, well, I admit I did have a bit of a *tendré* for him—he's so handsome and proper, and of course comes from ancient lineage—but we hardly exchanged two words. It was more like admiration from afar than true love."

"And this is true love?"

"Oh, yes! He is mysterious and quiet. If I didn't know better, I'd say he was shy. But that's quite unheard of for such a handsome man of fashion, and an earl's son besides. He's merely thoughtful and doesn't speak unless he has something important to say. Oh, and he's so artistic! I asked him to paint my portrait while he was here, and do you know he agreed? He painted the loveliest portrait of the Duchess of Devonshire. It's simply exquisite! He's developing quite an impressive reputation as an artist of both landscapes and portraits. I vow half of the fashionable houses in London are graced with one of his paintings."

"Yes, I've seen landscapes and portraits of his."

"I wish he had a twin so you could have one of him, too. He has brothers but none of them are coming. The eldest, the viscount, is off visiting his aunt and uncle somewhere, and the next eldest is at sea—a pirate, if you believe rumor, although I can't believe anyone in that family being such a scoundrel. And the next one is in London, but he seems to shun society. Scarred, too, I hear. Oh, but Christian is so handsome. He and his father look a great deal alike, both tall and broad-shouldered and blond. Mama says he looks like Hercules, but I think of him as Adonis." She sighed theatrically and pressed both hands over her heart.

Genevieve smiled at the romantic image her friend created. "Your mother approves, I take it?"

"Of course! And Father has already said he'll give permission promptly and not tease Christian when he seeks him out. Can you imagine? Me? Married to such a handsome man, and the son of an earl? Why, all my friends will be green with envy! Except you, of course, Jenny. You're a true friend."

Genevieve squeezed her hand. "I hope he makes you happy, Mattie, I truly do."

She made a silent vow to give this paragon a careful study to be sure he wasn't a clever *roué* who trifled with her friend's heart. After all the losses her dear friend had suffered, Matilda deserved true happiness. Genevieve would do anything to ensure Matilda found it.

Matilda sighed. "I suppose we ought to return to the others. Mama wishes me to help her greet our guests. The guest list is quite impressive, I assure you. Oh, Jenny, I hope someone comes who is suitable for you. It would be lovely to have a double wedding!"

Smiling, Genevieve said, "I hardly think a week-long house party is adequate time to fall in love with a stranger and decide to marry."

Earnest blue eyes met hers. "Sometimes love happens instantly and you just *know*." She pressed a hand over her heart. "It was that quick for me."

Genevieve nodded and kept her doubts to herself. She sent up a silent prayer that if this so-called perfect Christian Amesbury weren't good enough for Matilda, his flaws would become apparent before Matilda suffered true heartbreak.

They turned back to the house as more guests arrived. Carriages lined up and servants scurried to settle the arrivals.

Matilda halted before they entered the great hall. She took both of Genevieve's hands and pressed a kiss to her cheek. "I'm so glad you're here, Jenny. It's been torture to be in such raptures without anyone to share it with who really understands and listens."

Her words trailed off. Genevieve followed her gaze to a tall, distinguished older gentleman with silver streaks brushing his dark hair. He stood amid the chaos of boxes, trunks, and scurrying servants, surveying the scene with barely suppressed disdain. Sophisticated in his stylishly tailored riding clothes and lean form, he fingered his riding crop as if wishing he could control the servants the way he controlled his horse.

Matilda lowered her voice. "That's Lord Wickburgh, a viscount and an acquaintance of my father's."

"He's a very elegant gentleman."

"Yes. Very." For once, Matilda didn't elaborate.

Lord Wickburgh's gaze passed over the great hall. As his focus landed on Genevieve, he looked so hard at her that she turned her gaze downward. His stare contained a chill that settled into her backbone.

Admiral Widtsoe greeted the impressive lord, and soon the viscount ascended the staircase, presumably to his bedchamber. Genevieve let out a breath and worked the feeling back into her toes. Others arrived, and Matilda greeted them with her mother. Genevieve hung back so as not to be in the way and offered assistance when possible.

A young gentleman arrived with a couple. The bright-eyed older woman reminded Genevieve of a sparrow with her bright black eyes and the way she fluttered about. Matilda introduced them to Genevieve as Mr. and Mrs. Ashton and their son.

The young Mr. Ashton bowed low over her hand and offered a wan smile. "Delighted to make your acquaintance, Miss Marshall." The kindness in his eyes was at odds with the monotone quality of his voice and he gave her a rather lingering look.

Genevieve murmured a reply and blushed under Matilda's delighted grin.

Later came a very young man who didn't appear to have reached his majority, with his brown hair in the youthful-looking Cherubin style which sported short curls all over.

Mrs. Widtsoe clasped his hands. "So happy you are here, Sir Reginald. I hear you earned your degree from Oxford?"

"Yes, indeed I have, ma'am. My mother sends her love." He turned warm eyes onto Matilda. "Always a pleasure to see you, Mattie."

Matilda grinned. "Good afternoon, Reggie. I suppose you feel all grown up now, eh?" All at once, Matilda let out a strangled sound of glee, clearly forgetting Sir Reginald, and grabbed Genevieve's arm. "He's here!" Her urgent whisper drew Genevieve's focus.

Matilda gestured toward a breathtakingly perfect young gentleman. Genevieve had frequented art museums with sculptures and paintings of mortal men and gods, some so beautiful she could almost fall into a swoon over them. But never in her life had she seen one come to life. Though she'd always had a preference for dark-haired men, probably influenced by her penchant for reading Gothics, this stunning vision was a study in gold, from the gold of his glorious hair, to the lightly golden tones of his sun-kissed skin, even the gold threads in his waistcoat. His riding coat brought out the summer-sky blue of his eyes that glanced about and then darted to a man who could only be his father—a thinner, older image of the blond vision. The young gentleman's eyes narrowed in concern as they focused on his father.

This beautiful young man must be Christian Amesbury. No wonder Matilda was besotted!

In a hushed voice, Matilda said, "His father is the Earl of Tarrington."

The young Mr. Amesbury spoke quietly to his father, but the earl waved off his son's words. A faded version of a smile touched the older gentleman's mouth as he greeted Admiral and Mrs. Widtsoe. Matilda barely managed to pull her gaze of his son to greet the earl.

As if feeling the weight of Genevieve's stare, the stunning Mr. Amesbury glanced at her briefly before lowering his gaze, a half smile curving his full, shapely lips that conjured visions of stolen kisses underneath rose bowers.

Genevieve flushed. A pity she'd left her fan behind. Ashamed she'd been mooning over her friend's preference, Genevieve cast an anxious glance at Matilda. Her friend stared rapturously at the vision, her hands clasped to her bosom. Good. Genevieve's guilty secret remained safe.

Silent while his father greeted the hosts, Mr. Amesbury only looked her in the eye for an instant. But oh, what an instant!

A timeless sense of recognition hit her with all the fanfare of a royal parade but light as a cat's whisker. The empty place deepest inside her heart, one she'd not before known existed, cried out for its other half.

This must be what Matilda felt.

It must never happen again.

Genevieve was here to meet the gentleman of her friend's dreams, not form dreams of her own. She squared her shoulders and vowed to discover if his heart were as fair as his face. Most especially, she must learn whether he was worthy of her dearest friend.

CHAPTER 2

Christian Amesbury greeted his hosts, the Widtsoes, while keeping an eye on his father, the Earl of Tarrington. Leaving the healing waters of Bath and traveling to this house party might prove too taxing to the earl's failing strength. But this had been the first social event his father had expressed a desire to attend since Mama's death, so Christian had encouraged their attendance.

While still in the Widtsoes' hall, Christian searched for signs that their decision to come would prove too dangerous to his parent's health. However, besides fatigued, Father seemed well enough at present, even showing a keener interest in his surroundings than he had in months. Perhaps the trip would boost his flagging spirits and revive his vitality in a way Bath had failed to do.

Besides, Christian had never visited this rugged terrain before, and his artist's eye had already found new subject matter to paint. Not to mention, Admiral Widtsoe had commissioned him to do a painting of the abbey, and his lively daughter had already begged him to paint a portrait of her. The trip might be good for his father and him.

Father drew Christian into the conversation as he greeted his long-time friends. "You remember my son, Christian—my right-hand man."

"Certainly, my lord," the Admiral said. "Welcome, Mr. Amesbury. We hope you will enjoy yourself here. I hope you don't mind if I whisk your father away from time to time so we might catch up."

Christian inclined his head. "Of course I won't mind, Admiral."

"And you remember our daughter, of course," Mrs. Widtsoe said, gesturing to the pretty girl.

If memory serves, Christian had danced with Miss Widtsoe this past Season—only to humor his father.

Miss Widtsoe beamed at him with unabashed adoration. Christian resisted the urge to tug at his collar. The pretty girl watched him too closely. And she quivered a bit, rather like a poodle one of his mother's friends used to carry about under her arm everywhere she went. Still, as the daughter of their hosts, Miss Widtsoe deserved courtesy. He'd just have to be careful not to raise her expectations.

Christian bowed to Miss Widtsoe. As he lifted his head, he froze. Behind the hosts' daughter stood a young lady who captured Christian's attention. With a fascinating shade of auburn hair, the flawless skin of a doll, and exquisitely delicate features, beautiful seemed too blasé a word to describe her. She fixed a pair of rich, brown eyes on him. A shifting sensation inside him left him oddly off balanced.

"Lord Tarrington, Mr. Amesbury," the young Miss Widtsoe greeted them, although her eyes rested solely on Christian. Her smile revealed practically her entire set of pearly teeth. "I can't wait to show you around! I'm sure you, as an artist, will find many views of interest to paint here! And it's the *best* time of year, too, with all the summer blooms!" Though she never raised her voice above normal speaking tones, her enthusiasm turned her statements into exclamations.

Christian nodded, his only other defense when no appropriate reply came to him. Again, his gaze strayed to the exquisite young lady behind Miss Widtsoe. His fingers twitched in desire to paint her, to capture that air of purity and serenity he seldom found in adults;

normally only children had such undimmed light. A sense of timelessness crept over him. As if aware of his focus, she glanced his way again. Her brown eyes, ringed with an unusually thick fringe of lashes, moved about as if she searched his face for secrets best left hidden. He looked away before he tainted her beauty with his darkness, and instead studied the patterns on the floor.

Miss Widtsoe spoke again, reaching behind her and drawing the auburn-haired beauty next to her. "Genevieve, please allow me to introduce the Earl of Tarrington and his son, Christian Amesbury. My lord, Mr. Amesbury, this is my dearest friend in all the world, Miss Genevieve Marshall."

Genevieve. He tasted her name, repeating mentally, *Jenn-a-veeve*. Then he switched to the French pronunciation, *Zhahn-vee-ev*. A lovely name for a lovely girl. Of course, he could never call her by her given name. She must always be Miss Marshall to him.

As they exchanged their customary bows and curtsies, Father asked, "Are you related to Captain Marshall?"

Surprise widened her eyes and a smile curved her plump, kissable lips. "He is my father, my lord." A sweet contralto voice belonged to the vision.

"A good man," Father said. "Is he here?"

"Yes, my lord. He and my mother are resting after our journey."

"I look forward to renewing our acquaintance."

"As are they, I am sure." Her smile warmed.

Miss Widtsoe wrapped her arm around Miss Marshall's and smiled so hard Christian wondered if it caused her pain. Miss Widtsoe stood almost a head taller than her tiny, fairy-like friend, and where her figure was full, Miss Marshall's was lithe, graceful, as if she truly had been crafted to wear a pair of wings and flit among the flowers.

As a nod to his father's rank, the hostess took it upon herself to show them the way to their bedchambers rather than leave that task to a servant. Christian offered an arm to his father, but he waved off the aid and leaned on his cane instead, probably so as not to reveal the depth of his illness to his friends. How he'd managed to serve in Parliament this past Season was a mystery to Christian.

As they took their leave of the admiral, Miss Widtsoe curtsied. "I look forward to seeing you all at dinner tonight."

Her sunny smile brought an answering one to his lips. It was hard not to be cheerful amid such liveliness. She turned a pointed smile upon Christian. He bowed to all, his focus resting again on the beautiful Miss Marshall, and turned to follow the hostess.

After getting settled in his bedchamber and changing out of his traveling clothes, Christian checked on the earl. He found him reclining on a settee, sipping tea.

"Well, Son, you have already conquered the ladies without speaking a word, I see."

"Really, Father, we aren't at war. No conquering involved."

"This matchmaking business can feel like a war of sorts. Take no prisoners, Son."

Christian scoffed. "I'm not here to make matches. Do you require anything?"

"If I do, I'll ring for my valet. No need to fuss. I'll rest until dinner. Go amuse yourself. And for once, speak to a young lady. Or, if you can't think of anything to say, steal a kiss."

The image of the sweet, auburn-haired Miss Marshall edged into Christian's thoughts and heated his face. He nearly tugged on his collar.

The earl leaned his head against the tall settee. "You know, Admiral Widtsoe hopes you'll choose his daughter."

Christian cleared his throat. "Er...."

The earl's mouth curved in a ghostly reminder of the ready smiles he once wore when Mama was still alive. "But if you aren't ready to settle down, you could sow some oats—not with a lady of course—but in a new place with new possibilities, there are often willing women... maids—"

Christian had heard enough. "Rest well, sir. I shall see you at dinner—or tea if you are feeling well." He made his escape before the earl could begin ribbing him about his shyness around women or spout stories of how generations of Amesburys deserved their reputations of being philanderers. His father had wooed ladies of all classes and moral codes before he found and married Mama. His older brothers, Cole and Jared, seemed to share the earl's views. What his other living brother, Grant, thought of women was a complete mystery. But Christian never forgot his mother's admonition to treat the fair sex with respect, whether an innkeeper's daughter or a duchess.

Besides, wooing would involve speaking, and he'd rather face an opponent at fisticuffs or fencing than have to think of something clever to say to a lady.

He stopped by his room long enough to grab a sketchbook and an artist's pencil and went outside. Pausing, he turned slowly to find a good spot. Ah. There. A nearby hill. He took the shortest route out of the gardens to the hill to get a good view of the abbey. This seemed a good place to begin. He'd do several sketches first, all of different vantage points, before determining from which angle to create the final painting.

After finding a comfortable spot to sit, he eyed the structure. The multi-leveled tiers faintly reminiscent of Westminster Abbey but adorned with gargoyles and built out of dark stone, certainly created a forbidding, and fascinating, scene.

A replica of the abbey took form underneath his pencil. After adding details, he shaded in long, late afternoon shadows which only added to the ominous air. Just for fun, he added a gargoyle springing to life and flying off the building. He smiled. The earl thought his art a great waste of time, especially with the little fanciful turns it often took, but Christian couldn't have given up art any more than he could give up food. If only he could study under masters at the Royal Academy of Art. But he daren't follow that dream with his father so ill. And his family had always expected him to become a vicar.

Immersed in his work, he glanced up and gave a start. Two pairs of eyes stared at him. The Misses Widtsoe and Marshall stood watching him, with expressions of rapture and solemn contemplation, respectively.

He sprang to his feet. "Ladies." His pencil and pad of paper tumbled to the ground. With his face heating, he retrieved the items and offered a bow.

As they both curtsied, Miss Widtsoe giggled, her wide smile reappearing.

Miss Marshall held out a tiny gloved hand. "I apologize if we startled you, Mr. Amesbury. Please, resume your drawing."

He made a loose gesture to his paper. "I've finished this aspect." He would draw the abbey from a different vantage point another time. He tucked the paper under his arm and bowed to take his leave.

"We missed you at tea," Miss Widtsoe said. "People asked about you, but I didn't know what to tell them. Your father said you'd probably wandered off to draw somewhere, and it appears he was right."

"Er, yes." That explained his hunger. He hadn't noticed the passage of time while he'd sketched, but his stomach reminded him of the lapse. If the earl were at tea, he must be feeling well, an encouraging thought.

"Shall I have something brought to you? Cook makes the most amazing scones, as light as you would ever taste, and delicious with clotted cream! Or do you prefer lemon cake? I love lemon cake, and seed cake, too, but I'm careful not to overindulge, lest it adversely affect my figure." She struck a pose designed to attract his attention to her figure.

He only allowed himself a glance, but she was, indeed, very well endowed.

Before he thought of a response, she continued, "Anyway, I'm happy to order something brought to you. We try not to starve our guests, even those who wander off and miss tea." She grinned, revealing all her pearly teeth again.

Miss Marshall studied him with that quiet, assessing gaze. "We were about to return to the abbey to dress for dinner. Do you wish to walk with us?"

Unable to think of a gracious way to extract himself, Christian gripped his pad and pencil as he offered an elbow to each of them. Miss Widtsoe clung to him possessively, but Miss Marshall rested her hand on the crook of his arm with a feather touch. The top of her head barely reached his shoulder. Her petite form instilled a sense of protectiveness in him. She smiled gently at him.

He focused forward and headed down the path leading to the outer gardens. She glided without making a sound next to him as they walked. Everything about her was restful, and an answering calm came over him.

As Miss Widtsoe walked, she bounced as if barely containing great amounts of energy. "When do you plan to start painting the abbey?"

"As soon as I've decided which angle to use." There. He'd spoken without getting tongue-tied.

"And don't forget you promised to do my portrait, too. I saw the portraits you did of the Duchess of Devonshire and of Mrs. Clemmons, and I love your work! I simply must have a portrait, too! You haven't forgotten you promised to do my portrait, have you?"

He smiled, recalling the elegant Duchess of Devonshire and those moments when she'd revealed warmth underneath her frosty exterior. Perhaps he'd discover depth to Miss Widtsoe as he painted her. "I haven't forgotten."

Miss Widtsoe opened her mouth to speak but stopped when Miss Marshall asked quietly, "How do you choose which angle to use when painting a structure like a castle?"

"I sketch it from many different locations first, then choose my preference among them." Was it the topic that put him at ease or the lady herself?

"How did you like today's sketches?" she asked.

He glanced at the pad in his hand. "I only did one today."

She made a loose gesture to his pad. "Would it be prying to ask to see it?"

"Oh, yes!" Miss Widtsoe, who'd been uncharacteristically quiet, exclaimed. "I'd love to see it!"

He hesitated a moment but couldn't refuse Miss Marshall. If she disliked the additional live gargoyle, it made no difference to him.

Both ladies leaned over and studied the drawing. Miss Marshall let out a long breath, her eyes alight. "It's magnificent—so detailed and realistically proportioned. You have a unique flair. I love the gargoyle coming to life."

Miss Widtsoe shivered. "It looks like something out of a nightmare." As if fearing she had insulted him, she added hastily, "But it's very good! I can't wait to see the final product!"

Christian sifted through possible responses and finally said, "I hope your father will be pleased."

"I'm sure he will if this is any indication! You're so talented and it was so kind of you to accept his commission! I'm sure you have a great many other duties to attend to, but we're *so* glad you're here!"

Christian almost cringed under the praise she heaped upon him.

Then she landed the final blow. "I'm sure it will be simply perfect."

Perfect. How he'd grown to detest that word after the way his brothers had thrown it at him in that mocking, sing-song voice. *The perfectly perfect Christian.* Even years later, it still set his teeth on edge. Of course, with Cole so detached after he'd returned home from the sea, and Jared still away, and the always-aloof Grant taking up residence in London, Christian would rather bear that awful nickname if it meant having his brothers home. But no, they'd left for the war and hadn't truly returned.

Then Mama died and Father began to fade away too. It seemed everyone he loved left eventually, beginning with Jason's tragic death, a death that would forever haunt Christian and doom him to eternal loneliness.

"Are you well, Mr. Amesbury?" Miss Marshall's hushed voice pushed away his ghosts.

He snapped his head up. "Of course."

Her dark, assessing eyes peered at him. In a purely defensive, and probably cowardly measure, he turned his attention to Miss Widtsoe. "Can you tell me of the abbey's history? It might help me capture a unique tone in the painting."

With her usual exuberance, Miss Widtsoe launched into a history of the abbey while Christian tried to pick out the relevant parts that might prove useful to add mood to his painting. Her narrative filled the time that it took to arrive at the front steps.

"Thank you, Miss Widtsoe; that may prove helpful. Until dinner." He bowed to them both, not allowing his gaze to rest too long on either lady, but for entirely different reasons, and excused himself.

After pilfering a snack and dressing for dinner, Christian accompanied the earl down the stairs. In the drawing room, other guests gathered for drinks and conversation.

Wearing an abundance of bows and white silk, Miss Widtsoe beamed from across the room and bobbed slightly on her toes. How could he make it clear that he did not return her affection without wounding her sensibilities? Miss Marshall stood between an older lady with the same color hair, clearly her mother, and her friend. Also in fashionable white, she wore a simple, tasteful gown with clean lines that flattered her slender form. A green ribbon threaded through her auburn curls caught up in a more elaborate style than her chignon of this afternoon. She stood straight and still, focusing on every word her exuberant friend uttered, smiling with the sort of indulgent tenderness one often views in a parent when gazing on a favorite but mischievous child.

"Did you enjoy yourself this afternoon, Son?" the earl asked.

Christian removed his attention from Miss Marshall and focused it on his father. "I did a sketch of the abbey."

The earl made no comment. As his health declined, he'd grown more resigned, or perhaps apathetic, towards Christian's artistic pursuits—an improvement over the past when he vehemently criticized the waste of time. Besides, the admiral had made no secret about his delight over Christian accepting the commission. Perhaps

Admiral Widtsoe's interest lessened the earl's disappointment in Christian.

The butler announced dinner and Christian found himself in the uncomfortable position of escorting Miss Widtsoe into the dining room where he sat between the girl and her friend.

How the deuce should a gentleman extract himself from such an uncomfortable position? If Miss Widtsoe continued to make public claims on Christian, he'd be labeled a cad for raising her expectations and failing to come up to scratch. Moreover, his actions might call into question her reputation and harm her future prospects. Agreeing to paint her portrait sounded worse and worse.

He glanced at his father seated to the hostess's right near the end of the table, his conversation remained focused on Mrs. Widtsoe. She was an elegant, thoughtful woman with lively eyes; perhaps her daughter would follow suit as she matured and make a good wife—for someone else, not him. Christian had resigned himself years ago to living out his life alone.

On his left, Miss Widtsoe chattered, requiring few answers from him. On his right, Miss Marshall glanced at him throughout the meal, as if she viewed him as a puzzle that must be solved. Perhaps she was trying to ascertain if he were good enough for her friend, but he couldn't shake the fear that she saw too deeply inside him and wouldn't rest until she exposed all his dark secrets.

CHAPTER 3

Genevieve divided her conversation at the dinner table between Christian Amesbury and an older gentleman with thick mutton chops sprinkled liberally with gray. Matilda kept up a stream of diverting chatter, her usual charming wit and cheery disposition amusing everyone within earshot.

The mutton chop gentleman seated to her right launched into a tale of a recent safari. "Capital game there, Africa. Never knew if I'd be the predator or the prey, though." He chuckled.

"What was it like?" she asked out of pure courtesy.

As he rhapsodized about the land, with all its animals, her attention and, unfortunately, her vision, often strayed to the enigmatic Mr. Amesbury sitting at her left. He was a study in polite reserve and impeccable manners. Once he shifted in his seat, and a masculine combination of bergamot and a spice she couldn't identify wafted to her. She inhaled, letting the scent inspire images of strength and gentleness and something rather sensual. His hands, those strong but long-fingered, artistic hands, wielded his utensils as if performing a graceful ballet.

When Matilda finished relating an amusing story of a recent trip,

Mr. Amesbury asked Matilda in his soft, rich tones, "Do you wish to travel then, Miss Widtsoe?"

Matilda paused. "I..." she watched him with searching eyes, as if trying to choose an answer that would please him. "I suppose I would like to, a little, especially if my future husband wishes to do so. But I'd also be content to stay home with my children when the time comes." She shot an almost panicked expression at Genevieve, looking for reassurance.

Genevieve nodded her encouragement lest Matilda become overset about a perceived failure. Matilda's features relaxed and she returned her focus to Mr. Amesbury to judge his reaction.

He nodded and said, "I hope you are successful."

As the mutton chop gentleman wound down his description, Genevieve murmured a suitable reply and turned her focus back to her friend and her intended beau. A brief uncomfortable silence had fallen between them.

Genevieve rushed to the rescue. "Do you have any desire to travel, Mr. Amesbury?"

He paused and cast a glance down the table at his father. "I doubt my responsibilities will allow me that luxury."

"Oh, I'm sure you can if you really wish to do so." Matilda touched his hand and then withdrew her touch lest it be viewed as inappropriate. "Surely your father can do without you while you travel. A grand tour, perhaps?" Her face clouded. "That would take a goodly amount of time, though, wouldn't it?"

"Regretfully, a grand tour is out of the question at present," he said, his deep voice filled with regret. "I cannot be away that long."

Quietly, Genevieve asked, "What is it that ties you here?"

When he glanced at her, everything inside her went still. She'd almost forgotten how blue his eyes were, like the blue of a summer afternoon sky. His lips parted, again, filling her with visions of kisses.

What was wrong with her? Her self-appointed task was to ensure he was good enough for Matilda, not fantasize about kissing him. What kind of disloyal tart had she become?

He hesitated before speaking, "I don't dare leave with the earl's health so poor."

Interesting that he referred to his father as 'the earl.' "Because you oversee estate matters for him?" she asked.

Matilda cocked her head. "But you're the youngest. Doesn't one of your older brothers do that?"

His posture grew rigid. "They are all either out of the country or otherwise indisposed," he said stiffly as if he viewed her question as mildly insulting. The comment about him being the youngest, perhaps? But why should that irritate him?

He gentled his voice. "I've been doing it for years. I know how my father wishes matters to be handled."

"So, you don't travel lest the entire earldom fall into disrepair?" Genevieve gave him a teasing smile to soften the impertinent question.

He blinked, and his mouth curved, his body and features relaxing. "That, and to ensure the earl follows doctor's orders." A wry tone touched his voice.

She nodded. "How well I understand that. Mama doesn't always remember her medicine and must be coaxed into taking her walks and her naps. My dear Papa doesn't keep it straight, and the servants are too easily disregarded."

Matilda giggled. "Genevieve's mama calls her 'little mother' because she can be such a hen." She smiled at Genevieve.

For some reason, that interjection rankled. Surely Mattie meant it to be kind, or funny, and not condescending. Remembering her other dinner partner, lest she be considered neglectful, she turned to the mutton chop gentleman, but he'd turned his head to the lady on his other side and launched into a story about a herd that had stampeded.

From down the table, a dark-haired gentleman who had spoken with monotone voice looked her way. As their eyes met, he lifted his glass to her and gave her a kind smile.

After politely nodding at the gentleman whose name she could not recall, she returned her focus to Mr. Amesbury. He offered well-thought-out answers to Matilda's queries, even posing a few questions of his own. Contrary to his reticence that afternoon, he was much more engaging this evening. Perhaps he wished for solitude when he painted but expected conversation at dinner. Nothing in his manner gave Genevieve reason to disapprove of a match between him and her friend; therefore, there was no reason why she should continue to ask him questions designed to reveal his character.

Yet he fascinated her. She held her tongue so as not to intrude on Mattie's dialogue with him. Unfortunately, her friend continued to rain besotted expressions upon Mr. Amesbury. In turn, the object of her affections grew more and more stiff and quiet as dinner progressed. Was he uncomfortable with Matilda's openness, or did he fail to return her obvious preference for him?

Oh, dear. If he didn't return her feelings, Mattie would be crushed. True, she'd developed a 'grand passion' for any number of other gentlemen, but if this were real love, she would not so easily recover. Perhaps Genevieve could help Mr. Amesbury see Matilda's many qualities and why she'd make a desirable wife.

Dinner ended and the ladies left the gentlemen to their brandy and snuff. As she trailed out the door, Genevieve glanced over her shoulder. Christian Amesbury had declined snuff and picked up his half-full wineglass from dinner rather than accept port. Good. He seemed to lack many of the vices of other men. Genevieve left the room, plotting how she could help matters between Matilda and her chosen love.

An instant before she stepped out of the dining room door, another pair of eyes caught her attention. Lord Wickburgh, the thin elegant gentleman, eyed the entire length of her. She almost put her hands in front of her to ward off his improper stare. Genevieve hurried out.

As she followed the group of ladies to the drawing room, she cast off the improper stare Lord Wickburgh had given her. Instead, she turned over possible matchmaking encounters for her friend. Not being privy to planned activities, she couldn't very well arrange romantic meetings between Matilda and Mr. Amesbury. Perhaps the next time she had the opportunity to converse with Mr. Amesbury, Genevieve would mention Mattie's many accomplishments, and how kind she was and what a good wife and mother she'd make. Would that appeal to him?

She reviewed his qualities, what she knew of them. Responsible, judging by the way he managed his father's vast estate. Devoted, since he cared so much for his father. Respectful and thoughtful, by the way he spoke after giving careful consideration. Artistic, obviously. Cautious, if he had not yet made up his mind about Matilda. And sensitive that he was the youngest, which implied he'd been mercilessly teased by his older brothers, and perhaps snubbed by a lady of his choice who sought a marriage with an heir.

Genevieve set her teeth. A sudden desire to give a scathing set down to that unknown lady who'd mistreated such a kind gentleman seized her with such force that it quite halted her steps. Surely the love of a good woman would heal his wounded heart. Matilda's love, of course.

Perhaps those traits which he possessed were those he desired in a bride. Genevieve would simply have to ensure those sides of Matilda's personality surfaced in his presence. Matilda could be responsible, devoted, respectful. And while she lacked his artistic skills, she was an accomplished pianist. He was quiet and reserved compared to Matilda's enthusiasm and zeal for life, and that made them complementary.

Matilda appeared at her side. "What are you doing?" she said *sotto voce*. "Trying to make me look bad?"

Halting, Genevieve turned to her friend. "What do you mean?"

Clearly struggling against tears, Matilda tugged her arm to draw her away from the others. "You kept asking him all kinds of questions and hanging on his every word."

If Matilda had struck her, Genevieve would not have been as surprised. "Mattie, how can you say such a thing? I was only trying to help keep the conversation going for your sake. For a few moments, you both seemed uncomfortable."

Matilda blinked back her tears but still looked uncertain. "Then you meant nothing else by it?"

"Well, I admit I was trying to learn more about him so as to make a better determination of his character. I must satisfy myself that he's good enough for you. A handsome face and ancient family lineage are not enough to ensure a happy marriage, and I want you to be happy."

Pink colored Matilda's pretty, round cheeks and she chewed her lower lip. "Oh."

"Did I do something wrong?" Genevieve touched her arm and peered carefully into Matilda's eyes. Where Christian Amesbury's eyes were the crystal blue of a cloudless winter sky, Matilda's reminded Genevieve of a deep mountain lake.

Matilda let out a half-laugh, half-sound of distress. "No, Jenny, you've done nothing wrong. Forgive me. I'm afraid I questioned your motives and became a bit jealous. I shouldn't have."

"Jealous? Whatever for? You know I'd never come between you and your happiness."

Matilda's eyes grew shiny. "Oh, I know, but you're so beautiful. Most of the men in the room couldn't keep their eyes off you tonight. I'd forgotten how much they always do that."

"Oh, what a lot of poppycock! You're a perfect china doll. If you and Mr. Amesbury make a match of it, you'll have beautiful children, with big blue eyes and golden hair."

After fishing her handkerchief out of her reticule, Matilda dabbed at her nose. "You don't know what it's like going to social events with you, watching everyone stare at you and fall all over themselves to talk to you."

"Stop exaggerating. You are never at a loss for partners and you know it. My entire reason for being here is to spend time with you and to help you secure the proposal you desire. We need a plan."

Matilda's face lightened and she put away her handkerchief. They entered the drawing room painted to appear made of sand-colored bricks. Murals of white-clad, dark-eyed Egyptians wearing dark eye paint and posed with their arms bent at the elbows such as one would expect to see in a pyramid covered every wall.

Matilda made a dismissive wave at the decorating style. "Father's latest passion is Egypt… stuff." She led Genevieve to a settee carved curiously to resemble an Egyptian sarcophagus. "Now, then. What do you suggest?"

They sat with their heads together, discussing ways to feature Matilda's accomplishments and personality to her full advantage. To her credit, Matilda did an admirable job of keeping her voice down despite her energy while Genevieve made every helpful suggestion that came to her.

"What are you two whispering and giggling about?" Mrs. Widtsoe asked as she approached.

They both straightened guiltily. As Matilda blushed, Genevieve said, "We were speculating on what activity you have planned for this evening and what our role ought to be."

Matilda's mother smiled as if she knew the truth. "When the gentlemen arrive, I thought a few games of charades would be in order."

"How delightful," Genevieve said. "Perhaps until then, Matilda might favor us with a few pieces on the pianoforte so that the gentlemen can enjoy it as they arrive." She shot a meaningful look at Matilda.

"Oh!" Her friend sprang up, honey curls bobbing. "Yes, of course. You're so clever, Jenny." She went immediately to the pianoforte in the corner, surrounded by carved black Egyptian cats, and began a sonata.

Mrs. Widtsoe let out a contented sigh, her focus riveted on Matilda. With the setting sun bathing Matilda in golden light, filtered by sheer curtains over the windows, and a dreamy smile, she created a picture of such beauty that Mr. Amesbury would be a fool not to appreciate the sight.

"I hope she catches him," Mrs. Widtsoe said softly.

Genevieve stood next to her friend's mother and said in a low voice so as not to be overheard by other guests. "Mr. Amesbury?"

She nodded. "She certainly has set her cap at him. I hope she isn't in for another heartbreak."

Genevieve hoped so, as well. If only Matilda didn't give her heart away on a whim so often. Perhaps she couldn't help it. After all, deep down inside, everyone desires to be loved.

And Mr. Amesbury seemed easy to love.

"He seems a fine man," Genevieve offered.

"Young, but much to recommend him."

Genevieve smiled. Apparently, Mrs. Widtsoe shared Mama's opinion that most men were too young for the role of husband and father until the age of thirty. Mr. Amesbury looked as if he were only in his mid-twenties. "He seems steady and responsible, despite his youth."

"I believe you're right." The older lady's smile turned sheepish as she met Genevieve's gaze. "And one of the most handsome young men in all of Christendom."

"Oh, indeed." Genevieve returned her gaze to Matilda. It would not do to reveal the depth of her agreement with the lady's opinion. From now on, she'd dedicate herself to showing Mr. Amesbury all the many ways her friend deserved his consideration and love.

CHAPTER 4

When Christian followed the gentlemen into the drawing room to join the ladies, he glanced at his father. The earl moved slowly, his shoulders rounded in signs of fatigue.

Christian spoke softly so the men wouldn't overhear. "Shall I take you to your room, sir?"

"No need. I'm well enough."

"You look tired. We traveled all day; there's no shame in wishing to rest—"

"Yes, well, I came to spend time with friends, not hibernate in my room like an old bear."

Christian said nothing further. He'd get more insistent if his father appeared to be overtaxing himself. Still, the light in his eyes was an improvement over the apathy of most of the past year. Perhaps this house party would revive him.

The sweet chords of piano music beckoned to Christian as someone played with admirable passion and sensitivity. He entered the drawing room and paused to admire the Egyptian décor. The colors had been blended with skill to paint realistic-looking clay bricks. The Egyptian people, larger than life-size, were a bit stark but a fair imitation of their original inspiration.

Father looked mildly amused. "Egypt seems to be all the rage these days."

The last rays of evening sunlight slanted in through the windows and cast a glow on Miss Widtsoe sitting at the pianoforte, burnishing her gold curls and making her white gown luminescent. She was the creator of such a heartfelt performance? Surprising. But it shouldn't have been. She obviously held a great emotion under questionable restraint.

Seeing her in the unusual setting, bathed in sunlight, Christian paused, considering her portrait. He would have her turned sideways on the bench, not playing, but looking as if she had just completed a piece and was about to stand to receive her applause. It would reveal her talent for music and show her figure to full advantage. He'd give her face an angelic glow. Yes, that should please her and her parents. And her future husband—whomever that may be.

Off to one side, watching Miss Widtsoe with an expression of almost maternal pride, stood Miss Genevieve Marshall. She exuded an aura of innocence and serenity as well as a restraint that her friend lacked. Her russet hair lit by sunlight created a dazzling contrast to her peaceful expression. Delicate as a pixie, she belonged in a garden surrounded by flowers and waterfalls. Yes, that's how he'd paint her if he were commissioned to do so, though it would be inappropriate to paint her without permission.

"Pretty girls," the earl murmured. "Have you chosen a favorite or do you want them both?"

Christian's face flashed hot. "No."

"No matter. Plenty of options here, including the maids." He winked.

Christian drifted to an empty space near a group of men who were still engrossed in a discussion over the declining health of the king and whether the Prince Regent would become less dissipated once he took the throne.

Nearby, three young ladies whose names he couldn't remember sat discussing something about bonnets with Italian flowers, whatever those were. Miss Widtsoe's piano music blended with snatches of conversation that swelled and ebbed around him like an ocean current.

Miss Marshall sat in a nearby group of girls. She glanced over her shoulder at him but returned her gaze to the group. "Doesn't Miss Widtsoe play beautifully?"

The girls all murmured their agreement.

"She sings like an angel as well," she added. "Perhaps someone should play for her so she can entertain us."

"Do you play, Miss Marshall?" asked one of the girls.

"Oh, not well enough to accompany a singer of Miss Widtsoe's talent."

"Mr. Amesbury plays, don't you?" someone said.

His face flushed under the focus of so many pairs of eyes. "Er, yes."

Miss Marshall clasped her hands together. "Oh, that's perfect."

He winced. There was that word. He needed to build up an immunity to that word.

"You could play, and she could sing. You will, won't you? Please?"

The earnest pleading in Miss Marshall's big brown eyes, not to mention her exquisite face, propelled him into action. He stood. "If that is your wish."

She smiled and he almost took a step back from the sheer brilliance. A dark corner of his soul seemed cleaner somehow, less dark, from that single blast of pristine joy. She beckoned to him and led the way to the pianoforte just as Miss Widtsoe ended the piece she'd been performing.

"Matilda, Mr. Amesbury has agreed to accompany you as you sing. Will you do it?"

Miss Widtsoe's eyes widened and her tooth-revealing smile appeared. "Oh, I'd be happy to. Do you know 'The Soldier's Adieu'?"

"I know it in the key of B-flat."

She beamed. "That's well within my range."

Christian glanced at Genevieve Marshall, but she'd already taken a seat nearby. She faced forward as if anticipating her favorite opera rather than an informal and impromptu performance in a room full of people more absorbed in conversation than music.

As he played an introduction, Miss Widtsoe glanced over her shoulder at him, adoration clear in her cobalt eyes. How the deuce was he to make it clear he didn't return her affections? Accompanying her as she sang certainly wasn't helping his cause. His gaze strayed to Miss Marshall again. She'd set him up, the little matchmaker. He'd have to be wary of her, too. As he reached the vocal beginning, he nodded to Miss Widtsoe. She began to sing and did, indeed, have a lovely voice. He followed her carefully to give her full advantage.

He glanced about the drawing room. More and more eyes turned their way. The Widtsoes beamed in approval—hopefully of their daughter, not at him paired with her. Another young man with brown curls stared at Miss Widtsoe wearing a hopelessly besotted expression. Hmm. Perhaps he could be an ally in Christian's attempt to step out of Miss Widtsoe's favor.

Lord Wickburgh, the viscount, whom he'd only met today, stared in fascination as well, but not at Miss Widtsoe. No, his whole being focused on Miss Marshall. Rather than the interest of a prospective suitor, or the adoration of a lover, he watched her like a hunter sizing up prey and calculating the appropriate trap. A chill ran down Christian's spine and he played a wrong note but covered it up with a triplet that brought the melody back in correctly.

At the song's conclusion, Miss Widtsoe trilled beautifully. The listeners in the room applauded, some politely, others in clear appreciation.

After curtsying, she smiled at Christian. "I had no idea you played so beautifully. Do you know any piano duets? Do you know Mozart's The Sonata for Two Pianos K. Four-Forty-Eight? Or Fantasy in F minor by Schubert?"

Say no. Say no. He glanced at Miss Marshall. A mistake. She smiled as if he'd just handed her a longed-for gift. "I… do know them both."

He winced. Stupid! Playing duets with Miss Widtsoe would only raise her expectations. But he could not disappoint Miss Marshall. He couldn't begin to guess why.

"Let's do the Mozart," she suggested.

He scooted over on the bench to make room for Miss Widtsoe. She sat so close that their legs almost touched. He edged to the far side of the bench. If only he could extract himself from this. But he was already committed, for the duet, at least.

Letting her set the pace, he followed her. As the piece progressed at a satisfactory rate, his attention returned to Miss Marshall. Lord Wickburgh had moved in and now bowed to her. Mrs. Widtsoe gestured as if to make introductions. Miss Marshall looked up at the lord, her eyes wide and her smile forced.

Christian missed a note. "Sorry," he murmured to his duet partner.

Lord Wickburgh eyed her and fingered his cane as he spoke. Miss Marshall's glances became more furtive, her hands fidgeting in clear distress. How could Christian rescue her? He gritted his teeth. It wasn't his place. But he longed to intervene.

When they finished the duet, Christian glanced at his partner. "I believe your friend is in need of company."

Miss Widtsoe blinked, hurt and confusion in her eyes. He nodded his head meaningfully at Miss Marshall and Lord Wickburgh. She followed his direction.

"Oh. Oh!" She leaped to her feet. "Yes, thank you." She all but rushed to Miss Marshall's side. For all her faults, she was admirably devoted to her friend.

Christian sauntered to the group as if out for a stroll when his muscles raged at him to run. "Good evening," he said to one and all. He eyed Lord Wickburgh pointedly.

"Good evening," the lord replied, barely glancing at Christian. He continued to finger his ornately carved cane.

Christian took a closer look. When they'd first been introduced,

Christian had only made a cursory glance at the slender, elegant older gentleman with a taste for fashion and an air of cold superiority worn by most peers. Now, a deeper chill revealed itself. The lord glanced at Christian dismissively as adults often do to children and returned his focus to Genevieve. Wickburgh looked her over from head to toe, but instead of with appreciation for a fine piece of art, or even a leer for a desirable woman, something akin to puzzlement crossed his expression as if unable to determine why a girl half his age had captured his attention.

"Suffolk?" he said as if repeating something Miss Marshall had said. "Yes, I have land in Suffolk, among other places. I don't spend a great deal of time there, more's the pity. I divide most of my time between my county seat and London." He smiled coolly. "I assume you've been to London for the Season, bowed to the queen and all that?"

"Er, no, my lord," she said in subdued tones. "I've been to London —once—but not for the Season, and I've never taken my bows to the queen."

The normally buoyant Miss Widtsoe planted her feet and wound her arm through Miss Marshall's. "Miss Marshall and I have only been 'out' two years, you see, my lord, so even if she had been to London for the Season, it's unlikely her path would have crossed with such a mature lord as yourself."

Christian almost smiled. *Touché*. A clever way to remind the man he was too old for Miss Marshall. Miss Marshall had a loyal friend.

Lord Wickburgh's eyes narrowed. "*Our* paths have crossed, child, you recall."

"Well, yes," returned Miss Widtsoe, practically quailing under his unnerving stare, "but only because you know my father."

Miss Marshall stood and dropped a hasty curtsy. "If you will excuse us, my lord, I believe—"

He brought up his cane, blocking her path. "Stay." He tried to soften his sharp command with a smile. "I beg you."

Christian's hackles rose. "Forgive the interruption but I am come to ask Miss Widtsoe and Miss Marshall their opinion on a setting I'm considering for painting Miss Widtsoe's portrait. If I may show you both what I have in mind, I welcome your insight."

"Oh how lovely!" Miss Widtsoe enthused.

Christian nodded a farewell to Lord Wickburgh and held out an arm to the ladies. They each took an arm, offering him equal expressions of gratitude and relief as he led them to a far corner of the room.

"Thank you," Miss Marshall said quietly.

"What did you have in mind?" Miss Widtsoe asked. She practically batted her eyelashes at him.

Christian faltered. Surely Miss Widtsoe knew he'd contrived that statement as an excuse to extract Miss Marshall from the unwelcome attention of a gentleman. Perhaps she intended to ensure the ruse appeared believable.

He gestured to the pianoforte. "I thought perhaps I could paint you at the piano." He led her to the instrument. "Sit on the bench as if you are playing. Good. Now, act as if you have completed and are turning to receive your applause. There. Hold that pose. Miss Marshall, if you would be so kind." With her arm still on his, he stepped back to give her a look at the setting.

Miss Marshall glanced over her shoulder in Lord Wickburgh's direction. She drew a breath and then turned her full attention to her friend at the pianoforte. She took a moment to consider before nodding. "That's lovely. The wall painted in those subdued colors to imitate brick, and the light coming in through the windows gives her an excellent backdrop. Matilda, you take a look." The ladies traded places.

Miss Marshall sat surrounded by a halo of soft lighting, her mouth curved in an affectionate smile. The setting sun cast fiery burgundy lights in her hair in an array of colors it would take Christian days to mix and blend to get just right. If he were to paint Genevieve Marshall, he'd move the carved black cats out of the way, drape a sheer curtain behind the piano, add a vase of flowers, and perhaps some potted plants to invite the garden inside, accenting her fairy-like quality.

"I like it," Miss Widtsoe announced. "It would show off my talent for music, and I like the Egyptian influence. It adds a touch of the exotic, don't you think?" She beamed at Christian.

The vision of Miss Marshall filled his senses so completely that he barely managed to nod in acknowledgement.

"How soon can we start?" Miss Widtsoe asked.

He faltered, trying to remember what she wanted to start, and scrambled for a reply. "Perhaps tomorrow afternoon, to catch the best light."

"Perfect!"

It was all he could do not to wince. She enthused about the portrait, but his attention returned to Miss Marshall, whose focus shifted to something behind him. Her peaceful countenance clouded. He glanced back. Lord Wickburgh stared at her. Miss Marshall arose and joined Miss Widtsoe and him.

"Stay close," Christian said softly to Miss Marshall. "He'll get the message." If not, Christian would have to have words with Lord Wickburgh about leaving the lady alone.

She nodded.

Miss Widtsoe glanced between them with a puzzled frown tugging at her brows. "Jenny?"

Miss Marshall's mouth curved into a reassuring smile that failed to touch her eyes. "Don't mind me. I'm only being a goose."

Keeping his posture casual and his steps unhurried, Christian led both ladies towards Miss Marshall's parents who stood conversing with another couple. "I don't believe I've had the opportunity to meet your parents. Would you do me the honor of introducing me?"

"It would be my pleasure."

"Oh, the Marshalls are just wonderful people!" Miss Widtsoe beamed at Christian. "Did you know her father was a sea captain during the war? Why, his ship was instrumental in the victory at Trafalgar. That makes him rather a war hero, doesn't it?"

"Indeed."

The Marshalls turned at their approach, and Christian greeted them as Miss Marshall made the introductions to the distinguished gentleman and his diminutive wife, an older but attractive version of Genevieve. Christian made a casual glanced about the room. Lord Wickburgh stood engaged in conversation with another gentleman and no longer focused on Miss Marshall.

The hostess called for a game of charades. Throughout the evening, Christian covertly observed Lord Wickburgh, but the older man made no further attempt to approach Miss Marshall. Perhaps he'd gotten the hint.

Unfortunately, the more Christian tried to keep his attention off of the beautiful lady, the more he stared.

As the games ended, guests broke off into smaller groups, chatting and laughing. Others retired for the evening, including the earl. When Genevieve Marshall left with her parents, he relaxed; she'd be safe from Lord Wickburgh in their company. Christian would also be spared the agony of trying not to look at her.

Christian also bowed to the host and hostess. "Goodnight, sir, ma'am."

The overly enthusiastic Miss Widtsoe appeared at her parents' side. "Retiring so soon, Mr. Amesbury?"

"I wish to be well rested for the hunt tomorrow." He bowed and turned to leave, but her voice stopped him.

"Oh, of course. Do you enjoy hunting, then?"

"What I enjoy most about it is a good bruising ride through the countryside," he confessed.

"Oh, yes. My friend Jenny does as well. I believe I heard you like the steeplechase?"

He blinked. How did she know that? "I do, very much."

She smiled so brightly, so hopefully, that he practically fled.

As he prepared for bed, his thoughts circled back to Genevieve Marshall, no matter how much he tried to cast her out of her mind. Could he ever be deserving of the love of such a lady?

CHAPTER 5

Genevieve ducked to avoid a low hanging limb and tapped her horse lightly with the riding crop to urge him forward. She didn't dare fall behind the hunting party and give the men a reason to suggest she return home to sit with the ladies sewing while the men had all the fun. Besides, riding sidesaddle at breakneck speed over rugged terrain filled her with an exhilaration few other activities could provide.

The woods thinned and the group charged down a hillside following the barking, howling dogs. She galloped along with the hunting party, her body moving in harmony with the horse's stride. She laughed for sheer joy as the wind sang in her ears. Fresh, woodsy scents around her filled her lungs, reminding her of rides with her father back home.

Christian Amesbury glanced back at her again. Whether he checked on her so often out of simple chivalric duty, or a belief that she couldn't handle herself, she did not know. But each time he did, a warm flush lit up her toes. The other men gave their full attention to the hunt, except Papa who occasionally shared a grin with her.

As dogs barked, tack jingled, horses whinnied, and hooves pounded, the party raced along a ravine and then up the other side, winding between trees and scrub. The dogs' barking and howling reached a crescendo, and then all at once, they lost their prey. No amount of sniffing and false starts found the scent. Their quarry had vanished. Some of the men voiced their displeasure but many shrugged and said it was all part of the game.

Christian Amesbury wheeled around, grinning and rosy-cheeked from the chill morning air. "Race you back?" he called out to the nearest few riders.

Though not specifically included, his challenge was general enough that Genevieve joined in. They galloped, leaping over fallen trees and stumps, crashing through brush, and dodging rocks in their path. As they reached the perimeter of the abbey's gardens, Mr. Amesbury's stallion pulled ahead. His nearest two contenders leaned over their horses' necks and made a valiant effort, but Mr. Amesbury reached the paddock first. Genevieve arrived only seconds behind them.

The men laughed good-naturedly and congratulated each other on a fine run. Genevieve walked her horse around the perimeter to cool him before returning to the stable doors.

"May I help you dismount?" Lord Wickburgh appeared next to her horse. Classically handsome and elegant in his red riding coat, the older man smiled and extended a hand. But a chill in his gaze cooled her joy of the ride.

"Er, my father usually helps me," she said lamely, looking around for Papa.

She found him slapping Mr. Amesbury on the back and laughing with the men who'd encircled the impromptu race's winner. Papa seemed unaware of her plight.

"It's no inconvenience to me, Miss Marshall."

Since there seemed no tangible reason to resist and no graceful way to refuse, she accepted his help dismounting. His hands stayed longer than necessary on her waist. She stepped back and held onto her riding crop with both hands to put some distance between them.

His smooth voice reminded her of melted glass in a glassblower's shop. "Your riding habit is beautiful. It suits you."

"Thank you," she said breathlessly, looking down at her hands to avoid his chilling stare.

A stable hand arrived to take their reins.

The moment the servant left, Lord Wickburgh said, "You ride uncommonly well. I was surprised you chose to accompany a hunt—and surprised your father allows you to do something so dangerous."

"He and I often enjoy a vigorous ride together." She gathered up the train of her riding habit and laid it over her left arm. "If you will please excuse me, my lord, I believe I will change." She bobbed a quick curtsy and strode towards the house, her insides quaking.

Papa caught up to her. "Jolly good morning, eh?"

She hushed her disquiet from her encounter with Lord Wickburgh and found a smile to give Papa. "Lovely weather for a ride."

"That Amesbury fellow seems to have caught your eye, Jenny."

"Oh, no, he's not for me. Matilda has formed an attachment to him. I'm only trying to take measure of his character."

"Uh huh." His disbelief rang clear.

"Truly, Papa. I would never encourage the attention of a gentleman that my friend—"

"I know, daughter. I am not questioning your intentions. But he is young, handsome, the son of an earl..."

"He is gallant. And gentle. And intelligent." She might have listed at least a dozen more qualities she'd observed in him but stopped, lest her father misunderstand her praise. "I'm persuaded that he will be an excellent match for Matilda."

"Yes, he will be an excellent match for any young lady, even if he is a tad young for matrimony."

An uncomfortable prickling between her shoulder blades had her glancing over her shoulder. Lord Wickburgh stared after her. He nodded, then turned away, but something about it sent a tremor down her backbone.

Under her breath, she said, "Papa, what do you know of Lord Wickburgh?"

"Very little except that he is a viscount and a man of considerable wealth and influence. He has buried two wives."

"Oh, poor man. He must be lonely." That must have been it. She'd misunderstood him. What she'd perceived as a cold sort of ruthlessness must have been pain and loneliness.

"I'm sure." Her father's face clouded, and he cast a glance up at the window where he shared a bedroom with Mama during the house party. Did he worry that he might face widowhood soon?

Genevieve linked her arm with his. "Mama has been ever so much stronger lately. Why, the trip didn't seem to tire her much at all."

"Yes, I believe you're right."

"Don't you worry about her. Between you and me, we will make sure Mama lives a long and healthy life."

Papa kissed her temple, and they strolled into the house. After cleaning up and changing, Genevieve joined the ladies in the back parlor where they sat gossiping and sewing. Matilda sat at the pianoforte, practicing a particularly difficult piece, a Haydn, if she were correct. Genevieve sat next to her, careful not to jostle her on the bench. Following along, Genevieve turned the page at the correct time. Matilda stumbled over a particularly grueling passage.

"E flat," Genevieve murmured.

"I know," Matilda snapped. She stopped. Sighed. "Forgive me, Jenny. I'm trying to get this right so I can play it tonight for Christian. I want him to like me."

Genevieve put her hand on Matilda's back. "I don't think his good opinion of you will change if you fail to learn a new piece by this eve."

"I know, but I wish..." She turned sad eyes upon Genevieve. "I confess, I don't think he returns my regard. He's very kind but doesn't appear to share my grand passion. I have to try *something* to attract his notice." She returned to her music and worked at the passage until she got it right.

"You are a lovely and accomplished young lady," Genevieve said.

"And he does seem to admire you on some level. Perhaps when he draws your portrait you will have a better opportunity to become acquainted."

A gleam came into Matilda's eyes. "I wonder what his favorite color is?"

"Why?"

"I thought if perhaps I wore blue when he painted my portrait..."

Genevieve considered. "Hmm. He seems to favor blue. He wears it a lot. Besides, blue is lovely on you; it brings out your eyes."

Matilda's usual buoyancy returned to her expression. "I have a new sarcenet evening gown of Cambridge blue with a silvery-blue parted overskirt. Perhaps I should wear that for my sitting?"

"I'm sure it's beautiful on you. And even better if he favors the color."

"What else might I do to win his regard?"

"Well, having not made a match of my own, I can hardly say, but Mama says a lady should always ask a gentleman questions about himself and encourage him to speak, while speaking very little about herself."

"I've tried that. He doesn't say much." Matilda's voice turned plaintive.

"Perhaps you aren't asking the right questions. Have you asked him what his interests are?"

"Oh, yes. He's mad for the steeplechase, and he boxes and fences. Almost a Corinthian, isn't he? And... well, aside from art and music, I don't know much else."

"Try to word the questions so they can't be answered with a simple yes or no."

Matilda nodded thoughtfully.

A few gentlemen drifted in, including the Earl of Tarrington, but not Mr. Amesbury. The ladies continued chatting while the gentlemen filled in around them.

"Where do you think he is?" Matilda asked.

Genevieve didn't have to ask what "he" Matilda meant. "Probably out sketching the abbey."

Matilda let out a breath of glee. "I do believe I wish to go for a bit of a ramble."

"I do, as well." Genevieve returned her smile.

They took up hats and gloves, and changed into half-boots for walking. Genevieve grabbed a parasol to protect her skin from the sun's burning rays. After leaving behind the manicured gardens, they climbed nearby hills, looking for a place where Mr. Amesbury might have chosen to draw the abbey. They were both tired and almost willing to admit defeat and return to the house when Matilda let out a gasp.

"Oh! There he is!"

Sitting bareheaded amid a stand of poplars at the top of a hill, Mr. Amesbury sat as still as a painting. The dappled light shone on his golden head and played with the blue of his tailcoat.

Matilda made a straight course for him, but Genevieve pulled her back. "We must appear to be out for a stroll, Mattie, not hunting him."

Her friend made a sigh of exasperation but slowed her steps as they followed the rocky narrow path carved into the side of the hill. "You're right, of course." She let out a long-suffering sigh.

Genevieve admired the rugged beauty of the landscape and breathed the clean air.

After a moment, Matilda broke the silence. "Did you know we're going to have a ball tonight? After dinner, we'll roll up the carpets and dance. Mama even arranged to have some musicians play for us. Won't that be lovely? And Mama agreed that we can even *waltz*." She put a hand over her mouth as if she were scandalized but her eyes twinkled.

"Oh, dear. I never learned that dance."

"No? Pity. I learned with a dance master Papa hired this winter. It's been all the rage in Vienna for years, you know. I can't wait to waltz with Christian," Matilda said dreamily.

"Would you teach me how to do it?"

"Well, it would be difficult without a partner, but if you know the basic steps, you ought to be able to follow when you do have a partner." She cast a longing glance at Mr. Amesbury. "Shall we do it now?"

"Oh, no, let's not waste a moment of your time with him," Genevieve said. She looked back at where he sat, but he remained motionless as if he had not yet seen them.

"It will only take a moment to teach you the basic step." Mattie stood in front of her so Genevieve could follow her. "It's narrow here, and rocky, so watch your footing. Begin with your right foot taking a step back. One. Then bring your left through and to the left side and turn your body a half turn. Two. Then bring your right foot to your left and switch your weight onto it. Three. That's the first half. Then you begin again but this time stepping forward with your left and pivot on your right to spin around and complete the turn."

Genevieve tried to imitate. Matilda repeated with Genevieve following, her movements clumsy at first but then catching on.

Matilda counted, "One, two, three, four, five, six. One, two—ah!" She let out a sharp cry and went down.

Genevieve's breath strangled as Matilda pitched sideways over the edge of the hill. "Mattie!" She charged after her friend.

Matilda tumbled a few times before coming to a stop as the hill leveled off. She lay still. Stumbling and sliding in her haste to reach her friend, Genevieve rushed to her.

"Matilda?" She slid to her knees next to her friend's motionless form.

Matilda rolled over. "I'm all right. I think."

Genevieve almost sobbed in relief. She helped raise her to a sitting position. "Does it hurt anywhere?"

Heavy footsteps pounded to them. "Miss Widtsoe? Are you injured?" Christian Amesbury took long, commanding strides to reach them. Concern carved itself into his features, and his whole focus fixed upon Matilda.

With her face red, Matilda hurried to straighten her skirts to cover her legs. "I don't think so." She looked down but the shimmer of moisture on her eyes gave away her distress.

"Do you wish to rest here a moment before you try to stand?" Genevieve asked.

Biting her lip, Matilda nodded.

Mr. Amesbury crouched next to them both. He looked over Matilda. "Are you sure you're unharmed?" he asked gently.

Her eyes brimming with tears, she nodded jerkily, not in pain but in embarrassment. Poor dear. She'd been trying so hard to impress him. It was Genevieve's fault it had happened. She should never have agreed to a dance lesson in an area with uneven ground.

Mr. Amesbury's mouth pressed into a compassionate wince. He turned his attention to Genevieve. "Did you fall, too?"

"No. I ran after her. I'm quite well."

Matilda drew a shivering breath and pushed herself to a wobbly stand. Genevieve helped her and Mr. Amesbury held his hands out as if to steady her should she need his strength. As Matilda's took a step, she winced.

"Is your foot hurt?" Genevieve asked.

"My ankle. I must have twisted it. But I can walk."

Genevieve kept pace with Matilda as she marshaled her way down the hill, forgoing the path and taking the shortest distance back to the abbey. With each step, her face twisted in progressively more intense pain.

"Lean on my arm," Mr. Amesbury said.

Her face redder still and tears shining in her eyes, Matilda obliged, but her breath grew more and more labored.

"Perhaps you should rest," Genevieve suggested.

Matilda shook her head and pushed on.

Finally, Mr. Amesbury stopped and turned her. "You are aggravating your injury." He paused. "I could carry you back."

Matilda's gaze flew to his, hope and dread all mixed up. "Oh, no. You couldn't. I mean of course you could, you're certainly strong enough, I mean, you look strong enough but I…" She looked away as her face flushed an even deeper shade of scarlet, if that were possible.

"It's no trouble." His handsome face took on an earnest expression. "Unless you prefer me to go get help. We could perhaps bring a footman or a cart."

"Oh, dear. I'm so embarrassed." Matilda put a hand over her eyes.

"No need for embarrassment," Mr. Amesbury said gallantly. "It could happen to anyone." Looking truly concerned, he led her to a boulder and seated her upon it. He crouched next to her and took her hand. Very gently, he asked, "How can I assist you? What do you wish me to do?"

The very core of Genevieve's being melted at his compassion, his gentleness, his chivalry. Matilda had found the perfect gentleman. And he appeared—finally—to show true concern, perhaps even affection, for Matilda. Perhaps he'd held her in high esteem all along but was too shy to show it.

Genevieve should have been ecstatic at this encouraging step in the right direction. Instead, the opposite emotion reared its ugly head. Envy. Envy that such a desirable gentleman looked at Matilda. Envy that no one had ever behaved in such a way towards Genevieve. Envy that Matilda would probably marry Christian soon, and Genevieve would still be alone, left to compare every man she met to him, and who, naturally, would fall woefully short.

Oh, heaven help her, but the only man who'd ever turned her head was the love of Matilda's life. Genevieve was turning into a selfish beast.

CHAPTER 6

Christian studied the young woman, Miss Widtoe, in front of him. Were her tears a result of humiliation, or pain, or some other heartbreak he could not discern? Regardless, her distress spurred him to action. But to walk into the abbey carrying a young lady might throw her virtue into question.

"I'll go for help," Miss Marshall said quietly. She flicked troubled brown eyes at him.

And leave him alone with Miss Widtsoe, which might also tarnish her reputation as well as throw them alone together to further encourage Miss Widtsoe of his intention? A bad idea, all the way around.

There was no way to win. He refused to leave the ladies alone, which left him the choice of carrying Miss Widtsoe or sending her friend—both of which would give the wrong idea of his intentions, and both of which might put the lady's virtue and his character in question.

"No, please stay, Miss Marshall." Did his tone sound as desperate as he felt? Choosing what he hoped was the least bad of his options, he said, "Miss Widtsoe, do allow me to carry you home. We'll go in a side entrance, so you are spared further embarrassment." With luck, no one would see them.

She chewed her lip and then nodded. Looking up at him from underneath her lashes, her expression changed from discomfort to coyness. "You're so very chivalrous to offer, sir."

Christian almost groaned. Wonderful. Now, she'd view his carrying her as some sort of romantic gesture.

Miss Marshall's glance landed more on the side of gratitude. "You're very kind."

He had the urge to square his shoulders and draw himself to his full height. He slid his arms underneath Miss Widtsoe's legs and back, and lifted her. She snuggled against him and placed her arms around his shoulders. There was nothing for it. He started walking, Miss Marshall keeping up with him.

"I apologize for the inconvenience," Miss Widtsoe said in a soft, flirtatious tone.

He refused to look at her and put their mouths so close together. "Think nothing of it."

"It's fortunate that you came along when you did. I don't know how I'd manage, else."

"I am persuaded that your devoted friend would have assisted you."

"Yes, she would have. I've never had a truer friend!"

She must not be in much discomfort, judging from the way she was already lapsing into her habit of saying everything with an exclamation point.

Miss Marshall turned her head enough to send an affectionate smile at Miss Widtsoe, allowing Christian a glimpse of her face. Still, something shadowed her eyes. Did she fear for her friend's reputation? A disturbing thought. Christian was known as an upstanding gentleman, and Miss Widtsoe's behavior was, to his knowledge, exemplary. Today, throughout the entire incident, Miss Marshall had been present. And surely the circumstances necessitated some flexibility. So really, they had nothing to fear.

Still, had he made a mistake in carrying the girl home? But, dash it all, what else was he to do?

An uncomfortable silence fell. Christian asked Miss Widtsoe, "What caused your fall?"

"Oh, it was the silliest thing. Genevieve told me she didn't know how to waltz so I was showing her the basic steps, but I forgot I was on a narrow path and lost my footing."

Christian glanced at Miss Marshall, who winced as if she blamed herself for Miss Widtsoe's fall.

"It was foolish, I know," Miss Widtsoe continued, drawing his thoughts. "But I wanted ever so much for my dear friend to know how to waltz as I do."

He quirked a smile. "Perhaps in the future, you ought to restrict dancing lessons to a larger, flatter area, such as a drawing room."

With a giggle, she tightened her hold on his neck. "I am persuaded you are right. But then, perhaps it happened for a reason?" She smiled.

He deliberately kept his focus on the path.

Genevieve Marshall let out a small gasp. "Oh, no, Mattie! I hope your ankle is healed enough to dance tonight."

"Ohhhhh," Miss Widtsoe wailed. "How can I dance on it now?"

Miss Marshall's expression turned earnest. "We'll try every remedy we know. Perhaps if we wrap it and elevate it and you rest all day?"

"I suppose." Disappointment clouded Miss Widtsoe's features.

"We'll think of something, Mattie," Miss Marshall promised. "Your cook might know of a remedy. Perhaps your father will send for the doctor."

They reached the outer gardens. The strain of carrying the girl warmed Christian's muscles. He circled around to the back, skirted a ha-ha separating a field of sheep from the back lawn, and headed to a portico.

"Go to the side entrance off the terrace," Miss Widtsoe suggested. "No one should be in the library now, not on such a fine day."

He glanced down at Miss Marshall striding next to him so quietly that she seemed to float. Or perhaps his own heavy footsteps, even more so with a burden in his arms, drowned out any sound she made. Her bonnet hid her face from him. Still, the quality of her breathing sent wild little fingers of awareness over him.

For a brief, mad instant, he wished she were in his arms instead of Miss Widtsoe. And for entirely different reasons. But that would be a mistake in a dozen ways. Still, her nearness taunted him. She was not only one of the more beautiful ladies he'd ever seen, she was in possession of peaceful elegance and genuine kindness. His father would say something about still waters running deep.

She presented the exact opposite of Miss Widtsoe--one exuberant, the other restrained, not because she wasn't in possession of strong emotions, but she held them in check as if she only brought them out for special moments. One chattered freely with almost childlike charm, the other spoke after careful consideration, weighing each word to assure it contained the exact meaning to deliver her thoughts. And though Miss Widtsoe seemed cheerful and sweet, there were moments when he suspected her of being childishly self-absorbed. Yet Genevieve Marshall's unselfishness, the way she cared for others, and sought to show her friend in the best possible light while remaining quietly in the sidelines, won his respect.

Admirably, the young ladies were loyal friends. Which only served to remind him that if he spurned Miss Widtsoe's affection, he certainly could not pursue her friend. Not that he would, regardless of how tempting.

Miss Marshall's bonnet turned his way, revealing the fullness of her beauty. "Are you getting tired?"

He glanced at her as a wry grin tugged his mouth. "Are you questioning my manliness?"

"Of course she isn't!" Miss Widtsoe interjected. "She's just being the little mother again and taking care of everyone."

In truth, his arms ached. He shifted his bundle and tightened his grip. "I can get her to the house, never fear."

Miss Marshall glanced up at him again. Sadness shadowed her soft eyes. Surely she wasn't so upset about her friend being unable to dance? "I'll go ensure the room is empty." She trotted ahead.

He tried not to admire the grace of her stride nor the way wind flattened the fabric of her gown against her slender curves.

"Don't you just love Genevieve?" Miss Widtsoe chirped. "She is the dearest thing! I hope she finds a man to marry—someone who deserves her. But if she doesn't, maybe she'll live with me and help me raise my family. That would be sublime!"

"I'm sure she won't have any trouble finding a gentleman who will want to marry her. Someone worthy of her might be more difficult to locate, but she isn't meant to live as a spinster," he said.

"I'm sure you're right!" she gushed.

Had he spoken his opinion about Miss Marshall aloud?

"So," Miss Widtsoe said, "you come from a large family. Do you hope to have a lot of children when the time comes?"

He choked and finally managed, "I haven't given it any thought."

"Oh." She paused before asking, "If you could live anywhere, where would it be?"

He attempted to keep up with the questions she fired at him. "I like Bath. But anywhere? Perhaps the seashore—not Brighton, somewhere less crowded. I've always wanted to visit Italy, to paint there, but I'm not certain I'd want to live there. We have some property up in Scotland. Beautiful country. Perhaps there. Why do you ask?"

Miss Marshall opened a side door and vanished inside. Christian nearly broke into a run to catch up to her.

"Merely curious. I would love to see those places, too." Miss Widtsoe took another pause. "You excel at art and music. And you like riding and fencing and boxing. A gentleman of many interests, to be sure. What else do you enjoy?"

He wanted to squirm under all her questions. "I like to read."

Her exuberance faded. "Oh. I'm not much of a reader. Jenny enjoys it, but I find it tiresome to be in a room with someone who's reading." She stopped with a little gasp as if she'd feared she'd insulted him. "But

I applaud that interest in gentlemen. When I marry, I can certainly find other diversions while my husband reads if he so chooses." She cast an anxious look at him.

Christian barely managed not to wince at her obviousness.

Miss Marshall stepped out through a pair of French doors and gestured to him. "This way. It's empty."

Christian carried his burden inside and set her onto a nearby chair. As he straightened, he glanced at Miss Marshall, but her hat shielded her face. She sank down on her knees in front of Miss Widtsoe and began removing the half boot.

He took a step back. "I'll leave you now. I hope your ankle mends quickly, Miss Widtsoe."

She beamed at him. "I'm sure it will. Thank you so much for helping me. You are a true hero."

At that, Miss Marshall turned her head towards him, a secretive smile curving her beautifully formed lips. He wanted to push back her bonnet and run a hand over her silky head and lower his mouth to hers...

He almost groaned out loud. There were so many reasons why that thought was wholly inappropriate.

"It was nothing." He made a shallow bow and left.

He did not need a woman in his life right now. Caring for the earl and managing the estate consumed most of his waking hours, and a goodly number of hours he ought to be sleeping. His brothers would produce heirs to ensure the continuation of the Amesbury line, therefore, Christian had no duty to have heirs. Painting produced all the diversions he required. He would spend his life trying to atone for a host of failings and not drag some poor, undeserving lady into his world.

CHAPTER 7

Genevieve and Mrs. Widtsoe applied every kind of remedy upon Matilda's ankle, but by the time she planned to meet Mr. Amesbury for her first sitting, her ankle had still swollen enough to discourage the wearing of all but the softest slippers, and the skin had darkened to purple.

Sorrowful, Genevieve glanced at Mrs. Widtsoe. "No dancing?"

The dear lady shook her head.

Matilda's face crumpled, but her irrepressible spirit returned after only the briefest bout of tears. Of course, that rallying occurred the moment she received a note from Mr. Amesbury asking if she still wished to sit for her portrait today.

Genevieve almost shed a few tears herself. How could she help her friend? And how could she do it without allowing her jealousy to rule her?

As a maid arranged her hair, Matilda placed cool packets of lavender and chamomile over her face to help dispel signs of tears. "Never mind, Jenny. I will enjoy myself today at the sitting and tonight at the ball, regardless. And when you aren't dancing, you'll sit with me, won't you?"

Genevieve gave her a stern look but of course Matilda couldn't see it with lavender packets over her eyes. "Need you even ask?"

"No, I suppose not. I'm letting my insecurities show." She removed the compresses from her eyes. "How do I look?"

Matilda looked exquisite wearing an elegant blue evening gown. With only the sides caught up, Matilda's thick golden curls tumbled over one shoulder and down her back. Her skin was creamy as ever, and once more she smiling and bright-eyed. If she didn't turn Christian Amesbury's head, he wasn't a man.

Truthfully, Genevieve said, "You look like an angel."

Matilda rewarded her with a bright smile. "I hope he agrees."

They used a wheeled chair a footman had found in the attic to convey her down the corridor, and two footmen carried her, chair and all, down the stairs to the drawing room.

All along the way, Genevieve reminded herself that her task was to give the right nudges for Mr. Amesbury to fall in love with Matilda. Once Genevieve ensured Matilda's happiness, she'd give a thought to her own future. Perhaps she'd meet a fine gentleman later in the summer during their stay in Bath who would make her forget all about her improper fascination with Matilda's true love.

When they arrived in the drawing room, Mr. Amesbury was already there with an easel and a palette of paints. He wore a large, paint-stained smock over his clothes. Focused on something only an artist would see, he held his lower lip between his teeth.

Mama sat with Mrs. Widtsoe in the corner of the room, chatting quietly as they sewed, their voices creating a soft murmur. After wheeling Matilda to the bench next to the pianoforte, Genevieve helped her get settled and arranged her skirts with precision. Then she turned her attention to Matilda's hair, carefully placing her curls so they lay in the best possible arrangement.

She turned to find Mr. Amesbury looking at her. A soft smile curved his full mouth. His intensely focused gaze locked with hers as tangible as a caress. Her cheeks flushed and a place in her midsection quivered.

Gesturing to Matilda, she said, "Do you think she will do?"

As if remembering he'd agreed to paint her portrait, he glanced at Matilda, blinked, then focused. "The color suits her complexion and is an excellent contrast with the background."

Matilda offered an uncertain smile and glanced hesitantly at Genevieve. Genevieve wanted to yell at him. Didn't he see how much his opinion meant to Matilda?

He seemed to realize his error. "You look beautiful, Miss Widtsoe. Just right for a painting." An appreciative smile curved his lips as he gazed at Matilda. At last, he'd noticed her loveliness!

Matilda's signature smile blazed and all was well again. As Mr. Amesbury called out instructions to turn her knees slightly to the side, raise her chin and angle her head, Genevieve withdrew.

When she approached her mother sitting in the corner of the room with Matilda's, Mama nodded her way. "Jenny, dear, the rest of the guests are about to begin a game of croquet. Do join them on the east lawn."

"Very well." Lawn games appealed more than being in the room with the beautiful Christian Amesbury while he gently wooed her friend. Just as she'd hoped he would. Hadn't she?

She grabbed her gloves and tied her bonnet firmly underneath her chin, before hurrying to the east lawn. The guests were already pairing up. A slender young gentleman held his mallet in one hand and tossed his ball up in the air and caught it repeatedly. His action and his brown curls made him look like a mischievous boy. He stood off to the side alone, clearly in need of a partner.

As Genevieve approached, she threw out convention and called, "Sir Reginald, isn't it?"

Instantly smiling, he bowed. "Yes, Miss Marshall."

"Are you, by chance, in need of a partner?"

"I certainly am. Your arrival is most timely." He fixed warm brown eyes on her as he handed her a mallet and matching ball.

The cheerful young man with the fashionable Cherubin hairstyle proved an enthusiastic, and even skilled partner. He teased her into smiling, making outrageously flirtatious statements and inquiries about the state of her dowry. One part shocked and two parts charmed, she shook off her melancholy. Before long, she and Sir Reginald were laughing like old friends.

Clouds flirted with the sun as the merry group played, calling out dares, wagers, and jeers. The only blight in the afternoon came from Lord Wickburgh who watched Genevieve too closely. He'd left his cane somewhere, which confirmed that he only carried it as a fashion statement. Despite the long looks he continued to rain on her, he remained at a distance. Genevieve soon forgot him and focused on her friendly partner who reminded her a great deal of the little brother she never had. Without Matilda nearby to absorb all of her attention, Genevieve enjoyed getting to know the other guests.

Sir Reginald nodded his chin towards a group ahead of them near a spreading oak. "Mr. Ashton keeps looking at you. I believe you have captured his interest."

Genevieve glanced in that direction to catch the gaze of an attractive, dark-haired young gentleman she'd met previously but couldn't recall his name until Sir Reginald reminded her.

Maintaining eye contact, the gentleman nodded.

She bent her knees in the tiniest of curtsies, and said to Sir Reginald, "I can't imagine how. We've hardly spoken."

Sir Reginald grinned. "Speaking isn't requisite to admiring beauty."

"No, I suppose not, and I thank you for the compliment." She'd certainly admired Christian Amesbury before she'd exchanged a single word with him. With a sigh at what could never be, she focused on the game. They finished playing, not victors, but at least not last place.

Sir Reginald offered her a bow. "It was a pleasure to partner you this afternoon, Miss Marshall."

"The pleasure was mine, sir." She grinned at the guileless young man as if he were a dear friend.

As they put away their mallets and balls, a shadow fell over her. "Miss Marshall."

With a start, she met Lord Wickburgh's gaze. Quickly, she looked down to escape that oddly searching stare and curtsied. "Lord Wickburgh."

"You seemed to enjoy the game." Nothing in his tone sounded improper. Then why did he unnerve her so?

"Yes, I… I did, due to the company, I'm sure."

Sir Reginald eyed her curiously and took a few hesitant steps away.

She held a hand out to her partner. "Pray, excuse me, my lord. I promised Sir Reginald I'd walk with him after the game."

At her words, the young man squared his shoulders and offered her his arm. She curtsied to the viscount and took Sir Reginald's arm gratefully.

Several paces away, she said under her breath, "Thank you."

"Is he bothering you?"

"Not precisely, but he makes me nervous. Thank you for playing into my ruse."

"Always a pleasure, Miss Marshall. I did notice him looking at you several times." They fell silent as they strolled towards the house. "You and Miss Widtsoe are fast friends, I take it?"

"Yes, for years."

He let out a sigh. "She's the loveliest creature I've ever seen."

Genevieve smiled. "She does turn heads." At his smitten expression, she debated whether to discourage him. Perhaps it would be kinder to warn him that the way to Matilda's heart was barred. "I am persuaded she will make a match very soon."

His face fell. "With that Amesbury fellow." It wasn't a question.

She held her expression steady. "Perhaps. They have no formal understanding, mind you, but…." She let her voice trail off.

Another sigh. "I have only just reached my majority. I couldn't court her with a purpose until then, but I've admired her for years. Then when we danced in London…" Another sigh. "Do you think I'm too late?"

She wanted to tell him he was not too late, that he had a chance. The temptation arose to even help him try to wrest Matilda's interest away from Christian Amesbury. But that would be disloyal. And cruel to raise Sir Reginald's hopes where hope might not exist.

"I don't know if it's too late, but she has a clear preference for him. Whether he returns her regard is anyone's guess." There. That was honest.

The young man's mouth twisted to one side. "I see." He brightened. "I don't mind a little friendly competition. His father might be an earl, but my grandfather was the Duke of Suttenberg—not the present one, of course; he's a cousin—but *his* grandfather. And don't think I'm much younger than Amesbury, so my age shouldn't be a deterrent. I have reached my majority, after all." He paused. "Do you think she prefers blond over brown?"

Genevieve almost tousled his curls. "I can't imagine your hair would dissuade any sensible young lady."

He grinned. As his gaze fell on something off to the side, he pointed with his chin. "Look. I think the younger set have started a game of Blindman's Bluff. Shall we join them?"

She looked back at Lord Wickburgh. He was mounting the steps leading up to the abbey, absorbed in conversation with a gentleman his own age. She wouldn't have to worry about his disturbing presence if she stayed outside.

And Christian Amesbury remained inside with Matilda... where he should be. They should be together. And she should be happy for them. There was no compelling reason for her to enter the abbey at the moment.

"Yes, Blindman's Bluff sounds delightfully diverting." Anything to keep her away from temptation.

During the game, Genevieve laughed until her sides burned and her cheeks ached. Mr. Ashton continued to send her admiring glances, and Sir Reginald grinned conspiringly at her like an old friend.

When she found herself standing next to Sir Reginald, he winked. "I believe you have conquered Ashton."

Genevieve certainly had no desire to conquer anyone, least of all a man who had failed to engage her in conversation. "Nonsense."

"He can't keep his eyes off you."

"Perhaps he dislikes my bonnet and can't believe I'd wear it in public," she quipped.

"Have you looked in the mirror lately?"

The blindfolded person staggered towards them and they ducked to avoid the outstretched hands.

A footman announced tea, which dissolved the game. Guests moved in small groups and couples towards the abbey. With a meaningful glance at Mr. Ashton, Sir Reginald winked at Genevieve and started whistling as he quickened his pace to leave her behind. Shaking her head, Genevieve smiled. And people thought women were incorrigible matchmakers.

On the subject of matchmaking… had Mr. Amesbury finished the painting? Had he and Matilda enjoyed stimulating conversation? While Genevieve headed for the abbey at a sedate pace, footsteps rustled the grass beside her.

"Good afternoon, Miss Marshall." Mr. Ashton bent his elbow and offered it to her. "May I escort you back?"

"Thank you." She rested her hand lightly on his arm.

They walked in silence as Genevieve admired the rugged terrain, and the way the hills cast long shadows over the land. Wildflowers danced in the breeze and songbirds trilled as if all the world were a concert hall.

"Lovely weather, isn't it?" he said.

She looked up at him in surprise. Really? The weather? "Er, yes." Perhaps he was merely nervous, having never conversed beyond their brief introduction. "I confess, I have not played Blindman's Bluff in years. I can see I missed out on a lark."

"Yes, unexpectedly enjoyable." He spoke evenly, without any discernable emotion.

"I don't think I've laughed so hard in a long time."

"A welcome diversion, to be sure." He agreed in that same oddly monotone voice.

They walked on without speaking, and she tried to remember if she'd seen him smile or laugh during the game.

Genevieve fumbled to broach a topic with the solemn gentleman next to her. "Have you been here before? To the abbey, I mean."

"Yes, I live nearby. My father is the vicar here."

"I believe I did hear that."

"He is grooming me to take his place very soon."

"That must be a rewarding line of work."

"It will be sufficient." Did he speak in monotone because he didn't find the thought appealing? Or was that his normal tone of voice?

They reached the abbey and continued to the sectioned off part of the drawing room where other guests enjoyed tea. A summer breeze blew through open terrace doors, carrying in the scent of wildflowers and sunshine. Several older people conversed together creating a low murmur.

Matilda sat in her wheeled chair amid a group of young ladies, bubbling over with enthusiasm. As they reached the others, Genevieve curtsied to Mr. Ashton. "Thank you for escorting me."

"My pleasure," came the monotone reply.

Christian Amesbury drew her gaze. In the midst of admiring his fine form and handsome face as he sat painting Matilda, a new awareness spread through her, a desire to ease his burdens, to ask him about his hopes and dreams, to ride pell-mell through the countryside, even to simply sit with him and read as he created a work of art. Or perhaps forgo the book and simply admire him.

If he and Matilda made a match, those privileges would belong to Matilda. The thought sent a dart of pain into her heart. That was silly. Really, she hardly knew him. Surely her interest stemmed from a passing fancy.

CHAPTER 8

Throughout the afternoon, Christian tuned out Matilda Widtsoe's chatter and focused on the animated expressions of her face, trying to capture the best one for her portrait. Though lovely and pleasant, she had a draining effect on him. Still, on the rare occasion she fell silent, he asked her another question to keep her talking for the sake of the portrait. By the end of the sitting, he'd created an expression that combined a subdued form of her usual enthusiasm while capturing the liveliness of her eyes. He'd also sketched other rough likenesses of her, the piano, and enough decorations to suggest Egyptian flavor without overwhelming the main subject of the portrait.

Other houseguests streamed in, probably in anticipation of tea. Christian sat back. Satisfied with the proportions, he rolled his shoulders to loosen the tension.

When Miss Widtsoe took a breath from her steady stream of prattle, he said, "That will do for today."

Her mouth remained open as if she had stopped mid-sentence. Recovering, she closed her mouth and smiled. "This bench is getting hard anyway." She stood, visibly keeping her weight on one foot. "Will you help me to a settee, please?"

He leaped to his feet. "Your wheeled chair is here." No need to have more physical contact than necessary and give her another reason to mistake his intentions. He brought the wheeled contraption to her and held it steady while she settled herself in it, then he pushed her chair to the settee.

While he removed his smock and gathered up his painting supplies, she called, "May I see it?"

"It's not finished."

"I know, but—please?"

He tucked the easel under his arm and brought the canvas to her. "I'll add color tomorrow."

Her expression of expectation fell as she looked at the canvas, but she nodded and said with forced cheer, "I'm sure it will be lovely when you're finished."

She turned the full brightness of her smile on him but her praise was rather demoralizing, much like when as a child he showed his newest project to adults who patted him on the head and told him his art was fine when really they meant it was the pathetic scribblings of a beginner.

Genevieve Marshall sank down in an armchair next to Miss Widtsoe and leaned in to see the portrait. "Oh, my. The proportions are amazing, and you captured her lively spirit beautifully."

It was all he could do not to puff out his chest in pride. Before replying, he searched for a note of humility. "I'm gratified by your approval. I'll add color and finish it before I leave."

"I'm sure it will have no equal." Miss Marshall's admiration seemed genuine, without the coquettishness of so many ladies of the *ton*, including that of Miss Widtsoe.

Though tempted to remain basking in her soothing presence, he bowed. "If you will both excuse me, I need to go put this away."

"A footman can do that for you," Miss Widtsoe said with a flutter of lashes. Definitely a coquette.

"I prefer to do it myself. I have a rather particular way of storing it."

He returned to his bedchamber. After cleaning the paint off his hands and brushes, and checking to be sure he hadn't splattered paint on his face or clothing, he checked on his father.

He found the earl sitting next to the hearth, staring at the embers. Dressed in his breeches and shirtsleeves, with a banyan draped over his shoulders and tied loosely at the waist, he made no sign of awareness of Christian's presence. Next to him sat two creased letters.

Softly, so as not to startle him, Christian said, "Sir, do you wish to join us downstairs for tea?"

The earl let out a sigh and looked up at Christian, his eyes unfocused. He blinked and seemed to return to himself. "I'll have a tray here."

Christian stepped inside. "Don't you think spending a few moments in the company of others would be better than staying here alone?"

His father's mouth tugged off to the side in a loose smile. "I suppose you are right." As he stood, he summoned his valet, scooped up the letters, and handed them to Christian along with his signet ring. "Take care of these, will you, Son? I'll finish dressing." He took off the loose, robe-like garment and let it fall.

Sitting at the desk in his father's room, Christian read over the contents of the letters involving estate business. It was a shame Father took so little interest in estate matters or even parliament, which he used to serve so diligently. Mother's death had drained Father of all his *joie de vivre*. However, this trip seemed to have done him some good. He'd recover fully in time and with enough of the healing opportunities found in Bath.

Christian wrote out two replies the way his father would have wanted regarding the estate and sealed the wax with the earl's signet ring.

The earl returned, groomed and dressed. Christian matched his father's pace as they entered the drawing room. While his father walked on his cane to Mr. Widtsoe and Lord Wickburgh, Christian meandered towards a group of young men closer to his own age.

Mr. Ashton, the vicar's son, droned, "...a good match. Her dowry and behavior are respectable enough."

Sir Reginald shook his head, making his curls bob. "She's lovely and witty and charming, that's what, and if you don't appreciate her many fine qualities, you don't deserve her."

"Set your sights on her, have you?" Mr. Ashton asked with more emotion in his voice than Christian had heard thus far.

Sir Reginald shook his head. "I like her, but my heart belongs to Miss Widtsoe." He placed a hand over his heart.

Ah. So, Matilda Widtsoe did indeed have the attention of young Sir Reginald. Perhaps Christian could help facilitate a change of loyalty on the girl's part?

Casting off his curiosity over who they had been discussing earlier, Christian sidled up to the curly top. "Miss Widtsoe is lovely."

Sir Reginald gave a start and a decided straightening of his shoulders. "She is. I've known her for years—watched her grow up, as it were."

Christian almost grinned at the challenge in the young man's eyes and voice. "Childhood friends, were you?"

"Something like that." The challenge was flung back.

Christian nodded. "My parents were, as well. They enjoyed a very happy marriage."

Sir Reginald eyed him as if he didn't quite trust Christian's meaning. "Always a desirable arrangement."

Sir Reginald's gaze strayed to the girl under discussion and Christian followed his line of sight, but didn't get past Genevieve Marshall. She drew him like a moth to a flame. If he drew closer, would he find a long-absent warmth? Or get burned?

Before he knew it, he'd approached her and found himself standing in front of her in the center of a group of young ladies. Fortunately, Sir Reginald had accompanied him.

"Good afternoon," Christian said.

As all the young ladies nearby responded, he scrambled for something to say, since he had not intended to approach. *You're beautiful and restful and I want to know you better. Will you go for a long walk with me?* That hardly seemed appropriate. Or worse, *If I kiss you, will you kiss me back or slap me?*

He barely managed to avoid trying it. He daren't risk the consequences.

As Christian's panicked thoughts swirled in chaos, Sir Reginald came to the rescue and addressed the ladies as a group. "Mr. Amesbury and I were discussing the waltz and that many of you young ladies here might not know how. So, in preparation for tonight's ball, we have decided to offer our services as practice partners."

Christian glanced at him, brows raised, at the wild tale. That was brilliant, actually. Reginald held out his arms, half turning to encompass all the young ladies who held their teacups frozen in front of them, their mouths slightly agape.

Using his most charming smile, Christian added, "We realize it's a bit unconventional, but this is a house party, after all—not Almack's Assembly Rooms." Smiling, he extended a hand to Genevieve Marshall. "Care to have a practice waltz, Miss Marshall? I'm no dance master, but perhaps I can help."

Smiling, she rose and placed her hand in his. At her touch, an unraveled place inside him sighed and wove itself into the tapestry of his soul. It might be mad, but all his reasons for avoiding the idea of love or marriage no longer mattered. Having this woman—this incredible lady—in his life became a taunting wish.

"May I?" Sir Reginald bowed before another young lady.

As if a challenge had been issued, half the unmarried gentlemen in the room approached young ladies of their choice, bowed, and drew them into dance position. A murmur of one-two-three, four-five-six filled the room. The older adults' conversation died out, and a few sputtered at the strange, impromptu dance, but no one voiced a true protest. Not that it would have mattered. At that moment, dancing with Genevieve consumed Christian's every desire.

Well, not *every* desire. Taking her into a secluded room and kissing her senseless would be a preferred activity over dancing. But he must woo her slowly, making it clear he had honorable intentions.

"Shall I count?" she asked, a teasing half-smile curving her delicious lips.

Christian smiled at the gentle observation that they were standing in waltz position but not actually dancing. "I will, if you have no objection."

That luscious curve in her mouth deepened. "None at all."

"The best way to learn is to do. Keep your arms firm and put your hand here." He repositioned her hand to a spot higher on his arm near his shoulder. Did he imagine her quick intake of breath? "This is our frame. Keep some tension in your arms to maintain this distance. As long as we retain our frame, you should have no trouble following me."

She nodded, her eyes large and her pupils dilated—a sign of desire, unless he was mistaken. He'd spent enough time on the dance floor with ladies that he'd began taking for granted that ladies of all ages desired him. However, with Genevieve Marshall, he could not be sure if what he saw was desire. He might actually be in the unprecedented position of having to work to win her affections.

He looked forward to the challenge.

"Are you ready?" he asked.

"I hope I don't step on your foot."

He affected a mournful expression. "You appear to weigh about as much as a fallen leaf—if you step on me, I fear I might not survive the encounter."

Her eyes danced and her smile almost blinded him. He might never see another woman again. "I might surprise you."

"You already have, in many ways." Before he made a fool of himself right here and now, he said, "Step back with your right foot. Ready? One." He stepped forward with his left foot, guiding her back. "Two." He guided her to his right. "Three." He closed his steps. "You follow beautifully."

Again, came that blast of cleansing brilliance. "I love waltzing."

"We're not actually waltzing yet, that was just one half of the basic step."

"Silly me." A husky tone entered her voice.

He cleared his throat. "Now, we reverse. You step forward with your left as I step back and we turn to complete the circle." As they moved, he counted, "Four, five, six. That was a complete basic. Let's do it again just as before but without stopping."

While he counted, she followed him as he took her through the basic several more times. Then he turned her. She followed like an expert. He taught her several more moves, leading her and counting as he showed her the balance step, right turns, left turns, and the promenade. Each touch of her hand, the brush of her thigh, his hand on her back sent him over the moon time and time again. Through it all, her expression remained that of pure rapture.

He smiled down at the fairy-like girl in his arms who radiated purity and joy. "You can say it now, if you like."

"Say it?" She angled her head off to the side, looking so adorable that he almost kissed her right there.

"That you love to waltz."

"Oh, I do!" she said breathlessly. "But I'm a little dizzy with all this turning."

"Just wait until we add music."

"I can hardly wait." She grinned, and light filled a dark place inside.

Another voice broke in. "Gentlemen, I think the young ladies have had enough dance instruction for the afternoon."

Mrs. Widtsoe's added, "We wouldn't want to exhaust them before tonight's revelry begins."

Christian raised a brow and asked softly, "Are you exhausted, Miss Marshall?"

"Not a bit. But the point is taken."

"Or perhaps she merely wishes to limit contact for this very scandalous dance."

"Probably that, as well." Her eyes danced.

He had to tell himself to let her go twice before his arms actually obeyed. She gave him a conspiratorial smile, curtsied, and turned away.

As he joined the other gentlemen on the side of the room where he'd been standing, Sir Reginald said under his breath, "I'm relieved that I don't have to compete with you for the fair Matilda."

"No, indeed. My affections are definitely engaged elsewhere."

Mr. Ashton's gaze flicked in Christian's direction and his brow narrowed as if he were annoyed. Christian gave him little thought. Tonight, he would leap any hurdles to ensure he waltzed in truth with Genevieve Marshall.

CHAPTER 9

Genevieve joined Matilda's group of young ladies, positioning herself so she couldn't see Christian Amesbury. It wouldn't do to look at him too long or too frequently. His warmth and the texture of his skin remained on her hands as a ghostly reminder of where she'd been, and where she desperately wished to return.

Matilda spoke to her audience of young ladies, who either had not joined the dancing lesson or who had already returned, with her usual animation though clearly attempting to keep her voice down. "…I vow, with him studying me so closely as he painted my portrait, it was all I could do not to blush the entire time! He asked me ever so many questions about myself, my family, and my interests. I expect he will ask to speak to my father any day now!"

She spoke of Christian Amesbury, surely. Which meant Genevieve had misunderstood his intentions as they danced. Or Matilda nursed a grand delusion.

Though Genevieve had come to the house party fully expecting to meet the man Matilda would marry, the thought no longer gave her the pleasure it once did. But that was a selfish attitude. Matilda's happiness meant the world to Genevieve. Moreover, Christian

Amesbury had been in Matilda's heart long before Genevieve met him. Her only choice now lay in whether she would sulk like a child longing for a toy that belonged to another, conspire to betray her dearest friend, or help her friend secure the proposal she so fervently desired.

If only she could suggest that the object of Matilda's affection did not return her regard and that she should look elsewhere… like at the delightful Sir Reginald who loved her.

Rallying her good senses, Genevieve touched Matilda's arm. "I am persuaded that having Mr. Amesbury paint your portrait was an exceedingly fine idea—a perfect excuse to spend time with him."

Matilda beamed. "It was, wasn't it?"

Genevieve glanced over her shoulder at Mr. Amesbury who listened to one of the younger gentlemen with amusement. As the other gentleman came to the end of the story, everyone laughed, including Mr. Amesbury. His whole face lit in mirth. Genevieve barely resisted sighing at the stunning sight. Then she remembered. She wasn't supposed to look at him.

To cover up her mistake, she squeezed Matilda's hand. "I am happy you have attracted the attention of such a fine gentleman. He's perfect for you."

"He is perfect, all right," one of the other girls said.

Another added, "Perfectly delicious."

They all tittered.

"I'd like to spoon him up," said another.

More giggles.

How crass of them to speak about such a kind and honorable gentleman like that. Still, they had a point. Genevieve pressed her lips together to avoid chastising them. Or agreeing.

Matilda's expression fixed on Genevieve and darkened. "You certainly seemed to enjoy your little practice waltz with him."

"Er, I—yes, I did. He was kind to teach me. Your Mr. Amesbury is certainly a fine gentleman. You're are most fortunate to have spent the better part of the day with him."

Her words seemed to satisfy Matilda who resumed her usual sunny expression. After tea, they chatted and gossiped, all while Genevieve pointedly kept her attention on the ladies, and not on Christian Amesbury. But the act of refraining from looking at him almost caused physical pain. She rubbed her hands against the fabric of her muslin gown to brush off the lingering sensation of his touch. But to no effect.

She was a terrible friend!

"Come, Jenny, we should dress for dinner," Mama's quiet urging broke in from behind the settee where Genevieve sat.

Genevieve nodded. "Yes, Mama." She glanced back at her friend. "Do you need help getting to your room, Mattie?"

"I'll help her," Mrs. Widtsoe said as she reached the circle.

Genevieve followed her mother out of the room and upstairs. As they ascended the grand staircase, Genevieve admired the carved stone and gothic details found all over the Widtsoe's home.

"Are you enjoying yourself?" Mama asked.

"Yes, very much. We played croquet and Blindman's Bluff, and I own that I laughed quite with abandon."

"As did the others, I understand."

"Yes. and I am persuaded the practice waltz will be helpful for tonight's ball."

"I suspect it will. You attracted the attention of some gentlemen."

Genevieve lifted her shoulder in a dismissive shrug. "My partner in croquet, Sir Reginald, was diverting. Mr. Ashton escorted me back to the abbey."

"And young Mr. Amesbury taught you to waltz."

Genevieve blushed at the memory of his touch on her hand, her back, the small brushes as their bodies touched during the dance. No wonder people thought the waltz was daring. It certainly required a lot of close contact.

"Has anyone captured your heart?"

She hesitated a fraction too long in answering, "In so short a time? Of course not."

"Except, perhaps, one who has also captured the heart of your dearest friend?"

Genevieve sucked in her breath. It was pointless to deny it; Mama already knew. "Is it that obvious?"

"Probably not to others, but I see it. You try too hard not to look at him. When you do, you soften as I've never seen you do. And you positively glowed when you danced with him."

"It's pointless. Matilda loves him."

"Does he return her regard?"

"She seems to think he does. He's fairly reserved, but he was quick to come to her rescue this morning when she hurt her ankle."

"That is the mark of a gentleman—not necessarily of a young man in love."

Genevieve secretly agreed but tried to convince her mother of a truth to which Matilda clung. "He's attentive to her, and they had a lovely chat while he painted her portrait."

"He might merely be looking for the right expression for her portrait. Or he's simply being polite."

"I cannot hope for that, Mama. She loves him. And I want her to be happy. Therefore, I want him to love her."

Mama put her arm around Genevieve and gave her a sideways hug. "Matters of the heart are never easy."

While Mama retired to the chambers she shared with Papa, Genevieve went to her bedchamber and flopped on the bed. What kind of friend was she? Loyalty and honor were qualities her parents had instilled in her for as long as she could remember. Her friendship with Matilda transcended an interest in a gentleman.

Only one more evening. Genevieve could last one more evening. The house party would end soon. She and her parents would leave on the morrow and spend their summer in Bath helping her mother restore her health. She would never again see Christian Amesbury... except at Matilda's wedding.

Her maid, Hill, entered. "Do you wish to rest, miss? I can return later."

Genevieve sat up. "No, come in."

The maid set out the two evening gowns Genevieve had not yet worn at the house party.

After a glance, Genevieve gestured. "The silk ball gown, please. We're dancing tonight." Poor Matilda. She'd been so excited to dance with Christian Amesbury.

After a quick sponge bath, Genevieve dressed in a clean shift, slid on her silk stockings, tied them off above her knee, then stood while Hill tied her longs stays. Seated at a dressing table and wearing a dressing gown, she stared at her reflection without seeing it. Instead, she plotted how to survive the evening without allowing her discomfiting jealousy to affect her thoughts or behavior.

If Matilda were at a loss for company, Genevieve would sit with her. If Mr. Amesbury sat with Mattie, Genevieve would find an excuse to leave them alone. If he happened to speak with Genevieve, she'd only talk about Matilda. Matilda would attain her heart's desire and Genevieve would be happy for her—even if it killed her. Which was silly, really, since she hardly knew Christian Amesbury.

No matter how often she reminded herself of that fact, it never offered comfort.

"Are you unwell, miss?" her maid, Hill, asked.

"Oh no—merely woolgathering."

She should tell Hill to do her hair in a very simple chignon, something as plain as possible so as not to compete with Matilda. But she couldn't make the words come out. Besides, her hair was almost finished now, and to ask for a different hairstyle would be unkind to the maid who'd already combed her hair into soft curls. After Hill dampened the fine hairs on either side of Genevieve's face and curled them around her finger to make ringlets, she added a white ribbon as the finishing touch. It contrasted nicely against the color of her hair.

"Lovely, Hill," Genevieve said. "Thank you."

She stood and lifted her arms so Hill could lower the gown over her head. As the maid fastened the gown down the back, Genevieve eyed her reflection in the full-length mirror. Green ribbon threaded through the sleeves and around the bodice embroidered with tiny green leaves. The gown fit beautifully. Still, it was a pity she hadn't been blessed with curves like Matilda's, instead of the figure of a fourteen-year-old. Mama called her "elfin" but saw her through the eyes of a mother's love. Removing her focus from her reflection, Genevieve stepped into her dancing slippers.

Mama tapped on the door and peeked in. "Are you ready? Oh!" She clasped her hands together. "You look lovely, my dear. Positively lovely."

It was impossible to wallow in self-pity while her mother admired her with such enthusiasm.

As the final touch, Genevieve pulled on long gloves. "You do as well, Mama."

And truly, she did. With auburn hair the color of Genevieve's still untouched by gray, and a lovely face, her mother looked far younger than her age. Only the faintest lines around her eyes belied her departure from the first blush of youth.

Waiting for them in the corridor, Papa kissed her brow. "What a lucky man I am to escort two such lovely ladies."

"You look dashing as always, Papa." Genevieve kissed his cheek.

In the drawing room, half of the guests waited, sipping sherry and conversing. Matilda had yet to make an appearance, but Mr. Amesbury and his father had already arrived. Wearing a black tailcoat and a silver brocade waistcoat, Mr. Amesbury had an elegant sense of style. Next to him stood the cheerful, curly-haired Sir Reginald and the solemn Mr. Ashton, both sizing up Mr. Amesbury.

Did they view him as competition for Matilda? Did Matilda know she had so many admirers? If she knew, she might be less likely to set her sights on Christian Amesbury.

Genevieve squelched the traitorous thought. Matilda didn't form an attachment for him out of a lack of prospects; her preference came as a natural result of his kindness and charm. Being handsome and the son of an earl only added to his suitability. For many reasons, he was a perfectly desirable match, and Matilda was smart enough to recognize it.

Genevieve murmured to Mama, "Matilda isn't here yet. Should I look in on her?"

"Not necessary, surely. Do join the other girls," Mama gave a gentle nudge.

Genevieve moved to a group of chairs drawn up to make a conversation area.

"...only my first Season, so Mama says not to become discouraged," one of the young ladies said.

"That's all well and good for you," said another, "but next Season Mama is launching my younger sister. This house party is my last chance to receive an offer." The plain girl in a simple white muslin gown gave them all a pained smile. "Otherwise, I'll become a spinster —a burden to my parents. I'll probably spend the rest of my life in an old house on the moors caring for my oldest sister's children."

Genevieve sat in the empty spot next to her and gestured to the girl's neck. "What a lovely pendant."

The girl turned a startled glance at her and touched the necklace Genevieve indicated. "Thank you. It was my great aunt's."

Matilda arrived and all the girls turned their attention to her and her well-being. Moments later dinner was announced. Sadly, Genevieve sat nowhere near Mr. Amesbury and she must lean forward to even catch a glimpse of him. Instead, she sat between two older gentlemen and tried to be interested in their conversation. In addition, her place was as far from Matilda as possible.

Surely, the seating arrangements had been determined to give the guests a chance to converse with others, and not to deliberately separate Genevieve from both Matilda and Mr. Amesbury. Somehow, she couldn't quite believe that.

After dinner, the guests filed into the drawing room that had been transformed into the ballroom, with flowers and hundreds of candles blazing in the chandeliers and tall, wrought-iron candelabras. Local musicians played their instruments in that odd discord of pre-performance tuning. While Matilda sat like a queen on her wheeled chair up front where she would command a view of the room, several girls clustered around her, leaving no room for Genevieve. However, most of Matilda's current companions would be asked to dance shortly, which would leave her alone. When that happened, Genevieve would keep her company like a loyal friend.

The musicians struck up a quadrille. Heading up the set stood Christian Amesbury across from the girl in white muslin who'd expressed a fear of losing her only chance at marriage. Genevieve moved to join Matilda so she would not find herself alone, but before she had taken more than a few steps, a voice stopped her.

"May I have this first set?" Sir Reginald appeared at Genevieve's side, his hand extended and his warm brown eyes merry.

Genevieve hesitated. "I had planned on keeping Matilda company."

He glanced at Matilda. "Miss Widtsoe is surrounded by friends at present. Once the set ends, I plan to keep her company, but I feel I must first dance."

She cocked her head to the side. "You surprise me, sir; I would have thought you'd take every chance to be at her side."

He grinned. "I don't wish to make a cake of myself by sitting at her seat like an overeager puppy."

Genevieve gave in to the urge to tease him. "Are you using me to inspire a bit of jealousy in her?"

"Not entirely." With a covert wink, Sir Reginald took her hand and led her to the dance floor. He lined up next to Christian Amesbury and grinned impishly at her.

Using every shred of self-control not to look at Mr. Amesbury, she fixed her focus on her partner. As the music started, they took hands and danced past each other to the other dancers in their square, which led her to Mr. Amesbury. He looked directly into her eyes and smiled, a slow, sensuous curving of his lips that quite possibly turned her bones to clotted cream.

Trying not to fall flat on her face, she danced past him to the next gentleman where they repeated the steps. After she made her way around the formation, she arrived back with Sir Reginald, did the required little skip-step, and took hands as they watched Mr. Amesbury and his partner, the girl in white muslin whose smile practically illuminated the room, dance within the square. How kind of him to invite the plainest girl in the room to the first dance. Genevieve would probably be wearing a similar smile if she were his partner, only hers would be dimmed by guilt.

Under his breath, Sir Reginald said, "You're staring."

Dragging her gaze off Mr. Amesbury, she snapped in a terse whisper, "I am not."

His eyes twinkled. She lifted her chin, pointedly looking everywhere but at the dashing figure who commanded her thoughts far too often. Each time she found herself temporarily partnered with Christian Amesbury, he looked into her eyes as if he were trying to memorize her face.

Clearly, her imagination had gotten the better of her.

During the course of the dance, she managed not to collapse at his feet, and while she danced with the other gentlemen in the square, even kept her eyes off him —most of the time.

Upon completion of the set, Sir Reginald escorted her to her mother and bowed. "A delight, Miss Marshall." He all but sashayed to Matilda's side where he bowed over Matilda's hand and promptly took a seat next to her.

Matilda smiled at him flirtatiously. "Reggie, how kind of you to join me." She frowned briefly in Mr. Amesbury's direction who was bowing in front of one of the other young ladies lamenting her lack of prospects. Matilda returned her attention to Sir Reginald and smiled.

Mr. Ashton stepped into Genevieve's line of sight. "If I may have the honor?" he intoned blandly.

"Of course," she replied.

During the course of the country dance, she again danced a few steps with Mr. Amesbury as they came together in the middle, so closely they nearly touched as they circled facing one another.

His gaze again darted over her, his lips curving in a way that seemed to beg her to ask what he thought. "Stand up with me the next set?" he murmured.

A warm rush ran over her skin. "As you wish."

He smiled and she stumbled on stone feet. Must he be so handsome?

The steps took them apart on opposite sides of the line and brought her back to Mr. Ashton. He said nothing as they danced, but in his defense, the vigorous dance provided little opportunity to do so. Dancing always brought joy, and at the end of the first dance in the set, she stood laughing and trying to catch her breath. Her focus fell on Mr. Amesbury who watched her with such intensity that her heart fluttered. He inclined his head, smiling in a way that felt almost secretive. Only by sheer willpower did she manage a courteous smile rather than gaping at him. He turned his focus onto his partner, his expression smoothing over into polite interest.

"Today is the last full day of the house party. Everyone will leave tomorrow morning," Mr. Ashton said, stealing her attention.

She glanced at him, ashamed she'd had the bad form to stare at another while on the dance floor with a partner. What on earth he meant by that comment she could not guess. "Yes, I believe so."

He nodded. "Not much time, then."

"Oh, I think it's been a lovely few days. Of course, it's always a little disappointing when a party ends, but that's better than wishing for its end, don't you agree?"

He gave her a curious look. "I'm sure you must be right."

As she waited for the next dance in the set to begin, she allowed her gaze to roam the room. Lord Wickburgh stared at her. The lord stood still as a statue, gripping his walking stick with white knuckles. He, too, inclined his head in greeting as Mr. Amesbury had, but his gaze left her with an urge to duck behind a shield and a suit of armor.

As second dance began, she focused on remembering the steps and trying to not appear too breathless. Once again, she found herself partnered briefly with Christian. Every breath he took, even the smallest touch, the smolder in his eyes, sent her scenes spinning wildly out of control. At the conclusion, Mr. Ashton returned her to her mother. Genevieve fanned herself but failed to cool the burning in her skin.

Instantly, Mr. Amesbury appeared, his smile in place, his hand outstretched to her. "If you would be so kind." Did she imagine a sultry quality in his tone?

The heat intensified. She laid her hand in his and walked—or did she float?—with him to the dance floor.

He stepped closer. "It's the waltz."

"How lovely," she said, breathless. "I hope I remember how to do it. I'm not sure one brief lesson with a real partner is enough." Oh dear. Matilda had hurt herself teaching Genevieve how to waltz, and now she, instead of Mattie, was waltzing with Mr. Amesbury. Guilt shadowed her joy but failed to cool her feverish heat.

The music began. He drew her into waltz position, smiling down at her. Every candle in the room shone brighter. His scent drifted to her, a clean, masculine blend of sunshine, bergamot, and a sensual quality she could not identify.

He parted his lips. "I am honored to be your first, Miss Marshall."

Her first what? Kiss? Love? Her heart pounded at such thoughts.

"I hope to be a worthy waltz teacher," he added.

Waltz.

Oh.

Oh! Of course. How ridiculous she was being!

His arms firm, Mr. Amesbury took a step forward on the downbeat and guided her back. After only a moment of dancing, she moved with him with little thought, following his skillful lead with the music. He did several basic steps, giving her a chance to become re-acquainted with the new waltz from Vienna and the music's timing. A timelessness, a sensation of everything being right in the world while she danced in his arms, stole over her. A missing ingredient to the recipe of happiness had been added to her life.

But she had not known him long enough to know whether he

were her perfect match. He might be a passing fascination. Perhaps, in a few days or weeks, she would meet some other dashing fellow and forget all about Christian Amesbury.

And perhaps she would discover that fairies truly did open flowers and cupid's arrows were real—it seemed just as likely.

As they sailed across the floor, his smile faded to a solemn expression. "Miss Marshall, as a close friend of Miss Widtsoe's, you are best qualified to advise me."

Oh no. Her fever cooled. Here it came. He would ask her about Matilda's favorite flower, or if Matilda would prefer a new wedding ring or one that had been in his family for generations…

"I believe I have unintentionally raised her expectations."

Her thoughts stuttered to a halt.

At what must have been confusion in her expression, he rushed on, "I assure you it was purely accidental. In fact, aside from painting her portrait—well, and helping her when she twisted her ankle—I've made every attempt to appear uninterested while still being polite. Yet, she seems to think there is some sort of understanding between us."

Everything inside her went still. "Then you have not formed an attachment for her?"

"None. I never meant to give her that impression. I cannot imagine how she got that idea."

She didn't know whether to jump for joy that his heart remained unclaimed or weep for what would be a stinging disappointment for Matilda.

She moistened her lips. "Then I advise you to be direct. Quietly take her to the side, perhaps near the end of the evening, and tell her."

He winced. "I'm sure you're right, but I cannot imagine how I'll find the words to deliver such a cutting speech."

"The longer you delay, the worse it will be."

He nodded, his expression clouding. "She might accuse me of raising her expectations."

"That is a concern. Have you spent any time in her company in public?"

"No, none at all. The most time I've spent with her was painting her portrait. And helping her when she injured herself." He winced as if recalling a painful memory. Was he castigating himself for carrying Matilda and giving further fuel for her imagination? Or did he sympathize with her plight?

"That hardly signifies," Genevieve said. "Have you ever danced with her more than one set in one evening?"

His earnest blue eyes fixed on her face. "I've only danced with her once ever, despite being at the same soirees many times last Season."

"Have you sat with her and spoken for any length of time?"

"Never, beyond her portrait sitting."

"And I can assume, then, that you've never… kissed her?" Her cheeks warmed at the personal question. Or did they warm because she daydreamed of what it might be like to kiss him?

His blue eyes opened wide. "Heavens, no. I'm not such a cad."

She nodded thoughtfully. "In that case, it sounds to me that if her expectations have been raised, they were from her own desires. No one in society would expect you to make an offer, unless they believe what she's been saying about you."

A crease formed between his brows. "What has she been saying?"

"That she believes you return her feelings and expects a proposal."

He let out his breath in a long exhale. "I'd better speak to her before it gets out of hand."

She nodded, too conflicted to speak. He could be hers. But Matilda would surely be crushed if Genevieve encouraged him. And one didn't simply go about encouraging a gentleman for whom one's friend had a 'grand passion.' Not even if he had spurned said friend. Such an act would destroy the friendship.

"Are you up for the challenge of going beyond basic steps, Miss Marshall?"

"Absolutely."

He led her through several new steps. Following him came as naturally as if they'd danced together for years.

"You are an excellent student of the waltz," he murmured.

She smiled. "If I am, it is because you're an excellent teacher."

He opened his mouth and inhaled as if to speak but pressed his lips together instead.

In a flash of un-lady-like boldness, she asked, "What were you about to say?"

He shook his head, but his blue eyes suggested he carried secrets.

Gently, she pressed, "You've already confided in me regarding Matilda. Surely you can tell me what you were thinking just now."

His lips curved. "I never put much credence in the term love at first sight. But I am beginning to understand, at least in part, why people say that."

Her heart filled with light and song. "What are you saying?"

"More than I should, for now. Tomorrow, we all depart for home."

She nodded. "My family and I aren't going home right away; we're headed to Bath so that my mother might partake of the restorative waters."

A golden-brown brow raised. "My father and I are returning to Bath, as well. We've been there since the Season ended."

"I hope I shall see you there." Was that too bold?

A slow grin widened his mouth and curved those lips she longed to touch, to taste. "Oh, you can count on that."

The orchestra ended the song on a flourish, and he led her into a little dip.

"Thank you for the waltz," he said. "You were a delightful partner."

"You, as well."

They stood in dance position, not moving. His gaze moved over her face, his hand warm on hers, and his mouth parted. A distant drum thrummed in her ears in time with her heart.

He released her and stepped back. Around them, other couples had already left the dance floor.

She was making a cake of herself.

She wasn't sure she cared.

With an extended arm and a slight bow, he led her back to her mother. Genevieve sat and watched as he strode to Matilda, bowed, and after a brief conversation in which Sir Reginald appeared alarmed, he wheeled Matilda out of the room. At the doorway, he glanced at Genevieve before he exited.

He was about to break her friend's heart, but all Genevieve could think of was how completely he had captured hers.

Did that mean she had made assumptions about him and that a similar heartbreak as Matilda's was in her future?

CHAPTER 10

Christian pushed Miss Widtsoe's wheeled chair towards the door to the great hall in search of a place where they might have a conversation. Only his deeply ingrained manners kept him from rushing back to Genevieve Marshall's side to claim another dance. Those brief touches during the dancing had been torturous, leaving him longing for more. He'd always believed his own damaged heart to be insulated from the charms of a lady. Genevieve Marshall had proved him wrong.

Was it possible that he might have found that missing color in the palette of his life?

Serene and elegant but with a slightly impish curve to her lips, she curtsied to Mr. Ashton who spoke with her. Christian pitied the young man who was obviously smitten with her, but for whom she clearly did not return the preference. Was Christian also to be pitied?

No. She'd given him several warm smiles that she'd given no one else at the house party.

Just as he wheeled Miss Widtsoe out, he paused at the doorway. Genevieve glanced at him, that softness coming into her eyes, and her impish smile deepening. That same calm returned to him. Then, as if remembering herself, she demurely lowered her gaze and adjusted one of her long gloves. If only he could get her alone, he'd test that demure exterior to find the woman underneath.

Egad. He was starting to sound like his father.

Returning his mind to the unpleasant business at hand, he pushed Miss Widtsoe out to the main hall where a few others gathered. Good. They would be considered chaperoned out here. He pushed her to a small cluster of chairs in a corner.

Miss Widtsoe smiled at him expectantly. "You wanted to speak to me?"

He perched on the edge of a chair. "Yes." He swallowed. How did one go about this sort of business? He broke out into a cold sweat. "I fear there has been something of a misunderstanding between us."

"Oh?"

"Yes. It appears that… that is to say, it seems that you…" a breath, "…feel that there is a certain… understanding between us."

He swallowed hard and stared at the floor so he wouldn't have to look into her eyes. But that was cowardly. As a gentleman, he owed her eye contact. Witnessing her disappointment would be fitting penance for his carelessness.

He dragged in another breath and met her gaze. "If I have done anything to give you the wrong impression, I offer my humblest apologies."

Her expression remained fixed, hopeful, even.

This was not going well. He rubbed at the trickle of sweat at his brow and tried again. "You see, I never meant to give you the idea that I have any particular… erm… preference for you…" Deuce take it, he sounded like a complete cad.

Miss Widtsoe blinked. Her hopeful expression faded.

He closed his eyes to rally himself and then pressed on. "In truth, I've always believed I'd never marry. I manage my father's estate and watch over his care and I don't expect that a wife will fit into those duties." Not to mention he'd always believed that no one such as he deserved such a joyful union.

Miss Widtsoe's eyes grew shiny. "You... you don't feel any particular regard for me?"

He faltered at her emotion. "I admire you, of course. Any man would. But it was never my intention to court you—merely paint your portrait and a landscape of the abbey. When my father and I depart, I do not expect to see you again—ever." He winced at his own harshness. Each word sliced like a knife, causing pain to a girl who didn't deserve it. No one did.

Her lashes fluttered and her mouth quivered. "You don't have a grand passion for me."

Very gently, he said, "No, Miss Widtsoe."

She stared down at her hands twisting in her lap. "I see."

"I beg your forgiveness if I've misrepresented myself to you."

Her mouth opened, then closed.

He rushed to repair the damage, if possible. "There is much to recommend you, and half the gentlemen here are trying to catch your eye—Sir Reginald, for example. But I'm not—" He closed his mouth before he uttered that he was not for her, that he didn't believe they would suit. That was a bit too truthful, and hurtful. "I'm not free to pursue marriage just yet."

She said nothing, just sat with bowed head.

His heart twisted in compassion and regret that he'd taken the light out of her eyes. There appeared to be nothing more to say. He stood. "I'm so sorry."

As he turned away, she said in a voice devoid of any emotion, "It's Genevieve, isn't it?"

He paused. "As I said, I'm not certain it is my lot to marry—at least, not at present." Returning to the ballroom, he paused behind a potted plant to catch his breath. He felt like he'd just kicked a puppy.

Despite his weariness of heart, he moved back into the main area, searching for Genevieve, craving her soothing presence. The musicians packed up their instruments and guests clustered together. Genevieve stood next to two other young ladies, both of whom he had partnered earlier in the evening. She caught his eye like a red rose in a garden of white lilies, so lovely, so vibrant and yet so serene.

Remembering to don an appropriately *savoir faire* expression lest he appear a juvenile who'd discovered girls for the first time, he squared his shoulders and sauntered towards her.

Before he reached her side, Lord Wickburgh sidled up to her. Christian faltered. As a titled lord, the man certainly commanded greater precedence, and as his elder, he deserved Christian's respect and deference, but the man clearly frightened Genevieve. And his cold hardness raised Christian's hackles.

Lord Wickburgh bowed to Genevieve. The color left her cheeks and she lowered her head, clasping her hands in front of her as if trying to form a shield.

Christian had to do something. He got no further than a step before his father's voice broke in.

"The marquis appears to have selected his new bride." Standing next to Christian, the earl gestured with his glass at the scene. "He seems even more fascinated with her than you are."

"I'm not..." he trailed off. Denying it was pointless. Instead, he nodded. "She is remarkable."

"Apparently so." He paused, then said in as gentle a voice as Christian had ever heard the earl speak, "Her father may prefer a lord over a youngest son."

The words pricked his hope, but he refused to step back. "The Marshalls don't seem like social climbers."

"No, but most fathers want the best for their daughters, and they often weigh the wrong criteria such as money and status. I certainly made that mistake with Margaret." Sorrow filled his eyes.

Christian frowned. His sister's unhappy marriage became apparent the moment they returned from their honeymoon. "I'm not prepared to offer for her just yet, Father. At this point, all I plan to do is court her—her family will be going directly to Bath."

The earl nodded. "She has much to recommend her—desirable qualities and comes from a good family."

Tension Christian didn't realize he'd been holding eased back inside him. The earl approved. That meant more to him than he would have expected.

Father's next words came as a surprise. "You've spent all your life doing things to make your mother and me happy. It's time for you to do what makes you happy. I encourage you to follow your heart for a change, son."

Follow his heart. Could he? Had he done enough to make up for all he'd done so horribly wrong? Or was true happiness a taunting hope that would forever dangle just out of reach?

His father nodded towards Genevieve. "You'd best move quickly before Lord Wickburgh does. Otherwise, her father may choose the higher-ranking suitor for his daughter. Bath may not be soon enough. *Carpe diem.*" He pushed his fist into the air as if urging him into battle.

Did Christian truly need to act now rather than court her slowly in Bath? He'd wanted to move slowly in order to be sure of his heart. And to give her time to know hers. Surely, Captain Marshall would take his daughter's preferences into consideration and not rush her into a decision. And she preferred Christian to Lord Wickburgh.

Didn't she?

He watched them converse, Lord Wickburgh elegant and worldly, and Miss Marshall, gentle and reserved. She offered a small smile to the viscount.

Was she changing her opinion about the older man? He was in possession of a great deal of money, as well as the power and privilege of rank. Christian could only offer her a modest living and certainly no title.

Did he want to take the chance and offer for her?

He would have to find out. Standing in the shadows and watching another man pay court to her would serve no one.

For the first time in years, a flicker of hope lit inside. He might not have to live his life in complete darkness. *Carpe diem.*

Christian snatched a glass of lemonade from a tray and marched to her. As he reached her side, he nodded to the viscount and held out the glass to her. "Care for a glass of lemonade, Miss Marshall?"

She smiled, but it was restrained. "Thank you." As she accepted his glass, she glanced at Lord Wickburgh. "I wish you the best in your endeavors, my lord."

She sipped her drink and turned her body toward Christian, angling away from Wickburgh and pulling her shawl about her. Christian was right; she did not care for the viscount. In fact, she seemed afraid of him, judging from her rapid breathing, darting glances, and the fluttering of her left hand.

Though her words and action had been a subtle yet unmistakable dismissal, Lord Wickburgh held out an arm. "It's rather stuffy and crowded in here. Shall we take a turn about the garden and breathe some fresh air, Miss Marshall?"

She pressed her lips together and flitted her gaze at Christian. "I have already promised to do that with Mr. Amesbury. Pray, excuse us, my lord." She reached for Christian.

He readily offered her his arm, glad to assist in her charade and trying not to puff out his chest at her clear preference. But did she only want his company to escape a man who frightened her? She might be playing some kind of game.

Odd, moments ago he'd been certain, but now his confidence wavered. His decision not to marry had been a buffer to protect his heart. Now that he entertained the idea of a future of love and marriage, he'd never felt so… vulnerable.

Lord Wickburgh raised his walking stick and placed the tip of it in front of Christian like a barrier. "Have a care, boy. You'd do well to step aside like a gentleman."

If this arrogant bully thought he could cow Christian, he was in for a surprise. Christian said in even, low tones, "I will not aside for *you*. Not now, not ever."

The lord drew his brows together. "Watch your mouth, boy. I don't care who your father is, I'll not tolerate insolence."

Anger simmering in his core, Christian stepped in closer until they were almost nose to nose. How satisfying to stand a good two inches taller than the older man. "We are finished here."

He turned his back on the lord, replaced Genevieve's hand on his arm, and led her outside. Moonlight and Chinese lanterns guided them across the terrace and down the steps. Frogs and night insects sang a chorus and a sultry breeze ruffled stirred the air, teasing roses and jasmine until they perfumed the air. Christian drew several breaths to release his anger. Genevieve remained quiet until they reached a fountain deep in the garden.

She adjusted her shawl about her shoulders. "Thank you. I suppose it was cowardly of me to pull you into it and make up a story about our walk in the garden, but something about that man drains the courage out of me."

Christian had been foolish for letting his insecurities cast doubt on her character. Genevieve was genuine. She could be trusted. Did he dare trust her with his heart?

He put a hand over hers where it rested on his arm. "I'm happy to be of service."

"How did your conversation go with Matilda?"

He searched for the right words to say.

She squeezed his arm. "Forgive me. I do not wish to pry, but she is my friend."

"I tried to be as tactful as possible, and she seemed to take it well. But she was not in high spirits when I left her. I'm sorry to have been the cause of sorrow to your friend."

"She fancies herself in love all the time. She seemed to have developed a true attachment for you, but obviously, if you did not return her regard, she had no basis for her feelings. Still, I regret that she's hurt. She's such a dear friend; I would not wish her unhappy."

Christian led her towards a raised pond with a merry fountain. "She really has much to recommend her. I hope she meets someone worthy of her."

"I do, as well." She sank down onto the marble edge of the raised pond.

In the moonlight and amid the garden, her fairy-like quality became even more pronounced, as did that magical serenity she carried about her. He drew in a breath, inhaling her scent. Her peaceful presence soothed him. His focus fixed on her lips.

He sat next to her and took her hand. "Miss Marshall, I had never expected to marry. Since my father's decline, I have virtually assumed all his responsibilities for managing the estate. On a regular basis, I meet with his steward, tour the properties, handle his correspondence, and everything else required of him—except sit in the House, of course."

"It sounds like a great deal of responsibility."

"It is. But my oldest brother has returned home from the war, and I expect he will take my place soon. After all, he stands to inherit it all. Once that happens, I will no longer be needed in the capacity in which I serve now. When that occurs, my life will feel empty."

"Perhaps you'll find a new passion. You might concentrate more fully on your art."

"No doubt. But I recently realized that the reason I had never held out hopes for a family of my own was *not* because I was too busy caring for my father and the estate, but because I always felt rather as if I were... unworthy of love."

She tilted her head. Quietly, she asked, "Why do you feel unworthy of love?"

He shied away from the truth, from the horrible challenge that led to Jason's death, and the scattering of his brothers over the fight Christian caused between them and the earl.

He breathed through the pain lancing his chest. "I've done things that I deeply regret. Lost people I thought would always be there—through my own actions."

She slipped her hand into his and squeezed it gently. "Everyone deserves a second chance. To be loved. Even you. Especially you."

Her earnest expression, the tenderness in her eyes loosened knots in his soul that years of guilt and grief had tied. Could she be right? Did he deserve love? Despite his earlier determination to proceed slowly with her, his brain disengaged, and his body sought the sweetness of her lips. He leaned in and kissed her.

Her slight intake of breath should have stopped him, but her warm and malleable lips moved with his. Whatever was left of his reason vanished. He kissed her as if nothing beyond this moment ever existed.

CHAPTER 11

Genevieve's good sense always came through for her when other men tried to kiss her... until the instant Christian leaned in with that hungry expression. Instead of backing away like a proper young lady, she raised her head and met his mouth with hers. Fireworks at the park last summer failed to match the explosions of light and color inside her. Beyond glorious, kissing Christian instilled a sense of absolute belonging—to him, to the life they must share, or she would never again experience the wholeness of this single, perfect moment.

This then, was love. The seedlings of it had planted themselves in her heart the first moment she saw him, and each word, each glance, each touch had nurtured them until they flowered into the love about which poets rhapsodized.

She loved Christian, and nothing was ever so wondrous as the rightness of that knowledge.

Though uncommonly gentle, his kiss embodied everything passionate and lovely about human contact. The desire to immerse herself forever in his kiss consumed her. Enfolded in his arms, her mouth and soul at one with him, she sighed in glorious pleasure.

He ended the kiss before she was ready, but he showered kisses on her cheeks and brow. Finally, he just held her. Surely if she opened her eyes, she'd seen that her entire body was glowing with heavenly light.

His voice caressed her. "I'd planned to court you in Bath, then declare myself and ask your father's permission before kissing you, but I quite lost my head."

He had? Little sparks shot out from every pore. Was he declaring himself now? Did he love her?

She drew in a deep breath, filling herself with his scent. She ached to burrow in closer and breathe in more of it. Of him. "I cannot tell you how happy I am that you did." She should have blushed at the seductive quality in her voice, but he inspired a new boldness in her.

He pulled back enough to look at her. A hopeful half-smile touched his mouth, a mouth she'd rather be kissing. "You don't feel that I took advantage?"

She laughed softly. "Considering that I participated quite happily with you, it would be hypocritical. Do you mind that I didn't play the shocked little miss?"

"Not at all." He grinned at her, a vision that seemed to part the proverbial clouds and invite a heavenly chorus to break into song.

He kissed her again. Chaotic, hot desires mingled with that sensation of absolute belonging. His lips moved against hers, equal parts firm and gentle, and all passion. She ceased to exist except as a creature of desire.

He let out a husky chuckle. "We'd best go inside."

Disappointment rang through her like a bell. "I suppose we must."

He grinned, his eyes alight with joy equaling her own, and raised her to a stand. Hand in hand, they took a circuitous route past two other pairs of lovers enjoying the moonlight.

"Just so you know," he said, his voice low. "I still intend to court you properly and publicly in Bath."

"I can hardly wait." She grinned at him.

He grinned back, and his eyes burned from inner fire.

Christian released her hand before they crossed the terrace and came into view. The imprint of his hand left behind a lingering warmth. In the drawing room, a few groups clustered together, enjoying their last evening together. Her parents, it seemed, had already retired for the evening. There was no sign of Matilda.

"Goodnight," Christian murmured, his intense glance hungry.

She bade him a goodnight, barely managing not to throw herself into his arms again, and practically skipped through the open door leading to her parents' bedchamber.

"Mama, Papa, I have..." her voice trailed off at their serious expressions.

Her father spoke. "Sit down, Genevieve. We need to talk."

All the joy in her heart faded as dread took their place. She sank into a nearby chair. "What is it?"

"You have attracted some male attention."

Oh dear. They must have seen her in the garden with Christian. "Well, yes, but you see, his intensions are honorable, and—"

Papa interrupted. "This very eve, I have received not one, but two offers for your hand."

She blinked, hardly processing his words. But Christian said that he hadn't spoken to Papa because he planned to formally court her in Bath.

"Two?" she repeated.

"Mr. Ashton and Lord Wickburgh have both asked for my permission."

The blood drained out of her face. "Lord Wickburgh? Unthinkable!"

Her parents exchanged glances.

"And... Mr. Ashton... surely not. We've only conversed once or twice. Mr. Ashton is the most... bland man I have ever met."

Mama spoke up. "Consider carefully, Jenny. He is the respectable son of a vicar, who can offer you a respectably comfortable life when he begins his position."

Papa said, "Lord Wickburgh is a viscount—a peer of the realm with wealth, status, and power."

Genevieve waved her hands in front of her and shook her head.

Vigorously. "I'm not interested in marrying either of them. I'm in love with Christian Amesbury. And he has made his intentions known to me just tonight."

They exchanged glances. "He is courting Miss Widtsoe."

"No, he isn't. She only *wishes* she had his affections; he never said or did anything to encourage her. He has vowed to court me in Bath, and even plans to seek your permission when the time is right."

Mama put her hand over hers. "I know you've been infatuated with him since the beginning, but I caution you not to be too hasty. At least consider one of these other offers."

Papa took up the conversation. "Being a vicar's wife would come naturally to you, and it will allow you to live in the country as you wish and help parishioners. On the other hand, a viscount with ten thousand a year can offer you a life of luxury and position, not to mention anything money can buy."

She shook her head, unable to even imagine being married to the man who turned her cold with a single look.

Papa's voice grew stern. "He's a *lord*, Genevieve; so much more prestigious than a youngest son with little to his name."

She gaped at her parents. Before tonight, they'd always encouraged her to follow her heart. Besides, only days ago, Papa had said that Christian would be a good match for any young lady. Now they implied he wasn't good enough, and that she should choose a husband based on who offered the most advantageous position in society. Unbelievable.

Slowly, she shook her head. "I love Christian. I cannot abide the thought of marrying another."

Mama squeezed her hand. "He's handsome and charming, I'll give you that, but there is more to marriage than a pleasing face. And consider how he misrepresented himself to your friend. He might be a flirt or a rake who's simply mastered the art of being discreet."

How could they be so insistent about this? Rising to her feet and squaring her shoulders, she said in a calm, firm voice, "I have made my choice. I will allow no one but Christian to court me. When he asks me to marry him—and I'm confident he will—I will accept him."

Papa sighed. "Genevieve..."

"Furthermore," she continued, "Christian is expected to be a vicar when the position at his father's county seat becomes available. If he does, I'd still be a vicar's wife. Until then, he acts as his father's right hand running the family estate. In addition, his art grows more popular every day. I have no fear that he will be an adequate provider. Please trust that I know my own heart."

Silence fell.

Her parents exchanged glances.

Papa admitted, "He does have a comfortable income—some five thousand a year."

She huffed a laugh that her parents had implied such a large sum of money would reduce her to poverty. "That's more than many members of the gentry have. I'm sure we can do quite well on that, Papa."

Papa's stance relaxed. He waved a helpless hand. "Very well, Jenny. I trust you."

Mama smiled. "We had to make sure you were certain, dearest."

So, this had been a of test of her convictions. "Then you will refuse Mr. Ashton and Lord Wickburgh?"

"I will," Papa said ruefully.

Genevieve kissed them goodnight and went to bed where, despite the sparks shooting through her limbs, she slept like a baby.

In the morning, she rushed through her morning routine, donning her carriage dress in preparation for the journey, and went down for breakfast. Would Christian be up and about as well?

On her way, she passed Mr. Ashton speaking softly with the plain yet pleasant young lady from last night who wore the pendant Genevieve had admired. Based on the way they looked at one another, perhaps the vicar's son and the girl who didn't want to spend her life as a spinster on the moors would make a match.

Smiling, Genevieve passed them and headed to the breakfast room. Inside, she found Matilda, staring glumly into her plate of eggs.

Genevieve sat next to her friend and touched her arm in concern. "Are you well, Mattie?"

"You know, don't you? He told you?" Matilda raised her eyes.

Genevieve nodded. "He confided to me his concern that you had misunderstood his intentions. I advised him to clear it up before it was too late."

Matilda dropped her fork. "It was already too late. I thought he loved me. He deceived me."

"Mattie, he—"

"And I thought you were my friend. But you stole him from me. From the moment he saw you, he forgot all about me. And *you*—you encouraged him."

"No," Genevieve gasped. "I never meant—"

"You already had everyone else panting after you, but that wasn't good enough. You had to have him, too—the only man I ever truly loved!"

"It wasn't—"

"Don't ever speak to me!" Mattie stood and limped out of the room, her sobs trailing behind her.

Genevieve rocked back at the onslaught, cold down to her toes. She'd lost her dearest friend. She pressed a hand over her mouth. What had she done?

Sir Reginald strode past the door to catch up to Matilda. He called to her and they stood together, framed by the doorway, their voices only a murmur. He offered her his arm. Leaning heavily on him and limping, Matilda went with him into another room. Perhaps his loving heart would console her.

Genevieve had failed her friend. She'd allowed herself to love the gentleman for whom Matilda had formed an attachment. If Genevieve had she'd tried harder to point out Matilda's fine qualities, or if she'd removed herself from the house party, or been less friendly towards Christian, perhaps they might have made a match of it.

No. Who was she trying to fool? Her loyalty to Matilda didn't change the fact that Christian had never harbored a preference for Matilda. Her attachment for him was unrequited. In truth, she'd only fallen for Christian's handsome face and status as an earl's son. She didn't know him. Her tumultuous moods would never have suited his gentle and artistic nature. He needed someone steady and calm. Someone like Genevieve. And she needed him.

Where was Christian?

She peeked into the drawing room. There, on an easel, sat an exquisite, full-color painting of the abbey, in all its gothic glory. Next to it, sat a portrait of Matilda so lifelike that it might have been looking out a window at her, glowing with beauty, with a lively smile and an impish twinkle in her eyes. He must have worked all night to complete them.

Where was he? She wandered into the main hall where others were bidding the hosts goodbye.

"Mrs. Widtsoe," she called. "Have you seen Mr. Amesbury?"

Mrs. Widtsoe faltered upon seeing Genevieve. Her mouth turned down and her eyes took on an uncharacteristic hardness. She obviously blamed Genevieve for her daughter's heartbreak. "I believe the earl and his son have already departed."

"What? When?" Surely, he hadn't left without saying goodbye.

"Mere moments ago." She presented her back to Genevieve.

A frozen knot formed in her heart.

No. She was not losing him!

Without a shred of decorum, she raced outside to the main drive leading to the highway, searching for a coach with the Tarrington coat of arms.

No coach traveled down the drive. She was too late. Had she lost him as well as Matilda? A life without her best friend, and worse, a life without the only man she would ever love, stretched out in endless gloom.

CHAPTER 12

Genevieve stood in the drive alone. There had to be an explanation as to why he'd left. None came to mind, but she would not give up on him. Whatever had happened, she'd find him in Bath and remind him why they belonged together. She would be bold and fearless like a shield-maiden of old fighting for right.

Male voices reached her. Christian? She followed the voices to the side of the house. There stood Christian, wearing traveling clothes.

He hadn't left—not yet. The frozen knot in her midsection melted.

She nearly called out to him but stopped herself at the sight of the other man in his presence. Posture stiff, fists clenched at his sides, Christian and Lord Wickburgh faced off.

Christian spoke with hard, biting words, "As I told you last night, I refuse to step aside. I know for a fact that she has no desire to spend time in your company."

"You know nothing, boy," Lord Wickburgh said. "I'm warning you; she is mine. If you continue to interfere, you will meet an unhappy end."

"Threatening me will do you no good, sir."

"We'll see about that."

Christian's normally gentle voice lowered to a dangerous tone. "Stay away from her, or it is you who will meet an unhappy end."

Genevieve would never have imagined the hardness in Christian's voice. They stood, practically nose to nose, neither backing down, glaring hard enough to bore holes through one another.

"Christian, time to go!" The earl's voice called from the front steps.

Wickburgh let out a sneering laugh. "Go to your father, boy."

"Coming, Father," Christian said. To Lord Wickburgh, he said, "You are not to bother Miss Marshall again." He gave Lord Wickburgh a final, long look and strode away.

Genevieve stepped back quickly and headed towards the house. It would not do to let Christian know she'd seen the encounter. Her heart pounded. Seeing Christian locked in such a dangerous play with Lord Wickburgh revealed a new side of him. Dread at his danger, and excitement that he'd been protecting her, fighting for her, sent tingles of exhilaration down her backbone. He was like a knight of old jousting to win the favor of his lady love.

She dashed around the side of the house and hurried towards the front door, meeting the earl as he stepped off the stairs.

Lord Tarrington nodded as they passed. "Miss Marshall."

"My lord."

The Earl of Tarrington paused and half turned towards her. "I expect I'll be seeing you in Bath?"

She lowered her eyes. "I hope so."

He lifted his eyes to a point behind her. She turned. Christian, still grim, strode around the other side of the house towards her. When his gaze landed on Genevieve, Christian's stride broke. He resumed walking towards her, but his expression turned to wariness.

"Miss Marshall," he said, falling into formal speech, probably for the sake of his father.

"Ah, the coach is here at last." The earl bowed to Genevieve in farewell. "Miss Marshall."

"My lord." She curtsied.

"I'll wait for you inside, Son." He relied heavily on his cane as he made his way to the luxurious coach.

Christian nodded to acknowledge his father, not taking his eyes off Genevieve. Why the wariness in him? Perhaps he was still tense over his encounter with Lord Wickburgh.

She gave him a tentative smile. "I saw your paintings of Mattie and the abbey. They're exquisite."

Solemnly, he said, "I'm gratified you like them. Mr. Widtsoe seemed pleased."

Perhaps a little teasing? "Although I admit, I missed the flying gargoyle from your first sketch."

He moved his hand, but she missed whatever he'd hoped to express. Why had he retreated into the man of few words he'd been when they'd first met? His silence and palpable tension created a sudden jitteriness. Had she misunderstood his intentions? Had his kiss simply been the product of moonlight on the final night of a house party?

Her fears wormed out of her and into her voice. She whispered, "Were you going to leave without saying goodbye?"

He hesitated, his gaze flitting away. "I had not yet decided."

Her breath rushed out of her. "Did our kiss mean nothing to you?"

Eyeing her with such guardedness, he said nothing for a long moment. "It meant something to me. But it seems my suit is not adequate."

"What do you mean?"

True sorrow revealed itself in his expression. "I heard your parents."

She frowned and shook her head. "Heard them…?"

All at once, it came to her; he must have heard her parents telling her about the two offers for her hand, and how advantageous those matches would be.

He parted his beautiful lips, the very ones that had kissed her with such passion only hours ago. "You left your shawl behind, and I was returning it. The door was open so I couldn't help but overhear. They don't want you to settle for a youngest son. Perhaps you shouldn't." He pushed a hand through his hair.

Stepping closer, she said boldly, "They only wanted to be sure I knew my own mind. My own heart."

Those eyes, so blue, so intense, searched her eyes as if to find confirmation of her words.

Desperation squeezed her chest until she could hardly breathe, and it poured out of her voice. She took his hand. "I told them I would have you and no other. And they relented. My mother is thrilled, truth be told."

His expression softened, yet that wariness and vulnerability remained. He'd mentioned not feeling worthy of love, so she must be bold, leaving no room for doubt in his wounded heart.

"I would be miserable with anyone else—even a so-called advantageous match." She took his other hand and squeezed them both. "Christian, please trust me with your heart. I give you mine." She drew a breath. "I love you."

Hope and joy lit his face. He tugged on her hand, drawing her near. "Is that possible?"

"I love you with all of my heart."

His smile of joy should have inspired a heavenly choir of angels to break into song. He put hand on her cheek and looked more deeply into her eyes than anyone else ever had. "I love you, Genevieve Marshall."

His sincerity left no room for doubt. She laughed as tears filled her eyes. He kissed her so thoroughly she could hardly breathe. When his kiss ended, she almost begged him to do it again.

His husky voice vibrated through her. "I want to spend the rest of forever with you."

Surely her heart would explode with the love filling it past capacity. She'd never dreamed the power of those words.

She gave him an impish smile. "Forever may not be long enough."

His smile invited beams of happiness to shower all around them. "I have no title or coffers of money."

She leaned in and kissed the tip of his nose. "I would prefer not to starve, but if you can promise me food on the table and love in our home, I will be content—happy, even. Delirious."

"Then would it be presumptuous of me to ask you to marry me?"

"Would it be presumptuous of me to say it's about time you asked?"

He grinned and kissed her again until her feet left the ground and she floated.

A manly cough brought them back to earth. Horses snorted and stamped, and tack jingled, reminding them that the earl waited in the carriage.

Oh, heavens! She'd kissed Christian in full view of his father. However, she couldn't actually be as sorry as she ought.

Christian kissed her brow and stepped back. She almost laughed out loud at his rueful smile. "My father awaits. I'll come to you the moment you arrive in Bath." He took a step back, then another, as if he couldn't bring himself to turn around and walk away.

"I can hardly wait."

"There you are, Jenny," Matilda said. She came down the front steps, clasping her hands in front of her. "I came to say goodbye." She glanced back at Sir Reginald waiting by the front door who gave her an encouraging nod.

Matilda flitted her gaze to Christian who had halted halfway to the carriage. "Mr. Amesbury, I apologize for placing you in difficulty. I misunderstood—through no fault of yours. And I thank you for the lovely portrait. I've never seen its equal."

"It was my pleasure," he said graciously.

Matilda turned her gaze to Genevieve. Her face crumpled and tears filled her eyes. "Forgive me, Jenny!" She limped forward, her arms outstretched.

Genevieve met her and caught her in an embrace. "There is nothing to forgive. I'm grieved to have caused you pain."

Matilda shook her head. "You were only following your heart as you should." She glanced back at the curly-haired young Sir Reginald. "And I think it's time I followed mine."

Genevieve grinned at Sir Reginald, and his teeth flashed in return. "He's a fine young man, Mattie."

"Yes, he is. Curious. We've been friends for years, yet I never knew." Dreaminess came into her eyes for a moment. "Well, never mind. Goodbye for now. I hope to see you soon—perhaps in a church?"

Genevieve smiled at Christian who had only taken a few steps towards his family coach. She could not mistake his adoring gaze.

He replied without taking his attention off Genevieve. "Yes, in a church—as soon as possible." His smile promised many secret pleasures in the near future.

Matilda was locked in a gaze with Sir Reginald and has missed the entire exchanged. She pulled her focus of the young man who truly loved her and hugged Genevieve again. "Until then, goodbye." She hobbled up the steps with Sir Reginald at her side.

With a sultry gleam in his eye, Christian strode back to her with long, determined strides, and pulled her into his arms. "I love you, Genevieve." He cupped both of her cheeks and kissed her so expertly, so thoroughly, that her knees wobbled.

"Oh my," she said when she could speak. "I think we'd best purchase our wedding license as soon as possible."

He grinned. "Perfect."

Surely there could never be anything more perfect in all the world, than loving, and being loved by, Christian Amesbury.

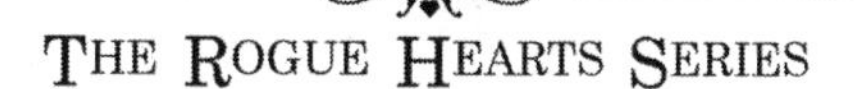

The Rogue Hearts Series

A Perfect Secret

Donna Hatch

CHAPTER 1

NORTHERN ENGLAND, LATE SUMMER 1819

For a woman determined to commit murder, Genevieve walked sedately, eerily tranquil, her heart beating slowly, her hands steady, her mind calm. Perhaps her serenity arose from a state of insanity, for only a lunatic would risk her immortal soul to an eternity of hellfire and brimstone.

Her blank existence, broken up only with moments of pain and fear when Lord Wickburgh played another cruel game, would finally, blessedly cease. As her life ended, so, too would the emptiness of her life and heart and womb.

Oh, how she'd always longed to hold a baby in her arms and coo into a baby's ear and smell that heavenly baby scent. Now, she'd never know that joy.

In trance-like calm, Genevieve followed the dappled pathway. Birdsong serenaded her as she sauntered along the woodland path, and the morning sun shone despite dark clouds growing at the horizon. A breeze carried the scent of the last few flowers of a dying summer. All of it mocked her, the perfect foil against the dark hole where her heart had once resided.

The river's roar deafened her as she padded on the planks of the bridge. Stopping in the middle, she gazed impassively down at the churning, muddy water. From recent rains, the normally placid river had swollen to a rushing torrent. Perfect. Even if she could swim, she'd never survive. The dark river no doubt hid all manner of danger and violence, similar in so many ways to her marriage, a sham that also hid all manner of danger and violence.

As she removed her shawl and let it fall, the crisp morning air raised bumps on her skin. The river would be even colder. Undaunted, Genevieve slid the sleeves of her gown off her shoulders and watched the fabric billow at her feet. Her petticoats, silk stockings and shoes followed. The weight of her clothing would hold her down better, but leaving it on the bridge for others to find would ensure that Lord Wickburgh, and all of society, would know where and how Genevieve had ended her life. The scandal of a wife who had committed suicide would be her one revenge upon the ice monster she'd had no choice but to marry if she'd had any prayer of saving her father.

After twisting her wedding band off her finger, she laid it down on top of her clothing, carefully placing everything near the edge of the bridge. Wearing only her shift and stays, she swung her legs over the railing and sat upon the narrow wooden slat.

The water beckoned, each muddy wave topped with a whitecap. A tree branch rolled over and over as the current swept it along. It surfaced, only to sink again. It reappeared again further downriver.

Would he look for her body, or might her clothes and ring be enough evidence of her death? Knowing Lord Wickburgh, a body would be required as proof. Otherwise, he'd never stop searching for her, like a miser who had to account for every penny.

Genevieve lifted her face one last time toward the sun but the clouds had closed in, threatening another day of rain. After bidding farewell to the stark ugliness of her life, she closed her eyes. Hell would probably be ugly, colorless, without music or light or scent. It would also be *sans* Lord Wickburgh . . . at least for a while, until he joined her in perdition. Perhaps she'd have her own fiery poker to keep him at bay.

Christian. She'd never see him again—not in this life, not in the next. A man of such high integrity would go straight to heaven after he left the earth. Dear, dear Christian! A faint stirring arose in the vacuum where her heart once rested. How clearly the tenderness in his blue eyes, the softness of his smile, the gentleness of his touch came to mind. And how clearly, too, his disbelief and hurt when she'd told him she chose to marry Wickburgh. That expression haunted her always.

It wasn't his fault that he believed her capable of such treachery. After all, she'd worked hard to lie to him. But deep inside, she'd hoped he would never believe she could be so vicious.

Sorrow gnawed through her chest, consuming her last spark of life. She blew out her breath to prevent buoyancy.

And jumped.

The water's icy blast hit and a current dragged her into a silent world of brownish-green, yet still no alarm arose. Instead, unnatural calm wrapped more securely around her. In a moment, it would all be over. As she grew numb from cold, the river carried her along gently, like a mother rocking her child. For the first time in years, peace enfolded her in its soft embrace.

She floated toward the safety of death.

CHAPTER 2

Profoundly alone, Christian stood in front of the family crypt, the white stone building glowing against the darkness. Only a faint hint of gray at the far eastern sky hinted at the coming dawn. He carefully laid his bunch of flowers at the entrance where the remains of a ten-year-old boy lay, a boy whose life was snuffed out long before his time.

Eighteen years ago today, Christian had held Jason in his arms while his brother, his advocate, his friend, took one last breath. Christian squeezed his eyes shut, but the images played out in his mind, as clear as the day they happened. Every detail, every sound, every sharp, accusing pain trampled him like a stampede, leaving only ruin in its wake.

"I'm sorry, Jason."

He'd never atone for causing his brother's death. Perhaps he should stop trying.

A bird fluttered over his head and perched on the roof of the crypt, twittering and singing a cheerful tune at odds with Christian's mood. He watched the bird sing, flutter a few steps forward, and fluff out its feathers. Viewing the bird's simple joy, Christian smiled in spite of himself. Now that his parents were both gone and his brother

Cole had inherited the title, Christian no longer had the responsibility of caring for his father and managing the Amesbury estate. Would it be so bad to indulge in a few dreams of his own now?

He'd dare hope his years of penance were through when he'd found such happiness with Genevieve. But that had been fleeting and false. He shoved away those memories for the lies that they were. Yes, it was time to leave.

Italy sang to him like a song of hope. Maybe he could convince his sister Rachel to go with him. It might entice her to leave her self-imposed exile and rekindle her zeal for living. Perhaps it would rekindle his own.

The grating of the gate swinging open broke the silence. He looked up at the sky shot through with streaks of pink as dawn crept closer. The family crypt loomed overhead, casting a shadow over him, just as Jason's death cast a shadow over Christian's life.

The gate slammed shut, his cue to leave. Christian took a circular route back to the gate to avoid seeing anyone. A shadow leaped in front of him. Startled, Christian dropped into a defensive crouch, reaching for his gun, until he recognized the form.

"Grant." Christian bit out the name, no less relieved than if a bandit faced him.

Dressed entirely in black, Grant stared, his cold gray eyes focused on Christian like a pair of claws. Grant had always been dark, but he'd come home from the war truly terrifying in his controlled, intense energy.

As Grant opened his mouth to spew a stinging insult, Christian took a step closer and stared him in the eye.

"Don't," Christian snarled through clenched teeth.

As he stalked to the main gate, he bumped against Grant's shoulder. Grant made a satisfying grunt as he steadied his balance. With his head high, Christian strode to his grazing Friesian, took up the reins and leaped into the saddle. He resisted the urge to look back at his brother. If Grant hadn't killed him by now, he likely wouldn't.

Christian urged the horse to a canter, heading back to Tarrington

Castle, but the thought of returning home to Cole and Alicia's love nest, complete with cooing and kissing in corners, left Christian faintly ill. And envious of their happiness.

Instead of heading to his ancestral home, Christian turned his horse to follow the river. The heavy overgrowth would provide a protective cover where he could continue his solitude. The roar of the rain-swollen, muddy river drowned out all sound. As dawn broke, sending golden rays through the clouds, he rode along the river.

His artistic mind nudged aside his grief enough to mentally mix colors he'd need if he were to paint the scenery. Silver and charcoal clouds billowed at the horizon of a rare, cobalt blue sky soaring above verdant green foliage. The first traces of autumn reds and gold tipped some of the leaves as if a great artist had begun gilding them with master strokes. Whitecaps topped the muddy rushing waves as the river leaped along its course and ducked underneath a quaint, weathered bridge.

A shimmer of white caught his eye on the old bridge. Christian narrowed his gaze and blinked in disbelief. Surely he was mistaken, but it appeared as though a woman sat on the railing. He blinked again, straining his eyes. He was not mistaken.

A woman sat with her legs dangling over the edge, the whiteness of her gown glowing against the weathered wood. She sat with lowered head as if she contemplated the river, her abundant auburn hair concealing most of her face and upper body. He'd only seen hair that color once. Its texture had put silk to shame.

But that was a lifetime ago.

As he continued trotting toward her, she shifted her legs until she sat dangerously close to the edge.

He let out a gasp. "What the devil . . . ?"

The woman jumped into the water.

Christian's heart leaped into his throat and an answering jolt shook his knees. He spurred his horse closer to the bridge, his gaze fixed on the water's surface. The woman vanished into the murky depths.

He didn't think; he simply acted. Before reaching the bridge, he leaped from his horse, threw off his tailcoat, and dove in. The freezing water hit him like a blow. His strength ebbed. Helpless as a leaf tossed on the savage current, he barely managed to keep his head up. The water tugged him down lower and lower, pulling him beneath the surface. Summoning all his strength, he fought the weakness, pushing upward. As his head broke through the surface, he took a breath. He scanned for the woman. No sign of her.

Christian floundered in the numbing cold as rapids overcame him again, pulling him down into a world of brown-green water. Shafts of light glimmered over his head.

He battled toward the surface, only to be dragged under again before he got a breath. His lungs screamed for air as mortal terror threatened to swallow him. He could die. Here. Now. He would never atone for his transgressions.

No. He would not die. Not today. Not for a long, long time.

With renewed determination, Christian forced stiffened muscles into smooth strokes and shot upward. As his head broke through, he drew air into starved lungs. The river widened and slowed, no longer lethal in its current. With the roar of the river deafening him, he looked wildly around for the woman. Nothing. He refused to give up. He had to save her. Still treading water, he searched the surface.

There. A bit of cloth. He launched himself toward it and reached out. His fingers closed over something, but they were too numb to identify what, exactly, he'd caught. As he made a fist and pulled, a solid form sailed toward him. Towing the mass behind him, he forced his numbed limbs to move him toward the riverbank. The moment his feet gained purchase on firm ground, he pulled harder, hauling the shapeless object toward him. His feet slipped and he fell to his knees. He glanced back. A feminine shape floated facedown and unmoving, her hair spread out around her like a dark halo.

"Heaven help me."

Christian wrapped his arms around the woman's torso and scrabbled up the slippery bank, hauling her limp body with him. He slipped in the mud and fell heavily, dropping the woman. Unwilling to yield, he put one arm around her waist and pulled her with him as he struggled upward, then collapsed on the muddy grass.

"Miss?"

The woman lay motionless beside him. He pushed on her back, hoping to force out the water in her lungs. No response. He'd heard of sailors reviving drowning victims by rolling them over a barrel. He looked around for a fallen log to serve as a substitute but found none. Again, he pushed on her back, harder. Nothing. He pulled her across his knees and pounded on her back between her shoulder blades.

"Breathe!"

Nothing. He pounded again. Dismay curled in his stomach. He'd failed to save her.

Finally, she retched, coughed, and drew in a ragged breath. Very carefully, he turned her over. His heart, that long-frozen organ, gave a painful lurch that hit him like a fist to his gut. His breath rushed out of him.

"Genevieve?" he gasped.

She'd dramatically changed. Still, he'd know her anywhere. No one forgot the girl who broke his heart and ran off with another man.

Horrified at the change, he stared. Still as death, Genevieve made no motion. She lay in perfect repose. What could have happened to her? Dark circles framed her eyes, her face had painfully thinned, and her once-lush figure had grown gaunt. Her coughing abated, but she remained unconscious.

Despite the lack of modesty provided by her wet shift and stays, his male responses remained dormant. Memories battered him, the sweet as well as the bitter. He pressed his hand into his eye sockets to shut them out. A low roar like the distant rumble of thunder filled his ears.

"Of all people, why you?"

Helpless anger coiled in his stomach. Pushing away the images and emotions that invaded his mind and his heart, he sucked in a breath and turned his attention to the matter at hand. What to do with her?

Long-nurtured resentment voiced an ugly temptation to simply throw the lying wench back into the water, or at the very least, leave her here.

But of course he couldn't do that. His duty as a gentleman demanded that he care for her, even if she were a lying gold digger. Very well, he'd take her home and see to her needs, then immediately ship her off to her precious husband.

With a sigh, he slid his arms underneath her shoulders and knees and stood holding her petite body. He carried her along the river as he retraced his steps. His gaze strayed to her face as if he could find answers to how she'd come to be here, and why someone so full of life and zeal would attempt the horrific act of self-murder. But she was no longer his concern. She'd toyed with his heart and then left him. She deserved unhappiness. What did he care if she tried to kill herself? He shouldn't care. He didn't care. He refused to care.

Gritting his teeth, he tramped to his horse who had followed his progress down the river and now grazed nearby.

"Good lad, Erebos. Take us home."

Struggling with Genevieve's limp form, Christian mounted his Friesian and urged the animal to a walk. Dark clouds blotted out the sun and cast gloom over the landscape. It matched his mood. Cold settled deep into his bones, and even deeper into his heart.

As the full realization hit him of how close he'd come to losing his life, Christian's hand holding the reins trembled. In his five and twenty years, he'd brushed up against death twice now. Only the fight which had left a scar on his face and ribs—courtesy of Wickburgh's lapdogs—had been as deadly as this battle with the river.

Christian took a steadying breath and looked down again at Genevieve in his arms. What could have driven her to such a state? No sane person attempted suicide. Perhaps she regretted leaving him and marrying a conniving scoundrel. With a scoff, he cast off the romantic notion. No doubt, she never gave a thought to the one whose heart she'd left in ruins a year ago.

A pattering of rain on the leaves blanketed the world in stillness.

Gray clouds closed in, weighting his spirits. Rain fell in a steady downpour. Christian's teeth chattered. His numb, stiff hands barely gripped the reins.

By the time Christian arrived at Tarrington Castle, he could scarcely move his body. After dismounting, he stumbled up the stairs to the front door.

The footman who opened the door remained calm and unruffled as if the earl's brother frequently came home dripping wet and carrying an equally dripping wet, unconscious woman. Normally Christian would find humor in the servant's trained composure, but at the moment, he cared little.

Mrs. Hodges, the head housekeeper, entered with swishing skirts. She frowned in disapproval at Christian as if he were a disobedient lad of six. "Master Christian, what is the meaning of this?"

Since he was no longer the child she once scolded with the ferocity of a lioness, Christian drew himself up, and called upon his most authoritative voice. "A guest room and the doctor, Mrs. Hodges."

Mrs. Hodges's gaze settled on Genevieve's pale, still face. The venerable woman actually lost her powers of speech. He couldn't enjoy the moment as much as he should have.

"Chris!" His brother Cole strode in, impeccable as usual as befitting the Sixth Earl Tarrington, and also stopped up short, his eyes widening.

Christian didn't bother to offer an explanation. He looked at the housekeeper and barked, "I gave you an order; now move, woman!"

Mrs. Hodges stared at him as if he'd bitten her.

Cole took command with the authority of a general. "Mrs. Hodges, send for Ann and have a fire started in a guest room. Vickery, fetch Stephens and Porter." Cole reached for the woman in Christian's arms. "Here, Chris, let me."

Unexplainably annoyed at his brother's interference, Christian glared at Cole and stepped back, holding protectively close the girl he'd once loved. But he didn't love her. Not anymore. He felt nothing at all for her except mild annoyance that she'd reappeared into his life, stirring up all kinds of memories he thought he'd killed.

Cole's eyes narrowed in concern. "You're shivering and your lips are purple. Go warm yourself. She'll receive the care she needs."

Without waiting for Christian's permission, Cole pulled Genevieve into his arms and carried her upstairs.

Christian had the oddest urge to race after Cole, punch his brother's face, and take back Genevieve. But the last time he'd fought for her, he'd been attacked and left for dead. Besides, she wasn't worth it.

Stephens, Cole's friend and valet, appeared, his Romany features settled into a worried frown. "Come. Let's get you warmed. Has someone sent for Porter?"

Christian pushed impatiently at his dripping hair. At the moment, he couldn't even remember who Porter was. Stephens tugged on Christian's arm and led him up the stairs. Groggy, Christian stumbled after him to his bedchamber. Porter arrived, making sounds of dismay. Oh, yes, Porter. His new valet. Too tired to speak or move, Christian stood in the middle of his bed chambers while Stephens and Porter stripped him of his wet clothing and wrapped him in a blanket. They seated him before a roaring fire and pressed a hot cup of tea in his hand. Christian burned his mouth on the tea but as he swallowed it, the icy lump in his stomach melted. A moment later, a hip bath arrived and the servants scurried to fill it with steaming water.

How fared Genevieve? She'd better recover quickly so he could tell her he didn't love her anymore and that he was coping just fine without her.

Then he'd throw her back to her precious viscount of a husband before she could steal away his fractured heart and grind it into powder.

CHAPTER 3

Hell felt heavenly. Safe. Warm. A fire crackled nearby and faint traces of the last summer roses wafted on the air. With her eyes still closed, Genevieve lay on her back, afraid to open her eyes. She stretched cautiously. Softness met her limbs. If she didn't know better, she would have thought she lay in a featherbed.

But that wasn't possible. Was it?

Genevieve opened her eyes to a blur of white. She blinked until she focused upon a white canopy with red flowers arched overhead. Disoriented, she blinked again. The feathers of a dozen pillows stuffed her head. She flexed her toes and fingers, running her hands over the texture of fine linens, the softness of a bed. She shifted again, testing her muscles. Dull pain met her motion, as if she'd fallen and had suffered bruises all over. Which meant she still lived.

She frowned. That was not possible. Her last memory was . . . .

Oh, Heaven help her, her last memory was throwing herself into a river in numb unconcern with the intent to actually commit the horrible crime of suicide. Her parents would be horrified. She was horrified.

A dim memory wormed into her mind of a strong pair of arms

holding her close, the rocking motion of horseback, a familiar scent, fleeting voices.

Realization dawned. Someone had rescued her. Genevieve looked beyond the canopy to the intricately carved ceiling and woodwork painted crisp white and rich blue. Late afternoon sunlight spilled through the velvet-draped windows. It all painted an incongruous setting for her plight.

She almost groaned out loud. She lay within a bedchamber of a house, probably near the river. In England. Near *his* northern estate. She still belonged to *him*.

"Good afternoon."

She jumped at the sound of a male voice and turned her head toward the speaker. She gaped. With golden hair, eyes as blue as forget-me-nots, and exquisitely chiseled, patrician features, none other than Christian Amesbury looked back at her.

Her heart started a slow, painful thud. Heaven help her, but he was even more handsome now than ever. Her dormant heart awakened. The only man she ever loved—the only man she would ever love—sat within reach. She ached to return to that optimistic girl she'd been when she met Christian. The complete opposite of her husband, Christian represented safety and love and everything good in the world.

Did he know she'd tried to drown herself? Fresh waves of shame heated her face and she wanted to pull the covers up over her head.

Christian leaned forward, putting his face at the same level as hers. Still as broad through the shoulders and muscular as he'd been . . . was it only a year ago?... he dwarfed the dainty floral chair upon which he sat. How was it possible he'd grown even more handsome? The only flaw to his perfection was a small scar at the outer corner of his right eye. How had he gotten that scar?

She moistened her lips. "Christian. Where am I?"

He sat back and folded his arms as his full, sensitive mouth curled into distain. "You're in Castle Tarrington, my ancestral home."

"I see." She'd known, of course, that Wickburgh had brought her within a few leagues of the Tarrington county seat, but never dreamed she'd see Christian. "How long have I been here?"

"About six hours."

Hours, not days. That was good. Wasn't it? She glanced at him, undone by his presence. And not a little disconcerted by the fearsome scowl marring his handsome face.

She babbled the first thing that came to her mind. "I didn't know you lived here."

His restless gaze flicked her way. "No doubt. Otherwise you wouldn't have come to the area."

No, but her husband never heeded her opinion so her objection would have been summarily dismissed. The hopelessness that had seized her and held her captive since she lost her baby—the same hopelessness that had spurred her to attempt to end her life—faded as she gazed upon Christian. Time had not dimmed her love for him.

From the way Christian glared at her, whatever affection he once felt for her had died.

She moistened her lips, searching for something to say to him. She focused on the black armband he wore. The newspaper had reported the passing of the Earl of Tarrington and of the succession of the title by Christian's brother, Cole, several weeks earlier.

"I'm sorry about your father."

He nodded. A new, decidedly haunted expression crept over his expression. As if catching himself in a moment of vulnerability, he straightened, pinned her with a hostile glare. "My sister-in-law had some clothes brought in for you." He made a loose gesture toward another part of the room. "Now get up and go back to your husband."

She gaped at the hardness of his tone. Where was the artistic dreamer she'd known and loved?

He continued barking orders at her. "I'll order a carriage and have them take you back to Wickburgh's manor."

Send her back! Alarm raced through her body and she shot to an upright position, ignoring the pain of her mysterious bruises, and held out her hands in supplication.

"Please don't send me back." Her voice sounded helpless, pleading, pathetic.

He spoke as if he hadn't heard her. "Or I could simply return you to the river. Unless you've changed your mind about killing yourself?" Eyes so blue and pale that they appeared to glow fixed upon her, accusation shining clearly through. "I admit, I never really knew you—obviously—but I never would have thought you capable of suicide. That's despicable even for you."

She deserved that. She really did. But his open hostility raised her hackles. He had no idea what she'd suffered. How dare he be so self-righteous and judgmental! Clearly, she'd been right; if Christian, instead of Wickburgh, had learned of her father's mutiny, he would have been horrified and rejected her. He probably would have marched down to the admiralty and personally reported her father.

Fisting her hands in the counterpane covering her, she threw open the gate controlling her fury and flung at him the word his brothers taunted at him throughout his childhood. "Yes, well, it must be difficult being so *perfect* all the time."

He stiffened at her use of the word 'perfect.' Good. She had his attention.

She drove in the barb deeper. "Clearly your only flaw is having to live among us flawed mortals who make mistakes."

With narrowed eyes, he leaned forward. "'Mistakes' is hardly the word I would use for what you did."

"You know nothing!" A sob tore out of her. She deserved his hatred, his judgment; she'd told the lies to earn it. Yet the full sharpness of his bitter anger stabbed her like a twisting blade.

He leaped to his feet like a restless tiger, turned on his heel, and strode to the door. "Go home."

He wrenched open the door and nearly trampled a maid carrying a tray. With a yelp, the maid staggered back, nearly upsetting the dishes. He caught her tray with one hand while steadying the girl with the other.

The maid gulped in a breath, eyeing Christian's hard set mouth and flushed face. "F-forgive me, sir. I-I brought yer breakfast, Miss," she stammered, glancing at Genevieve desperately.

Christian dragged his fingers through his hair and gripped the back of his neck. Stepping back, he blew out his breath. "Sorry, Ann."

He gestured for the maid to enter. With another wary look at Christian, the poor maid sidestepped him, giving him a wide berth, and entered the room.

Genevieve sucked in a breath, and blinked back hot tears welling up in her eyes. "Thank you," she managed, glancing at the maid.

As the maid approached, Genevieve braced her hands on the bed and resettled herself into an upright position. Pain shot out from multiple places. She hissed in her breath. After setting the tray on a bedside table, the maid arranged pillows behind her.

Christian hovered in the doorway, sending darting glances her way.

What could she say to him? She was sorry? She didn't mean all those things she said in Bath, or just now, for that matter? Any of that would only make matters worse. Her throat tightened and her eyes burned. The maid bobbed a curtsy and left the room.

Still standing in the doorway, Christian let out a long exhale and turned to leave. He might send her back to Wickburgh. Panic raced through her.

"Christian, wait."

With his back to her, he paused and stood fisting his hands.

Her heart thudded as she sought for the words to convince him to keep her secret. "You think me terrible for a number of reasons, and I have no right to ask you for forgiveness, nor for any favors."

He stood completely still.

She took a steadying breath. "But I beg you; do not send me back to Wickburgh."

Slowly he turned, folded his arms, and leaned his back against the doorframe in forced nonchalance. "Not blissfully happy as a viscountess, I take it?"

She had no reply. She wasn't about to bare the horror of belonging to Wickburgh.

"You can't stay here," he said flatly.

"No. That would be unwise for a number of reasons. All I ask is that you don't send me back to him. Please, just give me a day or two to regain my strength."

"And then?"

And then . . . what? Stalling, she eyed the tray of scones, clotted cream, and a cup of steaming chocolate. She poured cream and sugar into her cup of chocolate until the normally bitter drink became creamy and decadent.

The idea of a watery grave no longer held appeal. How could she have even thought of killing herself? Those actions seemed to belong to another person. Perhaps the water had knocked sense into her. But to go back to her ivy-covered prison ...

No. She'd never go back to *him*.

To avoid looking at Christian, Genevieve let her gaze drift about the room. Royal blue wallpaper with gold leaves adorned the walls. A corner of one piece of wallpaper had fallen loose near the window, just as her idyllic life had become unglued the moment she married Lord Wickburgh. More than unglued—completely unraveled.

How could she avoid going back to him? He'd find her like he did the last time she'd left. Of course, he might believe she'd died in the river. Her breath caught.

He might believe she'd died in the river.

A new plan formed. Daring. Dangerous. Probably doomed. But she could escape. If it worked.

Finally, she looked up at Christian who watched her warily. "I'm not entirely certain where I should go just yet. But I must get far away. And I desperately need everyone to believe I've drowned."

His forehead creased and he let out a huff in mocking amusement. "You want me to lie for you—you, of all people. Why would I do that?"

The cup in her hand shook at the venom dangling off his words. "I'm not asking you to lie for me. Just don't send word to anyone that

I'm here. Say nothing. Please." She leaned forward. "Tell no one who I am. Let him think I'm dead."

The crystal blue of his eyes turned to pure ice. "I want no part of this."

"Please." It came out as a half sob. "I cannot go back to him."

He shook his head, his shoulders sagging a little. "Very well. But I won't lie for you, *Lady* Wickburgh. Leave. Soon."

He closed the door. Cold seeped into her bones. Christian was so different. Had he changed so drastically, or had she not really known him? Their courtship had been short and blissful. Perhaps there was another side to him she'd never discovered during their short courtship.

At least she was safe for now, but this refuge could only be temporary. Remaining here would put her too close to her husband's reach. And that she could not abide.

CHAPTER 4

In the family dining room, Christian sat at the table, slowly drawing circles in his gravy with his fork. He glanced out the door in the direction of the stairs where he'd left Genevieve hours ago. The knots in his stomach left no room for his normally robust appetite.

His sister-in-law, Alicia, smiled gently, concern etching creases in her lovely face. "My word. I can't recall the last time you failed to empty nearly every dish on the table. Are you unwell?"

Christian let out a long exhale. "How long until she's able to leave?"

Alicia drew back in surprise. "Leave? Well, the doctor said she needs a day or so to rest. One doesn't recover from a near drowning in an hour." Her voice quieted. "And the doctor said she was *enceinte*."

"She's with child?" Christian's stomach clenched. Another man's baby. It made her betrayal so much worse.

"Not anymore; she recently miscarried."

"I see." Did her loss minimize her betrayal? No. Not at all. He didn't know what to feel about anything right now. Everything inside twisted into a tangled mess.

Alicia mused, "I wonder if the loss of her baby is what drove her to throw herself into the river. I've heard sometimes after a woman loses her unborn child, she can fall into a terrible melancholy." She looked down and rubbed her rounded stomach. "I hope nothing like that happens to me."

"I'm sure it won't," Christian said numbly.

Alicia buttered her bread. "Odd that she wouldn't give you her name when she woke. She was equally reluctant with me when I looked in on her. I wonder who she is. Her hands are fine and she speaks with the cultured tones of a lady, so she's clearly not a servant."

"No." Christian wished he could sink into his chair rather than lie to Alicia.

"I suppose she could be a governess, but she's awfully pretty for a governess. You grew up here, yet you don't know her?"

Christian watched the fork leave tiny lines as he drew it across the plate. "I haven't lived here in years, since before I went to Cambridge." He wasn't lying . . . exactly. "Father and I spent most of our time in Bath or with friends after Mama passed."

Alicia's expression turned wistful. "It would simplify everything if she'd tell us who she is. Still, she's hurting, frightened, and grieving her lost baby. We must be sensitive to her feelings."

He nodded silently. Sensitive to her feelings. What feelings? Maybe she didn't have feelings. She certainly hadn't shown any last year.

When the fork in his hand bent under his white-knuckled grip, he set down his utensils and pushed away his plate.

Alicia's voice broke into Christian's thoughts. "We need to watch her carefully. I fear she may try to harm herself again. Or leave before she's well enough."

Voices traveled from the great hall and a mild commotion reached their ears. Christian jumped to his feet. Had Lord Wickburgh come after his wife?

As Cole's voice boomed over the greetings of the servants, Christian relaxed. Alicia's eyes lit up and her face glowed. Cole appeared in the doorway wearing a wide grin.

"You're home," Alicia breathed, her face infused with joy.

"I have an excellent reason to be here." Cole's grin broadened.

With long strides, he came to Alicia, knelt by her chair, and gathered her in his arms. Cole was all tenderness when he kissed Alicia and placed his hand over her rounded belly. As the happy couple locked in a prolonged embrace, Christian mumbled an excuse and left them alone.

He cast a glare upward to the room where Genevieve lay. Fate had a cruel sense of timing to bring the jilt back into his life on the anniversary of Jason's death. The days' events left him frayed and worn and raw. Since he couldn't work off his frustration by boxing or fencing or racing, he'd paint to rein in his roiling emotions.

Christian went into his studio upstairs and lit every lamp in the room. Lamplight made a paltry substitution for natural sunlight, which is why he commandeered a room with windows all along the east wall. However, when seized by the need to paint this time of night, he needed to make concessions.

After removing his tailcoat, waistcoat and cravat, rolled up his sleeves and donned a large smock. Then he uncovered his easel and eyed his unfinished landscape.

After losing so many members of his family, Christian understood all too well the tenuous hold men have upon life. What would drive a person to such drastic measures as to purposely try to end her life? Not even Father, in his bleak and inconsolable grief after Mama died, had resorted to self-murder. No, he'd died slowly, a little more each day, of a broken heart.

He shouldn't be so affected by Genevieve. He lost her a year ago. No, he hadn't really lost her; she had never been his in the first place, clearly, or she wouldn't have jilted him.

He didn't need her. He was better off without her.

Drawing a deep breath, he blew away his scattered thoughts like so many dried leaves. After crushing the pigments with a pestle, he mixed his colors, then picked up a brush and focused on the painting.

With his brush, he outlined a landscape he'd viewed during his recent trip to the lake country.

Normally painting provided a reprieve from whatever thoughts haunted him, but tonight, they spiraled back to Genevieve. If she'd married him, they would have been happy. His whole existence would have been to make her smile. But she'd revealed her unfaithful heart.

Now, she wanted to flee her husband. Which just proved—again—that she wasn't capable of constancy. Was she even capable of love or did she view love as a game?

Refocusing on his painting, he finished shading in a tree before he began on the patterns of the lake. Creating life-like water had always proved a challenge that required his full focus, but tonight, instead of a clear lake, the muddy river that had nearly claimed both his and Genevieve's life tainted the painting.

It would have been so much simpler if he'd let her drown. He clenched his fist and put down his brush before he snapped it in half.

The clock revealed three o'clock in the morning. With a sigh, he washed his brushes and his hands. After removing his smock, he draped it over a stool and banked the fire. After a final glare at the painting with the greenish-brown lake, he blew out the lamps.

Shadows lurked in the corners along his path downstairs to the family quarters. He nodded to a sleepy-eyed footman at the bottom of the stairs, and then paused, casting a long look to the wing where Genevieve slept.

Why had she been desperate for her husband not to know of her existence? If they were simply estranged, they could live out their lives in separate houses and ignore one another. No, it was more than that.

Wickburgh had terrified her at the house party last summer. What had changed to make her want to marry that snake? Any sane woman would fear him.

Very well. Christian would help her if only to get her out of his life as soon as possible. Besides, anything that would cause difficulty for Wickburgh was sure to be a worthwhile endeavor.

A muffled scream sent Christian's heart racing. He bolted down the corridor, following the screams. They led him to Genevieve's room. Christian passed a footman running the same direction and burst inside.

Fully expecting to see an attacker over Genevieve, Christian raced in and flung back the bed curtains.

Alone and unharmed, Genevieve writhed in bed. Christian glared at her. What theatrics was this? And what did she hope to gain?

A maid appeared at the bedside and caught one of her flailing hands. "It's all right, Miss, yer safe 'ere."

Her face pale and the muscles in her neck standing out, Genevieve fought against an imaginary assailant while cries of distress wrenched from her. Absolute primal fear rolled off her in waves. The terror in her voice pierced his soul.

Softening in the face of such genuine panic, Christian touched her shoulder. "Jenny, wake up. You're dreaming."

She came awake with a shriek, wild-eyed, and jerked her hand out of the maid's grasp. Then she leaped away from Christian.

He gentled his voice and took a step back. "No one will harm you. You're safe."

She stared at him without recognition. Her gaze traveled to the burly footman behind him, and then to the maid at his side, her eyes wide and unblinking. Beads of perspiration stood out on her skin and her breath came in labored gasps.

Christian softened his voice. "You're at Tarrington Castle. You're safe."

Slowly, the crippling fear drained out of her and recognition entered her eyes. "Christian."

She heaved a shuddering sigh and fixed vulnerable, frightened eyes upon him. Dark as chocolate and fringed with thick lashes, the despair mirrored in them nearly broke his heart. Bruises dotted her arms and face, probably from the river. He'd found bruises on his own body, and he hadn't been in the river as long as she.

He should give her privacy to release her grief, not to mention his aversion to being so close to her. She'd betrayed him. Her misery was her just reward. Yet he could not leave her to face her demons alone.

Christian nodded to the footman and maid in dismissal before turning back to her. She wept bone-weary sobs as she sat hugging her knees. Grief and terror poured out of her and washed over him, leaving him breathless and shaken. Christian stood, appallingly helpless, at her bedside. Clearly, there was nothing he could do. Nor should he feel obligated to do anything for the jilt. He headed for the door.

"Don't leave, I beg you." Her voice rasped with tears. She wiped her tears.

He hesitated. Small and vulnerable, she sniffled and continued to rub her hands over her eyes. With a sigh, he retrieved a handkerchief from the nightstand and handed it to her.

"Thank you. Please forgive me for making such a scene. I often have nightmares . . . ."

Sympathy tapped the shoulder of his conscience. "Do you wish to tell me about your dream?"

She shook her head vigorously and pushed back at her loose hair. He'd known she wouldn't be happy with Wickburgh, but her stark misery cut through him like a knife. If only he could do something for her, protect her . . . .

No. Caring about her again would be supremely stupid. He should avoid her while she remained here. And do everything possible to forget her.

She moistened her lips. "Thank you for your . . . assistance. I'm sorry to have disturbed you at this hour."

"You didn't. I was still up."

She glanced at the clock on the nightstand next to a burning candle. "It's three o'clock in the morning."

"I was painting."

Her eyes opened wide. "Your artist's muse keeps you up at night?"

"Not usually."

"You never showed me any of your paintings, but your sketches were lovely."

He'd burned the sketchbook filled with drawings of Genevieve after she married Lord Wickburgh, one page at a time, each page curling and blackening like his heart.

He took a step toward the door. "It's late. You must be fatigued."

Her gaze fixed on him, so devoid of light and joy that her eyes seemed to belong to a different person. What had happened to her?

"You, as well. Thank you for your concern." Her stiff formal words failed to hide the pleading in her eyes, pleading him to help her, pleading him to protect her.

She sat in bed wearing nothing but a thin shift that did little to conceal her womanly curves. As if realizing her state of *dishabille,* she pulled the counterpane up and hugged it.

Oh, right. He'd left his waistcoat and tailcoat in his studio. He stood, half-dressed, in the bedchamber of a woman. Not that she was any temptation. Still, his presence here was inappropriate.

"Rest, Genev—er Lady Wickburgh. You're safe here."

He wouldn't let down his guard enough to trust her, or—heaven forbid—make the mistake of caring about her again. Wickburgh had no doubt been a cold and unyielding husband, but her terror suggested it was more than that. Christian's gut wrenched at the thought. Again, he wondered what had driven Genevieve to marry Wickburgh.

The wall he'd built around his heart developed a crack.

Whatever had happened to her was real and terrible, and his duty as a gentleman was clear. Very well. He'd send her as far away as possible and dust off his hands, glad to be rid of her. Then he'd resume his efforts to rebuild a life without her. As he left the room, he sealed the crack and built another wall around the fortress of his heart.

CHAPTER 5

Genevieve barely slept, always listening for the sound of *his* footsteps, her heart stopping at the tread of feet.

Christian was here. She was safe, for the time being.

As morning light spilled between the draperies, Genevieve plotted her next move. If only she could move without pain shooting out in every direction.

The door opened and her maid, Ann, perked in. When they made eye contact, she said, "Good morning, Miss."

"Good morning, Ann."

"I wasn't sure you'd be awake so early. I'll bring your tray straightaway."

"Thank you."

Moments later, the young Lady Tarrington entered, bearing her usual aura of serenity, and, despite being great with child, moving with grace. Lady Tarrington's smile bathed Genevieve in the brightness of her cheer. She'd only spoken with Genevieve a few moments the previous day. Now, Lady Tarrington lowered herself into a chair near the bed as if prepared for a longer visit.

"How do you feel this morning?" Lady Tarrington asked.

"Surprisingly well, thank you for asking." Considering she was supposed to be existing in endless torment amid fire and brimstone, she was quite well. Fortunately, she'd been saved from the river and her own stupidity. Now, at least, she had options.

"What can we do to make you more comfortable?" Lady Tarrington smiled so encouragingly that Genevieve was tempted to tell her everything. Almost.

Genevieve spread her hands. "You've already done too much."

"Not at all. You are welcome to remain here as our guest while you convalesce."

"It's very kind of you," Genevieve replied, "but I don't wish to impose on your hospitality."

Lady Tarrington drew in her breath sharply and rubbed her swollen abdomen.

Genevieve gave a start. "Are you unwell, my lady?"

Lady Tarrington shook her head, a peaceful smile touching her mouth. "I'm well. It happens a bit more often now. The *accoucheur* says it's all in preparation." She caressed her abdomen as if caressing a breathing infant.

What a cruel twist of fate that Genevieve must find herself in the presence of a lady joyfully awaiting the birth of her child when Genevieve had so recently lost her own, the one good thing that might have come of her horrible marriage. Sorrow burrowed a hole through her heart, leaving a raw, gaping wound.

Lady Tarrington's amber eyes opened wide as she looked at Genevieve. "Are you in pain?"

Genevieve tried to shake her head as a tidal wave of grief washed over her. Uncontrollable sobs seized her.

"I'll send for the doctor!" Lady Tarrington cried.

"No," Genevieve squeaked. "No. I don't need a doctor." She turned her head away and put her hands over her face.

The bed sank under a weight next to Genevieve and a small, cool hand covered hers. Lady Tarrington watched her with concern and sorrow. "Forgive me. I've been terribly insensitive. The doctor told me you recently lost a baby. And here I am going on about mine."

How long since she'd been touched in a gesture of friendship and affection! Starved for human contact, she gripped the woman's hand. Lady Tarrington gathered Genevieve into her slender arms. She was soft and soothing and sisterly. Welcoming long-absent contact, Genevieve clung to her. Lady Tarrington rubbed her back lightly while Genevieve unleashed her grief.

When her tears finally abated, Genevieve pulled away. "Forgive me."

Lady Tarrington's eyes were red-rimmed with shared sorrow. "No need to apologize. I cannot pretend to understand what you must have suffered."

Ann came in bringing her fruit and croissants. "Here you are, miss."

Wiping her eyes, Lady Tarrington helped place the tray. "First, eat. You were so chilled when you first arrived that we bathed you in hot water to try to warm you, but I'm afraid we failed to get all of the mud out of your hair. If you're feeling strong enough, I'll have Ann fill a bath for you."

"A bath would be lovely, thank you." Genevieve's tears returned, this time in gratitude. "You're very thoughtful. I wish there was something I could do for you."

"There, there. Don't cry or you won't be able to eat." Lady Tarrington's eyes shimmered.

Genevieve made an effort to choke back her tears. Lady Tarrington cleared her throat and blew her nose. Genevieve turned her attention to her breakfast tray. Her cup contained chocolate again. Sugar and cream sat in small containers and she added them both liberally to the bitter cocoa. After the liquid turned a shade of warm brown, Genevieve picked up the cup of chocolate. The sweetened drink slid comfortingly down her throat.

Lady Tarrington smiled. "You like your chocolate sweet and creamy, as do I."

Shaking off her sorrow, Genevieve returned the smile. "If I wanted to drink something bitter, I'd have coffee."

"Exactly!"

Genevieve held out the cup to her. "Would you like some?"

"Oh, heavens no. I've had two cups already this morning."

Bonded by such a quirk, they chatted comfortably of inconsequential things while Genevieve finished her breakfast. Outside the windows, the sun's glow painted stripes on the carpet.

Lady Tarrington gestured to a chair where gowns draped over the back. "I'm too big to wear these now and thought you might wish to borrow them."

"How kind. Thank you."

"We have lovely gardens if you desire to take a turn about them when you feel well enough to arise." She smiled. "And of course, you're invited to dine with us. We welcome your company."

"Thank you, my lady." Dining with Christian might be torturous, though.

Lady Tarrington's smile radiated true warmth. "You are safe here. Won't you please trust me with your name?"

Genevieve hesitated. If Christian hadn't told them her name, perhaps he'd chosen to help her, after all. Of course, he might not yet have decided. "My life depends on no one knowing my name, my lady."

"I see. Are you . . . wanted by the law?"

"Oh, no, I vow I've done nothing illegal." Expect commit self-murder, which, in truth, was against the law, not to mention a sin. She let out a helpless sigh. "There is no reason for the authorities to want me."

Lady Tarrington looked her over in an assessing way. "I believe you."

Why that meant so much to Genevieve, she couldn't say, but some of the tension left her shoulders. "Thank you."

"You're fortunate Christian pulled you from the river."

Genevieve's heart stuttered to a halt. "Christian pulled me out?"

Lady Tarrington nodded. "He came home carrying you like you were a crystal doll."

She closed her eyes. "He put himself at great risk."

"It must be in the Amesbury blood. They all have a strong code of honor and an innate need to come to the rescue of those in need."

"Lady Tarrington —"

"Please, call me Alicia."

"Alicia. What a lovely name."

"My mother was French."

After all Lady Tarrington's—Alicia's—kindness, Genevieve had to offer her something of herself. "You may call me Jenny."

Leaning in and taking her hand, Alicia said gently, "Jenny, if you aren't in hiding because you are a fugitive, why are you in hiding?"

Genevieve hesitated, but Alicia's concern nudged aside her caution. "Someone means to do me harm."

Lady Tarrington nodded slowly, her brows furrowing in concern. "Then of course you must stay until you find a safe place."

Ann appeared and bobbed a curtsy. "The bath is ready, ma'am."

Alicia stood. "I shall leave you in Ann's capable hands. Let her know if you require anything—anything at all. She'll make adjustments to the clothing that you require." She eyed her critically. "You're tiny; no doubt she'll need to take everything in a great deal. She's in training to be a lady's maid, so please I hope you'll help her with that endeavor by allowing her to aid you."

"Of course."

With another serene smile, Alicia left.

Genevieve sat up and swung her legs over but when she tried to stand, dizziness darkened her vision. She sat on the edge of the bed.

"Per'aps it's too soon for ye to be gettin' out o' bed, miss," Ann ventured.

"Give me a moment, and we'll try again."

Once the room righted itself and the grey fog around her vision lifted, she gripped Ann's hand. Ann put her other arm around her. Only when Genevieve could stand steadily did they move to the adjoining dressing room where she bathed. Ann handled her as if she were made of glass and scrubbed her scalp until her hair finally came clean. Genevieve lay back in the tub and soaked while Ann sat sewing.

After bathing, Genevieve sat patiently as Ann coaxed knots out of her unruly curls and wrestled them into a semblance of order.

"Just twist it into a simple knot, Ann."

Ann looked disappointed. "As you will." The maid coiled a chignon at the nape of Genevieve's neck. "Oi, ye 'ave such beautiful 'air, miss. Now that it's clean, it's such a lovely shade."

Genevieve smiled. "As a child, I was ashamed of my 'carrot top.' "

"Oh, no. It's 'most th' color o' cherry wood, it is. Verra distinguishing."

Very distinguishing indeed. Which meant she could not stay here. Eventually *he* would learn she still lived. And come after her.

She must disappear into the night where no one would ever find her. She hated the thought of betraying her host and hostess's kindness, but she'd probably have to resort to taking enough money to flee. Somehow, she'd find a way to repay them. Perhaps she could sneak back into Lord Wickburgh's house and take a few pieces of jewelry. It might purchase passage to Scotland and provide for her needs until she could secure employment—a governess, perhaps, or a teacher in a lady's seminary. But she didn't dare risk one of his servants finding her. He had a veritable army of ruffians he paid to do any number of unsavory activities, not the least of which was hold her prisoner with only her cat and, for a time, her canary for company. It had taken a miracle to escape. She'd need another miracle if she were to truly leave behind her former life.

After styling Genevieve's hair, Ann dressed her in a borrowed shift, stays, and stockings before lowering over her head a morning gown she'd hemmed while Genevieve bathed.

"Ach, the fit is all wrong and that color washes ye out," Ann grumbled as she fastened the buttons down her back.

Genevieve glanced in the mirror. The butter-colored gown, no doubt lovely on Lady Tarrington, seemed to drain all the color out of

Genevieve's already pale skin, and accentuated bruises she'd received from the debris-filled river.

"No matter. I'm not trying to impress anyone. And I'll only go for a short walk in the gardens and then return to my room."

Ann clapped her hand on her head. "Shoes. Ye haven't any have ye?"

"No, I'm afraid not." Wickburgh ensured she never owned a pair of shoes in an effort to prevent her from leaving the house without his permission. The moment they'd arrived at his nearby estate last month, he'd immediately confiscated the shoes she'd worn on their journey.

"Wait 'ere," the maid said.

Ann returned moments later with a pair of Lady Tarrington's shoes and placed them on Genevieve's feet. Genevieve wiggled her toes inside the large shoes like a child wearing her mother's slippers.

Ann frowned. "Those simply don't do—they're far too big. I've never seen such little feet."

Papa had called her his little elf. Genevieve smiled at the memory. How she loved him! How foolish she'd been to believe him not only invincible, but infallible. But at least Papa and Mama remained safe. That knowledge lent her strength each time Lord Wickburgh played another cruel game, like the time he'd chopped down her favorite tree, or killed her canary, or each time he turned his rage on her . . . .

Genevieve shuddered and focused on Ann's face. "Pray, don't trouble yourself, I'll simply remain in my room today."

"No trouble. I'll try again."

After a foray into the servants' quarters, Ann returned with a pair of shoes Genevieve could keep on as she walked. Ann still looked unhappy. "Those aren't good 'nuff fer a lady."

"They hardly show underneath the gown, and they'll stay on when I walk. For now, it's enough." If only she had something to give or do for Ann in return.

After donning a bonnet and a pair of gloves Alicia had provided, Genevieve went in search of temporary freedom. She wandered through the corridor, treading on plush carpet running the length of the corridor, marveling at the beauty of Tarrington Castle. The intricate woodwork in rich mahogany shone with constant care. Genevieve traced the elegant paper in gold and red *fleur de lis* on the walls. Portraits of distinguished ladies and gentlemen of by-gone eras marched down the walls. She smiled at the resemblance between the first Lord Tarrington and Christian. Crystal wall sconces shimmered in the sunlight from nearby windows, sending rainbows on the walls and floors. The décor outshone even the splendor of Lord Wickburgh's county seat.

She'd always thought of Wickburgh's houses as his homes. Never theirs. Of course, he'd never made any pretense about loving her. Their wedding night was proof of that. Losing the baby—the one pure thing to have come of their marriage—had been the killing blow.

Dark grief threatened to overcome her again, but she swallowed back her sorrow. She'd been given a chance for escape and she must seize it. There. That helped. The grief edged back until it only lapped at her like breakers on a seashore.

Squaring her shoulders, Genevieve descended the stairs. After entering several rooms, she found a large room at the back of the house. One wall completely lined by French doors opened to a paved terrace. Outside the house, she paused and breathed in the crisp morning air. Her tension eased and she drank in the beauty around her. She'd heard of Tarrington Gardens, but had failed to conjure the image that now met her eyes. Tendrils of mist clung to the trees, giving them a magical shimmer.

Entranced, she wandered along the winding gravel paths, stopping now and then to admire flowers blooming in unearthly beauty amid ponds, fountains, marble statues. At the entrance to the next garden, she halted.

Christian Amesbury sat bareheaded, his golden hair shimmering in the sunlight, a notepad balanced on one knee. Wearing a snowy cravat, grey and blue striped waistcoat, sky blue tailcoat and grey breeches tucked into gleaming boots, he emulated the perfect nobleman, fit for entrance into the most exclusive clubs in London. Yet the haughtiness of his class remained absent. He'd completely lacked the urbane boredom Londoners deemed appealing.

Apparently, he'd found that new, cool reserve during their separation. But now, so engrossed in his art, he looked so much like the Christian from her past that tears stung her eyes.

With a pencil in his left hand, he sketched. She glanced around the garden but failed to discover what had attracted his attention. Christian glanced in her direction with a ready smile. The instant he saw it was she, his smile faded.

He leaped to his feet. She'd forgotten how tall he was. His commanding presence and that new underlying tension seemed to add to his size.

He inclined his head in an abbreviated bow. "My lady. I didn't see you there."

She winced. "We needn't resume our formality, after everything that passed between us, do we?"

He stiffened. "That is exactly why we should, Lady Wickburgh."

Rather than explain how much she hated her title, and everything it meant, she gestured at the bench. "Pray, continue. I didn't mean to disturb you."

His gaze passed over her with such intensity that she almost stepped back. He was so different now. She couldn't reconcile the gentle man she'd loved a year ago to this new, hardened Christian. Perhaps she was too emotionally exhausted and beaten down to even try. It didn't matter. She must leave and never see him again.

His gaze dropped and he gripped his pencil with whitened fingers. She should leave now. Spending time with Christian could only mean disaster for her heart.

She took a step forward. "What are you drawing?"

He looked away as if he couldn't bear to look at her and made a vague gesture. Then his mouth twitched into a self-deprecating smile. She'd always loved how expressive he was. Although seeing him so clearly angry and disapproving opened up an ache in her chest. She'd done that to him. To them.

"I'm often fascinated by odd things, common objects other people find dull."

She nodded, as memories returned of them stopping as they walked together in Bath so he could capture something on paper. She indicated his sketch book. "May I see?"

He hesitated, no doubt uncomfortable showing her, who he most certainly considered The Jilt, anything so personal as his drawings.

Without looking at her, he surrendered the book. The first page held a sketch of a cluster of mushrooms, oddly shaped and distorted. A pixie peeped out from around them. She turned in the direction he'd been facing and spied them huddled in the shade of a fountain. They were exactly as he'd drawn them, but under his pencil lines, they took on an almost magical slant. His art had always had a fanciful flair. She flipped the page back to the previous drawing and saw a single hand, long-fingered, slender and graceful.

"Amazing," she said. "I adore the addition of the pixie."

He made no comment, much like the taciturn Christian she'd first met at the house party before their courtship in Bath.

The next page showed a pair of eyes, dark and soulful, filled with such despair that tears stung her own eyes. She quickly flipped to the next. On paper, Lady Tarrington wore a tender expression as she lovingly rested her hand on her rounded stomach. He'd re-created her quiet dignity and serenity. She glowed in maternal joy.

Genevieve ruthlessly shoved away her own grief and shut it behind a door. She glanced up at him. "You've done an impressive job in capturing her spirit. She's very kind. And so lovely."

"Yes, she is." His voice took on a wistfulness. "She makes my brother very happy."

She looked back down at the drawing. She had no gift for art but she'd read about the subject and had visited a number of public and private galleries, including the Elgin Marbles. Christian's sketches and paintings proudly displayed in homes she'd visited rivaled all the great masters.

She handed back the sketchpad to him. "I was sorry to hear about your father."

"Thank you." He stood gripping his sketchpad as if he expected a great wind to attempt to whisk it away. The ache in her chest sharpened at his clear emotional upheaval.

She cleared her throat. "I failed to thank you. I understand it was you who rescued me from the river at great risk to yourself. I'm indebted to you."

Despite his overt tension, the barest hint of a teasing note entered his voice. "Think nothing of it. I frequently go about rescuing ladies in distress."

She forced herself to smile despite the pain in her chest. "I'm not surprised. You would have made a wonderful knight, shining armor and all."

His expression was so uncharacteristically guarded that she couldn't determine his thoughts. If only she could tell him she hadn't really thrown him over, that she'd done it to save her parents. But that would not help matters. Somehow, though, there had to be a way to smooth over the hard feelings between them. She fidgeted with the ribbons of her bonnet and came up with nothing.

A breeze blew, carrying his scent to her. Oh, heaven help her, she'd almost forgotten how good he smelled, that unique blend of bergamot, sunshine, and another sensual smell that belonged only to him.

He cast a desperate glance at the house as if plotting his escape.

To break the silence, she drew a breath and spoke. "So, you live in London now? I thought you didn't care for the city."

He looked away. "London suits my needs."

She studied him, searching for an explanation. He once loved the country best, letting the splendor of nature inspire him to create beautiful paintings. "Are you still planning to go into the clergy?"

He shook his head. "I don't think so."

She waited.

He didn't elaborate.

She reached down inside and found a smile she could offer him. "Would you be willing to give me a tour of the gardens?"

Without looking at her, he shrugged and with forced nonchalance, said, "If you wish."

Surely a hundred other women had tried to heal Christian's wounded heart and win his love. She pictured another woman in his arms. Jealousy tied her stomach into knots. That, of course, was selfish. He deserved happiness, and she certainly couldn't give it to him. Yet for one mad moment, she almost told him everything and begged him to take her away.

Nothing changed the fact that she'd betrayed him and married another.

Moreover, she was the daughter of a traitor, and had sold herself for a blackmailer's silence. She was used and broken. Her unworthiness of Christian sliced through her wounded heart, and another piece fell away leaving an increasingly larger void inside.

She should leave. His presence only reminded her of what she'd sacrificed. And she clearly made him uncomfortable. But if she could help heal the wounds of the past, they might both find healing. There had to be a way to break through those heavy shields he held in front of him as if he saw her as a foe bent on destroying him. She owed it to him to try to help him if she could.

Christian cleared his throat and made a loose gesture that encompassed the garden in which they stood. "I suppose we can start here. This garden was designed by the seventh Baron Tarrington, back before my great, great-grandfather was given the additional title of earl."

He led her through each of the gardens, describing with obvious family pride, the background and its roots in mythology. Each successive Lord Tarrington had added his own garden with a unique theme. Caught up in his tales, Christian's reserve softened. His animated expression and eyes alit with excitement, combined with his rich baritone, kept her spell-bound. Her gaze riveted to his lips—full and expressive.

"Cole has yet to design his garden but he's mad about astronomy and Greek legends, and has a number of ideas."

Since she'd never met Christian's eldest brother, she could only picture a dark-haired, older version of Christian.

As they came to a new entrance to a garden, he quickened his steps to lead her past it. A haunted shadow darkened his eyes.

She glanced up at him. "What is it?"

He swallowed hard. "I don't go there. It's where my brother died."

She drew in her breath. She'd heard him speak of Cole, Jared, and Grant as well as two sisters. Had one of his brothers died since that summer in Bath? "Oh, I'm so sorry. I didn't know. Who?"

"Jason," he bit out. "Are you tiring?"

She almost stepped away from his fierceness. "A little."

Jason. An Amesbury brother she didn't know existed. Glancing over her shoulder to the garden Christian shunned, she wondered about the brother he'd lost, and the circumstances of the death that obviously tormented Christian. He'd never spoken of it. She eyed him as they walked, but his expression remained closed over, his thoughts guarded. He led her through the maze of pathways to the house. His posture stiff, he walked as far on the other side of the path as he could. If only she could soothe his hurt.

A pristine white lily blossomed in the middle of a nearly dormant flower bed. She gestured at it. "Look, a lily blooming so late in the year." She paused, bent down and admired the flower that had the boldness to bloom despite the rest of the world withdrawing from the looming winter.

Christian leaned down and picked it. He handed it to her. "You might as well take it inside or the cool nights will kill it soon."

She smiled up at him. "Thank you."

They stood only inches apart, so near that the heat of his body enfolded her, so near that his bay rum aftershave wafted to her, so near that she could touch him if she moved her hand.

So far away that they could never recapture what they once had.

Swiftly, he took two steps back, then made a gesture to the house. "Shall we return?"

She nodded and they fell into step, walking without speaking as the echoes of the past rang between them. Toying with the flower, Genevieve searched for something to say to him.

All too soon, they reached the house and she still hadn't found a way to reach him. She paused at the back door, desperate to stall for more time with him, and babbled the first thought that popped into her head. "Might I look for a book in the library?"

Again, he hesitated as if unable to bear spending more time in her presence. But ever the gentleman, he nodded once. "Of course."

He led her to a dark paneled room decorated in rich green floor-to-ceiling shelves filled with ancient books. The room had a comfortable, masculine feel. Over a settee hung a large landscape in oil.

She instantly recognized his style. "That's one of yours."

"Er, yes."

Genevieve sat sideways on the settee below it and gazed up at the painting. It clearly represented one of the Amesbury gardens, but it possessed a whimsical quality. The frame transformed into a window overlooking a world of fairies and sprites. The colors were more vibrant than any flowers Genevieve had seen, and the light slanting down through the trees glowed with magical brilliance. Utter peace and tranquility abounded in that beautiful world of his creation.

"It's astonishing," she breathed. "It almost looks real . . . only nothing is quite that beautiful. I wish it were a real place so I could go there."

The clock ticked while Genevieve sat entranced. Finally, she drew herself away and blinked at Christian. He belonged in that world. Golden, masculine, gentle. Too kind to be real. No longer in love with her. Perhaps betrothed by now. To someone else.

Of course, that was none of her concern. She'd relinquished any claim she might have had over him when she married Wickburgh.

She smiled up at him. "Your style reminds me of Thomas Gainsborough, only a bit more fanciful."

One side of this mouth lifted. "You're familiar with Gainsborough's work?"

"Don't look so surprised. I told you I have an interest in the arts."

"So you did."

She turned back to the painting. "Your style clearly reveals a preference for a Romanticism style of art, yet your compositions are unique."

A male voice boomed in the passageway, "Christian!"

"In here, Cole," Christian called.

As a dark-haired man with sapphire blue eyes entered, he stopped up short. His penetrating stare bore into Genevieve. She shrank back under the raw power of this man.

Christian made a gesture between then. "May I present my brother, Lord Tarrington—Cole to his family and closest friends. This is . . ." he clamped his mouth shut as if realizing belatedly that he was supposed to keep her name a secret.

"Jenny," she supplied.

Lord Tarrington bore the same urbane elegance so many of his class possessed. He was powerful. Dangerous. As a peer, Tarrington would feel duty bound to return her to her husband regardless of her wishes. She must leave. *He*'d find her. Tonight, she would go.

Drawing her courage about her, she dropped an elegant curtsy. "My lord."

Lord Tarrington's gaze remained unnervingly direct. "I'm happy to see you're feeling better. I hope you'll join us for dinner this evening."

She heard the command couched in his invitation. Though defiance arose in her heart, she remained outwardly deferential. "Of course, my lord. I'm grateful for your hospitality."

She turned to Christian, hoping she appeared calm. "Thank you for the tour, and for showing me your art." She glanced at Lord Tarrington. "My lord." She sank into a courtly curtsy.

Carefully controlling both her breathing and the gait of her step, she stepped around him to the door and walked to her room.

Ann waited for her there, a gown laid out on the bed. "'ave a nice walk, miss?"

"Yes, thank you."

"What's that?" Ann gestured to her hand.

Genevieve glanced down at the forgotten lily. "This is for you. To thank you for your excellent care." Although a small, neglected place in her heart cried out at giving up the flower Christian had given her, she didn't dare keep anything as a reminder of what he once meant to her. And she had nothing else to offer Ann for her kindness.

Ann's face lit up. "Oi, thankee kindly, miss." She drew a deep breath and then tucked it behind her ear. "Shall we dress ye fer dinner?"

"Yes, thank you."

Dinner. With the earl. Genevieve quailed at the thought of facing the earl again. He'd brought a new threat, a new danger. He was arrogant and powerful, too much like her husband. The idea of remaining in this house with such a man left her alternating between crippling fear and a savage determination to protect herself.

She'd endure dinner. Then, as soon as the house fell quiet, she'd flee before the earl figured out who she was and turned her over to Wickburgh.

Ann lit the lamps and helped her wash and dress. This time, Genevieve didn't stop Ann as she coiled her hair into an elegant upsweep, leaving soft tendrils to brush against the sides of her face. Not that it mattered. She wasn't trying to impress anyone. And she'd be gone before the night was over.

She squelched the image of Christian's face arising in her mind. It could never be. She hadn't received the forgiveness she'd hoped to find from him, but at least he seemed to have softened toward her. Perhaps she'd mended some of the hurt between them.

As the maid arranged the folds of the creamy gown, Genevieve produced a smile despite her heavy heart and gestured to the gown.

"It's a perfect fit, just as if it came from the *modiste*. Thank you, Ann, it was most expertly altered."

Ann bobbed a curtsy. "'Twas my pleasure, milady." She stepped back. "Oi, miss, yer beautiful, ain't ye?" She cleared her throat. "Er, that is, *aren't* you? My lady tells me I must speak proper if I am to become a lady's maid."

Genevieve touched the girl's hand. "You're doing very well."

As she left the room, she raised her head. She would never again be a victim. She'd prove to the world, and herself, that she was strong. Until then, she'd pretend to be strong.

Genevieve headed for the drawing room where the family gathered before dinner. Voices from the front parlor drew her attention. One voice was frighteningly familiar. Frissons of fear flitted down her back.

"My wife is insane and she needs help. She may still be out there, confused and alone."

Her heart leaped into her throat and strangled her. Blind with panic, she froze. "No. Oh, no. No, no, no."

"Miss?" A footman hovered in the corridor, his livery impeccable, but he wore a mildly distressed expression.

She couldn't speak or move or breathe. *He* was here to take her back. Back to misery.

Strong? No. She wasn't strong. But she would not become a victim ever again.

CHAPTER 6

Standing in the study behind Cole's chair, Christian fisted his hands and tried not to glare at Lord Wickburgh as he spoke of the woman Christian had once loved.

Wickburgh had changed little in the year since he and Christian had fought. Like most peers, he bore an air of arrogance, yet there was a hard set to his mouth and he stared at them through flat, soulless eyes that conjured images of a vampire.

Christian suppressed a shiver. How had Genevieve been so foolish as to marry him?

Wickburgh toyed with his walking stick. "She was out of her mind with grief over the loss of our unborn child. I fear the strain has driven her mad."

She'd lost a baby? Or was that another lie?

"I regret I never had the pleasure of meeting your wife," Cole said smoothly. "And I wasn't aware you'd returned to the area or I would have paid a call upon you."

Wickburgh made a dismissive wave. "We've only been here a short time and her health has been poor."

Cole rested an elbow on the arm of his chair. "Describe your wife to me, please?"

"Short, thin, very pale skin. And lots of red hair."

A horribly unromantic description by a supposedly loving husband.

Cole looked utterly bored, even going so far as to examine his fingernails. Which meant he was working hard to mask his thoughts. "If she's been missing for two days, it may be too late for her."

Wickburgh opened his mouth in feigned horror, yet his posture remained poised. "Don't say that, I beg you. I'm not giving up hope." He thumped his walking stick on the floor as if to convey urgency.

Christian swallowed a noise of disgust at the false emotion in Wickburgh's tone and reminded himself he shouldn't use the blackguard for boxing practice. At the moment, he couldn't think of a good reason why not.

Wickburgh continued, "All I ask is that you instruct your tenants to watch for her. I'm offering a reward for her safe return."

Christian could no longer tolerate the theatrics. "Surely if she were still alive, she would have returned to you by now. That is, if she wanted to return."

Wickburgh turned a cold eye on Christian and looked him over as if he were an impudent boy speaking out of turn in the presence of his betters. Christian resisted the urge to touch the scar on his face put there by Lord Wickburgh's thugs.

Refusing to be baited, Christian folded his arms without comment and stared him down as he imagined slipping a knife in between his enemy's ribs and leaving Wickburgh for dead.

"Of course she would want to return," Wickburgh said. "But she may not be capable of finding her way home in her mental state. Someone may have found her and taken her in until they can learn to whom she belongs."

"Belongs? Like a piece of jewelry?" Christian challenged.

The hard, flat eyes bored into him. "I am her husband. She belongs to me."

Christian clenched his teeth before he retorted something that would reveal too much. Even before their altercation in Bath,

Christian had disliked Wickburgh. There was just something supremely unsettling about the man. Regardless of what Genevieve had done, seeing her unhappy enough to go to such lengths didn't feel like justice; instead, it battered the ragged edges of his heart. Genevieve seemed vulnerable and fragile compared to the lively young lady he'd known a year ago. Wickburgh was clearly to blame.

Everything about her jilting him had seemed wrong. It was as if he'd stepped into someone else's story where the plot didn't match up with his own.

Still wearing his mask of urbane boredom, Cole said, "I'd be happy to alert my tenants to watch for your wife, Lord Wickburgh, and to pass on your description of her. However, you should prepare yourself for the likelihood that she's gone forever."

Christian added, "Any man who can't keep his wife didn't deserve her in the first place."

Wickburgh glowered, visibly biting back whatever retort he wished to fling at Christian but daren't speak it in front of an earl. Christian almost wished Cole away so he could have it out with Wickburgh once and for all.

"I'll notify you if we have any news." Cole stood, clearly dismissing their guest. "Keep us informed of the progress of your search."

No doubt aware that his host outranked him, Wickburgh followed suit, swinging his walking stick. "I'm most grateful to you, Lord Tarrington."

Wickburgh bowed to Cole, pointedly ignored Christian, and left carrying the walking stick like a scepter.

Christian let out his breath in a long exhale. "Scoundrel. I should have killed him when I had the chance."

Cole cocked a brow. "That would have been stupid."

"He's straight out of a nightmare."

"How long have you known that our river jumper is Lady Wickburgh?"

Christian hesitated. But Cole already knew Genevieve's identity.

All that remained was convincing Cole to keep her whereabouts from Wickburgh. "Since the moment I saw her face."

"What else haven't you told me?"

Christian dropped into a leather armchair. "She's the girl I almost married last year in Bath."

A light came into Cole's eyes. "The jilt."

Christian made a sound of disgust. "The jilt."

"Then Lord Wickburgh is the one you fought."

"How did you know I'd fought anyone?"

"I make it a point to keep track of my brothers."

Christian let out a snort.

Cole touched Christian's temple, tracing the scar there. "And I understand you have a worse scar in your ribs. Is Wickburgh responsible for those?"

"Not directly. He sent a group of ruffians after me."

Cole's eyes narrowed. "Can you prove that?"

"Just something one of them said." He paused. "No, I can't prove it."

"So, she threw herself into a river. Not happily wedded, I gather?"

Christian shrugged and looked away, lest Cole see too much, and fisted his hands.

Resuming his seat, Cole steepled his fingers and watched Christian. "You must feel some satisfaction that that she's unhappy with her choice."

"I couldn't care less."

"Uh-huh."

Christian leaped to his feet and made a point of pouring a sherry. His hands shook with unreleased anger.

"He wants her back, Chris."

Christian sipped the sherry. "She begged me not to notify anyone she's here. She wouldn't even tell Alicia her name. She plans to leave and let him believe she drowned."

"That seems drastic."

"She must have her reasons." Christian slammed down the glass on the sideboard table.

Cole's probing stare penetrated him. "You're still in love with her." It wasn't a question.

"No! I care nothing for that little jilt." He'd learned his lesson. A mistake he would not make a second time.

Humor laced Cole's voice. "Are you sure? 'Methinks thou doth protest too much—'"

"I like the idea of inconveniencing Wickburgh. I'd like to inconvenience him with the end of my sword."

"I see." Cole raised a brow. "Then by all means, help her. But don't kill her husband."

"I can't tell you how tempted I am to do that."

"That much is clear."

"I'd win, you know."

Cole laughed softly. "There are times when you sound too much like me."

Trying to shake off the anger still coursing through his veins, Christian shivered exaggeratedly. "Horrors."

Cole's smile flashed briefly before he sobered. "A solution will present itself."

Alicia appeared, dressed for dinner. She looked around the study. "Where's our lovely guest?"

An alarm bell clanged inside Christian's head. "Isn't she with you?"

"No. Her abigail said she left her room for dinner ten minutes ago. Do you think she took a wrong turn and is lost?"

If she learned Wickburgh had paid them a visit, she was running away. Christian raced to the door to find her before she disappeared.

CHAPTER 7

He was in the house.

She had to escape. Now.

With her heart drumming in her chest and perspiration dripping between her shoulder blades, Genevieve dashed down the servants' stairs to the kitchen where a cacophony of voices and smells met her. The head cook shouted at her assistants as they bustled about. Amid the chaos, Genevieve slipped out through the kitchen door.

Long shadows fell over her path as she dashed past the herb garden. The purple sky still showed a faint glimmer of red and gold in the horizon cast by the setting sun. Genevieve ran. Cool air stung her cheeks. She'd left the house without a wrap but didn't dare return for one.

Where to go? If Wickburgh had search parties, she'd be discovered no matter how far she ran. Perhaps she could hide somewhere on the estate until she found a better solution. Stumbling in her haste, she darted through the gardens, looking for a gardener's shed she'd noticed earlier that day. Where was it? She dashed along the path where Christian and she had walked so blithely only a few hours ago. The walkway wound through arched bowers, fountains, and statues. On she raced.

Eventually, the manicured area gave way to an open expanse of heather, bracken and ancient trees. A stream glimmered in the late afternoon sun, as if clinging to the fading light and attempting to ward off the encroaching darkness. It ran past a cottage, probably a dowager's house.

Darkened windows and bare flowerbeds revealed its disuse. Genevieve fled toward the possible sanctuary. Finding the door locked, she paused, searching for a way in. There. A rock about twice the size of her fist. She hefted the rock and threw it at one of the windows. Glass shattered the silence and sent shards flying inside the cottage. A ragged hole in the window glared back at her. One last piece of glass, dangling from the opening, fell and landed on the narrow porch. It scattered glass across the porch. She reached in through the jagged hole and fumbled for a lock.

Twigs snapped and leaves crackled as heavy feet pounded toward her. No time!

With a sob, she grabbed one of the larger pieces of glass at her feet. Poised to use the shard as a weapon if necessary, she whirled around and held her breath. A man darted out of the shadows into view.

A male voice broke through her haze of panic. "Genevieve?"

Christian had found her. Her relief only lasted a second. What if he'd come to fetch her and hand her over to Wickburgh? Her breath rasped.

Christian paused, eyeing her. His gaze flicked to the broken window behind her, then back to her. Taking a slow step toward her, he held out his hands. "Easy, Jen. No one will hurt you. I'm not here to drag you back to him."

Gripping the shard of glass, she searched his face but only found an intensity she could not identify. Was he concerned for her? Or worried that he might not succeed in bringing her back to Wickburgh?

He took another step closer and held out a hand. "Jen?"

Though he seemed to have softened toward her this afternoon, he may have washed his hands of the woman who threw him over for a lord. If she'd learned anything from Wickburgh, men were unpredictable. He might be following Tarrington's directive to send her back to her husband. Christian had no reason to defy his brother for her sake.

He stepped nearer, still looking at her in that disconcerting manner. "You have nothing to fear from me."

Hoping a display of cooperation would make him lower his guard until she could escape, she dropped the shard.

Creases formed in his brow. "Lord Wickburgh was here. Looking for you. But you know that, don't you." It wasn't a question.

Her muscles tensed, poised to run.

As if he were approaching a skittish foal, he took another cautious step forward. "We sent him away."

She searched his face for duplicity, or even any indication of his thoughts. The old Christian would never have lied, but this new, harder Christian was unreadable. She moistened her lips. "If he knows I'm here, he'll be back."

He shook his head. "He doesn't suspect you're here. He wanted us to notify our tenants that he's offering a reward for your safe return."

"Safe return." She let out a scoff. "He cares nothing about my safety." The chill night air settled in deeper. Shivering, she hugged herself.

"We told him we knew nothing of your whereabouts." He drew near enough to touch if she reached for him. "You can trust me, Jen."

She should run. It might all be some sort of ruse. But his words rooted her feet to the ground and she could only stand motionless. Christian removed his dark superfine tailcoat and laid it over her shoulders. She froze as his hands brushed against her skin. His coat, still warm from his body, smelled of him—earthy, wholly masculine, and oh so sensual. She clutched the lapels together and filled her nostrils with Christian's scent. Tears burned her eyes. She ached to trust him, yet fear held her back.

He reached for her. "Come."

Come. Wickburgh often ordered her to come, usually right before things got worse. Sudden fear sent a burst of cold energy through her veins. She took a step backward, judging the distance between them. She probably couldn't out run him. Still . . . .

He grew grave. "Genevieve?"

She lunged for freedom. His grunt of surprise sounded from behind her as she fled recklessly into the growing darkness, stumbling over obstacles in her path.

"Wait!" His footsteps pounded in pursuit.

She pushed herself harder and lost Christian's coat but charged onward. Though her lungs burned and her legs weakened, she ran on. His footsteps followed close behind her, growing steadily nearer. Too close! Blinded by fear, she plunged on without thought of caution. He caught her by the elbow, halting her, and pulled her stumbling against him.

Trapped! Hysteria bubbled up until rational thought fled. She screamed and struggled, but he held her in unyielding arms.

Her breath came out in sobbing gasps. "Let me go!"

His gentle voice wormed through her terror. "I'm not going to hurt you."

Too weak to fight him, she collapsed against him and wept.

His arms relaxed, no longer keeping her from escaping, merely offering comfort, enfolding her in his warmth, his strength. "You're safe here. He's gone."

Christian held her close, continuing to murmur words of reassurance while she sobbed. He fell silent and simply held her. She rested her head against his chest, solid, strong, safe.

Christian would never use his strength against her. He wouldn't have changed that much. Though commanding and larger than life, Christian was not dangerous. No one of Christian's ilk would change so drastically. He was no Wickburgh, nor ever would be.

Gradually, Genevieve's fear drained away. Calm edged in, pushing out the last of her fear. Peace filled her soul. She hadn't bathed in such safety since the last time she stood cradled in the circle of Christian's embrace.

She unclenched her fists and hesitantly put her arms around him. His stomach tightened, but he made no move. Her tears dried and she stood hiccupping within his arms, leaning against the tautness of his stomach, the leanness of his waist, the hard muscles of his chest. His heartbeat kept a steady rhythm underneath her ear. One of his hands rested on her back, the other at the side of her head, his thumb lightly rubbing back and forth across her cheek. He was warmth against the cold and the darkness, even the cold and darkness in her heart.

Night fell, enveloping them in total blackness until the moon rose. A nightingale trilled its song and stars peeped through the black sky. They remained motionless as if fearful of breaking the spell wrapped around them. Infused in Christian's warmth and strength, Genevieve clung to him, to the timelessness of this moment in his arms. Her fears melted away like ice under the sun's rays. All would be well.

A distant voice called, "Mr. Amesbury?"

Christian sighed and his voice rumbled against her ear as he said, "I think we've been missed."

When he released her, cold rushed at her. She longed to crawl back in his arms. But that was foolish. She must leave and build a new life of freedom and safety, and Christian had no place in that new life. He deserved better than a jilt.

And like it or not, she was married. She'd never tempt Christian to commit adultery. That was beneath them both.

Besides, he clearly no longer wanted her. He'd never trust her.

She shivered and rubbed her arms. Then remembered the coat he'd given her. "Oh! Your tailcoat. I—I think I dropped it . . ." Nervously, she glanced back the way she'd come. Looking up at him, she awaited a show of anger.

He appeared totally unperturbed. "'Tis nothing."

Heat crawled up her neck and over her face. Of course not. She kept expecting Christian to suddenly turn into Lord Wickburgh. Foolish. She should know better.

Wearing his striped waistcoat and shirtsleeves, he held out an arm, and smiled beckoningly, his teeth flashing white in the darkness. "Shall we?"

She gaped at the sheer beauty of the first genuine grin he'd given her since she'd arrived at Tarrington Castle. Pushing away a loose strand of hair away from her eyes, she placed her hand on the crook of his elbow, her gaze locked with his.

With the moonlight caressing his face, he smiled in true warmth. Perhaps he'd overcome his anger and she'd finally gained a measure of forgiveness. Her fears took a step back and she allowed herself one luxurious moment to admire him. Christian was so handsome and masculine with his head proudly held, his shoulders squared, and an aura of power and presence surrounding him, that he transformed into a knight of old, wielding his sword in defense of her honor and making vows of chivalry. She'd never find a more honorable gentleman or a more blatantly desirable man. Or anyone more forbidden.

Dragging her eyes away from his, she took a step and winced as pain shot up her foot.

"What is it?" he asked.

"My foot . . . I lost one of my shoes."

He chuckled softly. "Very well, Cinderella, I suppose I must carry you. We'll have to look elsewhere for a glass slipper, though." Without waiting for her permission, he scooped her up into his arms.

She waited for the rakish glint to enter his eyes, or a lewd comment to fall from his well-formed lips, but neither happened.

No, he hadn't changed much, after all.

With their mouths only inches away, his grin gradually faded as his lashes lowered, concealing his eyes, but the heat of his focus seared her lips. Her heart stalled and then tripped over itself. His lips parted slightly. Dread and excitement rippled over her. The force of his gaze held her captive.

She braced for his kiss, terrified, excited, confused. The gentle sensuality of his kiss a year ago came leaping into memory, the way his lips brushed against hers so gently, then hungrily, and later how they'd slanted over her mouth, possessing, claiming . . . .

Instead of moving closer, he went still. A breathless moment passed. Christian drew a shaking breath, turned his head forward, and began walking.

Shame rippled through her all over again. Christian was an honorable gentleman. He would never seduce a married woman nor would she let him sink that low. Twin rivers of relief and disappointment poured into a confusing pool of emotions. Pushing back the knowledge that she would soon leave and never see him again, she reveled in the temporary bliss of being in Christian's arms, and rested her head against his shoulder.

Lanterns bobbed in the darkness like fireflies. "Mr. Amesbury!"

"I'm here, lads!" he called.

A chorus of voices arose as a search party surrounded them. None of the men showed any surprise that their lord's brother carried what was probably a very bedraggled-looking woman out of the darkness, nor were there any looks of surprise at her compromised position or his state of *dishabille*. Christian acted as if nothing unusual were happening. Perhaps he carried stray women home all the time. He certainly seemed to be making a habit of it where she was concerned. It was a credit to the gentleman in him to save even the woman who'd rejected him.

She remained silent in the presence of so many strange men, and rested her head against her white knight while they all tromped through the brambles and heather.

Christian addressed a man nearest him. "Fleming, please send someone to come back in the morning and look for my coat. I appear to have lost it along the way."

"Yessir," the man replied amiably.

"Sorry," she whispered in Christian's ear.

"I'll send you a bill," he murmured lightly, his mouth curved into an easy smile.

As they reached the formal gardens and followed the gravel pathways toward the house, something wet and sticky tickled her cold bare foot. She rubbed it with her other foot, smearing dark liquid across the top of her shoe. She'd only had one pair of shoes, thanks to the charity of a maid, and now she'd lost one and ruined the other. She didn't dare borrow another pair; the maid probably didn't have another one to give her.

Light poured from the windows of the castle in greeting. Fear arose. She studied Christian's face, searching for guilt or a hidden agenda. Glancing at her, he flashed a reassuring smile. Animated, open, and guileless, Christian bore no lurking deceit despite that hardness she'd first seen in him. That had probably been a defensive measure he'd developed to shield himself from the wounds her presence reopened in him. It didn't mean he'd suddenly changed.

She squelched her apprehension and laid her head back on his shoulder while guilt for suspecting him swirled inside her in a dark maelstrom. Christian was nothing like Lord Wickburgh. He never would be. He would also never be hers.

CHAPTER 8

As her knight carried Genevieve toward the back terrace of the house, the other men split off, bidding Christian a good evening, and continued their boisterous talking amongst themselves. More comfortable than she ought to be in Christian's arms, she lay still, her head on his shoulder, bathing in the fleeting safety Christian's arms always brought her.

It wouldn't last, but she'd revel in it while she could. He carried her through open French doors into the back parlor. Lord and Lady Tarrington waited inside. Worry showed clear in Lady Tarrington's eyes but Lord Tarrington remained impassive as a block of marble.

"Jenny," Lady Tarrington cried. "I was so concerned. Are you well?"

Her face heated with embarrassment that she'd caused such a scene. She nodded. "Forgive me for worrying you."

Christian carefully lowered her to a settee. "She ran when she learned Wickburgh had come looking for her."

Genevieve gave a start, her gaze flying to Christian. Had he revealed her secret?

"I'm afraid it's quite difficult to keep secrets from my husband."

Lady Tarrington leaned forward. "You didn't think we'd turn you over to him when it was so obviously against your will?"

Genevieve stared at the floor. Lord Tarrington must have guessed the truth when Wickburgh arrived asking about her. She'd been selfish to expect Christian to lie to his family and foolish to think they wouldn't figure out she was the missing Lady Wickburgh.

"I'm his wife," she said softly. "He owns me."

"Of course he doesn't," Lady Tarrington said.

Christian lifted her bleeding foot to examine it. He frowned. "Alicia, ring for a servant, please."

The countess tugged on a pull at her elbow then sat calmly, smiling in sympathy at Genevieve. Christian sat back on his haunches and looked up at her.

"The men," Genevieve blurted. "They know…?"

"I paid them well for their silence," Lord Tarrington said from his position beside his wife. "Your husband will never learn from us, or anyone is our employ, that you are here." He paused and looked her over as if she were somehow sullying his divan with her filth. Or perhaps her own guilt for hurting his brother colored her perception. "He wants you back, Lady Wickburgh."

Genevieve's heart began an erratic staccato. She tensed, prepared to bolt again, but Christian could outrun her. And he'd proven she could trust him; she had no reason to flee again. Besides, she had nowhere to go. Her parents lived many days journey from here and she daren't drag them into her mess, not after all she sacrificed to protect them.

She swallowed against a choking lump, feeling very small, and folded trembling hands together. "Yes, I know he wants me back."

A footman arrived. "You rang, m'lord?"

Christian replied, "Bring me a bowl of water and some towels."

The footman bowed and left.

The earl continued, "Lord Wickburgh is telling people you suffered a collapse after you lost your unborn child and that you're insane."

Would they send her to bedlam or some other horrible asylum? She'd rather die than go there again.

At that, she lifted her head. "Do I appear insane?"

The earl's sapphire gaze probed her. "You did try to take your own life."

"Cole," Lady Tarrington gently admonished him.

Genevieve raised her chin a notch higher and stared him down. "Yes. Clearly, I was not in my right mind then. It was an act I sincerely regret and am not inclined to repeat."

"As his wife, it is your duty to return to him." Did she imagine the challenging glint?

Christian leaped up and faced Lord Tarrington. "She needs no reminder of her duty."

"The courts would tell her the same thing," Tarrington said evenly.

Christian took a step closer to his brother and folded his arms. "I've given her my word I won't tell him where she is. And so have you."

Genevieve stared at Christian's transformation. Brothers stood inches apart, glaring with enough heat to melt ice. Of similar height and build, they stood unmoving, nose to nose, Christian with clenched fists, his face set in hard lines. The earl stared back calmly. If he felt surprise at his brother's passionate outburst, he failed to reveal it.

"We have no right to interfere," the earl said. "She is married; therefore she owes her husband the truth."

"She owes that snake nothing."

"She owes him—"

"Cole, don't be a bully," Lady Tarrington interjected. "It's most unchivalrous of you." Humor tinged the firm rebuff while calm, golden-brown eyes fixed on the earl.

Lady Tarrington stood and approached the men, moving with surprising agility for a woman who would soon be in confinement.

Without a pause at the challenging stance between her husband and his brother, Lady Tarrington stepped unflinching between the men.

Genevieve gasped and leapt to her feet, prepared to throw herself into the fray to protect the gentle countess from such angry men. They dwarfed Lady Tarrington, those muscular, powerful men who could so easily hurt her. Without a qualm, she placed a hand on each broad chest.

"Boys, do behave yourselves. Lady Wickburgh—and her alone—should decide what's to be done." She patted their cheeks until they broke their gaze and turned their eyes to her. With equal contrition, they backed away.

Genevieve let out her breath in relief, her knees weakening, and sat back down. Christian shot a last challenging, defiant glare at his brother. Amusement lifted one corner of Tarrington's mouth, softening his hard stare. Christian's eyes narrowed and their crystal blue turned to steel.

"Christian," Lady Tarrington said in warning.

Lady Tarrington's soft reprimand prompted Christian to return to the settee. He sank in the cushion on the opposite end from Genevieve. The earl raised a brow and exchanged amused glances with Lady Tarrington. The countess touched his arm in a most familiar manner, intimate and affectionate. The last of Genevieve's alarm faded. Her year with Wickburgh had shaken her faith in humanity, even those clearly worthy of trust.

Lady Tarrington sat between Genevieve and Christian and took Genevieve's hand in hers. Drawing strength from the offered friendship and that aura of serenity that accompanied her, Genevieve clung to the countess.

"Now then," said Lady Tarrington, "what's to be done? Cole, what are her options?"

Tarrington sat in an armchair opposite the settee and rested an ankle on the opposite knee. "She has many options. For one, she can go home and request to live apart from her husband in a legal separation."

Annoyance flared and Genevieve spoke without thinking, her voice lowered to a tone that bordered on insolence. "Please do not speak about me as if I am not present. Or not of sound mind."

The earl inclined his head and looked her in the eye. Whether amused, or annoyed, she could not determine. "My apologies, Lady Wickburgh."

Genevieve met his gaze. "It's Genevieve. And I will not ever go back to Wickburgh."

The earl nodded thoughtfully. "You could arrange a meeting with your husband and your solicitor, and write up an agreement for a legal separation which states where you wish to live and the conditions, as long as they don't conflict with your original marriage settlement."

Genevieve said, "He would never agree to it." He wanted to control her, and he couldn't do that if they lived apart. Even bringing up the subject would merely invite a fresh round of his horrible games.

Tarrington rested his elbows on the arms of his chair. "You could also take your husband to court and sue for divorce. Parliament seldom grants them to women, but you could try."

Genevieve shook her head. "Suing for divorce is not an option I care to attempt, for a number of reasons." She picked up a decorative pillow and hugged it.

Lady Tarrington shook her head as tears brightened her eyes. "You poor dear. What has he done to you?"

Genevieve clamped her mouth shut, unable to speak of any of it.

Tarrington said, "If you remain wed to him, even if you leave, you will never be free to remarry."

She shook her head. "No, I will never remarry, regardless."

Christian shifted. "Where will you go?"

The footman returned, bringing a bowl of water and some clean cloths, and slipped away. Christian picked up the bowl, knelt in front of Genevieve and carefully bathed her foot.

Genevieve froze, surprised that he'd attend to a task normally left to the servants. Perhaps she truly had gained a measure of forgiveness.

The towels and water turned pink as he carefully cleaned her damaged foot in a surprisingly intimate manner. The touch of hands, both gentle and firm, sent spirals of pleasure through her. She should stop him. Enjoying his touch was wrong for a number of reasons. Yet she seemed powerless to speak. She chided herself for running from this gentle man moments ago and sat spell-bound as he cared for her with a softer touch than she'd imagined.

With his lowered head so close, she almost reached out and touched his hair shimmering gold in the lamplight. She curled her hand into a fist. No doubt he would believe her both faithless and wanton if she made her desire for him known. Desire. She paused. She hadn't experienced desire in so long that she'd almost forgotten how it felt. Sorrow edged against her like the lapping of waves that she'd had to give up such a remarkable man.

"I'm glad you weren't here to hear the things he said about you," Alicia said, "the way he tried to discredit you and paint you as a mad woman. It made me ill."

Tarrington lifted a brow. "You were listening?"

Alicia said without shame, "The door was open and I couldn't help but hear."

Christian said grimly, "He knows full well you jumped into the river, Jen. I think he believes you perished and is merely making a big show of playing the concerned husband before deciding how to announce your death."

Genevieve let out a long, slow breath. "Leaving him with the disgrace of having a wife who killed herself was my one revenge against him, and now he's removed even that." She should have known he'd find a way to escape unscathed. He must have bullied or bribed whoever found her clothes. "And even if the truth ever comes out that I drowned myself intentionally—or at least attempted to—he's already made sure everyone believed I was out of my mind with grief, which would garner sympathy for him instead of creating scandal."

Alicia tightened her hand on Genevieve's.

Christian's voice softened and the lines of his face gentled. "I promise you, we will give him no reason to suspect the truth."

The sincerity in his words wrapped around her like a warm blanket. She did not doubt him. Perhaps he could never love her again —nor should he—but at last she'd gained his forgiveness. Moved to tears by the lifting of that burden, Genevieve could only nod, hoping her gratitude showed in her face.

"Do you have a plan?" Alicia asked.

Genevieve nodded. "I do, my lady."

The countess smiled. "It's Alicia, remember?"

"Alicia. I shall apply for a post as a governess somewhere far away, out of Lord Wickburgh's reach. Perhaps Ireland or Scotland."

"A governess?" Christian repeated.

"I'm qualified," she said defensively. "I am well educated and can teach on almost any subject—even mathematics. My father has rather unusual views of appropriate education for young ladies."

Alicia clucked. "I hate to see a lady forced into employment. Don't you have family to whom you can go?"

Genevieve shook her head. "If I go to my parents, he'd hear of it. And I have no other family."

Tarrington expression turned pensive. "Who are your parents?"

"William and Cecily Marshall."

The earl blinked. "Captain Marshall? Of the HMS *Resolute*?"

She stared. "Yes. Do you know him?"

"Not well, but I had dealings with him while I served in the navy." A light of admiration shone in Tarrington's eyes. "He was a fine officer. A fine man."

"Yes." A fine man except for the mutiny. Bitterness frosted her heart. Still, he couldn't have known his actions would affect her so many years later.

Christian said, "I could take you to stay with Rachel."

"Your sister Rachel?" Genevieve asked.

Thoughtfully, he nodded. "She lives in a little hamlet near the Scottish border."

Alicia rubbed her rounded abdomen absently. "It's quite a remote area. You would go unnoticed there."

"I don't wish to be a burden, nor beholden, either," Genevieve added.

"She needs someone up there with her, believe me," Tarrington said.

Christian leaned forward. "I've been worried about her up there all alone, except for a few servants. Though I've encouraged her to get a secretary to help her with her cataloging, she hasn't yet. She needs someone up there with her. In fact, she needs someone to convince her to come home or travel abroad. Anything."

"She's a botanist, of sorts," Alicia explained, "and is gathering research for a book she plans to publish on the subject."

Tarrington let out a half laugh. "Honestly, it's all an excuse to tromp around the moor all day and avoid society." He rubbed his chin. "I can't blame her; I'd like to leave it all behind, at times."

Genevieve nodded slowly. "I could serve as her secretary. Then it would be a position, and not merely relying on her kindness."

"You could," Christian said slowly. "She could probably use the help. But you don't need to work. She'd be happy to have you as a guest." His mouth turned down as if he couldn't bear the thought of a gently bred lady forced to employment.

"I refuse to be a burden." She folded her arms.

Christian eyed her. "I'd hoped she would have grown weary of the isolation and come home, but except for a brief visit a few weeks ago, she has no plans to return soon. If ever. Trust me, if you stayed with Rachel, you'd be doing our family a favor."

"You might merely go for a visit, Genevieve," Alicia told her, "and reserve judgment. After you become acquainted with Rachel, you can make a decision whether or not you wish to remain—as her friend or companion or secretary."

Christian looked at her with that intensely focused gaze of his. "You'll love her, I know you will."

Genevieve held her lower lip between her teeth. If she were near the Scottish border, and in a small village, she'd surely be safe there. "Very well. I'll go. If she'll have me, I'll stay with her as her secretary or companion, whatever she chooses. I'll leave as soon as I can arrange transportation on a stage or a mail coach."

"Absolutely not. I'll take you in the family coach," Christian said.

Her gaze darted to him. "Oh, no, I wouldn't dream of imposing."

"I was already planning on going for a visit to convince Rachel to go on a grand tour—anything to get her out of isolation. If you and I can get her to go to France or Italy, you can travel with her as her companion. Then, when she's ready to come home, you can make more permanent arrangements for yourself on the continent."

She held out her hands. "Very well. It appears that I must accept your charity for a time. I thank you. All of you." She looked up at Christian. "How soon can we leave?"

"I had planned on leaving in the morning."

"Don't you think you ought to write to her first?"

"No need to stand on ceremony," Christian said. "When we arrive at her doorstep, I'll announce you are there to help her. She'll welcome you, believe me."

"You can't leave that early," Alicia interjected. "You'll need clothes and supplies."

Genevieve spread her hands. "I have nothing to pack. And as a secretary I won't need much."

Alicia's brow wrinkled. "I suppose not." Her face lit up. "I'll have more of my clothes and things made over tonight so you can take them with you. By the time I can fit in them again, they'll be terribly out of date and I shan't be able to wear them." She offered a self-deprecating grin. "It's bad form for a countess to wear last year's fashions, you know."

As they discussed the details of the upcoming journey, the last of Genevieve's reservations melted away and she basked in their warmth. In another lifetime, these people would have been her family.

If only her father hadn't been the victim of blackmail! If only he'd been honorable instead of participating in that horrible mutiny! She pushed back her self-pity and drew in a breath. It was done and it would not serve to dwell on what might have been.

She arose. "I bid you all a good night."

Christian rose, too. "I'll walk with you." He held out an arm.

Hesitantly, she took it. She glanced at Lord and Lady Tarrington to judged their reactions, but they had fallen into a private conversation, their heads close together. As she put a hand on Christian's arm, she kept her eyes on the floor. As they ascended the stairs, they fell silent.

Soon, she'd spend a great deal of time alone with Christian as they traveled. They'd have much time to squirm in awkward silence. If only she could explain why she'd jilted Christian. But, no, she didn't dare.

"Thank you again for your help," she said, breaking the silence.

He nodded.

Another moment of silence.

This time, Christian spoke, "I'm glad you've decided to visit Rachel. We'll leave right after breakfast."

She stopped walking as they reached the junction in the upstairs corridor and looked up at him. "Why are you willing to help me?"

He blinked. "Because you need it."

"What do you want in return?"

His mouth dropped open. "You're questioning my motives?"

"What could you hope to gain?"

"What do you think I want?" he demanded, his voice rising in anger.

"I don't know. I have no money with which to pay you. You're not hoping for a liaison, are you?"

"*What?*"

She flinched.

Christian turned away and sucked in great gulps of air, his hands clenched and his shoulders stiff. "You don't know me at all, do you?"

"I didn't mean to insult your honor. I've done nothing but hurt you and put you in danger and yet you're willing to do so much for me. I just don't understand why you'd be willing to help me."

"It's my duty as a gentleman."

Which was true. At the Widtsoe's house party, he'd always been quick to come to the assistance of any lady in need. But none of them had betrayed him.

"You are a true gentleman. But I don't deserve your chivalry."

He softened his voice. "I can't allow you to face that demon alone."

She bowed her head. "Thank you. I wish I had something to offer you in return."

"Helping Rachel will be repayment enough. Goodnight."

"Goodnight." She leaned against the door and watched him disappear into his room.

Thanks to the Amesburys, Christian especially, she would find a place of safety and rebuild herself into a new, free woman. She'd be alone, but safe.

CHAPTER 9

As the Amesbury family coach began its journey to the Scottish border, Christian settled into the rear-facing seat across from Genevieve and steeled himself against her presence for the next few days. If he'd had any sense at all, he would have hired a companion to travel with her. But he couldn't. Besides, she might help him convince Rachel to leave her isolation and do some traveling. Surely that would help her leave her sorrow behind. He had to do something to draw Rachel out of seclusion.

Genevieve, wearing a deeply hooded cloak despite the pleasant day, cast several anxious glances out the window as if expecting an army to suddenly appear and attack them. Or perhaps her reptile of a husband.

Seeing her so frightened nudged aside another piece of his anger for her betrayal in Bath. "We have two outriders escorting us, not to mention the coachman and footman who are both armed. As am I." He lifted his coat to reveal twin pistols at his hips. "We're quite safe."

"I wouldn't put it past him to watch your house and follow us."

"I can't imagine he would force you to go back with him, even if he did suspect you were here."

"He would." She said nothing more but continued casting furtive looks all around.

Perhaps she was right. During the house party, and then later in Bath, Wickburgh had watched her with such fanatical hunger that Christian could well believe Wickburgh had some sick need to keep Genevieve under his thumb.

They said nothing more as the carriage bumped along the rutted country roads. After passing several toll booths and changing horses twice, Genevieve's tension eased and she began to look out at the countryside out of curiosity, rather than the frightened, furtive glances she'd been casting all around.

"Feeling better now that we've put some distance behind us?" he asked.

She smiled. "Yes. Much."

He nodded while a dozen questions collided against his tongue. He clamped his mouth shut. He probably didn't want to know the answers.

And yet he was missing something, some key piece of the puzzle that eluded him. If only he could find it, everything would make sense; Genevieve's actions in Bath, her letter breaking off their unofficial engagement, her contradicting statements when he tried to stop the wedding, her clear misery now. Based on Genevieve's previous behavior, she would never have willingly married such a man. What had changed?

"Why is it that you're so worried about Rachel?" she asked.

He weighed his answers. "Right after our mother passed on, Rachel suffered a heartbreak and retreated from everyone. I fear if she doesn't come home soon, she'll turn into a complete recluse and remain mired in melancholy."

"So now she's researching plants?"

He nodded. "For a botanical book, or so she says."

"Has she always had such a scientific bent?"

"She's always been a self-proclaimed bluestocking, although never to this degree. I don't think she cares so much about this project as she needed an excuse to hide away for a while."

She stared at the carriage wall behind him, her finger absently stroking her lower lip. "And you hope that I can help draw her out."

He watched her finger caressing her lip, aching to touch those lips again and rediscover their warmth and softness. Foolishness.

He pulled his attention away from her mouth. "I hope you and I can convince her to come home. Or to go on a grand tour where she might find a reason to return to the life of the living."

She nodded. "I'll certainly do what I can. But I cannot imagine I'll have more influence on her than you."

"You may be the voice of reason to whom she listens."

"I'm not sure I'm the voice of reason," she said softly.

He wanted to press her for an explanation but held back. He probably didn't want to know. That she regretted marrying Wickburgh was clear, but whether she regretted *not* marrying Christian was another matter entirely. And he didn't care. He'd promised to help her, and he would, but he refused to allow himself to care for her again. He would not give her another weapon with which to wound him. As far as he was concerned, she was a waif who needed rescuing. A damsel in distress. A *married* damsel in distress. Nothing more.

"I can't thank you enough for your help," she said. "I know I am probably the last person with whom you want to spend time."

"You don't have to keep thanking me. I'm glad I found you."

She looked up at him with wide, startled eyes.

He shrugged. "If I hadn't, you would have drowned."

In the unlikely event someone else might have found her, true, they would probably have returned her to Wickburgh. Christian almost chortled at the thought of denying Wickburgh something he desired.

Her eyes shone in something that looked suspiciously like admiration. "You are a man of honor. Like a knight of old."

Shame at his glee for using Genevieve as a way to get back at

Wickburgh, Christian let down one of his shields and made a confession. "I always wanted to be a knight. I used to imagine I was battling a fire-breathing dragon and rescuing a princess, or sailing the seven seas, ridding the world of pirates."

"You are well suited for either role. But I must warn you, if Wickburgh ever learns you helped me . . . ."

"Wickburgh doesn't frighten me. And I always carry a gun now."

"Now?"

He hesitated, but there seemed no reason to hide the truth from her. "After I tried to break up your wedding, he sent his bullyboys after me as a warning not to cross him. I don't go anywhere unarmed now."

She leaned closer, her eyes traveling over his face. She reached up and touched his temple. "Is that how you got this scar?"

Her fingers traced his skin, sending the crackling of a lightning storm through him. He'd almost forgotten that sweet pain of desire shooting through him.

But she wasn't his. Nor did he want her.

He pulled away and found a semblance of a smile. "I won't show you, but I have an even better scar on my ribs." He touched his side where he'd been knifed.

"I'm so sorry you were hurt." Her voice cracked and she looked away, swallowing hard.

Tears for his sake? Or her own?

"I am to blame." She looked down at her hands, pressed her lips together and shook her head slightly.

Before Christian thought up a suitable response, the carriage hit a large rut in the road. Christian and Genevieve bounced out of their seats toward each other. He caught her as she bumped against him. As they half-sat, half-kneeled on the floor of the coach in each other's arms, the tension between them snapped and suddenly the drama of their history and their odd flight to the Scottish border seemed strangely funny.

Christian started to laugh. Genevieve joined in. They laughed together—deep, full, belly laughs. He'd forgotten the music of her laughter and the way her eyes glimmered and crinkled up on the sides.

The carriage lurched violently. With a groaning of wood, the carriage pitched to one side. Wrapping am arm around Genevieve, he braced his feet and put out another arm to stop them from falling.

The coach listed to one side and dragged its belly on the road until it scraped to a halt with a groan.

Christian threw open the door and got out, handing out Genevieve. The coachman let out a string of curse words as he leaped off the driver's seat and went to inspect the damage.

Christian glanced uncomfortably at Genevieve. "Easy, man. There's a lady present," he chided gently.

"Sorry, m'lady." The coachman took a closer look at the wheel.

Christian crouched down next to him. The wheel was ruined beyond repair. "Good thing we always carry a spare."

The coachman grunted. Christian took off his tailcoat and headed for the coach to toss it inside.

"I'll hold it for you." Genevieve held out her hands.

He handed it to her, rolled up his shirtsleeves and got to work helping the coachman and footman remove the broken wheel.

The outrider appeared then and swung off his horse. "I'll finish that, Mr. Amesbury."

"No need," Christian said lightly. "We've almost got it. Keep a sharp eye out for highwaymen."

"Aye, sir."

They finished changing the wheel for the new one stored underneath the coach. As Christian brushed off his hands, he glanced at Genevieve. She stood silently, looking down at his coat and running her hands over it as if she were caressing a lover. His throat tightened at the image. He flung it aside.

She was married to another man.

CHAPTER 10

As the coach pulled into a posting inn to change horses, night fell, enshrouding the land in twilight. Genevieve stepped into the crowded posting inn, keeping her head lowered, and tugged once more on the hood of her cloak to ensure no one would see her face. She curled her toes inside her shoes to keep them on. Even with three pairs of stockings, the borrowed shoes were still too big. The challenge of walking in them naturally required conscious effort. With his hand under her elbow, Christian led her through a room where shadows trembled in the dim candlelight.

A man coming the other direction bumped her with his shoulder. "Pardon me," he rasped as he passed.

That voice sounded vaguely familiar. Releasing her hold on Christian's arm, she stopped short and looked back. The stocky man wearing a coarse woolen coat paused in the doorway, stepping back as another pair of travelers entered. He nodded to the pair and turned his head slightly.

The blood rushed from her head down to her toes. Quickly, she turned to hide her face. That man looked a great deal like one of Wickburgh's thugs. She couldn't be sure. Maybe it wasn't him. If it had been him, was this a chance encounter, or had he followed her? It would be just like Wickburgh to give the man orders to make his presence known to torture her before he made a grab for her. But no, surely not.

Still . . . .

Christian spoke quietly to the innkeeper who led them to a private room. Careful to keep her face away from the main door, Genevieve followed Christian to the private dining room.

As the serving maid cleared the table of the previous diners' meal, Genevieve sank down into the chair Christian had pulled out for her. With her head down and her back to the door, Genevieve sat waiting for the man who looked like one of Wickburgh's men to pull her hood from her face and expose her secret. Her heart thundered in her ears. The smoke from the candles stung her eyes and the raucous laughter of locals and travelers closed in around her.

A moment passed without the man accosting her. The serving maid finally left and closed the door to their private room behind her.

Genevieve let out a shaking breath and trembled all over. Sheltered from curious eyes, she unclenched her hands from her cloak and pushed back her hood.

Christian touched her hand briefly but pulled away. "Would you rather have waited in the coach? I could bring you something to eat."

She shook her head and swallowed her fear. Leaving now would only draw attention. How foolish to think she could go out in public. But she'd spent the last several months locked inside and had been impatient to leave such restrictions.

Christian's concerned face filled her vision. "What is it?"

"I . . . ." if she told him she thought she'd seen one of Wickburgh's men, it might worry him needlessly. "I thought I saw someone I knew." She lifted her shoulder in a loose shrug as if to dismiss the matter.

Christian straightened. "Are you certain?"

"No, I'm not sure it was he."

"Did he see you?"

"I don't think so."

He nodded, his brows drawing together slightly. "I won't let anyone hurt you, Jen." His quiet, intense tones edged through the last of her fears.

Christian understood, somehow. He would keep her safe. Though she didn't deserve it, she had somehow garnered his commitment to protect her. If only she'd been able to protect him from the heartbreak she'd inflicted on him.

Perhaps they'd moved past all that and they could both rebuild their lives apart. Surely, she'd find a place of safety.

What could she do for Christian? There must be some way to repay him, or at least thank him, for all he was doing for her. At the moment, helping his sister was the only thing she could think of. Perhaps another opportunity would present itself. Of course, she'd never truly repay him; all she could hope for was a meaningful show of gratitude.

"Are you too tired to continue traveling tonight?" he asked. "We could stop here."

She shook her head. "I want to get there as quickly as possible." She snapped her mouth closed. It wasn't fair to inconvenience Christian to satisfy her desire to put as many miles as possible between Wickburgh and her. "Unless….do you wish to stay the night here?"

"Not necessarily. If we stop now, we'll have to find an inn again tomorrow night. If we go a few more hours tonight, we should reach Rachel's cottage tomorrow before nightfall. But really, there's no need to rush."

She dredged up a smile. "No, no need to rush. It's not as if we're racing to Gretna Green with enraged relatives on our heels determined to stop our wedding over the anvil."

If only they were.

He let out a half-hearted laugh. "No, fortunately."

Fortunately? Why? Because he no longer had any desire to marry her? Or merely that he was glad they didn't need to rush? It didn't matter.

There could be nothing between them ever again.

For better or worse, marriage was a lifetime commitment. She'd never be granted a second chance at love.

As the serving girl opened the dining room door to bring the food, the noise from the main room blasted in. Genevieve tensed. Wickburgh's man might be waiting out there. She went perfectly still, careful to look straight at Christian and keep the back of her head toward the door. The maid left, closing the door behind her.

Genevieve let out her breath, removed her gloves, and picked up her fork. Christian tucked into his meal like a man who hadn't eaten all day. In spite of herself, Genevieve smiled. He'd always had a healthy appetite—an endearing quality.

They ate in silence while Genevieve rejected every possible subject that came to her. Christian either didn't mind the silence or had no desire to have conversation with her.

After eating, they stood. She eyed the door, knowing she must go through it. With her hand on Christian's arm and her hood carefully over her head, she followed him out of the private dining room and navigated through the crowded inn. No one approached. As they returned to the carriage, Genevieve glanced back. No one seemed to notice them. And of that man she thought she'd seen, there was no trace.

"You're jumpy." Christian handed her into the carriage.

"I fear I'm not far enough away yet. Someone might see me."

"Are you well-known in the area?"

She settled her skirts on the seat. "No, my face is not known at all. I never left the house."

He halted with one foot on the step and one hand on the doorway. "Never?"

She shook her head.

"Why? As the wife of a viscountess, surely you were expected to make calls, see to the tenants, throw balls and such."

Genevieve's first inclination was to sidestep the issue. But she was so weary of all the secrecy between them. "He forbade me to leave the house. He wanted me where he could always find me. When he had to check on any of his other properties, or attend Parliament, he always took me with him and locked me away when we arrived."

He stared at her in clear disbelief. "You were a prisoner?"

She offered a wan smile and lifted a shoulder in a shrug. She couldn't bring herself to reveal those times when Wickburgh imprisoned her with only her cat for company and a twice-daily visit from her maid—besides the visits her husband paid on her to demand his husbandly privileges. She refused to think about that.

Christian's hand on the doorway curled into a fist and a muscle in his temple pulsed. A moment later, he got inside the coach facing her.

As the carriage began moving forward, he filled the carriage with his oh-so-desirable scent, with his very presence. She longed to feel his arms around her, ached for him in a way she hadn't for any other man. All her suppressed desire brought on by her long separation from Christian returned in raging force.

But that was wrong. Even though she was fleeing a husband she never loved, she was still married. Not only that but she was used. Damaged. More unworthy of Christian than ever.

He leaned forward and looked her earnestly in the eye. "As I said, I'll see you safely to Rachel's and then with any luck, onto a boat for the continent. You'll be free of him once and for all, I vow it."

Sorrow edged against her like the lapping of waves that she'd had to give up such a wonderful man. "You are a true gentleman. A perfect gentleman." Realizing what she'd just said, she pushed back the encroaching sadness to tease him a little. "Do your brothers still call you the 'perfectly perfect Christian?'"

His mouth quirked. "Grant does occasionally when he's in a particularly foul mood. Of course, Grant's usually in a foul mood."

She smiled. "I'm not certain I wish to meet Grant, but he is right. You are perfect in at least one way; you are a perfect gentleman and a perfect knight."

He shifted and looked away. "I'll try to live up to that high ideal but fear I'll fall woefully short."

"Better a short fall than a long fall, don't you think?" she quipped.

He smiled. "Yes, I suppose if one must fall, a short one is best."

They grinned at each other.

Well-being crept over her. She was safe, and she and Christian were conversing comfortably at last. "Well, you are as close to perfect as I've ever known. I mean that in the best possible way."

His smile faded and that intensely focused stare returned. He moved to her side of the carriage, his thigh brushing against hers, his presence large in such a confined space. Her heart gave a leap and began pounding against her ribs. The flickering light from the carriage lamps illuminated his face and gave him a warm glow.

He peered into her face as if seeking answers there. "At the Widtsoe's house party, you were clearly uncomfortable in Lord Wickburgh's presence—to the point that I had words with him about leaving you alone. In Bath, your opinion of him did not seem to change. Even at Lady Everett's soiree, you were still avoiding him. Why would you marry a man who frightened you?"

She opened her mouth, and then closed it. Focusing on her hands in her lap, she made a point to adjust her gloves.

He kept talking, as if voicing his thoughts helped him to understand them. "At the time, I assumed he was merely fascinated by your beauty. Later, I had the feeling he was rather obsessed with you, in an unhealthy way."

He was right, of course, but what could she say? He was obviously trying to make some sense of her cruel rejection.

He pressed on. "I assumed once he learned of our engagement that he would back off, but of course, that never became official."

She looked up at him then. "He . . . made his intentions known and I saw the . . . wisdom in his offer. My letter should have been quite clear." That letter had nearly killed her to write. How it must have hurt him to read those horrible words!

His eyes drove into hers with painful intensity. "In your letter, you stated you'd had a change of heart about us—I believe you used the word 'fickle'—and you said that we didn't suit, and that he met your ideal for a husband. But when I went to stop the wedding, you claimed to have been secretly engaged already and you were merely enjoying my intentions."

She went very still. "You must be mistaken."

"No, you were very clear on that point. As clear as you were on choosing to marry a lord instead of the youngest son—despite your protestations to the contrary at the house party."

She swallowed. Her spoken reason for marrying a lord must have cut him cruelly—which is why she'd used it as a last effort to convince him to leave. If only she could tell him the truth! Her eyes stung.

"I'm sorry I hurt you. I truly am." She looked away to hide her collecting tears.

"Why did you marry him? And please don't insult me by repeating any of those lies you told me in Bath. There was more to it, I know there was."

Her heart pounded so hard she feared it would knock her off her seat. Something inside her collapsed, and she could no longer keep up the ruse. "I wish I could tell you. But I can't."

"He forced you to marry him, didn't he?"

The fight left her. She couldn't lie to him anymore. She owed him the truth—at least, part of the truth. "Yes."

He let out his breath in a low, weighted exhale. "At last, something makes sense. How? What did he hold over you? I cannot believe your parents made you to do it."

"No. They were against it." She looked up at him desperately. "I cannot tell you more. I made a vow."

He blew out his breath and dragged a hand through his hair. "I wish you'd told me you were in trouble. I would have found a way around it."

She said nothing. There was nothing she could say.

"Did he ravish you?—is that why you felt you had to marry him?"

"No." Her face burned at the idea of Christian believing she'd lost her virtue before marriage. At least, he clearly did not believe she'd been at fault; his expression was searching, desperate even, but without any trace of accusation or judgment.

He said nothing for a long time, only chewed on his lower lip. She followed the motion of his teeth touching those full lips that had once kissed her so softly and with such heat. It seemed like a century ago instead of only a year.

"You're here now," he said quietly, "and I'll keep you safe from him, I give you my word."

She did not doubt it. The weight of her deception eased a little, and one corner of her heart filled with light and hope.

CHAPTER 11

The following day, as late afternoon sun bathed the countryside in golden light, the Amesbury-crested coach arrived in front of an unassuming cottage in the middle of a vast, windswept moor. Christian's fingers itched to draw it, to capture the texture of the limewash finish, dressed sandstone, crumbling slate wall running beside the cottage, the bracken and crowberry. His last visit had been too brief to indulge himself.

He glanced at Genevieve. She peered out the window, her eyes alight. He admired the curve of her cheek, the wisps of auburn hair that curled around her face. She hadn't jilted him. She hadn't thrown him over for a titled lord. He wanted to sing with joy. A great burden he'd been carrying lifted. It didn't change the fact that she was married. But it changed everything inside his heart. They could never be together of course, not as long as she remained married, but at least the pain of her rejection faded. For now, that was enough.

As the carriage rolled to a stop, Genevieve raised her brows in surprise. "Your sister lives here?"

"I warned you it was humble."

Her smile reached dazzling proportions. "It's absolutely charming! And better yet, he'll never think to look for me here."

He stared at her with open-mouthed surprise, completely undone at the beauty of her smile. That he could have provided her with a place to feel safe enough to smile so brightly brought warmth flooding over him. Her eyes locked with his and her smile faded, replaced with an uncharacteristic intensity. He tamped down the urge to trace a finger along her cheek. It would not do to rekindle old feelings for Genevieve. Knowing she'd been forced to marry Wickburgh did not make her any more available to him. But at least she hadn't callously thrown him over. The knowledge healed over the deepest of the wounds in his heart.

As they stepped out of the coach, a chill wind blew from the moor carrying the scent of heather and clean earth. She shivered. "I'm glad I have a heavy cloak. It's colder here."

"It's always windy here." He held out an arm. "Let's get you inside."

Mrs. Fletcher, a plump, motherly woman waved from the doorway. "Mr. Amesbury! I'm so glad you've come."

As Genevieve walked at his side, she seemed to step strangely. It wasn't quite a limp, but it wasn't her natural graceful stride, either.

He slowed his steps. "Are your shoes hurting your feet?"

She smiled up at him. "No. They're a little too big. But they'll do."

He made a mental note to take her to the cobbler. No lady should have to wear ill-fitting shoes.

As they reached the door, Christian gestured to Mrs. Fletcher. "This is our indispensable housekeeper, Mrs. Fletcher. Mrs. Fletcher, meet Mrs. Jennings." He let out his breath in relief that he hadn't stumbled over her alias.

Mrs. Fletcher beamed at Genevieve. "Welcome, Mrs. Jennings. I'll be glad to see Miss Amesbury have some company. I hope I can enlist your aid in reminding her to eat."

"Most definitely," Genevieve replied.

The housekeeper turned to Christian. "How long will we have the pleasure of your company, Mr. Amesbury?"

He shuddered dramatically. "Terrible trip. I hate the thought of making it anytime again soon. Unless she throws me out, I shall stay a few days and do some painting."

"Excellent. I'll tell Cook. She'll be so pleased to have someone appreciate her cooking the way you do."

Grinning, Christian glanced at Genevieve and said, "Don't tell my sister, but her cook is one of the reasons I made this perilous journey."

Mrs. Fletcher chuckled. "If I tell Cook you said that, it will earn you an extra serving of dessert, you smooth-tongued rogue."

"Ah! Just as I had hoped." He glanced at Genevieve. "A little flattery never hurts."

Genevieve smiled, her posture and expression more relaxed than he'd seen her since he fished her out of the river.

Shaking her head, Mrs. Fletcher chuckled again. "Manipulative whelp."

"Guilty," Christian admitted.

"You must be exhausted from your trip, Mrs. Jennings." Mrs. Fletcher said.

Genevieve nodded a beat too late, no doubt not used to her new name. "Indeed I am."

"I'll bring up some fresh water so you can wash. Do you want a bath first or food?"

"Food," answered Christian firmly. Then he glanced at Genevieve. "I . . . ah . . . I can wait if you wish to bathe first. I should get out of my dirt, as well."

She looked at him askance. "Certainly not. I've seen you hungry." She looked at Mrs. Fletcher. "You'd best feed Mr. Amesbury right away. He might eat the furniture, else. We can clean off our traveling dirt once we're no longer in danger of his voracious appetite."

Rachel appeared in the doorway. "Christian!" She threw her arms around him.

He hugged her and kissed her soundly on each cheek, making big smacking noises. She giggled. Stepping back, he eyed her carefully. Her dark hair was caught up in a careless chignon and her plain cotton gown was at least two years out of fashion, and black to show she was in mourning for Father, but the sorrow appeared to have faded from her eyes and her figure was trim instead of gaunt as it had been. Perhaps her self-imposed seclusion had been good for her, after all. Now all he needed to do was convince her to take Genevieve to the continent and help her find a safe place to live. Then Rachel could accompany him to Italy instead of returning to exile.

He gestured to Genevieve. "This is Mrs. Jennings."

Genevieve smiled tentatively. "Forgive me for coming unannounced, but I am looking for a position and I understand you might be interested in hiring a secretary or a companion."

Christian tried to catch Rachel's eyes to warn her to go along with this idea of keeping Genevieve, but her gaze was focused on Genevieve. "She'd be ideal for you," he added, still trying to attract her attention without being obvious.

Genevieve twisted her gloved fingers. "If you find that we don't suit, I will of course apply for a position elsewhere."

Rachel looked Genevieve over and finally glanced at him. Understanding dawned in the widening of her eyes and the appearance of a smile. "As a matter of fact, I have been meaning to place an advertisement, but I see you've saved me the trouble." She took Genevieve by both hands and smiled. "Welcome. I'm so glad you've come—Mrs. Jennings, is it?"

"Genevieve, if you please."

Christian thought back, trying to remember if he'd ever mentioned Genevieve to Rachel. She hadn't accompanied him and Father to Bath, and since he was terrible at writing letters, he was pretty sure he hadn't told her he'd even been close to proposing marriage, much less mentioning Genevieve by name. Besides, even if Rachel had known of Genevieve, she would have known her as Miss Marshall, not Genevieve Jennings. Regardless, he planned to convince Genevieve to confide in Rachel so she could better help protect her secret. Hopefully soon.

"Very well, Genevieve. I'm Rachel. I'm sure Mrs. Fletcher will see you comfortable."

"Thank you," Genevieve said. "You are under no obligation to keep me if I do not meet your requirements."

"Nonsense. I don't like most people but I'm already in perfect charity with you so I'm sure we'll get along famously. Come. Knowing Christian, food is the first order of business."

Rachel grinned at him and he breathed easier. Some of Rachel's spirit seemed to have returned instead of that painful apathy where she'd been wallowing for months.

With this obstacle overcome, Christian relaxed. The thought of food was welcome, as well. They settled in a small dining room where Mrs. Fletcher served a simple fare. As they ate, darkness fell outside.

"We don't usually eat so early," Rachel commented.

Christian grinned. "Good. Then I'll expect a heartier meal in a few hours."

Rachel lifted a brow, looking almost as imperious as Rachel's twin, Margaret. "You aren't a lad of seventeen anymore. Keep eating like that and you'll begin to grow horizontally."

"I hope you get there before I do."

Rachel threw her napkin at him. "Cad."

He grinned. Yes, she was definitely better. Perhaps now would be a good time to leave and allow Rachel and Genevieve a chance to converse without him underfoot. Hopefully, Genevieve would confide something of her situation to his sister and they could stop dancing around the truth.

He arose and offered a brief bow. "I'm going to check on the horses and make sure that troll of a stable hand remembers which end to feed."

"He's more deaf than ever," Rachel called after him.

In the stable, he found Cole's coach horses and his own Erebos, who'd traveled tied to the back of the carriage, well attended.

The stable hand, a wizened old man eyed him. "Who are you?" he demanded in an accent that had a slight Scottish burr.

"Christian Amesbury. We met a few months past when I visited my sister, Miss Amesbury, remember?"

The man put a hand to his ear. "Eh?"

"I'm Mr. Amesbury," Christian shouted.

"Ah. All right. Here. Get to work." The stable hand handed him a brush.

Chuckling, Christian cheerfully brushed Erebos. His stallion bumped him companionably as he worked, and he lingered over his silky coat and mane, enjoying the bond that strengthens during grooming. All the while, the old stable hand chattered away at Christian. Once he'd reacquainted himself with the man's odd accent, they carried on a bizarre conversation, Christian guessing at half the things the older man uttered, and the stable hand too deaf to hear most of what Christian said.

After Christian had thoroughly brushed Erebos, he moved on to Rachel's horses. They pawed at the ground as though they'd dearly like to go for a run. As silence fell, he realized the old man had wandered off. Christian finished brushing the horses in quiet. Enjoying the solitude, he began finalizing his plans. The nearest port was less than a day's journey. He'd take Rachel and Genevieve on a ship bound for France or Italy or wherever Rachel wished to go. It would be the simplest solution for both of their problems, at least for a time. Eventually he would have to find a more permanent answer for Genevieve.

The ancient stable hand stormed up to him. "Who are ye and wha'da want?"

In surprise, Christian held up a curry comb. "I'm brushing the horses."

The man's anger left as quickly as it had come. "Oh. Aye. When yer finished, go muck out the stalls."

Christian realized what a coward he truly was. He set down the combs and brushes. "I believe I hear my sister calling me."

"Eh?"

"My sister," Christian shouted. "My sister, Miss Amesbury."

"Who?"

"Your mistress. I think she's calling me."

The troll frowned. "Why would she call you?"

"She's my sister!" Christian turned and fled to the house to find the women.

At least Genevieve was safe. He vowed to keep her that way, whatever the cost. Whether he could keep his heart safe from her was another matter entirely.

CHAPTER 12

While Christian saw to the horses, Genevieve washed, changed, and unpacked. Upon finishing, she found Rachel, who led Genevieve to the study.

Rachel gestured. "Here's my project. As you can see, I could use a bit of help organizing."

Genevieve stared in dismay at the piles of chaotic clutter that crept over every inch of her employer's study. "A 'bit.' Indeed. Organizing the disaster before winter might require a miracle."

Rachel looked around the room with some puzzlement, as if she'd never realized how badly disorganized she'd become. "It's not so bad. I have a pretty good idea which pile belongs to what species of plant."

"Whatever we do, we must not sneeze," Genevieve said gravely.

Rachel chuckled. "We don't have to get to work right now. I expect you're weary from your trip."

"Oh, no. I don't mind getting started immediately."

"We'll both work on it, then." Rachel put a pencil behind her ear and moved to the first stack.

Genevieve picked up the top paper on a stack that threatened to topple if she breathed too hard. Much of what she read meant little to her, but the content gave her an idea of how it should be categorized.

She sorted papers into piles but found more topics than she had room to make piles.

Remembering Christian's hope for her to reach Rachel, she searched for something to say, but Rachel looked too engrossed in her reading, and they hadn't yet established a deep enough rapport for her to try to exercise any influence.

A male voice rumbled, "Unbelievable." Christian stood open-mouthed in the doorway. "I didn't think it possible, but it actually looks worse. What did you do, invite in a tornado?"

Rachel grinned unrepentantly. "Apparently. Where'd you find her?" She jabbed a thumb at Genevieve. "She's relentless. She fair took a whip to my back."

Genevieve peeped out at Rachel from behind a particularly fierce tower of papers. "You don't need a secretary. You need a general to conquer this."

Christian laughed and again, Genevieve's foolish heart leaped.

Rachel lifted her eyebrow and tilted her head at Genevieve. "You are utterly ruthless, you know."

Serenely, Genevieve said, "This may take years to sort."

"This is less than two years' worth of work," Rachel said in defense.

Christian sighed. "I believe I'll unpack my art supplies."

"You might get started on that pile," Genevieve suggested, motioning to one on the desk.

Christian recoiled in exaggerated dread. "Can I use a match?"

Rachel let out a cry of outrage. "And lose two years' worth of work? You're heartless!"

He grinned at Genevieve. "See? I'm heartless. Not perfect."

"Perfectly rotten," Rachel muttered.

He sighed heavily. "Surely there's something I can fail to do perfectly."

"You're failing to help us now," Genevieve pointed out with an overly sweet smile.

Grinning, he threw himself to the pile Genevieve had indicated.

Then he peered around it at Genevieve with a wide, boyish smile, mischievous and perfectly endearing. And perfectly dangerous to her heart. Soon, they would part, and he would leave her heart to herself. But then he'd be gone and she'd be utterly wretched without him. Only a few days ago, she thought she could never care for a man. She sighed, cursing herself for such foolishness as allowing her feelings for Christian to return.

That evening after another meal at Christian's request, Rachel read a scientific journal and Christian played the harpsichord. Sitting next to the fire, Genevieve picked up a small wooden embroidery hoop encircling a few embroidered leaves and flowers on a handkerchief with a pin, still threaded, stuck in the middle. Underneath it lay a pattern torn from a ladies' magazine.

"I started that months ago," Rachel said from her chair. "I don't really have the patience for embroidery. I'm not even sure why I thought to make the attempt."

"I love to embroider. Shall I finish it for you?"

"If you wish. It's yours, if you do. I have dozens." She resumed her reading and scribbled something on the paper.

As she plied her needle, Genevieve basked in the comfort of the cottage and in the Amesburys' company and friendship. She couldn't remember when she'd felt so safe and so hopeful. She prayed it would last.

A niggling fear whispered it would soon vanish like a wisp of smoke.

Later that night as she changed into her nightgown, she glanced on the bed. Her heart tripped. A rose lay on the quilt. Wickburgh used to give her roses to try to soften her after a particularly terrible incident between them. Often, the gesture preceded a new cruel game.

They'd seen no further signs of his men as they'd traveled, and she wasn't certain the man she'd seen at the inn was one of his. No, perhaps the rose had merely been a token of welcome from Rachel or Mrs. Fletcher. Or even from Christian. After all, he'd given her the lily. Perhaps the rose was another gesture. A gesture of what? Affection? Friendship? Surely not love.

Setting the rose aside, she pushed the matter from her mind and prepared for bed. For now, she'd focus on helping Rachel and enjoying greater safety and peace of mind than she'd known in a year. Later, she'd worry about how to build a new life.

Although, it would prove more difficult to build a life away from Christian.

CHAPTER 13

The following morning, while his sister and her new secretary tromped about the hills in search of some specimen as Rachel played botanist, Christian followed them, looking for the perfect scene for a landscape.

His gaze strayed to Genevieve. She'd lost the haunted expression, and her skin glowed in health and quiet joy. She was still as untouchable as ever.

He blew out his breath and refocused on his purpose. After finding a craggy ravine filled with late summer wildflowers, Christian sat down on a chair he'd brought out with him. He made several sketches before finding the focal point he wanted. As he set up a canvas, the housekeeper approached with a plate of tarts.

"Some sweets, Mr. Amesbury?"

"Bless you, madam." He devoured a tart and licked his fingers shamelessly. "However, I cannot believe you came all the way out here to bring me sweets."

"No, I offer you a bribe." Her eyes twinkled.

He chuckled. "I'm your humble servant."

"I need some supplies from the village." She held out a list.

"I'll saddle my horse at once." He pocketed the list, finished the tarts, scooped up his supplies, and went in search of Rachel and Genevieve. He found them next to a bluff, their heads close together examining a bit of greenery. "I'm going into the village. Do you need anything?"

Rachel waved him off, too engrossed in the study of the plant.

"Yes," called Genevieve. "I'd like some colored pencils. I thought perhaps we could mark subjects by color. And Rachel needs more ink and paper."

Christian nodded. After convincing the troll in the stables that he wasn't stealing the mistress's horse, he saddled Erebos and made his departure. Though the village was more like a hamlet, Christian found everything he needed, except a cobbler to get some shoes for Genevieve. The nearest one was miles away. Perhaps they could pay a visit to him or a shoemaker when he purchased passage on a ship to the continent. Genevieve hadn't complained, but wearing poorly fitting shoes couldn't be comfortable.

Prepared to return to Rachel's cottage, he crossed the road and headed for his mount he'd paid a village boy to hold. A voice hailed him.

"Christian Amesbury?"

He paused, carefully balancing his parcels, and turned. A tall, lanky man waved.

Christian grinned. "James Ingle, you old dog! What are you doing in this hovel?"

"Visiting my grandfather and trying to stay in the will."

"Oh? Who's your grandfather?"

"The duke on the hill."

Christian raised his brows. "The duke is your grandfather?"

Ingle chuckled. "Don't worry. Fourteen people would have to die before I'd inherit, thank goodness."

"Oh, that's a relief. You might have to be responsible, else."

"I shudder to think. Can I buy you a drink? The alehouse has a very rich, dark ale."

Christian nodded. "Let me put these packages away."

Ingle walked with him to where he'd left Erebos in the care of a boy. He let out a slow whistle. "What a beauty. A Friesian, eh? What's his name?"

"Erebos." Christian tucked away the parcels and adjusted his saddle bags.

Ingle rubbed Erebos's nose. "Is he a good jumper?"

Christian allowed himself a smug smile. "He's never lost a steeplechase."

Ingle clapped his hands and rubbed them together. "Ah! Care to test that against my Fleet?"

Christian snorted. "I've seen you race. I could beat you even if you were riding the mythological Pegasus."

James Ingle let out a hearty laugh. "Challenge accepted."

After Christian asked the lad to take the horse for another short walk to keep him warm, he walked with Ingle to the alehouse. Inside the darkened room, they found a table and placed their orders. A young serving girl brought them their tankards, leaning over to give them a full view of her *décolletage*. As she caught Christian's eye, she paused and looked him full in the face. Then she smiled, slow and seductive, a clear offer.

Christian smiled politely and handed her an extra coin, hoping she understood that he wasn't interested in her offer, but meant no offense. With a broadening grin, and a touch of relief in her eyes, she tucked the coin away. As she turned, she glanced back over her shoulder and smiled again before she moved to another table.

Ingle huffed. "Lucky devil. Does that happen to you everywhere you go?"

Christian took a long drink. It was indeed rich ale. "Does what happen?"

Shaking his head, Ingle snorted. "Never mind. So, what brings you to this remote spot?"

"I'm visiting my sister."

Ingle's face lit up. "Rachel is here?"

Christian chuckled. "Not that it should matter. She hates you."

"Why would she hate me?" Ingle was the picture of innocence.

"Because, among many other things, you threw her into the river!"

Ingle wore a look of puzzlement. "I was twelve. Twelve-year-old boys are supposed to be horrible to girls."

"She couldn't swim."

"I pulled her out again."

"By the hair."

"It worked, didn't it?"

Christian shook his head. "No wonder you're not married yet."

"I'm not married because I'm enjoying bachelor life too much."

"Yes, I have heard about the ways you enjoy bachelor life." To call him a rake would have been an understatement. It was a wonder the man hadn't caught some horrible disease, yet.

"Besides," Ingle added, "I'm not the marrying kind. You are, though. Why aren't you married yet?"

Christian went still at the reminder that he'd lost his chance to marry Genevieve. "I'm several years your junior."

"Oh, right. I keep forgetting. You followed Jared and me around so much, I guess I sorta accepted you as one of us."

"Accepted? You mean, when you weren't trying to frighten me with stories about the ogre that lived under the bridge?"

Ingle slapped his thigh and let out a gusty laugh. "I forgot about that one."

"It gave me nightmares."

Ingle sat back and sobered. "It's good to see you, Chris, really. How's Jared?"

"Believe it or not, he's happily married to a respectable widow with a son."

"Who would have thought? By the way, my mother shows off the portrait you did of her to anyone who visits."

Christian allowed himself a small smile. "I'm glad to hear it."

Ingle sipped his drink. "How are your sisters?"

"Margaret rules London society like a queen and avoids her husband. Rachel is feeding her bluestocking tendencies."

Ingle's gaze flicked to him, looking a little too interested. "Rachel's still not married, I presume?"

Christian looked at him askance. "No, and she's quite content to keep it that way, so don't get any ideas about my sister, you lecher."

Ingle chortled. "She's old enough to decide who she will accept as a caller."

"And I'm old enough to string you up by your lungs if you go near her."

Ingle gave a half laugh, but sobered as he studied Christian, obviously trying to decide if he were in earnest.

Christian glanced outside at the lengthening shadows. "I should go before it gets dark. Thank you for the ale."

"Tomorrow, then?"

Christian paused. "The steeplechase?"

"Unless you're inviting me to have dinner with you and your sister."

"Over my cold and lifeless body."

Ingle snapped his fingers as if he entertained a brilliant idea. "I have it. We'll raise the stakes a bit with a friendly wager. If I win, I may pay a call on Rachel and you put in a good word for me."

"You just told me you aren't the marrying kind, and I'll have to kill you if your intentions toward her aren't honorable."

Ingle held out his hands. "I just want to see her. For old time's sake."

Christian considered. Seeing a rake such as Ingle would be the last thing Rachel needed. But if Christian won, and he always won, he could secure Ingle's word as a gentleman that he'd stay away from her. Besides, Christian hadn't indulged in anything as exhilarating as a steeplechase in months and the lure was more than he could resist.

He nodded. "And if I win, you'll stay away from her. Forever." He gave him a stern look but Ingle only grinned.

"Agreed."

"Tomorrow at daybreak. Meet at the church?"

Ingle nodded. "Of course."

"You've run it before, so you'll have the advantage."

"Worried?" Ingle asked with raised brows.

"Just making a note of it so you'll appreciate how thoroughly I've beaten you."

Ingle laughed again. "Duly noted. And I see that you've also given yourself an excuse if you lose."

"I never need excuses because I never lose," Christian shot over his shoulder as he headed out the door. It sounded arrogant, and an awful lot like Cole—or Jared, for that matter—but a little psychological pressure on his opponent surely wouldn't hurt his cause.

As he rode back to Rachel's cottage at a near gallop, he laughed at the wind in his face, exhilarated with the speed. A rabbit darted across his path. He slowed. If he brought home a rabbit, he could convince Mrs. Fletcher to make her mouth-watering rabbit stew.

He picked up his gun, took careful aim at the zigzagging body, and fired. The rabbit dropped. As a youth, he'd been driven to shoot as well as his brothers. Later, when he realized he'd never go off on adventure like they had, but rather, his role was to care for his parents and help manage the estates, he hunted to bring home game rather than to prove himself.

Whistling, Christian retrieved the rabbit and put it in a bag on his saddle before returning to Rachel's cottage. He braved the wizened troll in the stable who was more pleasant about receiving horses than about letting them go. In the house, he presented the packages and the rabbit with a flourish to Cook and Mrs. Fletcher who rewarded him with a tasty morsel.

"Hmm," he mused. "I fetch, and you feed me. I feel like a hound."

Mrs. Fletcher laughed. "You eat better than most hounds."

Inside Rachel's study, he found Rachel and Genevieve, their heads bent over their paperwork. He whistled as he turned a circle amidst neat stacks and labeled boxes filled with notes. "I actually see progress."

"Nice of you to say." Genevieve smiled as if she knew a secret.

"Either be useful, or get out of the way," Rachel muttered as she tucked a quill behind her ear and blew at a strand of dark hair that had worked itself out of her chignon.

Christian made a tsking sound. "Productivity makes you grouchy. And ungrateful. I braved many dangers to bring you your parcels."

"Then you must have loved it," Genevieve said. "Did you manage to find a dragon to fight, as well?"

"Three." He set the wrapped packages on the desk, grinned at them both, and paused to bask in Genevieve's smile. "Good thing I remembered my sword."

Did she still think of him as a knight? If only he could slay her dragon of a husband and carry her off to his castle.

LATER, as they sat down to dinner, Genevieve said, "We're making amazing progress."

Rachel beamed at her. "I would never have accomplished so much without you."

"Hmmm," Christian mused. "That sounds like I'm about to receive the gratitude I so dearly deserve for bringing you an efficient and hard-working assistant." Christian placed a finger behind one ear in order to catch every word.

Rachel grimaced. "Yes. Very well. I admit it. You had a great idea."

"What was that? I didn't quite catch that."

"Thank you for bringing Genevieve to help me, you arrogant oaf." Rachel grinned.

Christian bowed his head graciously. "You are most welcome, O sister of mine."

Genevieve smiled at him with such affection that for a moment, he allowed himself to imagine what it might have been like to have married Genevieve and invited her into the family.

Rachel's voice cut in. "You're feeling particularly pleased with yourself—even more so than normal. What trouble did you get into when you went into town?"

"Trouble? *Moi?*"

Genevieve coughed into her pudding, her eyes dancing with mirth. "You might fool others with that innocent face, but it doesn't work on those of us who know you."

He grinned. At last, she'd thrown off the last of the haze of sorrow that had surrounded her and unburied the sense of humor that had delighted him in Bath. "But my innocent face has served me so well."

Rachel groaned. "You're looking far too smug. Don't tell me you found some poor, witless fool to challenge to a steeplechase."

He chuckled. Keeping secrets from Rachel had always been difficult. She seemed to read him like a fortune teller. "You are mistaken. I met up with an old friend and *he* challenged *me* to a steeplechase."

Rachel's face reddened and fire leaped out of her eyes. Her mouth opened, no doubt to spew some sort of dire prediction about the race.

"Christian!" Genevieve interjected, cutting off whatever Rachel was about to say. "I don't understand this insane need you have to take such a pointless risk. You are so sensible otherwise."

Christian leaned back in his chair and smirked. If she were this concerned over him, it must mean that on some level she cared. Not that he dared dwell on that thought. "It's not actually a pointless risk—there is a point to it. And racing is one of my few indulgences."

Rachel let out a sound of disgust. "Men! Why am I cursed with brothers bent on getting themselves killed? Don't do it, Chris. I cannot bear the strain of another brother putting his life at risk."

He sobered at the references to Cole's and Jared's recent near brushes with death. "We've already agreed upon it. As a gentleman, I cannot in good conscience call it off."

Not to mention, if he called off the race, he'd be forfeiting, and he'd have to allow Ingle to call on Rachel. Ingle might be an acceptable friend, but as a libertine, he was not an acceptable suitor for a respectable lady—especially Christian's sister.

Rachel threw her napkin at him. "Why won't you be reasonable?"

He considered. Perhaps he could use this to his advantage. "I might be persuaded to call off the race if you leave here tomorrow and board a ship to the continent."

She folded her arms. "Why is everyone so concerned that I'm here? I'm perfectly happy as an eccentric old maid living in the wilds."

"Old?" Christian bristled at the word. "Good heavens, Rachel, you're all of thirty-two, not ninety. Plenty of ladies marry at your age, and older, even."

"I won't be marrying at this or any age and I have nothing to say to anyone in society."

"I'm not asking you to re-enter society. I want you to come home. Or go to France or Italy, anything except sequestering yourself here alone with nothing to do but fester the wounds of the past."

"I am not festering wounds of the past, I am realizing a dream!"

"A dream you invented as an excuse to flee from civilization."

Rachel opened her mouth, then closed it with a snap. The fire left her eyes. She glanced at Genevieve, who was half standing as if to rush to her rescue.

Genevieve swallowed, glanced and Christian, and touched Rachel's arm. "Your family loves you. They're worried about you. I will gladly serve as your companion if you go on a Grand Tour." She offered a small smile. "I've always wanted to see France." She glanced at Christian. "And Italy."

She remembered his dream to paint in that location. Why that meant so much to him, he didn't care to explore.

Rachel let out her breath. She looked from Christian to Genevieve, got up, and stood staring out of a window. Finally, her shoulders slumped. "Very well. I'll leave. But not tomorrow. Give me a week, then I'll pack up my things and . . . actually, a Grand Tour might be just what I need. France. Italy. And Greece. I've always wanted to see Greece."

"Good." He let out his breath. At least that battle had been won.

The faraway look left her eyes. "Now will you give up your race?"

He weighed his options. If Christian forfeited, it would be the same as Ingle winning. But there had been no time limit set when

Ingle could call on Rachel. It was splitting hairs, of course, but he wouldn't actually be breaking his word if Rachel were gone by the time Ingle called.

"If you leave tomorrow, I will call off the race. If you leave next week, I'll convince Cole you should go to the continent instead of coming home and meeting one of his widowed friends." It might be stretching the truth a little, but Cole did have widowed friends he'd probably like to introduce to Rachel.

She made a face. "A widower. Just what I need."

He couldn't resist needling her just a little, if for nothing else than to enjoy the fire she was finally starting to show. "Aren't you going to ask who it is that Cole wants you to meet?"

Rachel stilled. "Do I wish to know?"

"He asked about you." He sipped his wine and glanced at her smugly.

Rachel's eyes narrowed. "I shudder to think."

He nodded sagely and tucked into his dessert as if completely oblivious to Rachel's curiosity.

"Well?" Rachel demanded. "Who was it?"

He grinned. "I thought you didn't want to know. It should be an interesting steeplechase tomorrow."

"Christian," Genevieve pled. "Please don't race. It's too dangerous. Anything could happen to you."

He gave her a measured stare. Her concern, while endearing, only served as a reminder that she no longer had any claim over his habits. The thought burned in his gut like a hot blade. And yet, again came that small pleasure that she worried for his safety.

He shrugged. "It's in Rachel's hands now."

"Who is racing against you?" Rachel asked.

Returning his focus to his sister, he sipped his drink, enjoying torturing Rachel far too much. "Why do you care?"

"I don't." She returned to the table. "It would be nice to know ahead of time who to look out for so when I come watch the race, I can avoid him. Or her. Is it a him or a her?"

"You're going to watch the race?" Vague alarm arose. He didn't want Ingle even seeing Rachel.

She took another serving of dessert. "I'd best have a first-hand account to report back to Cole when you kill yourself. Besides, I like hilltopping."

Genevieve murmured, "I used to enjoy hilltopping. I haven't done that in years."

Rachel turned to her. "Then you are long overdue."

She shook her head. "Oh, no. I won't be going. I'm not overly fond of crowds, you know." She sent Christian a warning look.

He nodded. "It will probably be dull. For you both."

Rachel turned to her. "I doubt there will be much in the way of crowds in such a remote area. The nearest hamlet is little more than a collection of tiny huts. If people came from a hundred miles in all directions, there would probably be less than a score of spectators."

"This is merely a challenge between two childhood friends," Christian said to both of them. "I'm sure you won't find it very interesting."

"Childhood friends . . ." Rachel's eyes narrowed as if sifting through memories. "Who is it? Tell me!" Her exasperation was reaching a breaking point. Time to stop toying with her.

He sighed. "James Ingle."

She stared at him in horror. "He's here?" The dismay was clear in her voice.

"Apparently he's some relation to the duke up on the hill."

"I didn't realize James Ingle had ties to anyone of significance."

"Distantly, I'm told." He watched her reaction.

Rachel chewed on her lower lip, no doubt debating whether she wished to see James Ingle and rekindle the love-hate relationship they'd once had.

"Will you win?" she asked.

Christian shrugged. "I haven't lost a steeplechase in years."

"I'd like to see you beat that . . . that . . . ." She dropped off. "And Genevieve will come, too."

"Oh, no. I think not," Genevieve said.

"You need to get out of the cottage. It would do you some good to be around people."

Christian ran a hand through his hair. He should have kept the race to himself. But Rachel didn't seem pleased at the prospect of seeing Ingle. Perhaps no harm would come of her being present. And to drag Genevieve out into public when she feared exposure seemed cruel. However, Rachel was right; Genevieve had been working hard and could use an outing.

Genevieve's long, slender fingers toyed with the stem of her wineglass. Christian admired the way the candlelight played in the curves of her face and in the shine of her hair.

She looked up at him. "I would like to go, but . . . ."

Rachel nodded. "Then it's settled."

" . . . but I fear that is not appropriate for a secretary."

Rachel gaped. "Genevieve, I'm surprised at you. We're on a first name basis, and you dine with us at night. You're not merely my secretary. I only pay you because you insist on working yourself to the bone. Otherwise, I'd be pleased to have you as my guest."

Genevieve faltered and shot Christian an imploring look. Perhaps it was time for her to confide in Rachel so they wouldn't have to keep up the charade. Moreover, Rachel would be hurt if she learned they kept a secret from her as if they didn't trust her.

As he opened his mouth to chide Rachel for trying to bully Genevieve into going somewhere she clearly did not wish to go, he reconsidered. Rachel hadn't expressed an interest in any social gathering in ages. Perhaps this would be the beginning of getting her to make appearances now and again. And if Genevieve didn't go, Rachel might not.

"It might be good for you both," he finally said. Surely this far from society, no one would recognize Genevieve.

Genevieve's brows drew together. "Perhaps you're right. I haven't attended any social event in over a year. I admit, the prospect has some appeal."

Wickburgh had kept her a prisoner their entire marriage? The scoundrel. Christian longed to seek out Wickburgh that moment and challenge him to a duel.

He drew a breath and pushed it out in a slow release. They passed the rest of the evening quietly, Rachel strumming her lap harp, Christian drawing, and Genevieve embroidering a handkerchief for Rachel, then curling up with a book.

As the hour grew late, Genevieve arose. "If you'll excuse me. I'm going to take a bath and retire. Goodnight."

After they bid her a good night, Rachel raised her brow and looked pointedly at Christian. "Exactly what are your intentions toward my secretary?"

"I have no intentions. She was in need of aid and I brought her to you."

"And why is it that you are still here?"

"You don't like my company?"

"You know that's not what I mean. But the last time you visited, you were only here two days. You seem to be settled in for a long stay." She shifted the harp on her lap.

"The last time I came, you traipsed all over the moor every day and muttered over your notes every evening. You weren't very good company. And I didn't think you'd stay in this self-imposed exile for so long."

Rachel pressed her lips together. "It isn't like you to be so evasive, Chris."

Christian stared unseeing into the flame of a nearby cluster of candles. "I'm only trying to help her. And I want you both to get on a ship for the continent with me. She needs to find a position abroad. Once she's settled, I'm hoping you'll join me in Italy for an extended stay."

She fell silent, plucking at the strings of her small harp. "I have the feeling there is more to her than she's telling me."

Christian kept his eyes on his drawing. "Everyone has secrets."

"She has the mannerisms of a very fine lady, and while she bears a great deal of sorrow, she's never spoken of her husband. Not once. I'm not entirely certain she's mourning his passing."

"That's something you'll have to ask her."

"I've seen the way you watch her."

He shielded his expression, donning a casual smile. "And why wouldn't I? She's beautiful. As an artist, I'm drawn to beauty."

"And that's all?"

Christian let out his breath in frustration. "She is not available, Rachel. Therefore, I don't have any desire for more."

She set down her harp. "I don't understand. She's a widow, so why would she be unavailable? You aren't bent on marrying some heiress."

Wordlessly, he moved to the pianoforte and began a sonata.

"You're in love with her," Rachel said, half accusingly, half in wonder.

His fingers stilled, poised over the keys. Was it true? Did he still love her?

"Who is she, Chris?"

If he didn't tell her something, she'd start asking questions Genevieve obviously wasn't prepared to have answered. "She's the girl I almost married in Bath last summer."

Rachel drew in her breath, then let it out in a long, "Ohhhh. She married a lord, didn't she?"

"Yes." He said flatly. Let her come to her own conclusions.

"How do you feel about all this?"

"Conflicted." He resumed playing, pretending to be focused on his music.

"There's no Lord Jennings in the book of peerages, nor do I remember a lord with the surname of Jennings."

Rachel said nothing more about Genevieve that evening and Christian relaxed as he played. His plan to get Genevieve to safety and spend time with his sister had worked well. If only he could quell his growing tenderness for the woman he could never have . . . .

CHAPTER 14

Genevieve eyed the horse in front of her and nervously fingered the strings on her bonnet. From the moment she awoke, a terrible foreboding had seized her. She'd tried to talk Christian out of the race, but he would hear none of it.

She reached a trembling hand out to the horse to let him smell her. "How did I let myself get talked into this?"

"Because you can't say no to me." Rachel looked unrepentant.

It was true. Genevieve had grown to adore Rachel in the short time she'd been here, and she wanted to see her new friend happy. Genevieve rubbed her eyes, burning and bleary from staying up so late mending one of Rachel's coats after she went to her room on the pretense of retiring. Rachel was so focused on her work that she never noticed her own needs. But Genevieve loved taking care of Rachel; for the first time in a year, she felt needed. At Wickburgh's estate, she'd been forbidden to leave the house to do her duty in taking care of the tenants and the servants. Now Rachel wanted her to go hilltopping with her. Of course Genevieve had capitulated.

"You have ridden before, haven't you?" Rachel asked, misunderstanding her fear.

"It's been a long time."

Christian stepped near and said in a voice only Genevieve could hear, "It's only a tiny hamlet. Few people will be there." A little louder, for Rachel's benefit, he said, "You won't fall off. A few minutes in the saddle and it will all come back to you. Up you go." Christian gave her a leg up.

The horse shifted under her in a familiar motion. Christian paused next to her, his hands out as if expecting to catch her as she slid off. After adjusting the skirts of her dark green riding habit that had once belonged to Alicia, Genevieve settled in on the side saddle. Christian glanced up at her with approval lighting his eyes. She tried to smile but her lips wavered.

Ever sensitive to her mood, he sobered, searching her face. "What is it?"

She opened her mouth, but couldn't express the growing anxiety that knotted her stomach, nor identify its source.

Rachel interjected. "Your mare is very gentle. She probably won't try to join in the race with the others, unlike this one," she patted her mount, "who will find it hard to resist joining the others like a herd."

Genevieve stroked her horse's smooth neck. "What's her name?"

"Pisces."

"Are all your horses named after mythical characters?"

"All the ones who come from Cole. He's mad about mythology and astronomy."

"He's horse-mad, too," added Rachel, "in case you didn't guess."

Christian mounted his Erebos and they set off at an easy pace. The wizened stable hand came tottering out, yelling and shaking his fists. Laughing, they spurred their mounts and rode out of shouting range.

"Where did you dig up that old fossil?" Christian jerked a thumb behind them toward the stable.

Rachel wrinkled her nose. "He came with the cottage. I think he must be a hundred and fifty."

As they rode through the hills, Genevieve's nervousness dissipated. The sun peeped over the mountains, painting the clouds pink and gold against a cobalt sky. On such a lovely day, worries faded away like morning mist. The sun burst through the clouds, lighting up the glorious landscape of verdant green hills and heather growing wild on the moors. Small animals scurried out of their way. She'd been under the mistaken impression that the moors were flat, but they were rugged, with rocky outcroppings. Over the last few days, she'd become intimately acquainted with the moor's wild beauty. She'd be sad to leave when the time came. They passed several low stone fences along the way, all the while the church steeple drew nearer.

As they approached the church where Christian and his opponent would begin their race, Genevieve's pulse quivered. Christian was a first-rate racer, but steeplechases were dangerous. The thought of him getting hurt made her heart seize up. But she'd forfeited her rights to urge him to reconsider when she failed to become his wife.

She glanced at him. As he eyed the layout of the land, his flushed face and sparkling eyes revealed his excitement. Everything Christian did, whether he painted, played music, rode, or loved, he did it with matchless, unapologetic passion.

She looked away, blinking back tears and swallowing against a lump choking her. Soon they'd part ways, probably forever, and his constant presence would no longer batter her with the constant temptation to release the hold on her heart and allow herself to fall in love with him all over again.

"Ingle!" Christian waved to another man who rounded a hill and approached them. He urged his mount forward.

Desperate to say something to him, she called out, "Christian."

He paused, looked over his shoulder, his brows raised inquiringly.

Thinking quickly, she held out one of the handkerchiefs she'd embroidered. "A favor for you, Sir Knight."

His brows rose in surprise. Grinning, he held out his arm, his pale eyes alight. "I'm honored, fair lady."

She tied her handkerchief around his forearm. "Good luck." She prayed he wouldn't be injured.

"Let's watch from up there." Rachel pointed.

"Don't you want to speak with James Ingle?" Christian said to

Rachel with a playful glint in his eye, and made a loose gesture to the distant figure approaching them.

Rachel pinned Christian with a glare that should have felled him on the spot. He grinned in return.

"Is he your opponent?" Genevieve asked.

Christian nodded. "An old friend of the family, of sorts."

He waved to the man who trotted up to them. The newcomer had dark brown hair and eye lashes that Genevieve envied. He also wore a rakish glint as his gaze fixed upon Rachel. "What a pleasure to see you again, Miss Amesbury."

"Mr. Ingle," she said coolly.

"You look even lovelier than ever."

"How kind of you to say." She might have been exchanging pleasantries at the royal palace for all the stiff formality she displayed. "May I present Mrs. Jennings?"

Mr. Ingle dragged his gaze off Rachel and glanced at Genevieve. He nodded politely and then did a double take, making a slow perusal a second time, his smile widening. "Mrs. Jennings. I'm delighted to meet you."

Genevieve inclined her head. "Mr. Ingle."

His expression openly admiring, he awarded her with what he no doubt considered an irresistibly charming smile. But his appeal fell short compared to Christian's.

His gaze danced between them and his smile delighted. "I'm honored to be in the presence of such breathtaking beauties."

"You waste your flattery, Ingle," Rachel snapped. "Come, Genevieve, let's find a place to view the race." As they rode away, Rachel muttered under her breath, "Scoundrel."

"Good luck to you both," Genevieve called to the racers.

Her attention lingered on Christian, wholly masculine in his buckskin breeches that hugged his muscular legs, and dark, fitted riding coat. He positively vibrated with excitement. Reluctant to leave, she followed Rachel. They rode on ahead a goodly distance and found a good vantage point to watch the race. Others arrived and lined up along the course. Genevieve tugged at her bonnet to ensure it hid her face from the sun and its propensity to make her freckle, and to shield her from any curious eyes. It also concealed her distinctive hair.

She glanced at Rachel. "Why do you dislike Mr. Ingle?"

"He's a libertine, a heartbreaker."

"A heartbreaker? Did he break yours?"

"Years ago—before he became so dissipated. Now he breaks the hearts of everyone else." Rachel pointed to a distant church on a hilltop. "They'll race to that steeple. This course is unusually rough. Christian will love it. I hope he doesn't get himself killed, the foolish, thoughtless, juvenile."

Genevieve smiled at Rachel's obvious attempt to change the subject as well as her sisterly concern. "I share that sentiment." She paused. "You love him very much, don't you?"

"He's a cork-brained brat. A ninnyhammer." Rachel smiled, clearly relenting. "I do love that pup."

"He's raced many times, though, hasn't he?"

"Yes, and I worry over him every time. I'm convinced he races far more than I know."

Genevieve had fretted over him both times he'd raced outside of Bath last summer. But now, the rugged course with so many stone fences, rises, rocks, and bluffs seemed downright foolhardy.

They waited while small groups of spectators clustered together on the nearby hills. The crowds grew larger and larger. Waves of quivers rolled through her stomach at faster and faster intervals. She drew a breath, trying to compose herself. They were in a remote village, and her husband would never have come this far north. And Christian knew what he was doing. Yet a terrible foreboding returned in full force, racing along her skin in little sparks.

The competitors lined up, their horses dancing against the reins. A gunshot split the air and the horses leaped forward. Genevieve watched in awe and horror as the horses plunged through the predetermined course over hedges and stone walls, and sending up a spray as they charged through a stream.

When the racers drew near Rachel and Genevieve's position, Rachel called. "Let's go. I want to see the finish."

Genevieve and Rachel rode along the hilltop. Genevieve's mount danced and pulled against the reins. Keeping a firm hold on the mare to prevent her from charging down the hill and joining the race, Genevieve turned the mare in a circle. The riders rushed headlong at a terrifying pace, hurtling over and around obstacles at the last possible second, neither giving any quarter.

"This is madness," Genevieve gasped.

"It is," Rachel agreed breathlessly. "You'd think he would have learned. He nearly killed himself in the fox hunt last autumn. But he's so mad for it. I think it's the one thing he does that always went against Mama's wishes. Of course, my brothers approve, the idiots. They say it keeps him from being too soft."

"I would never call Christian soft. He's certainly the most gentle man I've ever met but he's also one of the manliest as well."

"Ohhh," Rachel dragged out the word. Speculation flowered in Rachel's round eyes.

Genevieve rushed to explain. "You misunderstand. I have no expectations for him. He's kind. And he helped me when I needed aid. Nothing more."

Rachel tilted her head. "You never speak of your husband."

She cringed. "He's no longer in my life."

"It wasn't a happy marriage?"

Genevieve heaved a great sigh. "No, far from it."

Rachel saved her from answering. "My twin sister Margaret has a terrible marriage, too. Her husband spends all his time in gaming halls and brothels. And he flaunts his mistresses in public."

If only Lord Wickburgh had such ordinary vices.

"Here they come." Rachel gestured.

Christian and Mr. Ingle wound through the ravine, their horses running neck and neck. Genevieve and Rachel moved to the next hilltop within sight of the church. A white scarf fluttered from the branches of a tree near the front steps like a beacon to the racers, urging them to snatch the scarf and win the race.

The racers rounded the hill. Christian pulled ahead by half a length, but the other contender doggedly kept up. They took a final jump.

Something went wrong. James Ingle's horse stumbled as he landed. Horse and rider fell forward. Ingle hurtled forward and landed hard, rolling over once from momentum. With a cry of horror, Genevieve sat frozen. Rachel let out a sound of distress.

Ingle's horse got up and staggered. The man lay still. Genevieve urged her horse forward to lend aid with Rachel next to her.

Still running the course, Christian streaked ahead, unaware of the disaster behind him. An instant before he reached the fluttering scarf, Christian glanced over his shoulder. After a second glance, he pulled hard on the reins and turned Erebos in a circle, then ran back to Ingle. Christian leaped off before Erebos had come to a complete halt.

"Ingle!" Christian shouted.

The man floundered about on the ground convulsively. Christian grabbed him by the lapels and struck him hard across the face. Genevieve let out a gasp and urged her horse faster. She raced ahead and leaped off her horse. As she ran toward them, James Ingle sucked in his breath with a loud gasp.

Christian put his hands on Ingle's shoulders and shook him slightly. "James?"

Ingle struggled to breathe. "I'm all right."

Genevieve skidded to a halt and watched the exchange. Rachel caught up to her, tears streaking her face. Genevieve found the presence of mind to wonder about Rachel's emotional display for a man she claimed to dislike.

"Except now my face hurts," Ingle added. "Did you have to hit me so hard?" He rubbed his cheek.

Christian got up and stood bending over with his hands braced on his legs. "You were turning blue."

Ingle nodded. "The fall knocked the breath out of me."

"Anything broken?"

"I think my jaw is." He offered a rueful, if wan smile. "I'm teasing you, Chris."

"I know." Christian bowed his head, visibly shaken. "Saints above, you scared me."

Rachel muttered under her breath, "Men!" and turned away, wiping her cheeks.

Christian was unharmed. His opponent was unharmed now that Christian had shocked him into breathing again. Genevieve stood gasping for air and let the terror die down.

As a crowd gathered, Genevieve took a few steps to remove herself from the center of the crowd and looked for something to do, something to assuage her growing helpless anger over the risks the men had taken. Ingle's horse danced about nearby, his reins dragging on the ground. His eyes were wide and wild and his flanks heaved. She approached him slowly, crooning to him. Putting a hand on his neck, she continued to murmur assurances before taking the reins and leading him back to his rider.

Christian gave Mr. Ingle a hand up, and they went to Genevieve holding the horse. Ingle nodded to Genevieve in gratitude and began examining his mount for possible injuries.

Crouched next to Ingle, Christian ran gentle, practiced hands over the animal's legs. "He doesn't appear to be hurt."

Ingle nodded. "We were both lucky. It could have been worse."

He was right. It could have been worse. The full reality came over her. It could have been Christian. He might have been badly injured. Or killed. Something dark and horrible and angry took root and sprang into full bloom. She turned on them.

"Stupid, stupid men. Why must you be so reckless? You risk getting yourself killed for what? A bit of sport! Have you no care for your lives? Have you no care for others in your life? Well?"

Her chest heaved as her breath came in angry gasps. They stared at her outburst.

Her anger dissolved into shame and her face flamed. She shouldn't have made such an outburst. She had no right to scold either of them. She took a steadying breath. With trembling hands, she held out the reins to Mr. Ingle. He took the reins with open-mouthed astonishment. She glanced at Christian who gaped. Promptly, she turned her back on him and went to her horse.

As she looked about for something to use as a step, Christian came to her, alternately bewildered and contrite. "I'm sorry I frightened you."

She nodded stiffly. He gave her a crooked smile and offered his hand to give her a leg up. Silently, she accepted his aid. From atop her mount, she turned her head away from him, unable to look him in the eye. She'd just made a scene and attracted attention which was the last thing she should have done.

Christian strode away, mounted, and cantered to the tree where he grabbed the scarf. As he returned, he waved it tauntingly in front of his opponent's face, his tension relaxing into a grin. "I win."

Mr. Ingle laughed and shook his head. "I want a rematch."

"Poor loser."

Ingle nodded to Rachel and Genevieve. "Ladies. It was a delight. I hope we meet under more victorious circumstances next time." His gaze lingered on Rachel.

Christian gave Ingle a look that seemed to convey an entire conversation. Ingle cleared his throat and tugged on his collar. Apparently satisfied with whatever message he'd sent to Ingle, Christian paused to speak to a group of spectators closing in around him.

Genevieve focused on her riding gloves, making a point to avoid looking at Christian or Rachel. Tears stung her eyes and her hands shook. What would she have done if something terrible had happened to Christian? And why was she so foolish as to have made such a terrible scene?

When Christian returned, they turned their horses back around toward the road leading to the cottage. Rachel and Christian sent Genevieve puzzled looks, but she ignored them. As they rode home, no one spoke. The tension between them left nothing for speech. She'd had no right to be angry. She and Christian had no romantic understanding nor could they as long as she remained married. Even if she were free, her heart and soul were too battered and unworthy to offer to someone.

Her heart didn't seem to understand.

Riding next to Christian, Genevieve glanced at his profile. "I apologize for my outburst. I had no right to do such a thing. I fear I was a bit overset."

He looked over at her, touching her with his blue gaze, and his mouth pulled up on one side. "I flatter myself into thinking you were worried about me."

"I was," she admitted.

As they neared a stone wall, a gunshot roared through the mountains. A piece of rock on the wall exploded next to them, sending a shower of debris. The horses shied and they had to keep a firm grip on them. Christian pulled a pair of pistols and held them, poised, his eyes narrowed as he scanned the area.

"Good heavens," said Rachel. "Who could be hunting here? And why would they be so foolish as to fire while people are present?"

"Are you sure it was a hunter?" Genevieve asked.

"Who else would it be?" Rachel said.

"A poacher I suppose," Christian said. "But they aren't usually that careless."

Who else, indeed? Her unease returned tenfold. First the man who looked like one of Wickburgh's, then the rose, now a mysterious gunshot. It seemed too coincidental. She looked around but saw no one. No second shot sounded.

"Whoever it was is obviously gone now, the careless idiot," Rachel said. "He might have shot one of us."

Christian remained tense, still scanning the area. He said quietly, "That *was* close."

Genevieve slid off her horse and went to inspect the rock in the wall. Among the debris she found a bullet. It had indeed come awfully close to hitting one of them. In fact, the bullet appeared to have shot right between her and Christian.

That could not be coincidental. If one of Wickburgh's men—or even Wickburgh himself—knew she was here and had taken a shot at them, Christian and Rachel were in danger.

She was no longer safe. Not here. Not anywhere. And neither were the Amesburys if she remained with them.

After they arrived home, she forced herself to make polite conversation and try to behave as if nothing were amiss. However, a great weight settled with increasing heaviness every moment. For the remainder of the day, she must behave as if nothing were amiss. Tonight, she'd leave and draw Wickburgh away from those she loved.

CHAPTER 15

As the shadows stretched long, Genevieve smoothed a wrinkle from her skirt, and cast another anxious look around. If only she could smooth out the knots tangling in her stomach. From the vantage point at the top of the hill, no rocks or trees nearby appeared large enough to afford a hiding spot to a gunman. Still, she felt exposed and vulnerable away from the cottage. And worse, Rachel and Christian were exposed and vulnerable to Wickburgh's cruelty.

Rachel exclaimed over some perfect specimen of something that looked exactly like three others she'd found that hour. How dear Rachel had become to her. Leaving her—leaving Christian—would tear out another piece of her heart, but she must leave tonight. They'd think she abandoned them and would think poorly of her. But she'd be protecting them by leading Wickburgh away.

Snap! Genevieve jumped. Silly. Rachel had only stepped on a twig. Remaining outside with a gunman in the area left her jumpy, but if she revealed her fears, the Amesburys would try to intervene. She must do and say nothing to give away her plans, or Christian would try to protect her, thus placing himself in harm's way.

As Rachel kept up a steady stream of chatter, not needing input from her, Genevieve searched the area again for signs of danger. For a blissful moment, she allowed her gaze to rest on Christian who sat behind an easel, painting the sweeping valley below them. Blue paint smudged his cheek, almost matching the brilliance of his eyes. He'd shed his tailcoat and donned a smock. It never failed to surprise her how he could be dressed to the nines so stylishly that Beau Brummell himself would be green with envy, and the next moment dress so casually while engrossed in painting.

With his attention so utterly focused upon his subject, she allowed herself the luxury of looking him over. It may be the last time she'd have the opportunity. The sunlight shimmered in his hair. His eyelashes shaded his eyes when he lowered them, but the brilliance of his blue eyes seemed to leap out the moment he raised them to the view. His long legs, muscular and hard from frequent riding, stretched out before him. A tiny scuff marred the toe of one of his Hessians, a flaw over which his valet would no doubt weep and immediately remedy. His oversized smock failed to hide the breadth of his shoulders or the muscles of his arms. She marveled that this powerful man possessed such a gentle spirit, and such a sensitive, artistic soul.

She glanced at Rachel, then back at Christian. Both threw themselves wholly into their work. Were all the Amesburys so driven? So passionate? It left her breathless. And aching to throw herself into Christian's arms and rekindle what they once had.

She loved him. It was pointless to deny it. She loved him. And she'd do anything to protect him, even if it meant leaving tonight and never seeing him again. The thought smote her like a bullet in her heart.

"Do you see this?" exclaimed Rachel. "Amazing specimen."

Blinking back tears, Genevieve murmured a reply though Rachel required none. Rachel was an oddity, as well. The daughter of an earl, beautiful, intelligent, yet she sequestered herself away in the Scottish border engrossing herself in the study of plants. Rachel wore a serviceable gray gown not unlike her own, in total disregard for her social position. Her hair was twisted carelessly into a knot at the nape of her neck, several strands of her sable brown hair falling out haphazardly, and a broad-brimmed hat that looked at least a decade out of date perched upon her head. Only the pearl hat pin gave credence to her rank and position.

Rachel scribbled madly upon her papers and then sat back with a satisfied grunt. She grinned in an irrepressible way that reminded Genevieve of Christian.

"A most successful afternoon," Rachel announced.

"I'm so gratified to hear it."

"I'm hungry. It must be time for supper."

"Indeed." In truth, Genevieve's twisting stomach made the prospect of food unappealing, but she'd say anything to get the Amesburys inside and safe, anything to find an excuse to pretend to go to bed early and leave.

The gunman might not plan to shoot at them again so soon after the last attempt. Dragging out the suspense, letting her own terror build before the next blow, was exactly the type of game Wickburgh enjoyed playing. Still, no need to remain in the open unnecessarily.

Rachel looked up at her, smiling impishly, and glanced at Christian. "I wonder if he'll notice if we leave him here."

Despite her heavy heart at the prospect of leaving, Genevieve managed a smile. "Has he noticed in the past when you've left him?"

"Not usually. Unless he smells food."

As they gathered up their supplies, Genevieve eyed Rachel. "May I ask you something of a rather personal nature?"

Rachel crossed her legs where she sat on the grass. "I consider you a friend. You may ask me anything you desire." A knowing look gleamed in her eyes. "You want to know why I haven't married."

"Is it that obvious?"

"I get asked that often."

"I can imagine. I mean, you're bright, lovely, the daughter of an earl, and no doubt well dowered. Surely you've had offers."

Rachel nodded. "I received seven marriage offers. I accepted two.

One was considered by my father to be . . . unworthy. The other proved himself to be so and I found myself obliged to cry off."

"Do you ever regret it?"

Rachel looked down at the papers in her lap. "I don't know. Sometimes I'm so lonely I think I'll shrivel up and blow away like dust. My parents were desperately in love. They were seldom apart. When Mama died, Father lost his will to live. We took him to the seashore and Bath and did everything we could to revive him, but he slipped a little further away from us each day."

The image of the elegant but sad Lord Tarrington she'd met a year ago drifted into her memory. Christian had been so solicitous, so concerned. In the end, he hadn't been able to save the parent with the broken heart and no will to live.

Genevieve put an arm around her and gave her a squeeze. "I'm sorry."

"I'm not sure I want to risk dying of sorrow if my husband dies. And then I see my sister Margaret and her ghastly marriage. Being alone is better than being miserably married, I think."

Genevieve understood that all too well.

Rachel fixed a piecing gaze upon her that Genevieve found trouble meeting. "Would you rather have been alone than married?"

Genevieve swallowed. "Than married to him? Yes, without a doubt. But there was another . . . ." She picked up the papers in Rachel's lap and scattered around, and neatly stacked them.

"Christian told me you knew each other in Bath?"

"Yes. I . . . I admit I'd entertained hopes of marrying him."

"But?"

"I found myself . . . obliged to marry another."

She flushed. Rachel would probably think Genevieve had dallied and become with child. Let her. It was better than having to reveal the horror of belonging to Wickburgh.

Rachel nodded absently. "Then there's Cole and Alicia. They are every bit as much in love as Mama and Father were. Jared seems equally happy with his Elise. But they all chose well. That makes a difference."

"If you were to meet someone now, someone wonderful, would you give up your freedom to tromp about the moor and make scientific notations in exchange for a husband and a family?"

Rachel leaned back on her hands. "I wouldn't marry a man who would ask me to give it up. He'd appreciate my fine mind." Her mouth twisted in self-deprecating humor. "I doubt such a man exists. But if I met such a man, I would probably marry him, even at the risk of losing myself so deeply that if he died, I might, too. It's probably better than living my whole life alone and childless." She cast an almost guilty look at Genevieve. "Underneath my scientific mind, I have a bit of a romantic in me, too. Not to Christian's extent, but it's there."

"He is very romantic. Everything he draws and paints is more beautiful than it is in truth. It's how he sees the world."

"He does. Among the cynics and the critics, his kind of optimism and idealism is refreshing, don't you think?"

Genevieve smiled. "I suppose it is."

"But he has a dark side, too."

She waited.

"He's desperately sad about our brother who died."

"Jason?"

"Did he tell you?"

Genevieve shook her head. "Only that he had a brother—Jason—who died in the garden."

"I'm surprised he told you that much. He won't usually speak of him, or that day. Perhaps someday he'll tell you the rest."

Sighing, Genevieve looked out over the valley and the sharply angled mountains that pointed downward and trying to memorize the view so she could recall it after she left. "I doubt he'll have the opportunity."

"You're very young," Rachel said. "Give your heart time to heal, but don't let it scar over. Heal whole, not broken. Heal well, instead of bitter. Keep your ability to love and receive love intact. You may yet meet someone who can be trusted to keep your heart safe."

Genevieve examined the wisdom that had come out of Rachel.

Rachel added, "You two are like moths fluttering around fire. You're irresistibly attracted, but neither of you dare draw too near for fear of being burned."

Genevieve closed her eyes and winced at the pain shooting through her heart. "You're far too perceptive."

A hand covered hers. "I am. It's one of my worst flaws."

Genevieve gave her a rueful smile. "But you're here nursing a broken heart, too, aren't you?"

A fleeting look of pain crossed Rachel's face. "A bit. It's been healing to have something in which to immerse myself. But Christian is right; it's time to leave. I look forward to doing some traveling. Then maybe I'll return home and face off Cole's widowed friends. Not accept any of them, mind you, just put them in their place." She grinned.

Christian got up and stretched. He turned and flashed a sunny smile. "I need food."

Genevieve went to him and peered over his shoulder at his paining. "It's magnificent. One of your better paintings, I think."

He tilted his head, examining his creation. "Truly?"

"Absolutely. You have a great talent."

"I've been telling him that for years," Rachel said.

They carried in all their things, put them away, and Genevieve carefully put Rachel's file of the day's notes on the desk where she could review them later tonight and organize them before dinner. Before she left. As she looked around the study, she took no small pride in the organization she'd wrestled out of its former chaos.

After dinner, Genevieve excused herself. "I'm tired tonight. I believe I'll retire now." The sun hung low in the horizon, but darkness remained at least an hour away. They probably thought she had taken ill for going to bed so early.

Rachel looked at her in concern and slowly nodded. Christian gave her a searching look, but Genevieve fled the room without looking at him.

She must pack and take food. What else? The prospect of riding alone through unfamiliar land sent a chill of fear through her, but it couldn't be helped.

Footsteps followed. "What is it, Jen?" Christian's voice chased her.

She continued walking to her room without looking at Christian who matched her pace. "I told you. I'm tired."

"You've been quiet all afternoon. Are you still angry with me, or is something else bothering you?"

Genevieve halted in the narrow passageway just outside her bedchamber. Though she'd planned all day to tell him nothing and leave, the idea of simply stealing away in the night with no explanation made her feel a thief. The last time she'd acted without considering including Christian had led to a year of grief. For them both. He probably didn't still love her, but her leaving without a word would hurt him again.

It was easier to take care of others than let them take care of her. She'd already relied on him too much. But at that moment, the load just seemed too heavy to carry alone. A lifetime of loneliness stretched ahead of her like an endless, dark tunnel. She couldn't do that anymore.

She turned slowly around. "I . . . I think Wickburgh is behind all this."

"All what?"

She drew a breath to steady her voice and sat on the edge of her bed. "The first night we stopped for dinner, I thought I saw one of Wickburgh's men."

Christian nodded. "I remember."

"The night we arrived here, there was a rose on my bed. At the time, I assumed Rachel or Mrs. Fletcher left it as a welcome. But Wickburgh used to leave me roses, sometimes . . ." she drew a breath. He'd often left them to try to soften her before paying a visit to her bedchamber, but more often he left them before he began some cruel new game.

His eyes opened wide. "The rose was here?"

She nodded. "Then today someone shot at us. I think he was shooting at you. It'd be just like him to hurt you to punish me."

He drew in a deep breath and let it out slowly. "How certain are you?"

"It fits his style."

He rubbed this thumb along his lower lip, his eyes darting back and forth as if reading something invisible in the air.

She touched his arm. "You and Rachel are in danger. I need to leave. I'll go tonight."

"Wait. Just wait. Let me think. I can take care of this." He paced the corridor and rubbed the back of his neck. The determination of his tone again reminded her of the image of a knight preparing for battle.

She held out her hands in helplessness. "I'm sorry to have endangered you both. I've been such a burden, and now this. But when I leave, you'll both be safe."

He rested his hands on her shoulders. "You're no burden." He smiled grimly. Almost instantly, his eyes softened, grew tender. He tucked a strand of hair behind her ear. "You're right; you must leave, but not alone. I'm going with you."

"No. Anyone who helps me will be in danger. And you've already done too much. Far too much."

"I won't let you face this alone. Don't leave, Jen. I will take you safely away. You and Rachel. We'll leave together. All of us. Tonight."

She shook her head. "He'll hurt you. Or Rachel."

"You are not going off alone to fend for yourself. I will protect you. Do you trust me?"

She let out a sob and nodded. "Yes, of course I trust you. But I'd never live with myself if something happened to you."

"Nothing will happen to me. I can protect all of us. And Rachel is a good shot, too." He tilted his head. "Can you shoot a gun?"

"No. But I'm willing to learn."

"Then I'll teach you." He took her by the hand and led her back downstairs. "Rachel do you have a small handgun?"

Rachel looked up from her notes. "No sleep, after all?" She grinned wickedly, no doubt assuming they'd been kissing. She sobered at their expressions. "What's wrong?"

"Your gun?" Christian prompted.

"I have Mama's gun. It's in my room."

"You have Mama's gun?" Christian said. "How'd you get it instead of Margaret?"

"She has the pearl-handled gun. I have the one that shoots straight."

Despite his concern, Christian chuckled. "Devious, Rachel. You applied to her vanity, didn't you?"

"I'm a better shot than she is. A gun like that would be a waste in her hands."

Genevieve said, "I would like to learn to shoot."

Rachel turned to her. "Would you? Excellent. When shall we start?"

Genevieve spread her hands. "Now, if possible."

"I'll get my gun."

Outside in a brilliant sunset, Christian and the coachman who'd driven them to Scotland walked the area scanning the hills, probably looking for hidden gunmen. When he was satisfied, Christian nodded to the coachman who took up a watchful stance.

"You should have told me sooner," Christian chided her. "We could have set a watch all along."

Genevieve only nodded, too worried to defend her actions. After returning, Rachel presented her gun. Christian showed Genevieve the loading process of packing down the powder and ball, and went through the basic mechanics. His hands were steady and sure, and each time his skin brushed against hers, a soft shiver of pleasure spread.

"Rifles are typically more accurate," Christian said. "But Mama's—

Rachel's gun—is uncommonly precise. It shoots as well as my rifle, and I searched far and wide for one of its precision."

"Christian is as obsessed about the fox hunt as he is the steeplechase," Rachel interjected from nearby.

Christian grinned. "Almost. With four older brothers looking down their noses at me, I had something to prove."

Jason. Someday she'd discover what happened to him.

"Actually," Christian said with a glance at Rachel, "I like the racing better than shooting. Getting the fox is almost anti-climactic after all the hard riding. You are right-handed, I believe?" he asked Genevieve.

"I write with my right hand."

"That will make it easier. I write with my left, but I shoot and fence with my right."

"Why?"

He quirked a rueful smile. "Because if I'm ever in a duel, I'd have the disadvantage of exposing too much of my body as a target."

She raised her brows. "Do you do much dueling?"

"No. But a gentlemen should always be prepared. Here."

An image flashed in her mind of the day Christian had burst into Lord Wickburgh's library to break up the wedding. He'd made some mention of meeting Wickburgh at dawn. Because of her. She shivered.

Standing beside her, Christian positioned the gun in her right hand, showed her how to steady it with her left. He slid a hand under her elbow and raised it. Again, warmth spiraled outward where he touched her.

"Line up your target with this notch," he pointed, "and the end of the barrel here." His breath whispered on her neck, stirring the stray hairs that had fallen out of her chignon.

Drawing a breath, she tried to focus on his words, rather than on his proximity. Oh, how she ached to lean against him! She lined up the notch with the small ridge at the end of the gun, then lined them up with the target that looked suddenly very small and far away.

"This particular gun doesn't have a bad kick," he added softly, "but all guns do have one to some extent."

"A kick?"

"As it fires, the gun will jump back. Keep a tight hold." He exhaled a smile. "Not that tight. Your knuckles shouldn't be turning white. Now, don't pull or jerk the trigger. Squeeze it. Take a breath and then squeeze. Gently."

After she let out her breath and drew in another, she squeezed the trigger. She jumped as the gun practically leaped out of her hand. Her ears rang from the shot and the hills echoed.

Christian smiled. "A good showing, for a first try."

"I didn't hit the target," she said in dismay.

"It takes practice."

He had her reload and fire until her shoulders began to ache and she begged for a respite. Taking up the guns, Christian and Rachel easily knocked off every target lined up along the stone fence. They jeered and taunted each other good naturedly while Genevieve sat on a rocky outcropping and watched, admiring Christian's fine form, and envying Rachel's confidence.

Remembering the mysterious gunshot, she glanced around but saw nothing except the men Christian had assigned to watch over them.

After the last target fell, Christian squatted down in front of her. He looked at her soberly and took her hand. "Don't be discouraged, it does take practice. You did very well." He smiled.

She wondered how it was possible that she could live in the same house with this man for days and still be reduced to a stammering miss every time he smiled. She should be accustomed to it by now.

When darkness fell, they went indoors, Genevieve's mind racing in a hundred different directions.

Rachel cast a sideways glance at her. "When is someone going to tell me what is happening?"

Genevieve glanced at Christian. He nodded. Rachel should know if she were to accompany them to wherever Christian planned to take her.

Rachel took her hand. "Genevieve, we're friends. You can confide in me."

Genevieve shivered and drew a breath. "I..." She began haltingly. "I'm not a widow. I left my husband. I tried to make it appear as if I'd perished." She glanced at Christian, wanting to cringe each time she recalled the shame of trying to take her own life. "But he's here. He wants me to know he's coming after me."

Rachel digested that in silence as she took a seat on an armchair. "Does he mean you harm?"

Genevieve nodded. "And anyone who gets in his way."

Rachel shook her head, her brows furrowed. "If he were here, wouldn't he just appear at the doorstep and demand that you return with him?"

"He loves to play cruel games. Taunts me, tries to make me feel safe and then he does something . . . horrible."

Rachel blinked as if unable to fathom her meaning.

"I left once before. He had me declared mad and locked me in the asylum."

Rachel gasped. Christian looked like he was about to put a fist through a wall.

As memories threatened to drown her, a heart-wrenching sob tore out of her. "After three days, I'd had enough of that horrible place and agreed to go back to him."

Christian pulled her into an embrace. Genevieve nestled against him like a frightened child. With his arms wrapped around her, he held her close. How she longed to stay there. But she couldn't. Every moment they remained here brought them all closer to danger. She stepped out of his arms.

Rachel took several deep breaths. "And this time you thought you'd escaped him?"

"I'd dared to hope that he'd believe me dead and not look for me. But he found me somehow. He left a rose on the bed, just like the kind he used to give me. And the bullet was meant for Christian, I'm sure of it. I need to leave here, draw him away from you."

"I already told you; you are not going alone." Christian's tone was final.

"Certainly not," Rachel sniffed. "We're friends and we'll stand together."

"I do agree we should leave," Christian said. "We're too exposed out here. We'll go to London and find a safe place to stay while I work on a way to draw him out."

Genevieve fisted her hand in his sleeve. "No, Christian. He'll hurt you."

"You said you trust me."

"I do."

"Then stop worrying," he said in a low voice. "All will be well."

"I worry for your safety. You and Rachel. You are in danger, too."

"We can handle ourselves." The arrogant lift to his head made him look as lordly as his brother the earl.

Rachel patted the gun in her hand, a cocky grin tugging at the corner of her mouth. "We're friends, Genevieve. We're staying by you."

Christian exchanged a meaningful look with Rachel, then looked down at Genevieve. A fierce and possessive light entered his eyes. "I will not let him hurt you. He will have to find a way around me before he can touch you."

Tears stung her eyes. "That's what has me so frightened."

Rachel gave her hand a squeeze. "I'll pack and make arrangements for the rest of my things to be sent home."

"I'll pack as well." Genevieve went to her bedchamber. Her gaze landed on a gold ring glimmering on her nightstand.

A wedding band.

Her wedding band.

She stumbled backward. Panic robbed her of all coherent thought. A scream burst out of her. She staggered backward, stumbled, and fell onto her knees. Her lungs closed over. She looked wildly around, expecting Wickburgh to burst out from behind the furniture.

Christian charged in. "What is it?"

She pointed.

He looked at the ring, his eyes widening. "Yours?"

Nodding, she stuttered, "I-I t-took it off b-before I j-jumped into the r-river." Blinding waves of terror drowned her.

His breath came out in a loud expel. He rubbed his thumb across his lower lip.

Christian pulled her into his arms while she fell apart. He held her without speaking, smoothing his hand over her hair. He was strong and solid and safe. She clung to him as if her sanity depended upon it. She tottered at the edge of a cliff with a wind pushing from behind, and only a tenuous finger-hold protecting her from falling.

Christian's voice pulled her away from the edge. "I'm here, Genevieve. I won't let him hurt you."

Rachel's voice sounded next to her. "What's happened?"

Christian pointed to the ring. "Her wedding ring. She left it behind but it's here now."

Rachel let out an unladylike exclamation. "He wants you to know he's here."

"He'll torment me like this before he actually strikes." And he'd strike first at Christian or Rachel.

Christian took command. "We're leaving. Now. Pack very few things."

Genevieve reluctantly left the circle of his arms and with trembling hands, placed a satchel on the bed.

"I'm almost finished," Rachel said.

Christian and Rachel strode out.

Taking only the necessities, Genevieve gathered as much as she could take in her satchel. How could she get away without Wickburgh discovering her? There seemed no place she could go where he wouldn't find her. And now she'd put Christian and Rachel in harm's way. She should have left on her own without getting them involved.

If Wickburgh hurt them, Genevieve would never be able to live with her conscience.

Christian reappeared in her doorway moments later. "Here." He tossed her a pair of breeches. "They belong to my valet. The footman and one of the outriders are going to wear yours and Rachel's cloaks and take the family coach deeper into Scotland with the stable hand and one outrider. The three of us will leave together on horseback and you and Rachel will ride astride like men." He took a step closer and touched her cheek. "Know this; I will not allow you to face him alone. We all go together."

She almost threw her arms around him. Instead, she nodded. After he left, she struggled into the shirt, breeches, and coat.

The family coach left moments later with two footman wearing cloaks riding inside and an armed rider alongside. Christian, Genevieve and Rachel, all wearing breeches, dark woolen coats, and hats pulled down low, met outside the house. The coachman stood holding the reins of four horses. Nearly paralyzed with fear that so many lives were in danger because of her plight, Genevieve glanced around, half expecting Wickburgh to leap out at them. But that wasn't his style. He'd pick them off, one at a time. She only hoped the cover of growing darkness would protect them.

Christian gestured to the coachman. "Harrison is a good shot. He will ride with us and watch our backs," Christian explained.

She nodded. She trusted Christian. The grim warrior who stared back at her looked fully capable of far more than a gentleman's duel. He looked capable of anything.

CHAPTER 16

Riding between Rachel and Genevieve, Christian glanced back. Harrison rode behind them, his shoulders slumped and his mouth pulled tight as if in pain. The darkened road lay empty beyond. Evening shadows lurked like monsters awaiting a kill. The wind whispered in the trees like voices plotting their demise. Sweat poured down Christian's back despite the chill stinging his face. They pushed their horses as fast as they dared on roads still muddy from recent rains.

After riding all night and day, they'd reached a point of exhaustion he feared would make them careless. As they urged their mounts along the tree-lined highway, darkening shadows lay deep over the road. They rounded a bend and headed to the stable of the posting inn.

Dressed as boys in breeches and coats, with hats pulled down low over their eyes, Rachel and Genevieve lifted their heads. Dark circles lined their eyes standing out against pale faces.

"We're stopping for the night." Christian said. "We cannot keep up this pace."

No one argued.

After securing stalls for the horses and a private room for them to share for the night, Christian led the exhausted women inside. He gestured to Harrison. "I want you inside our room to guard the door."

Harrison hesitated, clearly uncomfortable crossing the lines of social class, but obeyed Christian's request. After a servant lit a lamp and the fire, he left without giving them a glance.

As Christian bolted the door, Rachel sank onto the large four poster bed, and Genevieve collapsed onto a chair by the hearth. Christian glared at the narrow settee by the window. Perhaps he'd be more comfortable on the floor than that small excuse for a couch. Within minutes, deep breathing of slumber filled the room. Christian went to the window and tested the lock. It held securely. Surely no one would notice four shabbily dressed, road-weary males and consider them ripe for the plucking. Harrison took up position in front of the door and fell asleep instantly.

Genevieve sprawled on a wingback chair. In sleep, her head lolled to one side, her face serene, her dark lashes kissing the smooth ivory skin of her cheek. Even with her hair flattened out by the man's hat and with strands that had worked loose from her chignon in complete disarray, she was lovely. His fingers itched to touch her face.

Emotions that he'd locked away when she'd left him pounded on the door to his heart, demanding to be set free. At that moment, he couldn't remember why letting them out to run their course would be wrong.

She sighed in her sleep and her hand twitched. He really ought to wake her and get her to bed rather than let her sleep in such an uncomfortable position.

He touched her arm and whispered, "Jen."

She stirred and blinked up at him. "Is it morning already?"

He whispered, "No. Go sleep on the bed."

"Mmhmm." She yawned but made no move, and within seconds, her eyes fluttered closed again and her breath deepened.

She looked so small and vulnerable that his heart squeezed. "Jen."

She stirred, but this time, didn't wake. He should leave her there. He shouldn't touch her. Each time he did, he risked opening up his heart to her and releasing all those old feelings. But if she stayed in that position, she'd be stiff and sore in the morning. Besides, he wanted to hold her, if for but a moment.

Sliding his hands under her, he carefully lifted her into his arms. She snuggled in against him. He carried her to the bed and lay her next to Rachel.

Her eyes fluttered and she caught his hand. "I love you," she murmured. "Always loved you..." She snuggled into her pillows and slipped into the rhythmic breathing of a deep sleeper, her face serene.

Christian stood with fists clenched. His world tilted and he struggled to find his place in it.

She loved him. He fought to bring air into the void in his lungs. She loved him. The locked door in his heart burst open and all the passion, protectiveness, and love he'd ever felt for her came pouring out like an ocean wave. She loved him.

And he loved her. He'd always loved her.

He'd get to the bottom of whatever had coerced her into marrying Wickburgh and find a way to free her. Most of all, he'd ensure Wickburgh got what he deserved.

Christian lay in front of the window, tensing at every sound. But no one touched their door. He finally slept.

When they left at first light, Rachel sidled her horse up to his. "What are you planning on doing in London?"

"Let a house where she'll be safe and hire a garrison of men to help me protect her."

"That's not a permanent solution."

"No."

Rachel searched his face and drew in her breath sharply. "You're going to challenge him, aren't you?"

He glanced back at Genevieve next to Harrison. She rode with her head bowed, her eyes shadowed with lack of sleep. "I hope it doesn't come to that. But I'm not convinced it was I who was his target. I think he was shooting at her."

"Doesn't he want her back?"

"I think he's realized he's lost her. And he's decided that if he can't have her, he won't let anyone else have her, either. If he wants me dead, it would only be to torture her first."

"He knows about you two, then?"

"He knows we were all but engaged in Bath. He must have assumed she came to me when she left him and knew to follow us."

"Chris, I know you and Grant are barely on speaking terms . . . ."

He tensed, anticipating her next words.

"... but I really think you should ask for his help."

He shook his head. The idea of asking Grant for anything made him want to smash something. "I can protect her. I'll hire help, if need be. I know men whom I can trust."

"Grant has contacts in the underworld and he may already know of a safe place where she can stay. It will take time for you to find help, but he can get men together on a moment's notice."

"No, Rachel. I am not asking that churlish, earth-vexing cretin—"

"Not even to protect her?"

Every nerve in his body skidded to a stop. Protecting Genevieve was more important than anything. But he could keep her safe. He didn't need help from Grant.

"He's the best, you know he is," Rachel said softly. "And despite all that's passed between you, you managed to work together to save Jared. Won't you work together again?"

He took a deep breath and let it out slowly. He didn't dare risk both Rachel's and Genevieve's safety merely to spare his pride. Rachel was right; Grant had so many contacts that he could probably raise a small army in an hour. Christian should know better than to cause delays that might risk their lives because of his bone-deep animosity toward Grant. Perhaps he should enlist Grant's help.

But could he trust Grant? He dabbled so much on the wrong side of the law, not to mention his already dark nature, that he might have become the kind of criminal he helped track down. Add to the mix how much Grant and Christian despised each other, and he wasn't sure Grant wouldn't prefer putting a knife in Christian's back or hurt Genevieve just to spite him.

No, that was unfair. Grant and Christian had worked together to help Jared only a few weeks ago. Ultimately, it was Grant's final intervention that saved Jared more so than Christian's. Moreover, his sisters and his sisters-in-law seemed to trust Grant, and Christian had learned long ago to trust feminine intuition. He couldn't really believe Grant would hurt any woman, despite his grumbles about the worthlessness of the fairer sex. Nor did he truly think Grant meant Christian any real harm. At least, not anymore.

He gritted his teeth and made up his mind. "Very well," he said to Rachel. "I'll send word to Grant the moment we arrive in town."

She nodded, satisfied and slowed a bit to ride next to Genevieve.

Christian let out his breath slowly, vowing to set aside his lifelong feud with Grant temporarily, at least. Protecting Genevieve was worth any cost.

CHAPTER 17

Christian paced in a private sitting room of the Nerot's Hotel in London. Grant's reply had promised he'd meet Christian at the hotel at five o'clock that afternoon. Though Grant was not technically late, it irked Christian to wait. But then, almost anything involving his brother irked him. Grant seemed to bring out the ire in most people. It might be Grant's smug superiority. Or his lack of a heart.

The mantle clock ticked, each second an invisible predator watching for a moment to strike out at Genevieve. The carpeted floors muffled his footsteps as he paced. He paused, his gaze resting on a rather good oil painting. Christian noted the techniques used, criticized the lighting, and then resumed his pacing. Filtered sunlight slanted in through the lace curtains at the windows where dust motes twirled. Where the devil was Grant?

Genevieve and Rachel slept upstairs, guarded only by Harrison. Every minute Christian waited downstairs left them vulnerable with only one man to guard them from Wickburgh. He glanced at the clock again. His brother was now two minutes late. It was just like Grant to torment him even now when the situation was so grave. Christian rubbed his hands over his face, the stubble on his unshaven jaw making a scraping noise. Fatigue taxed his patience. Each second, Christian's ire rose until he thought he'd explode.

Christian turned to glare at the door and then jumped. Grant stood in the threshold, utterly still, wearing that familiar, taunting expression that shouted he scorned everything about Christian.

"I hate when you sneak up on me like that," Christian grumbled.

Grant eyed him. "You look terrible."

Christian let out a weighty breath. "No doubt. We rode hard."

"If you're worried about security, you should be; even dressed like this, I got in without trying."

"It's a hotel, you fool, not a secured house."

Still, Christian chilled at the thought. All in black and cut from cheap cloth, Grant's clothes were more fitting for chasing footpads and cutthroats in the seedier parts of London than calling upon family in a respectable hotel. The long, ragged scar down the side of Grant's face only added to his fearsome appearance. All he needed was an eye patch to make a convincing pirate. And Grant was right; if a man dressed like a thug got in, surely Wickburgh or his lapdogs could, too.

"That's why I asked you to come," Christian said. "I need a safe place and some guards."

"How kind of you to bestow your righteous presence upon me. Decided to associate with the devil today, did you?" Grant taunted.

"No, just his favorite minion," Christian shot back, his temper rising. Why had he thought asking for Grant's help would be a good idea?

"Flatterer."

"There's something terribly wrong with you. Besides your taste."

Grant looked bored. "Oh, a fashion insult. I'm wounded. Truly."

"Are you going to help me or not?" Christian snarled.

Grant snapped into business form. "I am. Three of the best have agreed to guard her. I assured them you'd be most generous."

Christian waved away the cost. "Of course. But it will need to be round the clock."

"Which is why I've hired three."

"I'll be with her constantly, as well."

One eyebrow lifted. "Constantly?"

"Well, no, not at night." Heat rose up Christian's neck.

"No, of course not. Not you."

Christian glowered at the inferred insult regarding his purity. Grant knew nothing about him, but Christian wasn't about to enlighten him. "She's a lady," he ground out.

"Uh-huh."

"And she's married."

"Uh-huh."

"I am not having this discussion with you!"

"What discussion?"

Christian let out a sound of exasperation. "How soon can your men come?"

"They await you in the foyer."

Christian cursed him. "Why didn't you tell me?"

One corner of Grant's mouth twitched in suppressed amusement, or at least as close to amusement as Grant ever got. Tormenting younger brothers seemed the only thing Grant found amusing.

"Perhaps you should tell me the whole story rather than the cryptic message you sent me."

Christian sat, too weary to argue. Grant sat across from him and studied him with a disconcertingly piercing manner.

Beginning with meeting Genevieve at the house party at year ago and ending with their arrival in London, Christian told him the entire tale. Grant listened without expression or comment until Christian finished with, "… we came here to find a place where she can be secure until I can deal with Wickburgh."

"So, despite the news of her death in the papers, Lady Wickburgh is alive and in hiding—with you."

Christian paused. "Her death was in the newspapers?"

"Only last week. Apparently, they had enough evidence that she perished in a river near Castle Tarrington to declare her dead."

Christian turned over the implications. "He decided to announce her death only after he learned she was with Rachel and me." Which meant, Wickburgh had nothing to lose by killing her. He rubbed his hands over his face. He'd have to act quickly to save her.

Grant's voice broke into his thoughts. "Where is she now?"

"Upstairs with Rachel."

Grant straightened. "You dragged Rachel into this?"

As his fatigue and tension sapped his control, Christian fought to keep from shouting. "What do you think I should have done? Leave her all alone in that cottage? Wickburgh might have gone after Rachel out of revenge."

The brow quirked again, and a light of approval shone in Grant's cold, gray eyes. Christian almost choked. Approval? That had to be a first.

Grant's mouth lifted up on one corner. "I didn't suspect you capable of guessing what a dangerous man might do in retaliation."

"Yes, yes, I know; you think me too stupid to have considered it."

"Not stupid. Just naïve." His condescending tone twisted Christian's stomach.

Christian glowered at him. "You know nothing about me."

"If he's that dangerous, do you want me to kill him and be done with it?"

Christian choked at Grant's flat tone. He was serious. "What the devil . . . ? No, Grant. You can't just kill him, sorely as I'm tempted."

"It would solve everyone's problem."

Slowly, Christian shook his head in disbelief. "You are a scary, scary man."

"Thank you."

"Besides, he's a peer. One can't go about murdering peers without attracting attention."

"He sounds like something that lives under a rock."

"That's far too flattering for what he is."

Grant turned thoughtful. "This all started a year ago . . . is he responsible for the scar?" He tapped his temple and made a loose gesture to Christian's face.

Christian touched the mark on his own temple. “He hired some ruffians to give me a warning. One stuck a knife in my ribs and they left me for dead.”

Grant swore and made a reference to Wickburgh’s questionable parentage. The idea that Grant would be angry for his sake left Christian off balanced. They fell silent and Christian almost wished he could follow Grant’s idea of simply killing Wickburgh; it was the only way Genevieve would be safe.

He shivered, appalled at himself for having even considered murder. Of course, it wouldn’t be murder if he followed the Gentleman’s code and dueled him. Wickburgh might simply refuse, of course, but if he called him out in a public place, say White’s, he’d have witnesses and Wickburgh would be branded a coward if he refused.

Grant watched him. “I could make the murder look like a robbery.”

Christian gaped at him.

Grant laughed darkly. “You actually thought I was in earnest.”

“I’ve never pretended to understand you. I always assume you’re evil personified. It simplifies everything.”

“Indeed.” He smirked and Christian braced himself for whatever was coming. “It is rather delicious that the ‘perfectly perfect Christian’ has fallen for a married woman. Of us all, you are the last one I expected to be contemplating adultery.”

Christian growled, “Are you finished interrogating me? I’d like to meet your fellow cutthroats.”

“One’s a Bow Street Runner. The other two are retired Marines.”

“Do you know of a place where she can stay where she can be protected?”

Grant nodded slowly. “I’m surprised you didn’t take her to Tarrington House when you arrived in London.”

“If the husband knows she’s with us, he’ll easily learn where our properties are located.”

Grant lifted a brow. “Astute of you, I must say.”

He ground his teeth at the constant barbs Grant threw at him. Grant watched him with that penetrating stare that used to make Christian squirm. At the moment, he was too tired to care. Or simply immune after a lifetime of Grant's onslaughts.

Finally, Grant said, "Yes, I know of a few places. I'll make the arrangements." He rose and gestured for Christian to follow.

In the foyer outside the sitting room, three men stood silently. Two looked like pugilists. The third was leaner, taller, but equally formidable. Christian's step faltered as he recognized the taller one. Connor Jackson, a Bow Street Runner. Christian had encountered him a few years ago. He exchanged a brief nod with Jackson. All three men carried enough visible guns and knives to arm a small military regiment.

"Christian Amesbury, meet Connor Jackson, Sean McCullen, and John Barrow."

Christian inclined his head in greeting and motioned to them to enter the sitting room. Once they entered, he closed the door.

Grant began briefing them. "Your charge is Lady Wickburgh. Her husband wants her dead. He's already told the world she's dead, so he has nothing to lose by killing her. He's ruthless, cunning, and resourceful. You are not to allow anyone to approach her unless my brother or I give approval. We'll divide up time to be on guard while she's here. But when she leaves the premises, at least two of us will accompany her at all times. And we must assume anyone with her is also a target."

As the others nodded, Christian asked, "How soon can we secure the house?"

Grant's silver gaze flicked to him. "We can move her tonight once I've finalized the arrangements. You rest."

Christian stared at the rare gesture of humanity from the brother who'd always hated him. Too tired to needle Grant about it, he nodded and led the guards upstairs.

In the corridor, he gestured to Genevieve and Rachel's room. "Lady Wickburgh and my sister are in there."

Jackson took up post outside the door and gave Christian a reassuring nod. McCullen and Barrow disappeared in opposite directions down the corridor.

Christian stepped closer to the Runner and lowered his voice. "I didn't know you were back in England or I would have asked for your help directly."

Jackson glanced at Grant as if to say Christian was right to send for Grant. "I'm here now."

"I have a special assignment for you."

Jackson raised his brows.

"Find a replacement for this position and get hired on as one of Lord Wickburgh's bully-boys. Wickburgh is bound to show up in London sooner or later, and when he does, I want you already in place."

Jackson nodded slowly. "Word on the street is that he hires pugilists and former military men."

"You'll be perfect, then."

Jackson glanced behind Christian at Grant briefly before his gaze returned to Christian. "I know someone who can take my place. I'll send word to him and then apply for employment with Wickburgh."

It never ceased to surprise Christian how Jackson spoke like a well-born gentleman when he clearly came from the streets. One of these days, he'd learn the man's history.

Christian stepped inside his bedchamber with Grant following him. A tiny smile tugged at one corner of his brother's lip.

"You know Jackson, then?" Grant began a methodical search of the room to be sure it was secure.

Grimacing at the way Grant always moved like some kind of heathen assassin, Christian sat on the edge of the bed and struggled to remove his boots. "He helped me with something in the past."

Grant raised his brow but didn't comment on that. "It's a good plan, having Jackson on the inside." He grabbed Christian's boot and twisted it off. Then the other. "Sleep. We'll keep watch." Silent as a ghost, he stepped through the door and closed it.

Christian fell backward onto the bed without arguing. It seemed only moments later when he awoke with a start. He bolted up, listening. All remained still. Outside the windows, the setting sun cast the room in deep shadows. The usual street noises of Town tickled his ears—carts, horses, the clang of a bell. Still fully clothed, he climbed out of bed and opened the door. In the corridor, Grant and Jackson stood together talking quietly.

Grant turned. "The secure house is prepared. We'll take the three of you there when you're ready. Barrow and McCullen are there now."

"All of us? I had thought to take up residence at my usual bachelor's rooms."

"It would be easier to guard you if you are all in the same place."

Christian stiffened. "I don't need a guard."

"Everyone needs someone to watch his back. If you split up, he might target you. Can't have that, now can we?"

Speechless at Grant's concern for him, Christian stared. For years, he half expected Grant to shoot him in the back. To have Grant protecting him was beyond strange. Then again, they were brothers. Apparently, that meant something to Grant, regardless of their estrangement. Or maybe this was just business to him. And the thought of staying close to Genevieve to ensure she was safe held great appeal.

Jackson glanced at Christian. "My replacement will arrive tomorrow."

Rachel opened the door and blinked at them. "Grant? What are you doing here?"

Grant's mouth pulled into a semblance of a smile. "Protecting you and your secretary, as it were."

Rachel gave him a doubtful smile before launching herself at him and throwing her arms around him. "You're always there when we need you."

Grant patted her back, cleared his throat, and stepped back as soon as he could disentangle himself from so much sisterly affection.

The door opened wider and Genevieve looked out, her eyes

round. She'd bathed and changed from the boy's breeches she'd worn during their flight to London into a simple cotton gown. Lines of worry cut underneath her eyes.

Christian held a hand out to her. "Genevieve, come meet my brother Grant. He and some friends are helping us."

Grant, to his credit, affected a respectful bow. "My lady."

Christian introduced her to Jackson who kept his expression schooled in respect, but the light of appreciation shone in his eyes as he gazed at her. Christian gave him a warning stare, and Jackson pointedly removed his attention from Genevieve.

Christian squeezed Genevieve's hand. "We're moving to a secure location. How soon can you leave?"

"In a few moments." Her voice sounded steady, filled with quiet determination.

After returning to his room, Christian threw his few belongings into a bag. He ran his fingers through his tangled hair and wished for a shave but had no time for grooming. Less than ten minutes later, the women emerged wearing hooded cloaks and carrying valises. Genevieve glanced at Christian with trusting eyes.

He squeezed her hand and whispered, "Everything will be all right."

Followed by a watchful Grant, a porter took the bags and placed them into a waiting hackney coach outside the hotel. Christian gave an arm to each of the ladies and led them out. Jackson and McCullen followed behind, tense and watchful.

Outside, they descended the hotel's steps as fog rolled in. It roiled knee-high as they moved, muffling the clatter of coaches and the clopping of horse hooves. Lamplights cast an eerie glow over the scene. A group of men laughed raucously on the opposite side of the street. A breeze carried the pungent odors of the Thames and piles of manure in the streets that had yet to be cleared away. Genevieve held onto Christian so tightly that her fingers dug into his arm.

In silence, they crowded together inside the coach. The warmth of Genevieve's body next to him and her fragrance taunted him as if to remind him of what he couldn't have. He pushed that back. He needed to focus on keeping her safe.

The coach wound through the streets and stopped in front of an understated townhouse. Grant and Jackson leaped out of the coach before it had even stopped. They prowled around and looked up and down the streets. McCullen disappeared into the fog.

Christian paused, the hackles of his neck standing up. Surely Wickburgh hadn't arrived yet; the decoy carriage he sent from Rachel's cottage would have led him to Wales. But he couldn't shake the dark urgency that whispered Genevieve was in danger, and Rachel, too, by association.

After settling into their rooms and enjoying a well-prepared dinner, they met in a cozy library but the conversation lagged.

Grant arose. "I'm going to sleep now. I'll relieve McCullen in a few hours."

Rachel, too, mumbled a good night and left Christian alone with Genevieve. She sat hugging herself, staring into the fire.

Unable to resist, Christian moved to the settee and sat next to her. "Grant and his lads know what they are doing. And I'm here. Wickburgh won't get near you."

"But for how long? How long can we keep this up?"

"Until we can make him see that he needs to let you go."

"He won't."

"He'll have to."

"He'll hurt you and anyone who stands in his way."

Lightly, he traced her cheek. Her mouth parted slightly and her gaze turned intense. Hot need burned through his defenses. He brushed a finger across her cheek and traced the delicious curve of her lower lip. He leaned in, his hungry gaze fixed upon her mouth. Cradling her face, he lifted her chin up to him. Her hand touched his chest and slid upward to rest on his heart. Raising her chin toward him she leaned in.

Then she caught her breath and her body went rigid. She pushed him away.

Her reaction snapped him out of his fog of desire, and stark realization knifed through him. He couldn't dally with Genevieve. She deserved better. And it went against his principles to touch a married woman. He dropped his hands and leaned back.

Letting out her breath, she also moved away. He swore under his breath and dragged a hand through his hair. He'd almost made a mistake. She was not free.

"I'm sorry," he said hoarsely. "That was inappropriate."

She offered him a pained smile. Slowly, he raised her hand and pressed his lips against the soft skin. She held her breath, her eyes wide and watchful, cautious, wary.

Did she fear his touch? No telling what her husband had done to her to make her flinch each time he got close to her. But he had a pretty good idea.

He touched her cheek gently as a craving, burning need to protect her and love her as a man flamed brighter and hotter while another, even less honorable emotion joined in. Wickburgh had stolen the only girl Christian had ever loved, and abused her. The passion coursing through him flowed into a lake of anger filled with the uncharacteristic desire to find her husband. And kill him.

CHAPTER 18

In a sunny sitting room, Genevieve set down the book in her hands. Her thoughts swirled too loudly in her head, drowning out everything she tried to read. She felt safe here, but it was only temporary. Soon this standoff with Wickburgh would have to end. She only hoped it didn't end with Christian dueling him. They'd fight to the death, of that she had no doubt. Though Christian excelled at both swords and pistols, the idea that he'd put his life in such danger for her made her blood chill. She couldn't lose him, not again.

Christian strode in. Her heart gave an excited little leap. Despite the danger looming over all of them, seeing him never failed to warm and calm her. She could no longer deny that she loved him as much today as she loved him in Bath—perhaps even more now that she knew him better and had seen the lengths he went to protect her.

Oh, how it had pained her to push him away last night. But he deserved better than an affair with a married woman. No matter how much she abhorred her husband, she wouldn't cheapen her love for Christian.

Though he smiled, something serious simmered behind his eyes. He closed the door and took a seat next to her. "If I ask you a direct question, will you give me an honest answer?"

Her mouth went dry. He wanted the truth—all of it. "If I can."

For a moment, the only sound came from the ticking of the clock and the street noises outside as he visibly tried to organize his thoughts. "We had something in Bath. Something real."

Indeed it was real. Her memories of his love had helped her survive those dark nights as lord Wickburgh's wife. And she'd thrown such love away. But she'd done it to save her family. As much as it pained her, and obviously hurt Christian, she'd made the right choice. Still, the ache of losing him never went away. A hard knot formed in her stomach at all their lost opportunities.

He opened his hand out to her in a gesture of supplication. "I know you made some kind of vow of silence, but I need to know what we're facing. How did he force you to marry him? What was his leverage?"

Her voice froze in her throat. "I . . ." weariness tugged at her resolve. She'd carried this secret for so long, and the burden had been so heavy that she ached to let Christian share the load. But her father's reputation was at stake, even his very life.

"Jen?"

She let out a labored breath. If she told him, what would be the worst he'd do? Despite her earlier fears, he'd never report her father's crime to the admiralty or tell anyone else. Nor would he use the information to hurt or harass their family. And marrying him was out of the question, so she had no need to fear he'd reject her.

He leaned in. "You can trust me, Jen."

A sob tore out of her and she put a hand over her mouth. Of course she could trust him. No more honorable man ever lived. He'd never hurt her. He'd take her secret to the grave. She took a shaking breath and rubbed perspiring palms on her muslin day gown. She kicked off her borrowed, too-big slippers, and tucked her feet underneath her. Finally, she met his gaze. His intensely focused stare remained fixed on her, pleading, coaxing.

"What happened in Bath?" he prompted.

Her words choked in her throat. But he was risking his life and the lives of his family to save her; she owed him the truth. She gathered her courage. "I did it to save my parents."

He nodded and waited. Outside, a flower girl called out to passersby, a wagon rattled passed, and horse's hooves clopped in the street.

She moistened her lips. "He knew something bad about my father and was blackmailing him. That day he came demanding marriage to me. He said if my father refused, he'd go to the authorities." All the pain, the anguish, the terrible sense of betrayal when she'd learned of her father's crime came marching back into her soul, trampling her heart, stamping out her future.

"I should have known." He put a finger underneath her chin and lifted it until she looked him in the eye. The soft affection in his gaze was almost enough to make her burst into tears. "You were too loving, too soft in my arms to have been lying, or to have suddenly decided to marry a lord instead of a youngest son."

"I would have married you had you been the youngest son of a blacksmith."

He caressed her cheek. "You can tell me everything. All your secrets are safe with me."

Emboldened, she plunged in. "Many years ago, when my father was the second lieutenant in the navy, the crew mutinied and killed the captain."

Christian waited patiently, listening without condemnation. "Go on."

"Papa looked the other way. He felt he was doing it to protect the crew from further cruelty. Apparently, Wickburgh's brother got sick years later, and on his death bed, wrote a confession. He mailed the confession to Wickburgh who used it to force my father to make me marry him. I still don't understand why he was so obsessed with me in the first place, but he clearly saw the confession as leverage to have me. I was terrified Wickburgh would report him and Papa would be court marshaled."

She opened up her hands which she'd clenched into fists and ran them over her skirts again, their moisture leaving dark smears. "If Wickburgh exposed Papa, not only would he hang for mutiny, but the news would have killed my mother."

Grimly, Christian nodded. "Her health is delicate, isn't it?"

She nodded.

"And all your father's property would have been seized which would have left her penniless as well as branded the wife of a traitor."

She paused. "You do understand."

He gripped her hand. His touch was warm and steady. "Why didn't you tell me? I would have helped you."

She curled her fingers around his. He was so much larger than she, so much stronger, and yet she had no fear that he'd hurt her. He'd do what he must to protect her, but would never harm the innocent. "I couldn't bring myself to tell you; I feared you'd be horrified by what my father had done, and perhaps feel obligated to report his crime to the admiralty."

He jerked back as if she'd struck him. "Do you really think I'd do that?"

"I wasn't sure, but regardless, I'm the daughter of a mutineer. I'm tainted by his crime. You deserve better. I was so amazed that someone as wonderful as you would consider marrying me, and feared that it was too good to be real. Then when I learned what Papa had done, I couldn't tell you. I was so ashamed. And I knew you'd be horrified."

He ran a hand through his hair. "I can't believe you didn't tell me. That you didn't trust me."

Tears stung her eyes. "I'm so sorry. I cannot tell you how many times I regretted hurting you. I suffered every day with the knowledge that I could have been with you. But I had to save my family."

"Jen . . . ."

"I know I should have gone to you. Trusted you more. Trusted our love more. But now it's too late." Tears fell and another sob ripped from her chest.

He gathered her into his arms and squeezed. She clung to him. If ever there was anything right in the world, it was being in Christian's arms. He brushed her tears away with gentle fingers. Her senses filled with his bay rum aftershave mixed with his very own earthy scent. He tipped her chin up. Love shone in his eyes. He ran a finger down her cheek and cradled her face in both hands. Slowly, he lowered his head. Her heart swelled and warmth flooded her body.

Unwilling to wait another second, she rose up and kissed him. His warm, soft lips tugged gently, exploring, tasting, teasing. She'd forgotten how gently he kissed, as if he cherished her above all else in the world. She wrapped her arms around him and kissed him as if she were dying of thirst and finally taking a drink of cool, clear water. He slid his arms around her, gathering her in close, deepening the kiss. She opened up to him and welcomed him into her heart. All thought fled and she slipped into a state of feeling. Him. Her. Their union.

He ended the kiss and held her close. They sat quietly, so still, as if afraid to break the warm peace enfolding them.

Her heart fluttered like a flame on a new candle and every nerve tingled. How long since she'd been held like this, by this amazing man who made her complete! She'd been a fool not to keep him in her life. Saving her parents was important, yes, but if she'd gone to Christian, together they would have found a way to help everyone. If only she'd trusted him more.

In Christian's arms, courage returned to her. With him loving her, she was a better, stronger person. She was finished running and hiding. She'd confront Wickburgh. She would free herself of him and find a way to be with Christian. And she'd never, ever let him go.

Finally, he spoke, "I shouldn't have done that."

She smiled. "I kissed you, remember?"

"I cannot say I regret it." He gave her a squeeze before pulling away. "I've wanted to do that for days." Then his smile turned pained. "But like it or not, you're still married."

He was right. Shame washed over her. She should have known better than to kiss Christian until she was truly free. "I know. You'd never have an affair with a married woman. You're far too honorable. It's one of the things I love most about you."

He gripped the back of his neck with one hand. "You give me too much credit. Despite that taunt of my brothers, I'm not perfect. Far from it."

"I'm not saying you're a saint, but you are a good man. And I'll try not to tempt you until I'm free."

He took her hand and kissed it. Then he turned it over and kissed the palm. "I love you."

She sucked in her breath, tears of joy filling her eyes. "Oh, Christian. I love you. I buried it deep inside, but I never stopped loving you."

"I vow I will not rest until we can be together." He kissed her hand again.

She gave a half laugh through her tears. "Is that a proposal, Mr. Amesbury?"

"No, not yet, but I plan to propose properly as soon as you are free."

"That sounds perfect." Again she vowed to free herself of Wickburgh and never let Christian go.

CHAPTER 19

Early the next morning, Christian prowled the house, looking out every window, checking every door, exchanging words with the guards. They couldn't live like this forever. Sooner or later, he'd have to ferret out Wickburgh and deal with him.

Grant was sleeping, and Genevieve was in the garden, guarded, of course. Still, perhaps he should ensure she was well. As he headed to the back door, it opened and Genevieve, followed by one of the guards, came in.

The chill early morning air had turned her cheeks pink and her eyes sparkled. She smiled so brightly that his heart flipped over. How he loved this woman!

He shouldn't have kissed her. Despite the circumstances that led to her marriage, despite the man she married being a monster, she was still married. And that was a boundary he should never have tried to cross. He made a silent vow not to kiss her again until she could be free to truly be his.

"Good morning." She took off her hat and smoothed her hair.

Smiling, he brushed a stray curl back from her face. "You look radiant."

She smiled. "I feel wonderful. Being here with you has turned me into a new person."

He smiled, aching to take her into his arms. He'd lain awake in bed the previous night remembering her touch, her kiss, and her words of love.

She moved within arm's reach and smiled up at him. Unable to stop himself, he touched her face. She was so soft.

Soberly, she looked up at him. "I've been doing a lot of thinking. I want to sue for divorce."

Christian let out a sigh of relief. "I'm so glad to hear that. Because today I'd planned to give you all sorts of reasons why you should do that very thing."

"I realize it will be long, difficult and scandalous, but I refuse to be subject to his bullying." Emotions played across her face—a darkening fear in her eyes, the resolute set to her chin. Standing up to the man who'd terrorized her for the past year was an act of admirable courage.

His mind raced. She could sue on grounds that she was coerced into marrying Wickburgh, but that would drag her father into it, and they didn't dare risk that. Not yet. There must be a way to help her father with that problem, too. Perhaps his friend at the admiralty who helped him manipulate the near hanging that saved Jared's life . . . .

"If I divorce him, it may taint you," she said. "Possibly the whole family."

"It won't matter as much as you think it will."

"Your suing for divorce will embarrass and infuriate Wickburgh," Grant's voice rang out.

Christian jumped. He hadn't even noticed Grant enter. He let out a sound of exasperation. "Don't *do* that."

Grant leaned against the wall with his arms folded, somehow still managing to look as if he were about to spring into action. "He'll lash out at you both and hang the consequences."

Christian raised his eyebrows as Grant voiced the very fears nagging at him. "You sound as if you know him well."

"He's mentally unbalanced, which means he's completely above logical behavior." He turned a piercing stare on Genevieve. "If you expose his lies, he'll have nothing to lose by killing you or dragging you home and torturing you in ways he has not yet explored."

The color drained from Genevieve's face. Silence descended upon the room. It was frightening, really, how well Grant understood ruthless men like Wickburgh. Christian suppressed a shiver and rested his hand on his gun. Wickburgh would never touch Genevieve. Not as long as Christian breathed.

Genevieve spread her hands. "Now what?"

Christian glanced at Grant and their gazes held. For probably the first time in his life, he could almost read Grant's thoughts; it would never be over, not as long as Wickburgh was alive.

Christian would have to duel Wickburgh after all. Too bad he couldn't simply beat the man with his bare hands. One way or another, Genevieve would be free from Wickburgh's tyranny.

CHAPTER 20

Genevieve sat quietly in the sun-drenched front parlor, her hands folded demurely in front of her while Rachel fingered swatches of material. The modiste gushed over Rachel's lovely hair and willowy figure in her fake French accent. Genevieve almost smiled. Many of the *haut ton* were so obsessed with French fashion that they insisted on a "French" modiste to create their wardrobes. Silly, of course. Their success ought to be due to their design and workmanship rather than whether or not they were French.

She glanced at Christian who sat at a secretary desk catching up on correspondence. He seldom left her side, a clear mixture of wanting to be near her and fearing to let her out of his sight for safety's sake.

Grant Amesbury's silver-gray eyes watched with an overt alertness even as he appeared to lounge casually. Although he'd been perfectly terrifying at first, there was something reassuring about his commanding, albeit formidable presence. The other guards seldom appeared, spending most of their time patrolling the area; they clearly protected her with diligence.

Outside, horses clopped past pulling rattling carts. Merchants called to shoppers to try their wares. A pieman walked by and the fragrant savory smells of pies wafted in through the open windows.

Rachel moaned as she gestured at fashion plates scattered around her. "I cannot believe how much fashions have changed since I left the city."

Genevieve shook her head in surprise that Rachel suddenly cared now that she was in London, after being so unconcerned about her appearance at her cottage. Perhaps being the daughter of an earl prodded her to make a good showing in London where she would be in the public eye, if nothing else, for the sake of the family image.

The dressmaker held up a new swatch. "Ah, mademoiselle, dees one, eet ees more flattering for your complexion, I think, *non*?"

"I like it but I'm still in mourning for my father. I'll take the lavender silk." Rachel tugged Genevieve's arm, drawing her to the bolts of fabric the modiste had brought. "Now you pick some. No companion of mine will be any less than the height of fashion." She fired off a list of gowns she considered absolute necessities.

Genevieve shook her head. "Oh, I don't need—"

Rachel held up a hand and affected a regal air. "We're in London, my dear, not the country. Here we must uphold an image." She smiled and rolled her eyes.

Genevieve closed her mouth and nodded. If she traveled abroad, she'd need some clothes. She acquiesced to the process of measuring, tucking and pinning. Since September was far from the London Season, the modiste had few other orders and she happily bustled about finding new things with which to tempt them. By the time they had finished, Genevieve had ordered far more than her wages would earn all year. Staring at the daunting pile, she began mentally choosing items she could order now and which to order later.

"Now, now. Nothing goes back. It's all part of room and board, you see." Rachel nodded emphatically.

"No, I–"

"No use arguing with her," Christian called from the desk. "You should know by now Rachel always gets her way." He leaned back, his blue eyes twinkling.

"Did you put her up to it?" Genevieve demanded.

"I take offense to that," Rachel interjected with an exaggerated huff. "I put him up to many things. He never puts me up to anything."

"Do, it, Jen. And be sure to send for the shoemaker so you can have a decent pair of shoes." He gestured to her feet.

She laughed softly and nodded. "Now that, I won't refuse."

Mentally adding these purchases to the list of money she owed the Amesburys, Genevieve capitulated. Somehow, she'd pay them back. They didn't need her money, of course, but she refused to take advantage of their kindness and be an object of charity.

After Genevieve ordered enough clothes to satisfy Rachel, the modiste and her assistant gathered up her swatches and drawings and after promising to bring a few of the more essential items for a fitting tomorrow, they left.

A footman came in carrying a letter on a silver platter and held it out to Christian. He tore it open, his expression growing grave as he read.

She set down the dress engraving she'd been examining and went to him. "Is something amiss?"

He smiled but something hidden darkened his eyes. "The solicitor replied to my inquiry. He said the divorce may not be final for a very long time, if ever. It's a lengthy process and ultimately must be approved by Parliament. As Cole mentioned, women are seldom granted divorces."

"I'll wait as long as it takes," Genevieve said. Even if she married Christian today, it wouldn't be soon enough.

She smiled at the thought, but he looked pained. Had he reconsidered and decided marrying a divorced woman would be too much scandal to bring to the family? After all, he had his siblings' reputations to consider. Or had he realized how broken she was and decided he didn't want used merchandise?

One of Grant's men darted in and gestured to Grant. Christian's brother leaped to his feet with the fluid grace of a panther and slipped out of the room. Christian stood, keeping his gaze trained on the doorway. After a brief exchange of words, Grant came in. With a mere glance, he and Christian seemed to have an entire conversation. Christian took up a defensive stance next to Genevieve. Their state of alert sent Genevieve's heart pounding.

Christian's gaze darted to the windows and he stood blocking her from the windows with his body. In one hand he gripped a gun that seemed to magically appear.

Rachel turned to him. "What is it?"

"Something has Grant's man alarmed." Christian's wide and darting eyes took in the room all at once while his hand gripped his gun with white knuckles.

"Well, I'm going to go find out what it is," Rachel announced.

"No, you're going to stay right here where I can protect you." Christian's grim voice left no room for argument.

Rachel folded her arms and glared mulishly at Christian, but kept silent. A dark foreboding curled in Genevieve's stomach. Wickburgh was here. He'd found her. She'd never be safe from him. Sooner or later, he'd cut through everyone in his way to get to her.

A moment later, Grant returned. "Lady Wickburgh—"

"Please," Genevieve broke in, "don't call me that. I'm just Genevieve."

Grant paused. "There's a white cat outside. It's been disemboweled."

Genevieve's stomach lurched and she put a hand over her mouth. "I had a white cat."

Her poor cat! She'd always been such a sweet little thing, always content to purr in Genevieve's lap—often her one companion when she felt so alone. Too bad she didn't think to find a new home for the poor little thing before she left Wickburgh.

"Next to it was this note." Grant held out the note but she didn't need to look closely to recognize *his* handwriting nor his style of torture.

Thinking of you, my dear.

Christian cursed under his breath.

All the strength left Genevieve's legs and she had to sit down quickly. All her courage fled. "He's here."

"How could he have found you so fast?" Christian muttered. He said firmly, "We're moving you to a new location."

"Fire!" shouted a distant voice. "The house is on fire."

A woman screamed and feet thundered on the stairs. A cacophony erupted as servants began running and calling to each other.

"Stay with her!" Grant shouted. "It's a diversion." He ran out into the great foyer.

Christian put one arm around her and hefted his gun with his other hand. "Let's get out of the house. Rachel, stay close."

As they strode toward the front door, tendrils of black smoke curled along the ceiling, filling the house with the pungent odor of smoke. Genevieve coughed as smoke thickened. Shouts and thundering footsteps erupted all around them. Christian led her outside into the late afternoon sunlight and down the front steps. She glanced back at the façade. Flames lapped at the side of the structure and smoke puffed upward to a growing dark cloud.

A bucket brigade lined up along the street and began throwing water on the blaze. Christian's gaze fixed on those working to save the house. She understood. She ached to help, too, but if Wickburgh had started the fire, he'd have men ready to spirit her away the instant she was left unguarded. Genevieve's heart pounded. All this senseless destruction. How much lower would Wickburgh stoop?

She had done this, too, by allowing the Amesburys to help her. They were all in danger. Next time it would be worse than a fire. Next time, he might try to hurt Christian or Rachel. That bullet in Scotland had probably been only a warning. The next one would be intended for Christian.

The heat of the flames blistered her face and they all took a few more steps back. The setting sun cast long rays over the landscape and made silhouettes out of the buildings. Rachel stood watching the blazing house, her mouth open and her eyes round with horror.

A wagon filled with men wearing the badges of fire fighters careened around the corner and pulled to a stop in front of the house. The horses pulling the wagon snorted and stomped but remained almost calm amidst the smoke and chaos as the firefighters worked a large pump. After checking the fire mark on the house to verify the owner paid for fire insurance, one man directed a hose toward the fire and held it steady as a stream of water poured out. Others ran to refill the trough of water inside the fire truck, sometimes stumbling over those in the bucket brigade.

Christian stiffened, vibrating with tension, his gaze fixed on something across the street. She followed his line of sight. A man wearing a long dark coat stood watching them, unmoving. Cold foreboding crept down Genevieve's spine. The man trotted down an alley. Christian tensed as if to give chase, but never left her side. A sickening crack sounded next to Genevieve's ear.

Christian grunted and fell onto his knees, his hand on his head. A man with a bulbous nose stood over him holding the butt of a pistol. Genevieve let out a cry. Christian brought up his gun and pointed it at his attacker. A third man with pocked skin appeared and grabbed Christian's gun, forcing it down. It discharged, the gunshot deafening her and the smell of gunpowder combining with smoke from the fire. All three leaped toward Christian. Unarmed, he fought them with his fists, landing several solid blows.

Fumbling for Rachel's tiny handgun she kept in her pocket, Genevieve rushed to his aid. Someone grabbed Genevieve's arm, swung her around and struck her hard. Pain exploded from her face. She staggered back but his bruising grip kept her from falling. A second gun fired. A woman screamed. Rachel? The assailant dragged Genevieve into an ally. Dark anger boiled up inside of her and she bit and kicked her attacker.

"None o' tha'," a male voice rasped, exhaling the pungent odor of old onions.

She kicked harder and dug her nails into his arm. He struck her face again and black spots exploded before her eyes. Dazed, she collapsed, dimly aware of being hauled into a darkened coach. Someone threw her onto the floor. She lay, dizzy and panting, staring at a pair of boots.

"Well done," said a familiar voice. "I will see you generously rewarded."

Pinpricks moved down her neck and spread across her arms. She knew that voice. Her husband. Lord Wickburgh. He leaned back against the seat cushions, eyeing her coldly. The coach began moving, taking her further away from Christian.

Pushing herself up on her elbows, she looked him in the face. She'd almost forgotten how cold his eyes were, like the stare of a reptile.

She glared. "I will not go home with you. Not now, not ever."

After taking snuff out of a box and inhaling deeply, he looked her over without a glimmer of emotion. "Genevieve, you wound me. After all I've done for you."

"Done for me? Abusing me, locking me away, killing my pets . . . ?"

"Disobedient wives must be punished just as disobedient children."

"Disobedient?"

"Surely you didn't mistake my necessary use of punishment for lack of caring? You know I loved you, don't you?"

She huffed a disbelieving laugh. "You never loved me."

He drew his brows together. "I loved you more than I ever thought I could love."

She didn't miss his use of the past tense form of the word love. Perhaps he was right; perhaps he loved the only way a twisted sick mind like his could.

She drew herself up. "I am not coming back."

He let out a sharp laugh. "What makes you think I want you back now? You've been a disappointment. And you've clearly cuckolded me. No, I no longer want you back."

Terror trembled in the bottom of her stomach. "What do you want?"

"Nothing much. You've become too much trouble. You won't do as you're told, you've run from me—twice. Keeping you has been more trouble than you're worth. Since you won't stay with me, I shall ensure that you will never be with anyone else, either." He flexed his fingers.

He didn't want her back.

He wanted her dead.

Cold fear crawled down her spine like a hundred spiders. "You can't kill me. If I turn up dead—"

"You are already dead. We . . . ah . . . *found* a body that I've identified as you and given a proper Christian burial. I announced your death in all the papers."

She closed her eyes. Her parents. They must be heartbroken! Was there no end to Wickburgh's cruelty?

It stopped right here, right now. She would no longer subject herself to him. She was a worthwhile human being who loved—and was loved by—a wonderful man. She didn't deserve this. She'd never let him hurt her again.

Genevieve made a desperate leap for the door and yanked on the handle. He grabbed her and delivered a bone-jarring blow. She crumpled to the floor of the carriage. Lord Wickburgh struck her again and then kicked her. After days of living with Rachel and Christian, with a total lack of fear and pain, she'd lost her earlier numbness to his beatings.

Christian. Her last glimpse of him had been of ruffians overpowering him.

He could be injured. Or dead. Oh, what had she done? She'd failed to protect the ones she loved.

CHAPTER 21

In the street, Christian fought with his attackers and landed a solid punch. Without warning, the thugs fled. He took a few running steps after them, but remembered Rachel. He ran back to her as she pushed herself up from the street.

"Are you hurt?" He picked her up, searching for signs of injury.

"No." Her eyes were narrowed in anger rather than fear or hurt.

He looked wildly around. "Genevieve!"

Only firefighters and a milling crowd near the house met his gaze. He looked out over the carts and horses in the streets but saw no sign of her.

"Someone took her. In a black coach." Rachel spat out the words.

Sick with dread, he scanned the area. A darkened alley to his left seemed the most obvious place. "Stay here," he commanded.

He darted into the alley. A few dirty children played in an otherwise empty area. He ran through it to a larger street at the other end. As he looked both ways, his heart shivered.

She was gone.

He turned at the echo of footsteps and fell into a defensive crouch. Grant, with Rachel right behind him, ran to him.

"I caught one, but he was a diversion," Grant growled. "I can't believe I let myself get suckered into that one."

"She's gone," Christian gasped. Frustration chewed at his stomach until it left a raw, festering wound.

Grant's mouth tightened. "I found McCullen back there." He pointed to an ally across the street. "He's dead."

Christian winced at the loss of a good man as he continued peering into crowds for any sign of Genevieve. Desperate energy filled him. A coach turned a corner a block down the street, and a white object fluttered out of the interior. Had Genevieve thrown it?

He ran after it. With Grant at his side and Rachel only a few steps behind, Christian dodged traffic, keeping one eye on the coach. There. A bit of trampled white. He knelt and retrieved a white embroidered handkerchief.

"Genevieve's," Rachel confirmed.

Up ahead, a black coach with red wheels careened around a corner. Christian sprinted after the coach. It turned another corner. He raced after it, leaping over objects in his path and dodging pedestrians. His lungs burned but desperation spurred him on. The coach led him to the riverfront area. By the time he rounded the next corner, it vanished. He looked up and down the street. Nothing but the rolling fog.

Christian cursed and leaned over, bracing his hands on his thighs. He'd lost her. What to do now? A cold ball formed in his heart.

Grant appeared next to him. "He's going to kill her and throw her into the Thames." Grant was barely winded despite the pace.

"Heaven help us." With a madman like Lord Wickburgh, Grant was probably right. Since the world thought her dead already, no one would suspect him of murder.

"This way." Grant darted away.

As his pulse throbbed in his ears, Christian ran next to Grant through a narrow alleyway to the riverbank. Ramshackle buildings crowded along the edge, some so close they seemed in peril of toppling into the water. Christian raced along the embankment.

Ahead, a coach pulled to a stop, its coach lamps swinging eerily in the billowing fog and growing darkness. He ran toward it, desperation sharpening his senses. Was that the coach he sought?

A woman cried out in pain. Genevieve. She was in there. With that monster. And he was hurting her.

Something fierce and wild possessed him and he curled his hands into fists as he plunged toward the carriage. No one would hurt her. He'd defend her, even if he had to kill. Or die.

He would not lose the only woman he'd ever loved. It would be even worse than losing Jason.

CHAPTER 22

Genevieve stared at Wickburgh, horrified at the deranged squint in his eye and the twist of his mouth. He would kill her and then go after Christian and Rachel to remove witnesses to his crime. She relived all their many kindnesses, their jubilant zest for life, their companionable love. All that would be shattered. She imagined Christian lying cold and dead, his beautiful face frozen in a death mask. Dark terror engulfed her.

No. She would not allow that to happen. Somehow, she'd protect them. Him.

Through the blinding pain, a clear, quiet determination surfaced. Wickburgh would not harm Christian or his family. He would not break her. She'd suffered through his abuse, his threats, his cutting insults, his cruel games. No more. She would not allow this monster to destroy her. His cruelty would end. Now. Here.

Wickburgh struck her again. Pain flashed across her face. As she cried out, he continued to hit her. Whimpering and sobbing like the Genevieve of her past, she curled up around her abdomen as if to protect herself from the blows raining down upon her. Feeling her way in the semidarkness, she slipped her hand into her pocket and retrieved the small gun Rachel had lent her. The cold metal felt steady and sure.

Finally, Wickburgh stopped hitting her. A bell clanged nearby and water lapped against a shore or edge. The coach pulled to a stop. Her heartbeat ratcheted. He'd taken her to the riverfront where he probably planned to dispose of her body after he killed her. Wickburgh grabbed her by the arm and jerked her upward. The lamplight illuminated his face and his cold stare bored into her.

"Please," she rasped, stalling. "Please don't do this. I'll come back with you. I'll do everything you say."

His lip curled into an icy smile. "You've taken Amesbury as a lover. I won't keep a wife who has cuckolded me. I want you dead. I want to look into your eyes and watch you as I choke the life out of you." He wrapped his hands around her neck and squeezed.

Pain shot out from his fingers and her breath cut off.

Madness glinted in his eyes. "Die, you worthless, unfaithful trash."

Genevieve wrenched the gun out of its small holster and brought it up. She fired. The gunshot ripped through the evening stillness. There was a brief look of surprise. He fell back, clutching at his chest, writhing and gasping.

Genevieve stared numbly at him. Strange calm crept over her. She'd done it. She'd shot him.

Men's voices shouted from outside the carriage. The door wrenched open and Christian filled the frame. Sweat streaked his face and his chest heaved. His gaze searched her face, lowered to the smoking gun in her hand, and finally to Wickburgh lying back against the seats clutching his chest.

Very softly, Christian said, "Genevieve, give me the gun."

She blinked. A disjointed, surreal calm descended over her, and she couldn't think of what she was supposed to do. She looked up at Christian in the doorway. A thin line of blood trickled from his mouth and his eye had swollen.

Wickburgh had fallen silent and lay looking up at Christian with absolute hatred twisting his expression until he looked the very devil. "You!" he gasped.

Turning away from him, Genevieve reached for Christian as if he were her salvation from that creature of darkness. "You're hurt."

"Nothing serious." Christian held out a hand. "The gun, Jen."

What gun? She looked down at her hand clutching a pistol with white fingers. Slowly, as if her arm were filled with rocks, she laid her gun in Christian's hand. He tucked it away, put a hand under her elbow, and guided her out of the carriage. Her footsteps and the rustle of her skirts echoed in her head as if every noise were shouted. Outside the cool night air cooled the perspiration on her face. Next to the carriage, Grant stood pointing at pistol at Wickburgh's coachman who sat with his hands raised in surrender.

Behind her, Wickburgh made a wild leap out of the coach, ran past her, and jumped into the water. Grant ran to the river's edge and peered over. Still moving slowly as if in a dream, Genevieve dispassionately watched bubbles on the surface. Wickburgh never resurfaced. The bubbles popped and the river returned to its normal calm.

Grant cursed. "He's either dead or really good at holding his breath."

Genevieve looked up at Christian's grim face. He met her gaze and pulled her in close. "Let's get you home."

Grant waved his gun at the coachman. "Leave. Now."

The coachman snapped the reins and disappeared into the growing fog. With Genevieve's hand tucked firmly into the crook of Christian's arm, they started walking. Along the way, Grant hailed a cab. Silent and grim, Christian kept an arm around her as if he feared she'd disappear if he released her.

As they arrived at the house, the remaining guard, John Barrow, stood with his gun trained on the door. He relaxed as he recognized them. Rachel rushed to them. She let out a cry at the sight of Genevieve's face.

Barrow said, "We've prepared another place. Jackson's

replacement, Hinkle, is there keeping watch. I'll take you there now."
They bundled into a carriage and drove in tense silence.

Rachel took her hand. "You're hurt."

Was she? She wasn't sure. A terrible numbness overtook her until nothing remained.

Christian's jaw was set and hard. "He tried to kill her. I got there too late. She had to protect herself from him."

Genevieve shook her head. Had she really shot Wickburgh? After all this time she spent cowering in fear, she could have shot him a long time ago. She wet her lips. "I only wounded him. He got away."

"He surely drowned," Christian said.

Genevieve could not be so optimistic. As the horror of the night's events washed over her anew, Genevieve shook so hard her teeth chattered. Wickburgh had tried to kill her. He'd almost succeeded. Even after all the torment, she'd never believed he would try to murder her. Until tonight. The world spun and her limbs lost all strength.

Christian's voice broke through her haze of horror as he scooped her into his arms. "I have you, love."

She clung to his solid strength. He was the only thing real in her world of uncertainty. When the carriage stopped, Christian carried her inside and lay her on a bed. Desperate for his reassuring touch, she wrapped her arms around him, and held on as if he alone protected her from death.

"Don't leave me," she sobbed. "Please."

He went still, no doubt wrestling with the stigma to her reputation if he remained in a bedchamber with her. His compassion clearly winning out over his propriety, he encircled her in his arms, and rubbed her back. Muffled voices buzzed around her but she squeezed her eyes shut, willing them away. Finally, blessed quiet stole over the room.

Christian stretched out on the bed beside her and held her protectively close. His body warmth seeped into her, soothing her terrors. The steady beat of his heart and the soft rush of air as he breathed beat a comforting cadence. She immersed herself in his quiet steadiness, his fortitude. Peace and contentment settled over her.

How long they lay like that, she couldn't guess, but when her shoulder began to ache from lying on it so long, she shifted. He loosened his arms until she'd resettled, and simply held her. He made no move to seduce her, merely offered her comfort. His sense of honor would never allow him take advantage of a woman in distress.

Although, at the moment, she had a hard time convincing herself that making love to Christian would be wrong.

CHAPTER 23

Christian lay next to Genevieve, listening to her deep breathing. Unable to sleep, he lay still, offering what comfort he could. At first, his body craved her so deeply that it took all his will not to peel off her clothing and show her just how much he loved her. But he refused to take advantage of her, and his bone-deep anger at Wickburgh for trying to kill her gnawed at him, leaving him tattered and raw.

Coming so close to losing her intensified his desire to have her for his own. He wanted to hold her every night, wake up to her every morning, and spend the days with her. First, he must set her free.

Though this house was two streets away from the old one, the smell of smoke from the fire Wickburgh had set permeated the air, just as the threat of Wickburgh and his cruel and murderous games permeated his life. Wickburgh had been wounded, true, but rodents like him didn't simply throw themselves into rivers and die. They had to be exterminated.

The clock in the hall struck midnight. Careful not to wake Genevieve, Christian disentangled himself from her limbs and eased out of bed. He covered her with the counterpane and slipped out of the room, through the open door—he'd at least thought to make that small nod toward preserving her reputation—past Barrow standing guard, and down the stairs. The new guard, Hinkle, prowled around the house. No doubt, Grant patrolled outside. Or slept.

In a small library, Christian poured himself a brandy, gulped it down, and poured a second before taking a seat. He hunched over with his arms braced on his knees.

Wickburgh had almost won tonight. That monster had endangered his family and tried to kill Genevieve. Christian had almost lost her. He wouldn't fail her again. He'd die before he'd lose her.

Grant had sworn out a warrant for Wickburgh's arrest, but the constables had yet to find him. It would be too convenient for Wickburgh to be dead already.

"Chris." Grant stood in the doorway.

Christian remembered the brandy in his hand and tossed back the contents. Not in the mood to banter with Grant, he refilled his glass without replying.

Grant's mouth curved slightly on one side. "Your face will be colorful tomorrow. Didn't anyone teach you to block a shot?"

Without looking at him, Christian said dryly, "You know us baby brothers; we just can't seem to handle ourselves."

Grant sobered. "You handled yourself well."

"I should have killed him last year when I had the chance."

"Probably. But killing a person, however deserving, always marks the killer."

Had that been a stab about Christian's role in Jason's death? The image of Jason's lifeless body on the ground burst into his mind, along with all the sharp guilt that always accompanied it. Pushing back the image, Christian watched him narrowly, but Grant only appeared thoughtful, not condemning. Regardless, Christian would do anything to protect Genevieve. Even kill. As soon as the scoundrel reappeared. Christian downed his glass.

Grant leaned against the doorjamb. "Planning on drinking yourself under the table?"

"Will it help?"

"No."

Christian drank another anyway.

"This isn't like you."

Something about the confusion, or maybe the condemnation, in Grant's voice fueled his anger and it bubbled up inside him. "No. I'm tired of being like me. I think I'll be someone else." He tossed back another drink and finally, blissful numbness sank into his muscles, unbunching them.

"Pigs must be flying now; otherwise you wouldn't be getting drunk. Don't tell me your next act will be to visit a brothel."

"Know any good ones?" Christian quipped half-heartedly.

Without any warning, Grant strode to him and slapped him. His cheek stung. Shocked, Christian stared, too surprised to even register anger.

"Get a hold of yourself," Grant growled. "The world does not need more careless rakes. It needs honorable men like you."

Christian stared in stunned silence. Grant's words echoed in his head. *Honorable men like you.* He ran his hand across his stinging cheek. Grant wanted him to remain honorable, the very thing for which he'd mocked Christian their whole lives. The idea was as laughable as it was sad.

Well, he'd be honorable. He'd kill her husband honorably. No jury convicted a man for dueling if he followed the gentleman's code.

Grant added, "Don't lower yourself for an image you think you want and realize later you despise."

"I'll despise myself if Wickburgh gets near here again. I will finish this."

If only Jared were here. He'd serve as Christian's second just for the adventure, but Jared was a married man now and Christian wouldn't risk him. James Ingle would probably do it, but he was still rusticating in the country. Christian sifted through friends who might act as his second, but he doubted any were in London during this time of year. Many had gone to the country or the seashore or abroad.

Grant narrowed his eyes. "You're going to challenge Wickburgh to a duel, aren't you?"

"If I can find him, yes. I cannot allow Genevieve to live in constant fear. The only way to stop him is to kill him."

Grant raised his brow. "Turn him over to the law."

"He may hire someone to finish her while he awaits trial. And we risk him being acquitted; you know how hesitant peers are to convict each other."

Nodding slowly, Grant went still as if plotting his next move. "If you go after him, you might get hurt."

"I'm a very good shot."

"True, but duels are unpredictable." Grant poured himself a brandy and examined the glass as if judging its color. "Who will be your second?"

"I don't know yet."

He turned to face Christian. "Then allow me to serve in that role."

Christian stared. This night had been full of unexpected twists. "You would do that?"

"If you can't trust me to have your back, who can you trust? You know, since Jared and Cole aren't nearby." He quirked a faint smile.

"You jest."

"Believe it or not, I don't really wish for your demise."

Christian snorted. "When did that change?"

Grant's mouth twisted. "Probably sometime during the war. I waxed rather poetic about home and family while I was amidst all the carnage. If you need a second, you can count on me."

Maybe it was the alcohol, but Christian's throat tightened. He coughed into his hand to cover up his emotion and managed, "My thanks."

Now all they had to do was wait for Wickburgh to crawl out from underneath the rock where he'd been hiding.

Then Christian would put an end to Wickburgh's cruelty.

Permanently.

CHAPTER 24

By the light of the early morning rays, Genevieve stared at the note in her hand addressed to *Mrs. Jennings* in Wickburgh's erratic scrawl.

Her breath froze into a solid lump. He'd called her by her brief alias Mrs. Jennings to mock her. Fearing the note would somehow conjure the man who wrote it, she held it away from her body. Then, donning her courage like a shield, she broke the seal and unfolded the paper.

I deeply regret our recent separation and have a great desire to see you. Come to your parents' home so we may be reunited. I am so enjoying my visit with them and we need your presence to be complete. Come this afternoon for tea. Do come alone, please. I give you my word your parents will be safe if you honor my request for your return.

I remain

Your obedient servant

W.

. . .

CRUMPLING THE NOTE INTO A WAD, she squeezed her eyes shut. Her parents. Once again, that monster threatened her parents.

No longer. This afternoon, his threat would end. She would defeat him.

She put a hand on either side of her head. If she obeyed Wickburgh, he'd kill her. And if any shred of honor remained in Wickburgh, it was his word; he always kept his word. Which meant her parents would be safe if she sacrificed herself.

Every nerve in her body urged her to run to Christian. But Wickburgh had already tried to kill him. She couldn't risk his life. She had to take care of him. Keep him safe.

Still, the last time she shut Christian out of her life, she'd regretted it. It was time to allow someone to help her, to be a true partner who would help carry her burdens. She'd never act again without letting Christian be a part of her decisions, just as she should have confided in Christian last year when Wickburgh demanded she marry him.

Ignoring the pain in her face and ribs from Wickburgh's fists, and in her neck where he'd tried to squeeze the life out of her, she donned a robe and went out into the corridor. With his gun at the ready, one of Grant's men loitered in the hall.

"My lady?" he called out.

"Where is Mr. Amesbury? Ah, Christian?" she added, remembering there were presently two Mr. Amesburys in residence.

He pointed down the corridor. "Do you need something?"

She waved him back and ran past an open window where early morning light filtered in and cast a patch of sunlight on the carpet. Ignoring the rules of propriety—after all, she'd lain in bed with him last night—she knocked at Christian's door. Without waiting, she flung it open to a room enshrouded by darkness. "Christian, I need you."

A lump moved in the middle of the bed and a tousled head appeared among the blankets and pillows. "Jen?"

She moved to the bedside and held out the note. "He's after my family again. He's going to hurt them."

With a rustle of sheets, Christian sat up, his nightshirt gaping open to reveal a broad, bare chest. He groaned and put a hand to his head. "Sorry . . . what?"

Ignoring the delicious sight of a sleepy, rumpled Christian in bed, she stepped closer and shook the crumpled note. "He sent me a note demanding I meet him at my parents' house alone this afternoon. He's threatening them if I don't come."

Holding his head as if he feared it would roll off, Christian swore under his breath. A faint odor of stale alcohol wafted to her. She wrinkled her nose. He'd picked a fine time to overindulge.

"What, exactly, does it say?" He shifted, and rubbed his hand over his face, clearly trying to become more alert.

She quoted the letter in a shaking voice.

He let out his breath. "You are not going alone. What kind of fool does he think you are?"

"He knows I'd do anything to protect my family."

"And so you shall. But not on his terms." Then, unexpectedly, he took her hand in a firm grip. His mouth curved into a disbelieving smile. "You came to me. I can't tell you how much that means." He kissed her fingers.

His pale blue eyes, if a bit bloodshot, shone with a light all their own. Warmth edged through her fear and she managed to smile. All would be well. She'd been a fool to try to do everything all alone last year. There was greater strength when two people united against opposition.

He shifted. "Give me a moment to dress and I'll meet you in the breakfast room. We'll formulate a plan to ensure you and your family will be safe from him forever."

His calm, determined voice quieted the last of her fears. Together, they would succeed.

Genevieve stepped outside Christian's room and jumped, a cry escaping her mouth as an ominous shadow moved in her peripheral vision. Where the other guard had been moments before, Grant leaned against the wall, his arms folded, looking like a snake coiled and ready to strike.

She sucked in her breath and put at hand on her chest. "You startled me."

Grant lifted a brow as a sardonic twitch tugged at his mouth. "Apologies, my lady."

Genevieve studied him. Was he mocking her? Aside from the ragged scar running down the side of his face, Grant resembled his brothers enough to be almost handsome, except for the fearsome scowl he wore and the scorn that darkened his gray eyes, especially when he looked at her. He probably viewed her as a trollop who had toyed with his brother's emotions, abandoned him, and then came back to seduce him into helping her get rid of her husband.

Next to Grant stood another man who looked like a cutthroat. The pair of them were truly terrifying. Her instincts urged her to run back into Christian's room. Instead, she drew herself up and affected a lofty air, looking pointedly at the other man.

Grant jerked a thumb in the stranger's direction. "This is Hinkle. He's also from Bow Street. He's taken Jackson's place."

"Why? Where is Jackson?"

"He went on a little errand."

The stranger touched his forelock in a respectful greeting. She nodded in return. What kind of little errand Jackson might be doing for Grant left her faintly alarmed. But, despite Grant's fearsome exterior, he appeared to be loyal enough to Christian to truly protect them. Or perhaps he merely took pride in his skills. Either way, Christian's brother looked more like an assassin than a protector. Desperate times…

She moistened her lips and nodded as if all were well. As she strode down the corridor to her room, the middle of her back between her shoulder blades prickled as if Grant were aiming a knife at it. She shivered and kept her head up, walking with all the dignity of a queen to her room. Hastily, she dressed and rushed to the breakfast room but found it empty except for a servant placing breakfast dishes on a sideboard.

Moments later, Christian strode in, all strength and confidence, washed, shaven, and dressed. Except for slightly red eyes, he gave no sign that he'd been jug bitten. He looked fit for making social calls, if one overlooked the bruises on his cheek and a swollen eye.

"I'll confront Wickburgh," he announced.

"Not alone, you won't." Grant's voice boomed from the doorway. "He'll have his bullies, and they'll be armed. The lads and I will accompany you."

Christian's face flushed and his eyes narrowed. He drew a breath and rubbed a hand down his jaw, turning thoughtful, "Yes, yes, perhaps you should. Has Jackson sent word?"

"Not yet."

Genevieve glanced between them. "What is Jackson doing?"

Christian explained, "He's posing as a mercenary seeking employment as one of Wickburgh's toadies."

Grant continued, "He hasn't come back, so I assume he succeeded. Or he's dead."

Genevieve let out a gasp at the casual way Grant suggested someone's death. Grant glanced at her, his mouth twitching. Had that last comment been some kind of joke? If so, Grant definitely had a dark sense of humor. His gaze flicked to Genevieve, yet his inscrutable stare gave no clues as to his thoughts. Genevieve shivered. Beyond mysterious; Grant was dark and frightening.

Christian turned to her. "Since Jackson is Wickburgh's newest minion, he won't be entrusted with sensitive information. But we can count on him to worm his way into the action, and he'll come to our aid when we need him."

Genevieve nodded slowly. "How much do you trust him?"

"Completely." Christian tugged on his lip with a faraway look in his eyes. "Until we hear from him, we'll assume we're on our own. If Wickburgh is expecting you in time for tea, we need to leave within a few hours if we're to free your parents."

Grant went utterly still except for his narrowed eyes darting back and forth as if plotting steps for some complicated scheme. "He may be unhinged, but he's intelligent. I'd wager he has an elaborate scheme."

"He does," Genevieve said. "We can count on that."

Waving impatiently, Christian nodded. "Fine. But let's make sure."

"Agreed" Grant said. "Let's scout the area."

Christian's eyes widened as if surprised at Grant's suggestion and he leaped to his feet, his fingers twitching. Then he paused, his gaze flicking to Genevieve. His shoulders sagged almost imperceptibly. "No. I won't leave her here alone again."

She stood and went to him, linking her fingers with his. "I'll go with you."

"Absolutely not," two voices stated.

Undaunted, she looked up at them with pleading eyes. "I need to see if my parents are well." She paused, and added, "I can shoot."

"No," Grant said.

Christian shook his head. "You aren't going anywhere near Wickburgh."

She let out her breath in a huff. "We're not marching into battle, only scouting."

Grant scowled. "You aren't trained to scout. You'll be too noisy and give away our location."

Christian squeezed her hand. "I know you want to be there, Jen, but—"

"Please, I shall go mad if I stay under lock and key another day."

"You're not coming with us," Grant said.

Raising her chin, she glared at them mulishly. "Then I'll follow you."

Christian exploded, "Genevieve Eliza Ann, if you do, I swear—"

"You'll what?" she demanded.

Christian's anger diffused at her challenging stare, but his determination never faded. "It's too dangerous."

Grant let out a sound of exasperation. "Blasted wench, don't be stupid. That madman wants you dead."

Archly, she said, "Then we'll have to be clever about our disguises when we leave."

"No, Jen." Anguish darkened Christian's eyes. "I cannot risk losing you again."

She waved her hands. "He won't expect it. He thinks I'm some cowering little mouse who won't be bold enough to do something like this."

Taking both of her hands in his, Christian turned her to face him. "You've staged your death, masqueraded as a secretary, disguised yourself as a boy, ridden astride all the way to London, and shot Wickburgh when he was trying to strangle you. You're no covering little mouse."

"Let's hope he thinks I am."

"Jen...."

"If you care at all for me, you'll bring me with you."

"If you care at all for me, you'll stay here where I know you'll be safe. Please don't do this to me. I couldn't bear it if anything happened to you." He cupped her cheek and looked down at her with such love that her resolve crumbled.

He was right. She'd be a fool to leave the protection of the house. And she'd be selfish to try. Christian didn't deserve to be hurt by her again, and she'd most certainly hurt him if she were injured or killed. Strange, but though she'd never been really good enough for him, and even less so now that she'd married Wickburgh, Christian truly loved her.

Gently, he traced her face, lightly tracing her bruised cheek and swollen lip. "Are you in pain?"

"Not much." She shrugged lightly. "He didn't break anything this time."

Christian's jaw tightened. "Stay here with me and be safe, Jen. Let me protect you. If something happened to you, too, I'd die. I cannot lose anyone else. I just can't do it."

The pleading in his eyes undid her and the fight rushed out of her in a great exhale. "Very well. You go with Grant and—" She stopped, staring at the wall where Grant had stood.

Grant had vanished.

Smiling ruefully, Christian led her to a small sitting room. Seated on a settee, he held her as if he feared she'd disappear right before his eyes. "I'll stay here with you." His mouth curved upward as he put an arm around her. "It's the only way I can be sure you will stay put."

As she slid an arm around his waist, she nestled into his shoulder. Perhaps it was improper for a married woman to sit in such a way with a man, but nothing about their situation was normal. And after falling asleep in his arms last night, it didn't seem to matter anymore.

Then his words came back to her. "When you said you couldn't lose anyone else, were you referring to your parents? Your brother?"

He fell silent for a so long that she gave up on getting an answer. His hand lightly tracing her arm as it rested across his abdomen. "I don't like to speak of it."

"I don't mean to pry, but sometimes it helps to allow someone else to share your burden as I'm sharing mine with you."

His breathing turned ragged as if he were remembering a hard run.

She snuggled in more firmly against him. "Just know that I love you and I will help you any way I can."

Still he said nothing, his body tense, his hands clenched, his breathing erratic. Just as she had resigned herself to remaining outside that part of his heart, he began speaking. "When I was six, my brother Jason died."

When he paused, she prompted, "You were close?"

"Very much." He took a series of breaths. "It was my fault."

She wrapped her arm more tightly around him. "How was it your fault?"

"I was trying to prove I was as big and brave as they."

He closed his eyes and pressed his hands over his face. As if from a far-off place, he started talking in low, halting tones as he relived that tragic day from which he carried a crushing burden of guilt and grief.

CHAPTER 25

Long-rejected memories washed over Christian like an incoming tide, ferocious, hungry, battering and eroding his heart and soul.

That horrific day so long ago, played out in sharp, cruel details... how he'd been running with all his might to keep up with his brothers, desperate to prove he wasn't a baby who should have stayed in the house with his sisters. As usual, he'd been unable to keep up as they raced to the tree. His six-year-old self had been sure he'd outrun them all one day.

Christian's brothers had disappeared around a corner in the gardens, the shaking of shrubbery all that bespoke their passing. Drawing from some inner well of speed he didn't know he possessed, Christian had darted around the corner and skidded on loose gravel. His feet had gone out from underneath him and he crashed to the ground. Pain burst from his thigh and elbow. Now, he would be last. Again. But he wouldn't quit.

Blinking back hot tears of humiliation, Christian scrambled to his feet and charged down the stone path toward Zeus's Garden. He flew headlong through the arch of roses, past statues, dodging fountains and flowers and shaped shrubbery.

His brothers' voices led Christian to their tree. Perfect for climbing with low, strong limbs spaced as evenly as a ladder, they'd imagined it as a pirate ship, a navy frigate, a castle where a dragon lived, or a deep, dark dungeon filled with ogres.

Hanging from a branch, Grant mocked Christian. "Sorry, Chrissy, you're last. Go back home and sew and draw and play music with the girls."

Christian stuck his chin out. "I don't sew."

"Rules are rules," Jared said with a taunting smile. "Last one here has to go back and play with the twins. Maybe they'll put bows in your pretty blond hair."

"Aw, come on, let him stay." Jason's voice broke in. "Look, he fell and scraped up his leg and arm and didn't even cry."

"'The perfectly perfect Christian' is too perfect to cry," Grant sneered.

Christian clamped his mouth shut as Grant taunted him with that all too familiar, sing-songy phrase that never failed to make his blood boil. He wasn't perfect, but he did try to be good for Mama's sake. Which was the only reason he didn't climb up the tree and punch Grant in the face.

"Let him stay," Jason urged again. "He's not bothering anyone."

Grant let out a snort. "You're too soft on him."

Cole, highest in the tree and holding a paper he'd rolled up into the shape of a spyglass, let out a long-suffering sigh. "You can be the cabin boy. Ahoy there!"

The tree was a ship, today.

From his perch on one of the lower tree limbs, Jason leaned down and held out a hand. "Come on up, Chris. I'll help you."

Christian shook his head. "I can do it by myself."

He would prove he could climb just as well as they could—without help. He stood below the lowest limb and jumped, his fingers curling around the branch as he caught it. After swinging his legs, he hooked his ankles around the limb and hoisted himself up.

"I'll bet you can't reach that one," Jared said to Cole, their voices filtering down from above like falling leaves.

"Watch me." Cole inched away from the trunk and tucked his feet below his body. After shifting into a crouch, his legs wobbling a little, he jumped toward an upper limb, and caught it. Within moments, Cole, Grant and Jason began leaping from limb to limb like sailors climbing the rigging of a ship.

Eyeing a branch far away from the others, Christian climbed. He'd jump to that far one, and prove he was as strong and able as the big boys. He ground his teeth against the throbbing pain in his elbow and leg, and hauled himself upward.

"Where are you going in such a hurry?" Jason put up an arm to block Christian's climb.

"Up there." Christian pointed to the isolated branch near the top. "I'm gonna jump to it."

Jason looked up. "That one up there? You're mad."

"I'll show you. Bet *you* can't jump to it."

Jason let out his breath slowly as he looked up. "That's a long way from the other branches."

Christian nodded. If Jason admitted he could never do it, even on a dare, and Christian did reach it, they'd see how big and brave he was. "I dare you to try."

Jason hesitated.

"You're too scared," Christian taunted. "But I'm not. I can do it."

Grant's voice cut in. "Jason's not scared of anything."

A bead of perspiration trickled down the side of Jason's face and his hand trembled as he wiped it away. He jumped. His body made a graceful arc, his legs straight, his arms reaching outward. The tip of his fingers grazed the coveted branch.

And slid off.

Jason fell.

Christian stared in horror as down, down, down Jason's twisting body plunged, slowly, like one of Christian's nightmares when it becomes impossible to run even when a monster is in pursuit. Someone screamed—a terrible keening noise that rent the air. Jason landed on the ground below with a thud that tore through Christian's body like a lightning strike.

Jason lay unmoving.

All sound faded away except for the wild pounding of Christian's heart, and that terrible, terrible scream. Christian reached the ground without knowing how he got there. Faintly aware of searing pain in his hands, he collapsed on the ground beside Jason, reaching for him but terrified to touch him. Dizzy and out of breath, he gulped in air and the screaming stopped.

"Jason?" he rasped.

Other noises, other shapes, swarmed around him in a fog of confusion, but his vision fixed on Jason's chest struggling to rise.

Christian put his forehead on Jason's brow and wrapped his arms around his brother. "Jason, wake up. Open your eyes."

Jason's breathing grew more labored. He made a terrible rattle, then fell silent. All motion in Jason's chest stopped. Christian's own heart stopped. All the world stopped.

Hands peeled Christian off Jason and shoved him away. Voices, frantic and shrill, poured in all around him but he stood alone in a sea of horror. Adults shoved past him, crowding around Jason's motionless form. A dull roar built up in Christian's head drowning out everything but the image of Jason lying so still.

Not moving.

Not breathing.

Not living.

Somewhere the far reaches of his mind registered the knowledge that Jason would never open his eyes, never play, never laugh.

Someone shook Christian so hard that he bit his tongue. "What happened?"

Christian pushed back the suffocating fog. "He fell." His voice sounded far away as if someone else were talking through the other end of a hollow log. The truth wrenched out of him. "I dared him to jump. And he fell."

The ground had rushed up then, smashed Christian in the face, and had hurled him into darkness...

Genevieve's voice reached into the darkness and pulled Christian back to the present moment, to her. "Oh, my love, it wasn't your fault."

How much he'd told her and how much he'd simply relived, he did not know.

Now that he'd started talking, the rest of the story kept pouring out. "Mother never sang or smiled after that."

Genevieve sniffled.

"Jared's antics grew more and more reckless until about two months later, during a prank, someone got hurt—not seriously, but enough to cause concern. I ran for help. Father . . . I'd never seen him so angry. He started whipping Jared." He swallowed. "I felt every blow as if I were getting whipped. I wished it were me instead of Jared. But I was so frightened, I did nothing. Cole interfered. It led to a terrible row. Cole and Jared left home that day. Cole joined the navy. Jared joined a privateer." His voice shook.

Silently weeping, Genevieve let him talk.

"Grant never forgave me. He had been closest to Jason. Jason understood Grant. After Jason's death, Grant barely spoke to me except to tell me he wished I'd been the one to die. I started actually fearing that he'd try to kill me."

"Oh, no. I can't imagine..."

"A few month later, he convinced Father to purchase a commission for him in the Army. In a matter of a year, my mother lost all her sons. Except me." Self-loathing dripped off those last two words.

Hoarsely, through her tears, she managed, "She's lucky she had you."

"I caused everything to go wrong. Mama's health declined. I tried to make up for it. I did everything to try to make her happy, but she never recovered, only slipped further and further away. Then her health took a sudden turn for the worse. Her death threw Father into a melancholy. I'd hoped time in Bath would revive his health, but his heart had already died when she did. I couldn't make him want to live. It's my fault Jason died. It's my fault my parents died."

Genevieve let out a sob. "Oh, my love, of course it's not your fault."

"If I hadn't been trying so hard to prove I was something I wasn't —" His voice cracked. He coughed into his hand and cleared his throat.

She raised up, put a hand on either side of his face, and looked directly into his eyes even while tears streaked her face. "You must stop blaming yourself. It was an accident—a horrible, terrible, heartbreaking accident. You didn't kill him, Christian. He was a boy, and boys do foolish things. Sometimes those foolish things cause tragedies."

Fearful hope edged into him. Her impassioned statement rang of truth. But was she right?

She wiped her tears with the back of a hand. "I love you. You are the most honorable man I've ever met. Let go of all your guilt and stop punishing yourself."

She wrapped her arms around him and guided his head to her shoulder. Leaning against her, he slid an arm behind her and wrapped her in a tight embrace.

She whispered, "Let it go."

He drew a shuddering breath.

"I wish I could crawl inside and heal all your hurt. After all you'd already suffered, you must have thought yourself truly undeserving of love. But you do deserve love. I feel that in every inch of my heart."

Did he? Did he truly?

"Rachel gave me some wise advice. She said, 'Give your heart time to heal, but don't let it scar over. Heal whole, not broken. Heal well, instead of bitter. Keep your ability to love and receive love intact. You may yet meet someone who can be trusted to keep your heart safe.'"

"I hope you can trust me."

He did. To his surprise, he did trust her.

She smoothed back his hair and kissed his brow. "You are good and honorable and kind. You love your family fiercely and loyally. You're strong and courageous and you fight for what's right. You are my Prince Charming. I promise you, I will spend the rest of my life proving to you how much I love you and how rare and remarkable you really are."

He let out his breath in a half laugh. "I look forward to that. I must say, though, that you are doing a fine job of it right now."

"Then I have a good start."

"I don't deserve you, but I do love you," he said softly.

He kissed her then, pouring all the heat of his love into that kiss. Every brush of her lips chased away the last vestiges of pain. He was whole. He was home.

After he ended the kiss, he held her and breathed. Each inhale brought in a cleansing sensation, and each exhale pushed out long-held sorrow. Genevieve's arms tightened as if she could not bear to let go. They sat wrapped in their embrace while the world faded away until only the two of them remained, healing each other and creating new hope. How much time passed, he could not guess, but no one disturbed them.

Christian's hushed voice broke the silence. "Just so you know, I'm not as honorable as you think."

"Oh?"

"I vowed to myself that I wouldn't kiss you again until you were free to be mine."

"Mmm. I suppose it's not your fault I'm such a tempting morsel." She lifted her head and smiled at him.

He cupped her cheek, kissed her brow, and pulled her against him again. "I might break my word again before the day is through."

Stolen kisses would never be enough. He must find a way to force Wickburgh's hand to give her up. Of course, sending him to prison or getting him transported might do the trick. He had to try. If nothing else, he'd challenge him to a duel.

He would not lose Genevieve again.

CHAPTER 26

Nestled in Christian's arms, all traces of the fear, hopelessness, and pain that had been her constant companions since her ill-fated marriage to Wickburgh dissipated, leaving a new serenity. Christian had healed her. With him, she was whole.

Grant strode into the room and announced, "The Marshalls are not there."

Genevieve lifted her head from Christian's shoulder. "Where are they?"

"According to the servants, your parents received a visitor—their son-in-law—and they left with him."

Genevieve leaped to her feet. "If I don't go, he'll hurt them, he'll torture them."

"We won't let that happen." Christian's grim but quiet tone pulled her back from the edge of panic. He stood and took her hand. "Trust me."

She nodded. "I do trust you. But Wickburgh—"

"Is no match for us." Again, the image of a heroic knight superimposed itself over Christian's beloved face. Though everything chivalrous and gentle, he was strong and protective.

She nodded again. "What do we do?"

Grant answered. "I stationed two men there to watch the Marshall's house in case they return."

Christian lips twitched sardonically. "How many men do you have at your disposal?"

"A plethora. And yes, you're paying dearly for them."

Christian waved it off as if the money were meaningless. As a youngest son, he wouldn't have the family wealth at his disposal, but in Bath he'd mentioned some investments he'd made. Perhaps those investments had paid off.

"How long ago did the Marshalls leave?" Christian asked.

"Early this morning. My men are tailing them. They'll send a messenger as soon as we learn their final destination. We'll have to play his game for now. But not by his rules."

He and Christian exchanged a charged look. Though they clearly had their differences, and now that she understood why, Genevieve could hardly believe they worked together as well as they did.

As if they conversed in a mental language, Christian nodded slowly. "He wants her to come alone. 'Alone' is a very relative term, don't you think?"

A dangerous gleam lit Grant's gray eyes. "It's too dangerous for a lady to travel by horseback."

Christian nodded. "She'll need to travel by coach. With a coachman and a footman." He gestured to himself and to Grant.

Genevieve caught their meaning. "And perhaps even an outrider or two?"

Grant's brow raised and she had the impression she'd just passed some sort of test. "Precisely."

Christian grinned darkly as if he were contemplating the worst sort of mayhem, which, really, seemed incongruous with the Christian she once knew. The new Christian was more complex than the sweet dreamer she'd known before. Or maybe she hadn't known him as well as she had first supposed. Still, she trusted him completely, perhaps even more so.

He gentled his voice to address Genevieve. "We'll be right there with you, armed to the teeth and ready for battle. No one will hurt your parents. And at last, you'll be free from Wickburgh."

"Think any of the servants' livery will fit us?" Christian asked Grant.

"There are some very strapping lads as footmen," Grant said. "I'm sure we can find something."

A dark gleam lit Christian's eyes at the prospect of a coup, and his hand gripped a bulge in his coat roughly the size of a pistol. An even darker gleam brightened Grant's eyes. Genevieve almost smiled. She might not want to meet Grant in a dark alley, but he'd be a good person to have on their side as they faced the man who wanted her dead and would use her parents without mercy.

Christian called out orders to the nearest guard, his tone leaving no room for hesitation. The guard dashed away to do his bidding. Despite the gloom hanging over them, she smiled. How she loved this man!

His resolute and fierce expression softened. "I'm proud of you. You're so brave. We won't fail, I promise you."

"I know. I have complete faith in you."

He kissed her again and turned to work out details with Grant.

Brave. Yes, she was brave. She would do whatever she must. Her courage had often failed her when defending herself against the demon she'd married. But always, her courage rose up, bright and fierce, when protecting those she loved.

She would never be a victim again, would never allow Wickburgh —nor anyone else—power to keep her from her parents, her friends, and especially Christian.

She prayed Papa and Mama would remain unharmed even while Wickburgh used them as bait. The moment he viewed them of no further use, he'd dispose of them. Or worse, keep them prisoner to play his vicious games with them.

Genevieve listened to Grant and Christian plan the rescue, her determination growing every minute. Yes, she'd do whatever she must to protect those she loved.

CHAPTER 27

Wearing the coat and hat of a coachman, Christian stood next to the back door, pulled Genevieve into his arms, and tried not to crush her. Her soft body molded into his and his senses filled with her scent and her sweetness.

The temptation to discard the plan and carry Genevieve off to France or Italy, somewhere she'd be safe—and where they could finally be together—sang through his veins. First, her insane husband had to be stopped. Otherwise, she would never be safe, and neither would her parents. For the moment, he'd enjoy this moment holding Genevieve.

"I'll be right there with you," he said huskily into her hair.

She buried her face into his shirtfront. "I know you will. I'm not afraid."

Heaven help him, he loved this woman so much that it gave him renewed strength. He drew back and held her at arm's length. "Do you have your gun?"

She nodded. "It's in my pocket." She patted the front of her pelisse.

"And the dagger?"

She lifted her skirts to show a hilt peeping out from inside her right riding boot.

His blue gaze bathed her in intense light. "If anything goes wrong, run."

She nodded.

He gripped her shoulders. "I mean, it, Genevieve; don't stay and play heroine."

"I know." She placed a cool, steady hand on his cheek. "All will be well."

He wished he could share her optimism. With a man like Wickburgh, anything could happen. Their plan would probably go wrong at some point, so he'd have to make snap decisions. He clenched his fists. The idea of gambling with Genevieve's life and the lives of her parents turned him to ice.

Grant, dressed in the fine livery of footman, spoke quietly to one of the Runners. If the situation weren't so dangerous, Christian would rib Grant about his fancy attire. But Grant understood Christian needed the better disguise of the coachman or Wickburgh would recognize him if they were seen.

"Our first priority is rescuing the hostages," Grant said. "If we lose Wickburgh, let him go. You can still challenge him another time."

Genevieve's mouth dropped open and disapproval lurked in her eyes. "Challenge? To a duel?"

Christian met her gaze without apology. "One way or another, this ends." If things got rough and Wickburgh got shot, no one would mourn his passing.

She nodded slowly, eyeing him as if she'd never seen him before.

"What is it?" Christian asked.

"He probably deserves whatever he gets, but I don't want you to become something that would . . . ." She trailed off.

He touched her arm. "Tell me."

"I just never thought you ruthless enough to duel someone."

He stiffened. "Ruthless? Dueling is a matter of honor and I will do whatever I must to protect you."

"I know, it just seems so close to murder. And you aren't cold blooded."

"No, I assure you, my blood is very hot right now. But I vow to keep a cool head. Our goal is to free your parents, keep you safe, and bring him before the authorities."

She nodded again, her forehead creasing. Then she lifted her chin and put a hand on his chest right over his heart. "I trust you, Christian. Be careful. I couldn't bear it if you got hurt."

Pride and love swelled his chest and softened the hard edge forming around him. It reminded him of his true goal to protect Genevieve and rescue her parents—not kill Wickburgh. She was right; he wasn't cold blooded enough to kill a man. They'd subdue Wickburgh and let the Bow Street officers take him to the magistrate where he'd face the law for his crimes. No punishment would be too harsh for that monster.

Voices boomed through the great hall from the front door. Christian's ears perked. Those voices sounded like Cole and Jared. He paused, listening.

A second later, the eldest two Amesbury brothers strode in dressed in riding clothes, looking so much alike that many people mistook them for twins. Their flushed faces and glittering eyes reminded Christian of wolves on the hunt.

Cole grinned. "Chris!"

"Having an adventure without us?" Jared grinned gleefully.

Cole's gazed flitted over Christian and Grant, no doubt taking in their odd state of dress. "You are. I'm insulted." He turned to Jared. "Are you insulted?"

Jared nodded. "Oh, absolutely."

Cole made an imperious wave. "We're insulted. We demand satisfaction."

"But first, we're going with you to defeat your foes," Jared added helpfully. "Then we'll demand satisfaction."

Christian's head spun at the way they fired off their ridiculous comments.

Jared's eyes gleamed as he gazed at Genevieve and his grin

broadened. "Belay that. You must introduce me to this ethereal goddess at once."

The sudden urge to plant a fist in the middle of Jared's fool mouth seized Christian. "You aren't going with us. I thought you were still in France with your *wife*."

Jared ignored him. Instead he took Genevieve's hand and raised it to his lips. "Dear lady, I am Christian's favorite brother, Jared Amesbury, at your service." He kissed her hand again. "I cannot understand what you see in him—too perfect by half for all of us—but it's certainly clear what he sees in you."

Christian shouldered him aside and pried him off Genevieve's hand. "Stop slobbering on her, you great oaf. Go away, both of you." He made a shooing motion to Cole and Jared.

"And miss out on a lark?" Cole opened his mouth and eyes in mock horror, looking more like a fish than an earl.

"Not a chance," Jared said.

"Then stop babbling," Grant snarled from the corner.

Cole cocked a brow at Christian. "Yes, quite. What is your plan?"

Christian sighed. Secretly, he appreciated their offer to come to his aid. But he hated the idea that they thought he couldn't handle himself. Still, with a madman like Wickburgh, and Genevieve's life as well as her parents' lives on the line, he'd be foolish to turn them away.

"Very well. You can take the place of our outriders."

"How soon do we leave?" Cole asked.

"Immediately." Christian glanced at Genevieve. "She's expected for tea and it's about a two-hour drive from here."

Rachel arrived. "Cole! Jared!" She threw her arms around them and kissed them both soundly. "I'm so glad you're here."

Christian turned to her. "We're leaving one of Grant's men here to protect you."

Rachel pointed to a gun tucked into a belt around her waist. "Maybe I'll protect myself."

"Don't get overly confident."

She put her arms around his neck. "Don't worry about me. You be careful. Come back whole."

"That's the idea." He hugged his sister and released her quickly.

Grant handed Christian a bag grimly. "Real men's clothes. I plan to change, if possible, after we learn where Wickburgh is keeping the Marshalls."

Perhaps it was Cole and Jared's presence, but despite the tension, Christian snorted in suppressed laughter. "Really, Grant, worried about your apparel? I'm surprised at your vanity."

Grant glowered. "I have a reputation for not looking like a peacock, unlike you dandies."

Cole and Jared guffawed like a couple of village brats. But since Grant was the object of their laughter, Christian allowed himself a smug smile. Despite the grimness of their mission, even Genevieve chuckled. With their nerves so tightly strung, emotions ran high—even humor.

Christian slung Grant's bag over his shoulder. "After I stow your bag inside, I'll bring the coach around front."

Grant headed for the foyer, quiet as a whisper. Hopefully Grant would have the sense to stop moving like an infernal assassin and start walking with the heavier steps of a footman. Otherwise, if any of Wickburgh's henchmen were watching the house, they'd see through their ruse.

Genevieve stood by quietly, as serene as a painting, but her cheeks were flushed, the only indication to her nervousness. No doubt she feared for her parents. It was so like her to worry for them more than for herself. Christian gave Genevieve's hand a quick squeeze, tugged his hat low over his face, and headed for the servant's entrance, fingering his hidden weapons.

Outside, Christian's nerves tingled on high alert. While trying to appear casual, he scanned the streets, searching for signs of threat to Genevieve. Every call of the pieman or flower girl, every cart that rattled by, and every horse that snorted took on sinister intentions. He found no imminent threat. The weight of his pistols helped, but seemed too far away. He headed for the mews. Moments later, coach wheels clattered on the cobbled street as he drove to the front door.

Cole and Jared waited in the street in front of the house, already mounted, their faces sober but their eyes alight at the prospect of adventure. With just the right amount of subservient confidence of a footman, Grant trailed Genevieve as she descended the steps. Christian hunched over on the driver's seat and relaxed his gloved hands on the reins. He tried not to look interested. Or frantic. Grant handed Genevieve into the coach, stowed the carriage step, and swung onto the back for the ride.

On horseback, Cole and Jared led the way as they left London behind and followed the road through Hamstead Heath. The rambling grassy ridge offered a lovely view of London, but Christian kept his eyes trained ahead, barely glancing at the ponds and ancient woodlands nestled in the popular public area. No signs of danger. Yet. Christian remained alert, his senses straining. Cole's Arabian cantered ahead while Jared's blue roan flanked the coach. Both experienced military men, they would keep a sharp eye out.

Jared glanced up at Christian and grinned. Daft fool was enjoying himself far too much. But Christian allowed himself a smile in return. His brothers were here. In spite of their differences, they'd come to help him. Together, they would not fail. A comfortable familiarity settled into Christian and the knots in his shoulders relaxed.

Two hours later, they reached the hamlet where Genevieve had grown up. The closer they drew to her childhood manor where Wickburgh would lay the first piece in his trap for Genevieve, the more Christian's gut tightened until the knots folded in on themselves. He straightened and fortified his courage. He would not fail her.

He turned the coach and began a slight climb through a country road lined with shrubbery turning golden at the beginning of autumn. Wind gusted through the hedgerows, making them whisper as if passing along news of their arrival, and sending a chill down Christian's spine.

After turning down a narrow lane, the coach arrived in front of the Marshall's manor, an ivy-covered brick house from the Tudor age. Though he'd almost married her, he'd only visited the house the Marshalls had let for the summer in Bath, and had never seen her family country home. The comfortable manor suited the Marshalls. He couldn't reconcile the proper gentleman he'd seen in Captain Marshall with a man who'd commit mutiny. There had to be more to his story.

Christian slowed the carriage in front of the house, his skin sparking. As the wheels came to a rolling stop, Grant leaped from the back of the coach, placed the step, and opened the door, all while bearing the appropriate servitude manner of a footman. Christian kept his gaze forward as the carriage subtly shifted underneath him while Genevieve climbed out. Careful not to look at her, he waited as she mounted the stairs to the front door of the manor. Before she reached it, the door opened.

"Welcome, my lady. You are expected," a man said calmly in the cultured tones of a gentleman.

It was Connor Jackson. Christian went utterly still and hoped his expression hadn't registered any recognition in the likely event that other eyes watched him. Christian glanced at the Bow Street officer casually.

Jackson's face was as impassive as a statue as he opened the door and ushered her in. Turning, he made a shooing motion at Christian and Grant. "You've delivered your charge, now return to your master. No need to wait. My lord will see her home."

Christian ground his teeth. Though he was clearly following orders to continue the ruse, Jackson's words still rankled. The idea of letting another man protect Genevieve while he turned away made him want to burst into the house, weapons drawn, and confront Wickburgh immediately. But that would endanger Genevieve's parents, wherever they were being held. Besides, Wickburgh would be at a different location. Christian would have to see this game through and let Wickburgh's lapdogs lead the rescuers to their master.

Grant inclined his head to Jackson, turned on his heel, and leaped onto the coach as if he hadn't any concern.

Cole and Jared turned their horses around, Cole taking the lead as an outrider with Jared following the carriage. The moment they rounded a bend in the road and were no longer in view of the house, Christian slowed the team to a stop. Cole continued on ahead.

"Jared!" Christian leaped down from the driver's seat as his brother cantered to him. "Give me your horse. I'm going to follow them. You, Cole, and Grant take the coach to the posting inn and get the other horses we sent ahead."

Jared shook his head. "Not a chance. I'll go with you. When we find out where they've gone, you can stay and keep an eye on things while I come back and guide the others to where they've taken the Marshalls."

Cole galloped back to them, too far ahead to have heard their discussion. "We're going back, yes?"

"I should go instead of Chris." Grant swung down from the carriage.

Christian's stomach tightened and heat flushed his face. "I am not leaving her there!"

Grant sneered. "Yes, you and your cool head will help her really well right now, not to mention your utter lack of experience tracking dangerous criminals."

Christian marched up to Grant and stood nose to nose with him. "I am not the little brother you left behind when you went away to war. Get out of my way." He whirled around and grabbed the reins from Jared, who stared at him as if he'd never seen him.

"You'll get yourself killed, idiot," Grant hissed through his teeth.

Cole raised a brow and his mouth twitched on one corner. "The three of you go together. I'll take the coach back and pick up the horses. Leave me a trail so I can find you, or send one of your men." He tossed his horse's reins to Grant and swung up on the driver's box.

It was Christian's turn to stare. Cole, the self-appointed leader of the brothers, was letting someone else take the lead?

He shot his brother a look of gratitude. "Good. Let's go." He swung up onto the saddle of Jared's roan.

Grant went still and peered ahead, sending Christian's muscles on high alert. Two men on horseback materialized out of the bushes. Christian palmed his gun.

Grant relaxed and dashed to them. After speaking to them quietly, one rode to Cole, while another followed Grant.

Grant gestured. "They're moving Genevieve. A cart left the Marshall's house with her in it."

Christian mounted. "Which way?"

Grant gestured up the road and said to Jared, "Ride double with me."

Jared glared at Christian. "I'm riding behind Grant while you take my horse—how is that fair?"

"Quit mewling like a babe. Nothing's fair." Grant tore off the tailcoat and cravat and tossed them into the interior of the coach. "If I had more time, I'd change out of these infernal togs." He gestured to his satin knee breeches and brocade waistcoat.

"We don't," Christian snapped.

Grant shot him a look normally reserved for the completely stupid, and mounted. Christian urged Jared's horse forward. Christian, his brothers, and one of Grant's men galloped as a group toward the Marshall's house. He craned his neck, searching the road up in front of them as it wound among the hills. Far ahead, a governess cart bumped along the road.

Christian urged the horse to a gallop. Grant and Jared, riding double, remained beside him. Grant's man followed behind.

"Steady," Jared said. "Don't get too close or they'll know they're being followed."

Christian reined a little, slowing the horse to a comfortable trot, all the while his instincts screaming at him to run. When they came to a crossroads, they paused. With the winding road and hilly countryside, the cart had vanished. Christian cursed. Grant peered up ahead with narrowed eyes.

A glimmer caught Christian's eye. "What's that?" He pointed to a small metal object winking in the sunlight next to the road branching off to the left.

Jared slid off the horse and picked it up. He held it out. "It's a signet ring."

Grant grunted. "It's Jackson's. He's leaving us a breadcrumb trail."

Jared put on the ring and Christian urged his horse forward. As they crossed over a small bridge and began climbing a hill, the hackles in Christian's neck rose. An instant later, Grant held up his hand to halt them. They slowed, scanning for signs of danger.

"Stay here." Grant slid off his horse and crept soundlessly forward.

"Not on your life," Christian muttered as he followed behind, careful to keep his footfalls quiet.

How Grant managed to move like a phantom was beyond Christian. Usually it was sinister enough to raise the hackles on the back of Christian's neck. Today, he was grateful for his brother's uncanny ability. He tried to match Grant's stride, mimicking his posture, the way he moved, the placing of his feet so soundlessly so as not to be discovered by Wickburgh's lapdogs.

Grant crouched as they approached the low hill and then flattened himself on the ground. Christian lowered himself to his stomach next to him. On their bellies, they inched forward and peered over the rim into a shallow dell. A small crofter's cottage crouched next to a dry stream. The roof had collapsed, and the shutters hung drunkenly over the tiny windows. An unoccupied governess cart waited behind an overgrown shrub.

Grant watched silently, making a careful perusal of the cottage and area. Christian's tension climbed, and every muscle in his body urged him to leap up, race down the hill, burst into the cottage, and save Genevieve.

"Steady," Grant whispered.

Christian focused on slowing his breathing. They waited. Jackson's tall, lean form moved in front of the window. He looked out to survey the area, then he stepped away.

A guard walked around from behind the cottage, gun held loosely in hand. A second guard appeared from the other side, exchanged glances with the first, turned, and strode back like a sentry. Two guards. Possibly more hidden in the trees. They couldn't simply storm the structure. Besides, they didn't dare risk Wickburgh killing his hostages. And Genevieve. No sound came from the cottage.

Christian battled back images that Wickburgh had already killed Genevieve; Jackson wouldn't let her get hurt. Christian eyed his brother. Grant was a crack shot from his time serving as a sharpshooter in the war. Christian could probably match him, but now was not the time to test his skill. The stakes were too high.

Christian whispered to Grant, "Can you get off a clean shot at that range?"

"Only if my target happens to walk in front of the window. Jackson knows that; he'll do what he can."

Grant inched backward. Christian kept up with him. Behind them, Jared and the guard who'd come with them both stood with a pair of pistols primed and ready for a fight. When Christian and Grant had scooted back out of sight, Grant took his rifle off the saddle, and sent the man who'd come with them back to guide Cole to them.

Grant glanced at Christian. "Circle around and try to get in close while the guard is on the other side of the cottage."

At last! Christian gripped both his guns. Moving low and swift, careful to tread lightly so as not to give away his presence, Christian darted from bush to boulder. Pausing, he peered around his cover, then ducked back as the guard circled around again.

Wait. Breathe. Wait.

Christian peeked out. The guard turned and headed back the other way. Christian dashed to a hedgerow and crouched behind it.

"Who's there?" a voice called.

Heavy footsteps neared. Christian gripped his gun and prepared for a fight.

CHAPTER 28

Genevieve stood in the main room of the rundown cottage with her hands folded together and hoped Wickburgh didn't see them shake. Where in the world had that proud and wealthy man found such an unlikely place?

"I have come as you asked, *husband*," she let derision drip off her words. "Now set my parents free."

"Of course, of course." Wickburgh jerked his chin toward one of his men.

Grant's associate, Connor Jackson, fully immersed in the role as one of Wickburgh's cronies, strode to the door leading to a smaller room and opened it.

Genevieve drew in a steadying breath. Surely Christian and the Amesbury brothers were on their way. She trusted them.

"Bring them out," Jackson said to someone inside.

"On your feet, then," said another voice.

All other thoughts fled as first her mother, then her father walked out. Both looked calm and unruffled, as if being captured and held prisoner were a daily occurrence. Genevieve had feared the strain would have caused her mother's heart to give out, but she seemed well enough. Serene, even. Perhaps Jackson had managed to assure them of his true allegiance and that rescue was on the way.

Her father saw her first. His eyes opened wide and his mouth worked. "Genevieve!"

Her mother stared at her in disbelief. "My dear! You're well? When we'd heard you'd perished . . . ." Her eyes shimmered and her lip trembled.

Genevieve rushed toward her parents but one of Wickburgh's men grabbed her arm and pulled her back.

"No, none of that," Wickburgh said.

Genevieve kept her focus on her mother. "I'm well, Mama. Are you . . . ?"

Her mother offered a pained smile. "I'm unharmed, dearest."

"How dare you," Papa said to Wickburgh. "How dare you keep us here! Release us at once."

Wickburgh made a tsking sound. "You forget yourself. I make the demands—not you."

Anger welled up inside Genevieve. "Free them."

"No need to be hasty. We have unfinished business here. Please be seated." He gestured toward three wooden chairs lined up in a row.

One of the men waved his pistol at the chairs in a clear directive. Genevieve exchanged glances with her parents who stared at her in mingled disbelief and joy.

Genevieve cursed herself for not having the presence of mind to send them word that she was alive the moment she'd learned Wickburgh had reported her as dead. Once she and her parents sat on the hard chairs, a gunman handed ropes to Jackson and one other man.

Jackson stood behind Genevieve and tied the ropes loosely. Something cool and metallic slid into her hand. A knife? She closed a fist over it and schooled her features into submissive dejection. Jackson gave them a tug as if testing their strength. He moved to Papa sitting next to her and tested his bindings tied by the other guard.

"All of you," Wickburgh said. "Out. And keep your eyes open. This little whore's lover will appear and try to cause trouble. He's annoyingly tenacious."

Darkness twisted in her stomach and tied itself into a harder, tighter knot. All his torment, all those hours she'd cried and cowered. What a fool she'd been. She should have poisoned his food and saved her family and Christian. She'd be a murderess, if she had. The thought didn't fill her with the horror that it should.

As Jackson crossed in front of her, walking between her and Wickburgh, he mouthed the word 'widow' and made a meaningful look toward Wickburgh.

Widow? What did that mean? She peered out of the window through the crookedly hanging shutters but saw only the countryside. Widow? What was he telling her? And why Wickburgh? She mulled it over as she kept her gaze focused on the floor as if afraid. She glanced up at Jackson. He looked pointedly at the window. Then he stepped out of the cottage with the other guard, leaving her and her parents alone in the cottage with Wickburgh.

Not widow—window! Jackson wanted her to look out the window. But why? Maybe he wanted her to jump out the window. Or push Wickburgh out of it. Why? The fall wouldn't hurt him. What was Jackson trying to tell her? Slowly, she fingered the cold metal in her palm, a little longer than a nail file and had the serrated edge of a tiny knife. She turned it over and sawed at her bindings, careful not to let her shoulders make any motion.

"So, my errant little wife finally returns to me." Wickburgh's shiny boots paced in front of her vision.

She froze and hunched over as if cowering in fear.

Window. Wickburgh. It came to her in a rush. Jackson wanted her to get Wickburgh to stand in front of the window. Christian was an excellent shot. Perhaps he believed Christian could shoot Wickburgh through the window.

"You've led me on a merry little chase, my dear," Wickburgh added.

A pity Jackson couldn't arrest Wickburgh now, but Wickburgh

had too many men, and Jackson would be overwhelmed in an instant. If Christian and his brothers were already outside...

Wickburgh's voice changed timbre. "I despise merry little chases."

"I thought you enjoyed games," she taunted.

He pressed a hand over his chest, his mouth twisted in pain. Only then did she notice his flushed face and glassy eyes, signs of fever from the wound. "Then you had the gall to shoot me. Most unladylike."

She let out a caustic huff of laughter. "I'm not certain beating and strangling one's wife is entirely gentlemanly."

"The last time we were together, I'd only planned to kill you. But now, I find it necessary to make your punishment a bit more . . . elaborate."

He moved away and stopped in front of her father. Anger nudged away all other emotions. Christian was right; Wickburgh needed to be stopped, by any possible method. Genevieve continued sawing at her ropes. If only they hadn't searched her at her parent's house and taken the gun she'd tucked into her boot, she could shoot him again. And this time, not merely wound him. Now, she had nothing but the tiny knife Jackson had slipped her.

"But where to start?" Wickburgh said, looking at her father. "No, not you; you must be taught a lesson, as well. I think I shall start first with the one you've all been protecting. It would be poetic justice for you to watch her die." He looked pointedly at Mama.

"No," her father rasped, straining at his bindings.

"Leave them out of this," Genevieve gasped. "You promised!"

Her bindings loosened. She must have sawed all the way through one loop. She worked desperately at the remaining ropes.

Unmoved by their pleas, Wickburgh sauntered lazily toward her mother, his fingers twitching. He raised both hands and spread them, reaching for her neck.

With a cry of distress, Mother began gasping and pressed her hands over her chest. She slumped over. Her heart!

"No!" Genevieve screamed.

"Someone's coming!" Jackson shouted from outside.

"You monster!" Her father's body hurtled past her toward Wickburgh. Metal glinted in his hand as he raised his arm and brought it down in a savage thrust.

Wickburgh stiffened and let out an inhuman scream. Papa wrenched a knife out of Wickburgh's back and gripped it with white fingers. Wickburgh twisted around and lurched at Papa. As Papa brought down his arm to strike again, Wickburgh grabbed the weapon. They struggled, each straining to control the blade.

"Jackson! Smith! Get in here!" Wickburgh yelled.

Frantically, Genevieve sawed at her ropes with shaking fingers, her attention divided between her father fighting with Wickburgh, and Mother who had sagged against her bindings, her eyes closed.

Sounds of combat exploded outside, the all-too-familiar sounds of fists hitting bodies. Jackson was probably battling Wickburgh's men outside, preventing them from rushing to answer Wickburgh's call.

A gunshot roared through the air. Had Christian arrived, or had something gone wrong? Her ropes snapped apart and Genevieve's arms sprang free. She leaped from her seat and flew at Wickburgh, her small knife in her hand. Still struggling, Wickburgh kneed her father in the groin. Papa went down, coughing. As Genevieve threw herself upon Wickburgh and embedded her knife into his back, she wrapped both hands around the hilt and used her weight to try to steer him toward the window. He twisted around and threw her off. She staggered back. He backhanded her. Pain ripped through her face. The force of his blow slammed her against the floor.

Outside, gunshots ripped through the air. Bullets splintered the wooden walls. The shutters blasted apart. Debris showered the room. Genevieve flattened herself against the floor to avoid lethal projectiles. Oblivious to the danger, Wickburgh kicked her father where he lay on the ground.

Genevieve screamed. "Stop! Leave him alone!"

"Oh, no, my dear," he said calmly, oddly contrasting with the battle raging outside. "I will kill them both while you watch, starting with your dear Mama. Then when they are dead, I will kill you. Slowly.

Very slowly. I give you my word." His mouth twisted into a deranged smile.

Genevieve scrambled to her feet and rushed at Wickburgh. The door flew open so hard that it banged against the wall. Jackson staggered in, his gun raised. Another gunshot rang out. Jackson jerked backward and collapsed on the floor.

Genevieve screamed.

"Genevieve!" Christian's voice cut through the gunfire.

CHAPTER 29

With Genevieve's scream echoing in his head, Christian took careful aim at one of Wickburgh's minions racing toward the open door of the cottage. He squeezed the trigger. The thug who shot Jackson crumpled. Jackson lay unmoving in the open doorway of the cottage. With steady hands, Christian reloaded his guns. Bark exploded off the tree inches from Christian's shoulder. All fell silent for a moment while opponents found cover and reloaded.

Genevieve screamed again.

"I'm going in!" Christian hefted a gun in each hand.

"No!" Jared shouted.

Christian propelled himself out from behind the tree. As he sprinted to the cottage, gunfire broke out all around him as Jared and Grant cleared a path for him. Christian reached the cottage, vaulted over Jackson's inert form, and landed in a crouch. Genevieve, with wild panic in her eyes, was locked in a struggle with Wickburgh, each trying to control a small dagger. Dark blood oozed from multiple locations on Wickburgh's tailored coat, and his breath dissolved into wheezing.

Genevieve's mouth was set into a grim line and a purple bruise spread over one of her flushed cheeks. That monster had hit her again. Calm fury turned Christian cold. Shaking with rage, he stowed his guns in the waistband of his breeches and put one hand over Genevieve's and Wickburgh's locked fists. He wrapped an arm around Genevieve's waist.

"Easy, Jen," he said softly into her hair. "I have you."

Christian steadied the knife in an upright and harmless position with one hand. She released her hold on the dagger and Christian pulled her back. With Genevieve safely out of the way, Christian gave the blade a sharp jerk. Wickburgh lost his grip on the weapon and it came away in Christian's hand. Still locked in eye contact with Wickburgh, Christian tossed the knife behind him. It clattered on the floor. Outside, the gunfire halted. Smoke drifted through the air, burning his eyes and throat.

Wickburgh turned a murderous glare on him. "Amesbury." Loathing oozed from his voice.

Christian pulled out both guns and trained them on Wickburgh. He should just shoot him now. Wickburgh was dangerous, violent, murderous. He didn't deserve to live. If they took him to the magistrate, they risked Wickburgh being acquitted. As long as Wickburgh lived, Genevieve would be in danger.

Christian could take her to the continent, but he'd always be looking for signs that Wickburgh had found them. If Wickburgh refused to grant her a divorce, he could never marry her and be a proper husband. Their children would grow up with the stigma of being illegitimate. And he'd be separated from his family.

Still. He couldn't kill the man—any man, even one such as this—in cold blood.

"You've lost." Christian's quiet voice echoed eerily in the small cottage.

Madness glinted in Wickburgh's eyes and spittle dripped off his mouth as he roared, "Amesbury!"

Christian held his guns steady. "If you make any move, I'll shoot you."

Wickburgh's eyes bulged and his face turned purple. "I'll kill you both!" He lunged.

Christian squeezed both triggers.

Three gunshots roared through the air. Two holes blossomed in Wickburgh's chest and one opened up in his forehead right between the eyes. Wickburgh fell backward with a thud and lay staring.

Christian stared. He killed him. He'd never killed a man before. He felt oddly empty. Hollow. Numb. Wait . . . three?

Grant appeared next to him, his gun still smoking, and muttered a disparaging remark about Wickburgh's parentage. "He died too quickly."

Christian stared at the savagery in Grant's tone. But he agreed. Labored breathing behind him caught his attention and he turned to Genevieve.

Clutching her chest as if her heart pained her, she met his gaze with wide, horrified eyes. A second later, she turned to her parents. "Mama . . . ?"

Mrs. Marshall, tied to a chair, averted her gaze from Wickburgh's prostrate form and looked at her husband who was slowly pushing himself to a seated position on the floor. Christian tucked his guns away, offered Captain Marshall a hand, and pulled him to a stand.

Genevieve stumbled to her mother. "Mama?"

Mrs. Marshall smiled gently. "I'm unharmed, dearest."

Genevieve let out a sob. "I thought you were having a heart attack."

Her mother smiled. "Yes, well, I thought perhaps you and your father needed a diversion so you could finish breaking free. Buying myself a bit more time could be beneficial as well."

Genevieve smiled wanly and shook her head. "You terrified me. But that was good thinking." She retrieved the knife from the floor and cut her mother's ropes.

Captain Marshall staggered to his feet and pulled Mrs. Marshall into his arms. Genevieve gave them a searching gaze as if to reassure herself they were well. They wrapped their arms around her, too, and all three of them enjoyed a family embrace.

They were safe. At last, they were free from Wickburgh's threats.

Genevieve was free.

Christian stood alone, strangely disjointed and out of place. Remembering Jackson, he moved to the Bow Street officer and felt for a pulse. When he found one, he let out his breath in relief. A dark stain spread from Jackson's shoulder down his arm.

Jackson moaned and squinted up at him. "I suppose I'm not dead." He spoke with the strong tones of a fighter, not the weak rattle of a man moments from death.

Christian grinned. "No, just a teeny tiny hole in your shoulder."

As Jackson turned his head, he hissed in his breath. "What did you do, hit me while I was unconscious?"

Someone let out his breath in disgust. "Ah! I knew I'd miss all the fun!" Cole strode in and looked around. His eyes fell on Wickburgh and his lip curled in disgust. "Messy, that."

Christian made no attempt to reply as he gently probed Jackson's head. Jackson gritted his teeth and grunted when Christian's fingers found a sizable bump. "I think you hit your head when you fell. Probably what knocked you out."

Pale, but not deathly gray, Jackson sat up, wincing and holding his shoulder.

Christian eyed him in concern. "Perhaps you should lie back down."

Jackson waved him off. "I'm fine. Don't coddle."

Christian stood and glanced at Genevieve to reassure himself she was well.

Pulling away from her parents, she looked into Christian's eyes somberly. Then her lips curved upward.

"You really are my white knight." She ran to him then and threw herself against him.

He wrapped her up tight and closed his eyes. She was safe. Safe at last.

Holding her tiny body close, he buried his face into her hair. "I fear my armor is a bit tarnished, but if you'll have me, I'm yours."

"You don't have to be perfect to be a good man."

Perhaps not. For the first time in years, he felt truly worthy of love.

CHAPTER 30

Genevieve nestled against Christian, safe within the circle of his arms, as he guided their horse on which they rode double. His strong and steady heartbeat drummed a soothing cadence. He tightened his arms around her and kissed her temple. Wickburgh's violence against her and her family, not to mention witnessing his death, threw her into a state of numb disbelief. By the time the magistrate and coroners had finished and they were all free to go, shock faded, leaving only quiet sorrow. Christian's comforting presence wrapped her in comfort and safety. She might never forget the murderous light in Wickburgh's eyes, his madness, his brutality. The image of him lying lifeless on the floor of the cottage played over and over in her mind.

She shivered. Christian stroked her hair, kissed the side of her head, and simply held her. He'd been quiet all evening, merely touching her gently, and offering her his strength. Pure love for Christian enfolded her in its sweet embrace but the residual horror of the day tainted her joy.

Behind them, her parents' voices, subdued from the day's terrifying events, mingled with Jared's and Cole's. Grant rode beside

Christian silently, his dark presence no longer frightening. Jackson, hunched in the saddle, seldom spoke.

"Please stay for the night," Mama said for the second time. "It's late and you're all fatigued."

"Quite right," Papa added. "You especially need rest, Mr. Jackson."

"I don't wish to impose, sir," said Jackson, but his voice was strained. "Besides, the surgeon patched me up well enough. I'll be all right."

Mama made a tsking sound. "After the way you came to our aid, the least we can do is offer you our hospitality while you recover from your injuries."

"Nasty business, gunshot wounds," Papa added.

"You may as well accept," Genevieve said, her voice strangely hollow in her own ears despite her attempt at a light-hearted tone. "Or they'll hound you all the way back to the manor."

"Perhaps we should accept," Cole said. "It's dark and highwaymen might be about."

Jared scoffed. "They'd best fear *us*."

Grant's voice floated back to them in the still, night air. "We need to retrieve the carriage."

"The innkeeper wasn't happy about that arrangement," Cole added with an unrepentant grin.

In the end, they agreed to stay with Genevieve's parents. After reclaiming the carriage and offering the innkeeper enough coin to pacify him, they arrived cold and exhausted at the Marshall family manor.

"Bring food at once and prepare guest rooms for each of our brave rescuers," Mama told the servants.

The housekeeper laid out a cold meal fit for a small army. Christian, as usual, tucked into the feast as if he hadn't eaten in days, and the other men ate with equally hearty appetites. Too overwhelmed by the day's events, Genevieve only picked at her food.

Afterward, they collapsed onto various chairs and settees in the family sitting room. Genevieve curled up next to Christian, tucking her legs underneath her body and nestling against his side. He wrapped his arms around her, leaned his head back against the back of the settee, and closed his eyes but his breathing remained light and the pressure of his arms stayed strong. She looked forward to sleeping in his arms like this every night. Soon.

If it were her choice, she'd abduct Christian and run off to Gretna Green this instant. But she didn't wish to bring more discomfort to the Amesbury family. They'd already done so much for her. The least she could do was marry their brother properly.

Jackson sprawled against the cushions of a settee with one hand holding his shoulder where he'd been shot. He suddenly raised his head. "Did you find my ring on the road?"

Jared took the ring off his finger and handed it over. "Good clue."

With an audible sigh of relief, Jackson slid the ring on his finger and let his head fall back against the settee.

Mama's shoulders drooped and she blinked her eyes slowly as if she could hardly keep them open. Cole yawned, and Jared rubbed his eyes. Only Grant and the other Bow Street officer remained watchful and unmoved.

"Mama, go to bed," Genevieve said. "I'll see to our guests."

Mama nodded without argument and arose. "Good night. I trust you'll be made comfortable."

Genevieve stood and hugged her, leaning into her mother's long-absent embrace. "I love you, Mama," she whispered. "You were so brave today."

Mama let out a tired snort. "If you'd all stop coddling me, you'd see I'm not the delicate flower you all seem to think I am."

Genevieve smiled. "Yes, Mama."

Mama squeezed Genevieve tightly. "I love you, too, dearest." She turned to Papa. "Coming, dear?"

"In a moment, love. I'd like to speak to Genevieve and Mr. Amesbury."

The housekeeper came in. "All the guest rooms are prepared."

Jackson stood, but swayed. Grant and the other Bow Street officer leaped to his side in a flash. They supported him as they followed the housekeeper up to their rooms.

Cole looked at Jared and arched an eyebrow. "Think our wives will worry if we don't come back tonight?"

Jared shook his head. "Elise isn't a worrier. She'll assume I'm out enjoying some lark with my brothers. She'll keep Alicia company."

Jared clapped Christian on the shoulder. "That was good fun. Let me know when you plan the next *coup*."

Christian opened one eye and grunted at him. Cole grinned and Jared chuckled. Genevieve smiled at the brotherly affection between them, loving them for Christian's sake and for the way they'd all come together to help him. To help her. To help her parents.

Cole sobered. "Well done, Chris."

Jared nodded, his grin lighting his sea-green eyes. "Maybe I should have brought you on my ship, after all. I could have used someone with your cool head and fighting skills. You would have made a first-rate pirate."

Christian opened his eyes and raised his head. He opened his mouth as if to say more, but merely nodded, looking a bit dazed. Cole gave him another searching look and smiled. Abruptly, he turned on his heel. He and Jared left together.

Christian let out his breath and rubbed his face. "Strange, after all these years, that their opinion still matters so much."

"Of course it does. They're family." She squeezed his arm.

Christian put a hand over hers and slid forward to the edge of his seat, eyeing Papa. "Sir. I'm sure you have concerns about your daughter and me."

"No, son. I am not here to interrogate you about your relationship with her or even your intentions. I gave up that right when I stood by and allowed her to pay the price for my crime."

"Papa." Genevieve crossed the room and sat next to him. Though she'd secretly harbored the very same thoughts, hearing him expressed them in such self-loathing softened her heart. "Don't go on so."

Papa shook his head. "I should have confessed my crime years ago and faced the consequences. I should have never allowed Wickburgh to rob me of my own daughter. Genevieve paid dearly, and so did you when you lost her."

Christian opened his mouth, but Papa held out a hand. "Hear me out. I'm a mutineer. My only defense was my reluctance to implicate my shipmates in removing a man who had no business being in command. Later, I kept silent for fear of hurting my wife. Instead, I hurt my daughter. And I hurt you. I can never make restitution. There is no taking back any of it." He stopped and swallowed.

Genevieve kept silent to allow him to express all the thoughts and feelings of his burdened heart. Tears stung her eyes. What a terrible load he'd carried! No one deserved that kind of torment.

Papa turned anguished eyes on her. "I haven't shown it, but I dearly love you, child. I hope you will find all the love and peace and joy you so richly deserve." He hung his head a moment. "I only hope you will find it in your heart to forgive me someday—not because I deserve it, but because I've seen how the cancer of un-forgiveness grows and destroys."

"Of course I forgive you, Papa." She touched his arm and squeezed it.

Christian asked. "What exactly happened, sir—on the ship?"

Papa's eyes glazed over as if reliving the past. "The captain was a monster. He'd taken cruelty to a whole new low. He'd already flogged to death several men, and the crew were on half rations despite land being only a few days away. He refused to go ashore to replenish our stores."

Genevieve stared, shocked to hear of such a thing happening in the Royal Navy.

Christian nodded. "My brother Cole had a similar experience on his first vessel. Go on."

"When the first lieutenant tried to reason with him, the captain threw him into the brig and threatened to court martial him for insubordination."

Papa scrubbed his hands over his face. "Then he ordered us into battle when our ship was still damaged, and we were clearly outgunned. The men started an uprising. I looked the other way while they killed the captain. When it was over, I released the first lieutenant who assumed command." He clenched and unclenched his hands.

"How old were you then?" Christian asked quietly.

"Seventeen."

Genevieve pictured her father, so young to make such difficult decisions. Tears burned her eyes that he'd faced such a terrible choice.

Papa continued, "We lied about the captain's death to the admiralty. The crew vowed to remain silent. Except, apparently, Seton —Wickburgh's brother. I'm sure he felt he needed to confess if he were dying. I probably would, too. I wish that I had confessed. I wish I hadn't put you both through all of that."

"Papa." Genevieve knelt in front of him. "I love you. I made my choice freely to help you and Mama."

She wrapped her arms around him. Speaking those words healed over the raw wounds in her heart. Long harbored, unacknowledged resentment fell away like old scales. Years of sadness, even blame, were cleansed.

At first, Papa sat utterly still. Then his arms went around her, and he crushed her against him. "My little one," he murmured. He kissed the top of her head. Then his shoulders began to shake. "I'm so sorry, child."

"Shhhh, I forgive you. It's over. It's all over. Now, all I need from you and Mama is to live long lives and spoil your grandchildren."

His tears dissolved into laughter. He pulled back and looked searchingly at her. Then glanced at Christian who stood nearby. "Is that a wedding announcement?"

Genevieve smiled. "Not officially, but I hope one will be coming soon." She looked up at Christian, but his face was solemn.

"Sir." Christian took another step nearer. "We've all done things we regret. I bear you no ill will." He held out a hand.

They shook formally. Christian's gaze slid Genevieve's way briefly before he returned his focus to Papa. "I vow I will spend my life doing everything I can to make Genevieve happy. I'm only a youngest son, but I have lucrative investments—"

"Don't mention it, son. You've more than earned my respect. Neither you nor she needs my permission. You have my blessing, most wholeheartedly. Be happy. Both of you."

Christian smiled. He turned to Genevieve and took a shuddering breath. "I bid you both a good night."

She took his arm. "I'll show you to your room."

Walking arm in arm, they mounted the steps and she led him to the guest wing opposite the family wing. The housekeeper passed them coming the other direction.

"The blue room?" Genevieve asked.

The housekeeper nodded. "Shall I?"

"I'll show him in." Genevieve led him to the door of the bedchamber and paused on the threshold. "I still can't believe it's over."

He lightly traced spirals across her bruised face. "Are you in pain?"

"It's not so bad." She closed her eyes and leaned into his touch.

"Is it really over?"

She opened her eyes and looked up at him. "Why wouldn't it be? The magistrate said there wouldn't be any legal action taken against you and Grant, not even a hearing."

She paused, still uncertain whose bullet had actually delivered the killing blow. Not that it mattered. They'd both fired. And it was clear Wickburgh meant to kill them all. "What troubles you?"

"You said there was a letter in Wickburgh's possession?" he asked.

She nodded. "Yes. As we agreed, he let me hold the letter during the ceremony. Then when the wedding was final, I burned it."

Christian stared. "He let you burn it?"

"He promised me before I married him that I could. He was a cunning and cold man, but he always kept his word. Always." She shivered, pushing against the recollection of a few terrifying times Wickburgh had made her a horrible promise and kept it.

"Could anyone else know of it? Family? Close friends?"

"He does—er, did—have another brother, but he has been abroad for years. He knows nothing about the letter or the reason I married Wickburgh." She shoved all those memories into a dark room and slammed the door shut. They had no place in her life, now. Only her family mattered. And Christian.

Christian kissed her brow. "You need time to heal from all of this madness. I'll try to be patient and give you all the time you need."

She rested her hand against his cheek, the slight scrape of his one-day's growth rough against her palm. "I love you."

He let out his breath in a great exhale. "I don't think I'll ever grow accustomed to hearing that."

She lifted her face up to him and slid her hand behind his neck in a clear invitation. Gazing at her with love in his eyes, he lowered his head and kissed her slowly, powerfully, with contained passion. Despite his gentleness, heat exploded from his touch and his exploration of her mouth turned hungry. She gave herself to his mouth, glorying in the privilege of finally touching him, kissing him, without any moral barriers between them. She leaned into him as years of loneliness and heartache melted away until they were alone in the world, no past, no sorrow, only love. When they were both breathless and aching, he cupped her cheek and ended the kiss.

Christian audibly swallowed. "I'd best go now before I ravish you right here and now."

She smiled, her body tingling in places she'd thought long dead. "I don't think it's considered ravishment if we're both willing."

He tapped her on the nose and kissed it. "Don't tempt me. I won't have it said we *had* to get married. And I refuse to have any doubt as to who is the father of our child."

She blushed down to her toenails. "I can picture a house full of blond little boys and laughter."

He grinned. "We're doing this backwards. First the proposal, then the discussion of children. Will you marry me, Genevieve?"

Healed and whole, she smiled. "Well, I suppose since I've promised to give you a houseful of sons, I ought to be married to you at the time."

He grinned. "I'm tempted to have Cole get a special license and marry you as soon as possible, but I want to do this right. We'll purchase a marriage license and marry in a church."

"If you want no chance people will speculate whether or not our child is yours, we will have to wait three months to marry so at least a year will have passed before a child is born."

Christian's eye narrowed in pain. "Three months," he gasped. "I'm sure I cannot wait that long."

She smiled. "Marry me and I'm sure we'll figure something out."

"Tonight wouldn't be soon enough for me." He kissed her again, turned her around and gave her a gentle push. "Good night." He closed the door but there was a soft thud, as if he had let his head drop on the other side of the door.

She placed her hand on the door in an attempt to have one last touch of Christian before going to bed.

Free of the threat that had hung over her family for a year, free of Wickburgh, free to marry Christian, Genevieve waltzed to her room humming, her lips tingling from Christian's kiss.

At least in this moment, love did make everything perfect.

CHAPTER 31

Dearest Christian,

You are the joy in my smile, the light in my eyes, the love in my heart. Today, when I finally become yours, I will be the happiest woman who ever breathed. I vow to love you and to receive your love with all my heart throughout all time. When we are both gone from this life, heaven will be our new home where I have no doubt our happiness will grow and our love will continue throughout eternity.

I eagerly await your arrival at the church today where I will be

Forever yours,

Genevieve

Christian let out a whoop and turned to Jared. After kissing his startled brother soundly on both cheeks, he flung open the door and shouted, "I'm getting married today!"

Surrounded by his brothers, Christian skipped up the church steps and practically ran inside.

Jared put a hand on his shoulder. "Steady, Chris. Show some decorum, will you?" He grinned.

The organ music began. Christian, heedless of the guests, practically danced as he stood next to the altar while Genevieve, a vision of loveliness in an apricot creation that made her skin glow, glided serenely down the aisle. Her smile filled his soul with such light and joy that he half expected to float off the floor.

When they were finally declared man and wife, Christian had to restrain himself from scooping her up into his arms and carrying her away that instant.

The second the wedding breakfast ended, Christian did just that. He swung her up into his arms and raced toward the carriage waiting in the church driveway.

Genevieve let out a gasp of surprise. She laughed. "You are ever impetuous."

"I know what I want. No need to wait around."

It was quieter here away from the guests. Only the soft strains of a harp playing for the guests floated to him in the air.

She wrapped her arms around his neck and snuggled in. "I had no idea when you gave me that first shy smile you'd be such a force to be reckoned with."

"Just wait." He grinned wolfishly.

A figure dressed head to toe in black stood by the carriage. Christian halted. Grant, wearing a beautifully tailored superfine tailcoat, waited. Christian gaped. He hadn't noticed the suit until now. When was the last time Grant had worn such tasteful attire? Probably Jared's wedding. It was probably the same suit. The coachman leaped up onto the box and waited with the reins in his hand.

Silent as a wraith, Grant approached. He gave Christian a searching look. "Well, done, little brother." A rare, true smile curved Grant's mouth. He stepped back and opened the carriage door.

Stunned, Christian only stared at him. He nodded, unable to speak. After setting down Genevieve next to the carriage, he held out a hand to guide her in.

Instead, she turned to Grant, rose up on tiptoe and kissed his cheek. "Thank you," she murmured.

Grant looked winded. She smiled, glanced at Christian with a come-hither smile, and stepped into the carriage. Christian offered Grant a hand. They clasped hands, eyes meeting eyes. A dozen things he ought to say flitted through his mind but he couldn't seem to voice them. Grant nodded and let go of his hand. Nothing needed to be said. Despite their differences, their history, they were brothers. They'd always be there for each other when it mattered.

Inside the coach, Christian settled next to Genevieve. As the carriage moved forward, Christian took Genevieve into his arms. "Good day, Mrs. Amesbury."

She smiled. "I love the sound of that. I love you."

"I love you." He wrapped an arm around her and drew her in close.

She snuggled in next to him and sighed. "I'm so happy. I have you. And I finally have a pair of shoes that fit!" She giggled and held up her feet to show her slippers. "They aren't glass slippers, but I think they're lovely."

"Very well, Cinderella, I'll try to be your Prince Charming and see that you are never lacking in slippers that fit properly."

His kiss started gently, but quickly burned brighter and hotter. Together at last, bonded by trial and hardship, they drove toward their future.

ABOUT THE AUTHOR

Award-winning author of more than twenty best-selling Regency Historical Romances, Donna Hatch is a hopeful romantic and an adventurer at heart. Each story she writes is filled with heart and plenty of swoon-worthy romance. Donna sings, plays the harp, and ballroom dances. Her family, including six children and two cats, recently left their native Arizona for the Pacific coast of the U.S. No matter where they live, she and her husband of over twenty-five years are proof that there truly is a happily ever after.

For sneak peeks, announcements about new releases, and giveaways, please subscribe to Donna's newsletter https://donnahatch.com/subscribe/
Website: https://www.donnahatch.com
Blog https://www.donnahatch.com/blog
Facebook https://www.facebook.com/RomanceAuthorDonnaHatch/
or
https://www.facebook.com/DonnaHatch.Author
Book Bub https://www.bookbub.com/profile/donna-hatch
Twitter https://twitter.com/donnahatch
Amazon https://www.facebook.com/RomanceAuthorDonnaHatch/
LinkedIn https://www.linkedin.com/in/donnahatch/
Pinterest https://www.pinterest.com/donnahatch29/
Instagram https://www.instagram.com/donnahatch.author/
Goodreads https://www.goodreads.com/author/show/2072970.Donna_Hatch

OTHER TITLES BY DONNA HATCH

Need more chocolate for your romantic soul? Other titles by Donna Hatch:

The Rogue Heart series:

The Stranger She Married

The Guise of a Gentleman

A Perfect Secret

The Suspect's Daughter

Courting Series:

Courting Countess

Courting Country Miss

Music of the Hearts Series

Heart Strings

Novellas and Short Stories:

"Sabrina's Hero"

"Unmasking the Duke"

"Matchmaking Game"

"Constant Hearts"

"Emma's Dilemma"

"The Reluctant Bride"

"Troubled Hearts"

"When Ship Bells Ring"

"A Wager for Love" *Timeless Romance Anthology, Wedding Wagers*

"A Perfect Match"

Christmas Stories

Christmas Secrets

"A Christmas Reunion"

"Mistletoe Magic"

"A Winter's Knight"

Fantasy

Queen in Exile (Out of Print)